Acclaim for the novels of
BRENDA JOYCE

BEYOND SCANDAL
"Master storyteller Brenda Joyce
weaves threads of mystery,
intrigue and passion into a tale
that Gothic fans will relish and
romance readers will devour."
Romantic Times

THE GAME
"A stunning tale of power and passion set
against a rich Elizabethan tapestry.
Don't miss it!"
Virginia Henley

AFTER INNOCENCE
"An extraordinary woman...
an emotional roller coaster.
Publishers Weekly

PROMISE OF THE ROSE
"A powerful story, rife with compelling
characters, political intrigue
and steamy sensuality."
Los Angeles Daily News

BRENDA JOYCE

Violet Fire

AVON BOOKS ◆ NEW YORK

This is a work of fiction. Names, characters, places, and incidents either are the product of the author's imagination or are used fictitiously. Any resemblance to actual events, locales, organizations, or persons, living or dead, is entirely coincidental and beyond the intent of either the author or the publisher.

AVON BOOKS, INC.
1350 Avenue of the Americas
New York, New York 10019

Copyright © 1989 by Brenda Joyce Dworman
Published by arrangement with the author
Visit our website at http://www.AvonBooks.com
Library of Congress Catalog Card Number: 88-91373
ISBN: 0-380-75578-5

First Avon Books Printing: May 1989

AVON TRADEMARK REG. U.S. PAT. OFF. AND IN OTHER COUNTRIES, MARCA REGISTRADA, HECHO EN U.S.A.

Printed in the U.S.A.

WCD 10 9 8 7 6 5

Prologue

New York City
November 1, 1873

"Rathe, I'm so glad you could come."

Rathe Bragg's smile was easy and devastatingly charming as he shook Albert van Horne's hand. He had just stepped into the huge, marble-columned foyer of van Horne's Fourteenth Street mansion. The ceilings were twenty-five feet high and decorated with intricately painted cherubs floating on a bank of clouds. A staircase and massive rosewood and brass banister curved upward toward the mezzanine, the steps carpeted in royal red from the Orient. Classical busts frowned at Rathe from green marble bases, and a chandelier the size of two grand pianos hung from the ceiling, shimmering with thousands of crystals. Rathe had seen his share of fabulously appointed homes, but even he was impressed.

"It's my pleasure, Albert. You know that," he said warmly, meaning it.

Albert van Horne, who had been financing the railroads since before the outbreak of the Civil War, returned Rathe's smile. He threw his arm around the young man's shoulders and together they strolled through a vast black and white marble-floored hall. "How are you, Rathe?"

"Fine, sir, and you?"

"As hale as possible, I think," van Horne replied. "I've heard rumors that you'll be leaving us again shortly."

"Yes sir, I'm afraid so."

"I have some business I'd like to discuss with you before you go." Van Horne shook his head. "Rathe, you'll be thirty in a few years. You just got back from Europe and now you're off again. It's time you thought of settling down. Build yourself a home. Put down roots."

"I'm afraid it's business—not pleasure—that's taking me away this time. I've invested in a mining venture in Vancouver. We've had a helluva time getting this operation off the ground. I'm headed up there to find out what or who is holding up the works."

"You think it could be a matter of human error?" Van Horne asked.

"Possibly *calculated* human error," Rathe returned, with a surprising, hard chill to his tone. He was a beautiful man, tall, broad-shouldered, lean-hipped, bronzed from a lifetime out of doors, his hair a riot of gold, his face perfectly sculpted. Yet now, all of his easy charm, so irresistible when coupled with his blond good looks, was gone. He suddenly seemed menacing.

They entered a huge and opulent salon, with thick Persian rugs underfoot and a frescoed ceiling overhead. The salon was nowhere near full, for tonight's dinner was just an intimate gathering of twenty or so, all in formal evening wear.

Rathe glanced around the room, nodding at those nearest him and seeking out Mrs. van Horne, a bland-looking, overweight woman. "Jocelyn, it's wonderful to see you again," he said warmly, then kissed her hand. "I see you've done some redecorating. The place looks beautiful."

"Oh, do you think so?" Jocelyn asked worriedly, biting her plump lower lip and crossing her arms over her massive bosom. "I do wonder if the reds and purples really go together. You have such good taste, Rathe. Tell me truthfully, do you really think they're all right?"

"Fit only for kings and their queens," he said, grinning and sweeping her a mock bow. "My lady."

She giggled.

Thadeus Parker, a real-estate magnate and a good friend, clasped his hand firmly. "Good to see you, my boy. Heard you've been up to more crazy escapades. Climbing cliffs in the Alps?"

Rathe grinned. "We call it rock climbing, Thad, and it's quite a sport."

"Quite a way to kill yourself, if you ask me."

Rathe chuckled. "That's half the thrill. But I have no intention of getting myself killed—there's too much I haven't done yet."

"It's a good thing you were born under a lucky star," Parker said. "Because one fall is all it takes. You know, Rathe, most men would give anything for your luck."

Rathe raised an eyebrow. "In business, at cards, or with women?"

Parker laughed. "All three!"

"How's Elizabeth?" Rathe asked. "And the girls? The last time I saw those two I was in jeopardy of losing my heart twice over!"

Parker beamed. "Elizabeth is very well, thank you, and of course, the girls have heard you're in town and are begging to see you."

Parker's daughters were thirteen and fifteen and actually too plain to have admirers swooning at their feet. "I'll stop by tomorrow," Rathe promised. "I've brought them a few gifts from Paris."

"You spoil them," Parker chastised gently.

Rathe chuckled, exposing two deep dimples. "How could I not spoil those two?" And he meant it.

He nodded at a steel magnate, a textile king, the publisher of the New York *Evening Post,* and the famous socialite lawyer, Bradley Martin, and his wife, Cornelia. He was about to move toward the latter when something hard came banging down on his arm. He could tell by the feel of the blow that it had come from old Mrs. Anderson's cane. He turned, smiling, and was rapped once again. The diminutive, white-haired woman glared. "You come in here and talk to everyone in the room but me, you scoundrel!"

Rathe took her clawlike hand with its huge emerald ring and kissed it gallantly. "You're too quick for me, Beatrice, and you know it."

She scowled. "You haven't come to visit me in a week, boy!"

"I came yesterday, remember?" he said gently, still holding her hand. The redoubtable widow had been the wife of a prominent banker and the hostess nonpareil of her generation. She was thus still deferred to and invited to all of society's functions, although some thought her senile. "Did you enjoy the French chocolates I brought you?"

Her faded blue eyes suddenly lit up. "I did indeed! Next time you bring me two boxes, not one!"

He had to smile. "Beatrice, you didn't eat the entire box already, did you?"

"Of course not," she huffed.

He fingered her shawl, another gift from him. It was made of the most delicate silk, a vivid, shimmering green which clashed terribly with her pale blue gown. "I see you like the shawl?"

She melted. "It's beautiful, Rathe. I wear it every day. But next time you go abroad you must take me with you. Then I can buy my own shawls and candies. I haven't been to Paris in far too long. I'm not getting any younger, you know."

Mrs. Anderson was well into her eighties. "It's a long, hard trip," Rathe said softly, seriously. "When I arrive in London, I'm exhausted for a week. A terrible trip."

"Hmm." She pursed her mouth. "Yes, I remember, it's a very long voyage. Maybe it is too much for me at my age."

"You just tell me what you want me to bring you next time, Beatrice, and I will."

"You're a good boy," she said, touching his cheek.

"Thank you," he said. Then, with a twinkle in his blue eyes, he winked. "I know."

Her cane came down again on his arm. "Pride goeth before the fall."

Rathe just grinned.

Van Horne walked over to them with a striking blond woman. "Have you met my niece, Rathe?" he asked. "Patricia Darning? Perhaps you ran into her husband while you were in London?"

Rathe turned to the beautiful blonde. He took her hand and kissed it casually. "No, I don't believe I had the pleasure of meeting Mr. Darning. But I am acquainted with his lovely wife," he said, dimpling, "which is how I know that Darning is a very lucky man."

Patricia was staring at him intensely. "Thank you. I hear you just came back from Europe?" she asked politely.

"Yes. The Alps. Paris, London."

"How nice," she murmured.

Rathe turned his attention back to van Horne. "By the way, when I was in England visiting my brother I stopped at a Devon stud farm and purchased a colt and two broodmares. The mares are proven, but Albert," Rathe said as his eyes flashed, "the colt is superb. A real winner."

"Why don't you tell me all about it tomorrow over breakfast at the club?"

A dazzling smile broke out on Rathe's face. "Good. And we can discuss the business you mentioned earlier, as well."

Van Horne agreed and moved away, mingling with his other guests.

"I missed you today," Patricia said in a low, careful voice. "I came by your hotel, but you weren't there. I waited for an hour, Rathe."

"I'm sorry, Trish, but I was in a meeting." He smiled, glancing around the room. Then, because no one was paying them any mind, Rathe held her gaze with heady promise. A small smile tilted the beautiful curve of his mouth;

his hand touched her waist, his thumb moving sensually across her satin gown. He leaned close. ''We can make up for lost time later, don't you think?'' His drawl was pure west Texas, both smooth as silk and rough as sandpaper.

''Meet me upstairs in the blue guest room in half an hour,'' Patricia whispered, and then she walked away.

For a brief moment, Rathe gazed after her. He was remembering their last hot interlude. But lately, Patricia had started hinting that she would be amenable to divorcing her husband, Darning. She had also begun questioning Rathe about his half-brother, Nick, who, although a quarter Indian, like himself, was the current Lord Shelton, Earl of Dragmore.

The fact that Nick and Rathe's mother was the last Lord Shelton's daughter was no secret, yet Rathe never referred to it. How Patricia had found out was beyond him, but apparently she had been doing some detective work. And when a woman began investigating, well, it meant she had certain serious intentions.

Rathe supposed he ought to put an end to her machinations by telling her the truth. He wasn't ready to settle down; he doubted he would be for another decade—at least. It wasn't that he was against marriage, because he wasn't. Someday he would meet the right woman and have a family, the way his father had when he'd met his mother. But that day was a long way off yet and there was a whole world waiting for him out there. After Canada he was going to sail to China on a merchant clipper in which he had recently purchased shares. After all, he had never been to the Orient before.

Still, he couldn't help feeling a touch sorry for Patricia, though he had never made her any promises, and she *was* already married. Why was it that women all wanted to marry him? Especially the proper kind. Even before he had made his first million, they seemed to start thinking about the altar just as soon as they laid eyes on him.

Rathe chatted amiably with van Horne's guests, finding

the time to say a few brief words to everybody, but exactly thirty minutes later he was entering the blue guest room and closing the heavy rosewood door behind him. Patricia was waiting with a look no man could possibly mistake. Rathe pulled her slowly and completely against him. "Hello, Trish," he murmured, and then his mouth found hers gently, stroking and sensual. He plundered with his tongue, fully aroused now, pressing his hot hardness against her, rubbing lithely back and forth. She moaned. He cupped a small breast and kneaded it.

"Oh, Rathe, Rathe," she gasped, her hands wild in his thick sun-streaked hair.

"I know, darlin', I know," he groaned back.

Her dress was full-length, the latest style from Paris. It boasted a fashionably full bustle and a set of collapsing hoops, which annoyed Rathe immensely—especially at times like these. He pulled it up to her waist with skilled determination. His hand immediately went to her thigh, delicately tracing its inner softness to the wonderfully full and swelling joining of her legs. She sagged against the door. Deftly he found the opening in her scanty silk drawers, then the damp, warm flesh, stroking gently, searching, gliding insistently. She shuddered and whimpered.

He kissed her softly, barely, teasingly. His tongue played and tormented. "Come on, darlin', come on, reach for the stars," he drawled thickly, urgently.

She moaned, a low, ragged sound, then tensed and cried out, again and again.

"Darlin'," he whispered, swiftly unbuttoning his trousers. Swollen and thick, he bent his knees, and thrust in. She gasped. He did, too.

With her legs around his waist and her back against the door, she rode him as he moved, hard, rhythmically, his face buried in her neck.

"Rathe," she whimpered, "I think—*oh.*" She sobbed.

With his own guttural cry, he exploded, spasm after spasm of his hot seed filling her.

After they had regained their breath and as they re-

adjusted their clothing, Rathe squeezed her waist fondly.
"Sweet," he murmured. "Now let's go before we're
missed."

She gave him a look of utter adoration.

Twenty minutes later they sat to dinner amidst white
linen, crystal, and Chateau Rothschild. The conversation
soon turned to everyone's favorite scandal, the Woodhull
affair.

Victoria Woodhull and her sister had been running an
extremist women's weekly, which advocated, among other
things, the right of women to love whomever and whenever they chose. Recently, Victoria Woodhull had accused
Henry Ward Beecher, a leader of the National Women's
Suffrage Association, of having an affair with Elizabeth
Tilton, the wife of a reformist editor. Woodhull had gone
on to call Beecher a hypocrite and coward for not supporting free love publicly. Then the Women's Suffrage Association responded by breaking with the Woodhull sisters,
who were arrested for printing obscene literature. At the
present, the papers were ablaze with the scandal, and the
public hungry for any bit of gossip they could provide.

"I, for one, think Woodhull's guilty," Cornelia Martin
announced. "Imagine, printing stories on free love in her
little newspaper—of course it's obscene material."

"That entire paper is obscene," said van Horne. "Advocating free love for women and men? My God, it's athe-
istic!"

Rathe couldn't help grinning at that. "I happen to think
free love is an interesting idea," he murmured dryly.

Patricia glared at him. Some of the men chuckled.

"Keep your nasty opinions to yourself, young man,"
piped up Beatrice Anderson. Rathe met her scowl with an
exaggerated wink.

"From the very beginning," van Horne went on, "these
crusading women have been nothing but promiscuous immoral free-lovers and man-haters—that's quite obvious."

"Quite," agreed Thadeus Parker.

"Actually, I am entirely in support of women's suffrage," said the publisher, Bradford Ames. "But as long as they've got these rabble-rousers trying to destroy our American institutions, why, I'm afraid they'll never get the vote."

"Do you think she'll be found guilty?" Patricia asked, referring to Victoria Woodhull.

A rousing argument ensued, carrying them through dinner.

Afterwards, the ladies adjourned to the salon for coffee and sweets, while the men retired to their brandies and cigars in the library.

"I'll take two," Rathe said, a cigar clamped firmly between his teeth.

The library was almost silent, except for the low sound of male voices and the occasional clink of their brandy snifters. Rathe casually picked up the two cards the dealer slapped on the gleaming oak table.

He had shed his black cutaway evening coat and his silk tie. His sleeves were rolled up to his elbows, revealing large strong forearms. His silver and blue waistcoat hung open across a broad expanse of chest. He puffed on the cigar, watching closely as van Horne took two cards, Parker one, Bradford Ames two, and Martin three.

The library, like the rest of van Horne's home, was boldly opulent. The rug was Oriental, a pattern of twining red and turquoise and gold. The walls were a gold brocade, the draperies gold velveteen. The woodwork was mahogany, the furniture rosewood, the work of the famous New York furniture-maker, Henry Belter.

"I'll call," Rathe drawled.

Suddenly from outside the quiet room there came a shriek. It sounded like "Liberate!"

"What the hell was that?" Ames asked, pulling on his elongated mustache.

Rathe shrugged. Then there was the sound of glass shattering and another high-pitched scream that most definitely sounded like "Ladies liberate!"

For one instant, every man in the library froze. Then Rathe was on his feet and striding forcefully to the door. As he opened it there was another crash, and from somewhere in the vicinity of the foyer, the vibrant cry: "Down with male tyranny!"

And then came another scream, this one hysterical and unmistakably Mrs. van Horne's—"Get her off my piano!"

Rathe was at the library door before any of the others and racing down the hall. He stopped short at the sight that greeted him—and laughed.

A tall slim woman clad in a shapeless wool dress and a bonnet that hid half of her oval face was standing on the piano in the middle of the plush parlor, while the women stood and gawked.

"Ladies," she cried, "we are not just God's human beings, we are citizens under the law—under the Fourteenth Amendment. We are entitled to the vote just as the freed Negro is!"

"Stop her," wailed Jocelyn van Horne. "She's going to ruin my piano!"

"How did she get in here?" van Horne demanded furiously. "Get her out of my home!"

At that, the woman calmly pulled a gun from beneath her shawl. The crowd gasped. "Not until I finish what I came to say," she cried, glaring fiercely around the room. "Your servants couldn't stop me," she went on, gathering force as she spoke, "because I have right on my side and I *will* be heard." She waved the gun in the air. Cornelia Martin screamed and Thad Parker made a lunge for the intruder, which she deftly eluded. Rathe was busy studying her weapon. It was an old Colt five-shooter from 1840 or so—he seriously doubted it would still fire, a fact which amused him greatly.

"Ladies," cried the woman, "only gross injustice could have brought me here tonight. I have sought you out, braved the male tyrants at your door, broken through the walls that imprison you to preach the message of liberation. Tomorrow is Election Day. I beg you, I implore you—go out to the polls! Demand your rights! Follow the example of our fearless leader, Susan B. Anthony—"

"You are trespassing," yelled van Horne. "I warn you to get down from that piano now, or I will send for the police."

Rathe was smiling.

The woman's oval face was no longer the delicate white of ivory, but heavily flushed. "Ladies," she went on, ignoring van Horne completely, "why is it that as soon as we marry we cease to exist in the eyes of the law? From that moment on, our husbands own us. They take our property, deprive us of our rights, and administer chastisement at whim! If single and the owner of property, we are taxed to support a government that gives us no representation. We must demand a say in our government. I beg you all, tomorrow march to the polls!"

"Rathe, do something," Jocelyn urged frantically. "My God, I'll never live this down. I'll be ruined. A free-loving man-hater besieging my own home!"

Rathe's mouth hurt from smiling. "Come on down, ma'am," he cajoled softly, reaching out a hand as he took a step forward, about to swing onto the piano stool.

She pointed the gun straight at his chest. "Stop right there! I'm not finished. I—"

One of van Horne's man servants was stealthily approaching. Jocelyn was signaling to him desperately. The woman swung around just in time. As she did so, the gun went off, obviously by accident, causing her to jump and everyone to shrink back.

"Send for the police," van Horne shouted to the room in general as his wife collapsed to the floor. "Look! My wife has fainted! I want that woman arrested!"

The suffragette woman was thoroughly aroused now. Wisps of red hair were escaping her bonnet to frame her face. "Tomorrow we must go to the polls! We must attempt to end this male tyranny, this domination based on strength and might, not right!''

''I cannot believe this,'' Bradford Ames said.

''She is crazy,'' Patricia agreed.

Triumphantly now, the woman cried, ''It's not just a matter of voting! We must liberate ourselves from all domination! Don't allow these perverted philistines to use your bodies for their own lusts! Liberate yourselves completely! We are equal!'' She was so excited her arms flailed like a windmill, and two accidental shots followed, flying harmlessly into the paneled ceiling.

Rathe started laughing again.

''Can you believe this?'' Thadeus Parker asked.

''This is an outrage!'' shouted van Horne. ''Where are the police?''

''I have never seen anything like this.'' Rathe grinned at Thad. ''And I've seen quite a bit, believe me.''

''We must take charge!'' the redhead cried. ''The time is now!'' The occupants of the salon all cringed as another shot exploded from the gun, this time purposefully aimed at the ceiling. Rathe grinned again—he couldn't help it—and shook his head. If she wasn't careful she was going to get herself into trouble.

''Has anyone sent for the police?'' Parker asked.

''I just sent the coachman,'' Ames replied.

''We cannot collude!'' shouted the woman hysterically. ''To marry one of these tyrants, to bear his children, to keep his larder and to warm his bed—that is collusion.''

Rathe smiled. Was she a little bit unhinged? Did she expect women to give up men? Give up matrimony? He chuckled and started forward.

She whirled to face him, pointing the gun at his chest.

He made out a small, pointed chin and full coral lips set in a frown of determination. ''Come on down heah, darlin'.''

''Don't come any closer,'' she warned. ''Philistine! Philanderer! Tyrant!''

He leaped onto the piano knowing she had no shots left.

There was a long mahogany table behind her covered with porcelain bowls, Oriental vases, and other bric-a-brac. She lunged toward it; he lunged after her. His arms closed around her waist, pulling her against him. Her body was as warm and soft and feminine as any woman's. She struggled. He chuckled again. "You should count your bullets, sweetheart," he drawled softly.

"Pig!" she screamed.

He saw it coming just in the nick of time—a vicious and unladylike elbow at his groin. He spun away and she leaped from the piano onto the table, stepping precariously, causing the dishes and vases to clatter to the floor.

A huge grin broke out on Rathe's handsome face and he leaped after her, sliding on the thickly waxed wood. He knocked over two snifters full of brandy and more glass crashed and broke. She screamed, grabbed a vase at the end of the table, and hefted it menacingly. Rathe skidded to a stop, with difficulty, hands held high. His blue eyes sparkled. "Put the vase down," he said coaxingly, his tone honey-sweet.

"Despot," she cried, and she threw it.

He ducked. So did van Horne and two other guests, all in her line of fire. It missed everyone and broke against the wall. Rathe charged. She shrieked as he lifted her and slung her upside down over his shoulder, then slipped to the floor as if she were weightless. His hand settled on a perfect palmful of buttock, too intimately. She started twisting and kicking and then grabbed handfuls of his hair. "Let me down, you beast!"

He used one hand to grab both of her wrists and held them down by his chest. "What do you want me to do with her?" he asked.

"Hold her for the constable outside," van Horne ordered.

Rathe strode out of the salon and down the hall amidst excited murmurings while his burden spit and hissed from his shoulders.

"Unhand me, you—bastard."

He laughed and stepped out into the night.

"Do you promise to behave?" he asked.

"Yes," she gasped. "Just put me down."

He released her hands, and unable to help himself, slid his free hand over her firm round buttocks again. Disguised though she was in the baggy dress, there still was no mistaking the fact that she had an exceptional figure. She swung a fist toward his ear for his efforts, the blow glancing off him harmlessly, and he slid her to the ground gently but slowly—her body slipping down against his. The top of her bonneted head came to his chin; she was tall for a woman, and for a second they stared mutely at each other.

It was dark in the street, but Rathe got a vague impression of fragile features, high cheekbones, and big, dark eyes. He thought, surprised, *Why, she's pretty.*

She looked into a face unshadowed by a hat and saw perfectly sculpted features and sensually full lips. It was the most handsome face she had ever seen, and for some reason, that made her even more furious.

He smiled.

She glared.

"Don't worry," he murmured, his hands tightening on her shoulders. "I won't let the police get you."

For one more instant their gazes locked, his warm, hers ice-cold. And then she kicked his shin as hard as she could.

He buckled at the knee; she fled into the night.

Chapter 1

Mississippi, 1875

Grace O'Rourke sat perfectly erect, shoulders stiff and squared, gloved hands clasped primly in her lap. She looked out from beneath a gray bonnet at the passing countryside—green and lush and so very hot in August. They had passed through rolling, wooded hills and small, cultivated plots of land, by vast fields of cotton, shimmering white in the sun, ragged shacks with sagging roofs, and huge, partially destroyed antebellum mansions, with blackened-out windows, a testimony to the recent past. The train was already chugging its way across Mississippi. In a very few hours she would arrive at her destination. Unconsciously, her hands tightened.

She made a nondescript figure in her dowdy gray traveling suit. There was a light dusting of freckles over her perfectly small, slightly upturned, classically Irish nose. A pair of gold-rimmed spectacles also rested on that nose, but could not disguise wide, almond-shaped eyes of the most remarkable color—violet. Her mouth was lush and full, especially when relaxed and not primly pursed in thought or vexation. The hat hid every single strand of her fantastically red hair, a near impossible accomplishment, for it was a hip-length mass of untamable curls. Her eyebrows, arched above the ugly glasses, were a darker auburn, almost but not quite the exact same shade as her hair.

Grace was very anxious. She was terribly afraid that something might go wrong, that she might lose the job she was traveling to Natchez to claim. A very proper appearance was crucial. Her suit, however unflattering, was her best and that, along with the glasses, which she did not need, and the bonnet concealing her hair, made her look, she thought, properly matronly. Properly governess-like, she hoped. "Oh, darn," she finally whispered to herself, releasing some of the anxiety that had been building in her over the last few days.

The couple sitting in front of her turned to stare.

Grace smiled immediately, ignoring the man, whose red face and veined nose bespoke intemperance to her discerning eye. The woman was plump and sad-eyed, a sister in need—Grace could just feel it. They had boarded in Nashville. Grace had been waiting for the right opportunity to strike up a conversation. "It's such a shame," she said softly, gesturing at the still-magnificent ruins of yet another antebellum plantation.

"Yes, it is," the woman responded, twisting to look at her.

"I'm Grace O'Rourke, from New York City," Grace said, smiling and extending her hand. She felt a twinge of worry about using her real name, even though it was unlikely anyone would recognize her so far from home.

"I'm Martha Grimes, and this is my husband, Charles."

Charles turned too, after taking a sip from a beautifully wrought silver hip flask. "My pleasure, ma'am."

Grace nodded and turned her attention back to Martha. "Where are you from, Martha?"

"You wouldn't know it—a little town called Two Corners, fifty miles south of Nashville."

"No, I don't know it. What brings you and your husband south?"

"We're visiting our daughter in Natchez," Martha said, beaming. "She's just had her first."

"How wonderful. I'm on my way to Natchez, too. I'm a teacher."

Charles turned. "Hope you ain't one of them nigger teachers."

Grace stiffened, flushing. Do not respond, she told herself sternly. Do not. She ignored him. "Actually, a dear, old friend of mine has arranged a position for me at a plantation called Melrose. As governess."

"How wonderful," Martha said. "How many children will you have?"

"Just two," Grace said, with a deep sigh. She was so unbelievably lucky to have gotten this position. The pay was more than generous, and it included room and board. She would be able to send all of her income back home to help out her sick mother. And she would not have to augment her salary with part-time employment, the way she had done in New York.

Once she had been a New York City public schoolteacher, but she hadn't worked in ten months—ever since she had been arrested.

Grace was the daughter of abolitionists. Her father, Sian O'Rourke, was an easygoing Irish doctor who had died in the Civil War, accidentally shot while trying to tend to the wounded in the midst of battle. He and her mother, Dianna, had been active participants in the Underground Railroad and the American Anti-Slavery Society. Her mother had begun to question the role of women in society as early as the forties. With Sian's full support, she had attended the first convention for women's rights in Seneca Falls, New York, in '48, and had been lecturing and organizing ever since. After the War and her husband's death, she had turned all her attention to the women's suffrage movement, first as a member of the American Equal Rights Association, and when that divided into two camps, the radical National Woman's Suffrage Association.

It was only natural that Grace should join the cause from the time she was an adolescent. As a child she had heard many heated debates between her parents and their friends. Sometimes she had sat on her father's warm lap, held close to his chest, while he smoked a pipe, the fervent conversation echoing around the kitchen as the abolition-ists and women agitators met and planned. Sian was as quiet as her mother was volatile—he had always teased her that her hair and her temper had most definitely not come from his side of the family. But when he did speak, never raising his voice, everyone stopped to listen. Those were wonderful, exciting times.

They lived in a small apartment in the city, with just the one bedroom for her parents. Grace slept on a cot in the kitchen. Both Sian and Dianna gave her her lessons, and Grace was reading avidly by the age of six—anything she could get her hands on. There were always plenty of pamphlets around. Sian was proud of his daughter's abil-ity, and both of her parents always had time to answer her questions.

Sian rarely had cash, though. Most of his patients were too poor to offer any payment other than a few eggs or a home-cooked meal. Dianna was an excellent seamstress, and through her efforts, kept food on the table. Grace learned to stitch at an early age, although she hated it; she preferred her books to all else, but was expected to help her mother—and she did.

She knew as a youngster that she wanted to be a school-teacher. At first, her father was surprised. "Are you sure, Grace?"

"Da, look how you and Mum have taught me. Imagine if I'd grown up in one of those fancy mansions on the river. I'd be some simpering idiot, now wouldn't I?"

Sian smiled.

"But you taught me to think, you made sure my eyes were open to the world, to all its injustices. How can the slaves ever be freed, how can women ever escape male tyranny, if children aren't taught to think, to question what they see and hear and are told?"

Sian wrapped her in his warm, familiar embrace. "I'm proud of you, Grace." She was only twelve.

She was going to teach children to think for themselves, as her parents had taught her. It became the family mission to scrape together the money she needed for school. It was no easy task, especially when the War began, and her father died. At fourteen Grace took employment as a maid for the extra income. Even during school she worked part-time, went to class, studied, and found time to work alongside her mother in the National Woman's Suffrage Association.

In '66, at the age of eighteen, she had attended the National Women's Rights Convention with her mother—her first one. It was an exhilarating experience, one that left her flushed with excitement for days. She had attended many more since. There had never been any question that she would follow in her parents' footsteps organizing and agitating and teaching others in order to correct the injustices of the world.

She was twenty-three when she finally attained her hard-earned teaching certificate.

Now Grace gazed absently out of the train's window. Ten months ago she had lost her teaching job. A proprietor of a men's haberdashery had had her arrested for disturbing the peace. It had not been her first arrest. Two years ago she and five other women had been arrested for trying to register to vote amidst shocked males and dismayed, confused election officials. All charges had been dropped as the country had turned to watch the spectacular trial of Susan B. Anthony for exactly the same offense. She had been found guilty of violating the voting laws and fined, but she had resolutely refused to pay. To this day she was successfully avoiding payment.

It still made Grace furious whenever she thought about her own last arrest. It wasn't fair. Yes, she had hit the man, but he had grabbed her in a most intimate place—and damned if she wouldn't hit him again if she had the chance! She had succeeded in sending most of his customers fleeing from the store, outside of which two women were handing out pamphlets inviting the men to attend a women's suffrage meeting especially for their edification and enlightenment. Fortunately, she had only been fined and had managed to borrow the money to pay. But it was too late; the damage was done. She had been dismissed by the city's Superintendent of Public Schools. Her career as a New York City schoolteacher was over.

To make matters worse, during the past two years Grace had watched her mother grow paler, thinner, and more fanatical. She worried that her mother was pushing herself too hard. Six months ago the fatal blow had fallen—her mother had been diagnosed as having tuberculosis.

Grace had been desperate for a job. Her mother needed special care that only the city's finest hospitals could provide. And in New York she was now notorious as a crazy women's rights agitator, thanks to the headlines she had made during her last arrest. Not only had she lost her public school position, but as she soon discovered, no private schools would hire her. She had not even been able to find a position as a tutor. No one would hire her—not even for a clerical position.

"Are you married, dear?" Martha asked, interrupting her thoughts.

Grace thought of her dear friend, Allen Kennedy. "No." She could read Martha's thoughts as if they were spoken aloud, feel her pity. The poor thing, Martha was thinking, she's a spinster.

Grace's lips tightened into a narrow line. She hated that word, *spinster*. It was the most unfair, chauvinistic word, and a perfect example of the tyranny of the male sex over women. And she could be married if she wanted to be. Allen had asked her twice.

Allen.

Dear Allen had come to her rescue, and Grace clutched her reticule with his letter in it closer to her bosom. Allen was also a schoolteacher. They had met three years ago during a city-wide meeting of the National. The guest lecturer had been Victoria Woodhull, and Grace had been the first to raise her hand during the question-and-answer session afterward. She had been angry, although she hadn't let it show. The Woodhulls, Grace fervently believed, had irreparably damaged the women's movement by advocating free love. It had alienated too many potential followers. Instead of asking Victoria a question, Grace had used the opportunity to call her to account for sidetracking the movement. Later, Allen had sought Grace out. He not only agreed with the inexpedience of advocating free love, but like herself, he was against it morally as well. They had had a long and exhilarating talk and had become fast friends.

Allen had left New York last year, before the fiasco of her last arrest, having taken a position in one of Mississippi's new public schools, teaching the children of newly freed slaves. He had asked her to marry him for the second time just before he left, but Grace had refused. Although she loved Allen and had the utmost respect for him, she had no desire to marry him, even though he was the most enlightened man a woman could hope to find. Allen did not understand, and Grace really didn't either. She tried to tell him, and herself, that she just had no interest in marrying.

She sighed, then caught sight of Martha Grimes again. Why linger over the past, she told herself, when a willing subject presented herself?

"May I join you, Martha?" she said, pointing toward the place Charles Grimes had just vacated.

Martha agreed happily and Grace slipped into the seat beside her, digging into her reticule and pulling out a pamphlet. "Do you like to read?" she asked, her face flushed now, her eyes sparkling.

"Of course," Martha said, but Grace had already handed her the papers. "This includes the text of a wonderful speech by Elizabeth Cady Stanton," Grace cried enthusiastically. "On marriage. On divorce."

Martha stared and Grace held her gaze. "You know," Grace said in a hushed, tense voice, "when men enter into a partnership, if it's not mutually beneficial, it's an accepted, indeed, expected practice for them to dissolve that partnership and go their separate ways."

Martha bit her lip, clutching the papers to her plump breast.

Grace drove on. "Why is it that only we women suffer to endure? When a child attains a certain age, his subjection to his parents' authority is dissolved. Why is it a wife's subjection is eternal? Did you know that in some countries widows are burned on the funeral pyre with their dead husbands?"

Martha's eyes widened.

"Why is it," Grace said, her voice rising, causing heads to turn, "that women are doomed to servitude for their entire lives?"

"I don't know," Martha whispered weakly.

Grace gripped her arm. "Martha, I will be forming a local women's organization in Natchez, if one isn't in existence already. Please, come and hear us. Just hear us. I want to help you." She removed her spectacles, which were slipping off of her nose from her excitement, to stare intently into Martha's eyes.

"I couldn't," Martha managed. "Charles . . ."

"He doesn't have to know," Grace said vehemently.

Martha blinked, weakened. "I don't know . . ."

"I'll let you know when our first meeting will be," Grace said, squeezing her hand. "We're all in this together, Martha. All of us."

Chapter 2

Allen was waiting for her at the railroad depot in Natchez.

At the sight of his familiar form, Grace felt a surge of affection. She turned to the Grimeses, clasping Martha's palms. "Do take care, and I'm looking forward so much to seeing you again."

Martha glanced guiltily at Charles, then squeezed Grace's hands back.

Grace turned to wave to Allen. He was a solid, nearly portly man in his late thirties, with graying sideburns and warm brown eyes. "Grace! Grace!" His excitement was etched all over his face.

She beamed and descended to meet him.

"It's so wonderful to see you," Allen declared, holding her hands tightly.

"How are you?" Grace asked.

"Just fine," Allen said, but not before she saw shadows flitting across his eyes. "At least, now I am."

Grace frowned, wondering what he meant.

Allen paid a Negro porter to take her bags to a waiting cheviotte. He climbed in after Grace, raising the reins. Grace twisted to take in the sprawling city. White clapboard houses with picket fences and carefully tended gardens graced this section of town, although the smokestacks of a factory could be seen on a distant ridge, billowing gray clouds into the horizon. "Where's the Mississippi River?"

23

Allen pointed. "On the other side of town." He touched the tip of her nose. "What are those?"

Grace smiled. "Spectacles, Allen. Surely you can see that."

He chuckled. "Dare I inquire as to why you're wearing glasses? Has your vision taken a turn for the worse?"

She laughed, a rich, vibrant sound. "No, Allen, my eyesight is fine. Actually, this is part of my proper governess disguise."

He smiled wryly, then took one of her gloved hands. "I missed you, Miss O'Rourke."

She didn't hesitate—Allen was her dearest friend. "I missed you too, Allen Kennedy."

"How was your trip?"

"Dusty. Allen, how is everything? You've told me so much about the school in your letters that I can't wait to see it."

Allen hesitated. "Just fine."

Grace stared at him speculatively.

She knew, mostly from reading the newspapers, that teaching public school in the South was no easy profession. The new educational system had been instituted by the Republican Congress just after the War. There was tremendous local opposition to the schools, as well as to much of the "radical" Republican Congress's legislation.

The lines in the South were, for the most part, concisely drawn. Most Southerners were conservative Democrats, who had fought for secession and who now saw their entire way of life disintegrating before their eyes. Just after the War, under the Andrew Johnson administration, they had enacted the harsh Black Codes, which, in effect, kept the newly emancipated Negroes in economic and political slavery.

Then the Republican Congress had taken it upon itself to reorganize the South, beginning with the three Reconstruction Acts in 1867.

These acts put the South under military supervision. All the rebels were immediately disenfranchised, and the new state governments were required to ratify the Fourteenth Amendment, which gave the freed Negro basic civil rights, including the right to vote. With Negro suffrage, the Republicans assumed control of the Southern state governments, although in many localities the Democrats were strong enough to control local and county governments, or at least exert various degrees of influence upon them. According to Allen, this was the case in Natchez, where the Democrats held several municipal positions, such as the sheriff's office, although not all.

He had written her at least weekly but most of his letters had lauded the progress of his pupils, all freed Negro children, or described the beauty of the Mississippi countryside. Grace sensed an omission, but she couldn't quite pinpoint what it was.

"Let me tell you about Melrose," Allen said. "The Barclays were one of the great Natchez planter families. Melrose was a huge plantation at the time of the War. Of course, its foundation was cotton. But like the other great Natchez planters, the Barclays eventually diversified, buying into Northern industrial interests. The plantation is actually across the Mississippi in Louisiana, though Louisa Barclay prefers her home in Natchez and resides here most of the time. Louisa was only sixteen when she married Philip Barclay—he was already middle-aged. She was widowed shortly after the War when Philip died in his sleep at a ripe old age."

"So they didn't lose Melrose because of the War?"

"No. Philip was too well off. Rumor has it they had no trouble with the taxes. Melrose is thriving, from what I gather." And he grimaced.

"Allen, what is it?"

"Nothing," he said, attempting a smile. "I just hope this is the right thing for you, Grace."

"Don't worry about me," she said firmly.

After a hot, dusty drive, they finally arrived at Melrose. The house was a red brick Greek Revival mansion with massive white columns and a white pediment. Grace's stomach began to twist into knots as they approached along the paved, curving drive, the scent of magnolia hanging thick and heady all around them. "Allen, you don't think they'll find out about what happened in New York, do you?"

"Not if you can stick strictly to teaching," Allen said gently, with a touch of reprimand. Grace resolved not to agitate for her sisters or any other oppressed classes—at least, not publicly. And then she knew instantly that she was fooling herself; she could never give up the causes she believed in. Somehow, she would have to be very discreet.

At the impressive front door Allen left her with a young Negro girl who was about fifteen. Her name was Clarissa and she was one of his students. He then promised to pick Grace up for church on Sunday and dinner afterward.

Minutes later, Grace found herself standing in a large high-ceilinged hall, rich with wood paneling. "You just wait heah a bit, ma'am," Clarissa instructed her, smiling brightly. Grace instantly liked the young woman. But wait she did—a good half an hour. By the time Louisa Barclay appeared, Grace was simmering with annoyance, and trying not to show it.

Louisa was very close to her own age, raven-haired, blue-eyed, and beautiful—a perfect Southern belle. Once they were ensconced in an elegant parlor, she looked Grace up and down carefully. Louisa was all elegance and vitality, her day gown cut scandalously low, exposing a good deal of bosom, as white as the magnolia blossoms outside. Her hair was arranged in a mass of artfully casual curls, held in place by gold combs. She fluttered a hand-painted Chinese fan.

Grace stood still, her every joint aching from the days of bone-jarring travel, her glasses fogging from the humidity and her own body's warmth. She wanted to remove the spectacles, so she could see better but she did not dare. Perspiration gathered under the crown of her hat and between her full, although carefully concealed, breasts. She immediately sensed that Louisa was vain, arrogant, and demanding. She was afraid to breathe, afraid she wouldn't pass muster, and at the same time furious for having to take this position. Louisa pointed the fan at Grace's head. "Perhaps you'd care to take off your hat?"

Grace did, controlling her red-hot Irish temper with difficulty, keeping her eyes down so Louisa wouldn't see her anger.

"You have red hair." Louisa sounded shocked.

Grace said nothing.

"You never said so in your letter. It's been my experience that red-headed women are loose. My daughters must have only the best influences. At least you're not young."

Grace bit her lip. Usually her age was not a sore spot, and she did want to look older for this job. But somehow, just now she felt tired of people making allusions to it. She remembered Martha Grimes asking if she was married, and how that had bothered her. But maybe she should face it. She was a spinster—she was twenty-seven.

Louisa shrugged. "Oh well, at present I am desperate to see the girls taken care of. They are to be instructed in sewing, embroidering, and etiquette every morning from ten to one. Dinner is precisely at one-fifteen. In the afternoons, they may nap. From three to five you may give them their reading and geography lessons. Supper for the children is at six. You are to eat with them, unless you wish a tray in your room. Breakfast for the children is at nine. You may take your own breakfast anytime you like. I expect you to spend Saturdays keeping them amused— picnics and so forth. Sundays are your own. Hannah will show you to your room and introduce you to the girls."

Grace could not bring herself to say yes ma'am to this woman, and was fortunately relieved from having to do so when Louisa left and a tall, statuesque black woman of about forty appeared, with Clarissa trailing behind her.

Hannah flashed Grace a warm smile. "Don't you worry about her," she said. "Just stay out of her way and things will be just fine. Miz Barclay likes to think she's royalty, and expects everyone else to think so, too.''

Grace smiled, pleased she had found at least one ally. ''I'm Grace O'Rourke,'' she said, extending her hand.

The woman blinked, then laughed. ''Women shakin' hands?'' She waved at her. ''Come on, you must be exhausted. You met my girl, Clarissa?''

''Yes, I have.'' Grace dropped her hand. ''Why shouldn't women shake hands when they meet each other? Men do.'' Stop it, Grace, she said to herself instantly. Don't go starting up.

Hannah flashed her an amazed look. '' 'Cause we *ain't* men. Clarissa, go and fetch some fixin's for Miz O'Rourke, mebbe some nice, cool lemonade an' a piece of that cake Cook made.''

Grace bit her tongue, hard.

''Yes'm,'' Clarissa said, her eyes wide and curious on Grace. She flashed her another smile before running off to do as her mother bid.

Grace's room was on the second floor, tucked away in the back. It was probably the smallest room in the house, but Grace didn't mind.

She stared at the walls, then touched one. Fabric. Blue and white fabric. She caressed one of the intricately carved posters of the linen-draped bed. The wood was smooth and cool. Hannah followed her gaze. ''Ain't you ever seen mosquito netting before?''

Grace shook her head. The coverlet was white, and lace-trimmed. There was a big, plush dark blue chair with a footstool, perfect for reading at night, and a beautiful pine bureau, with a lace doily, wash basin, pitcher, and mirror. On the other side of the room was a small escritoire. She couldn't wait to sit down at it and write. There was even an immense rosewood wardrobe. She strode to the window.

Below, a green lawn fell away to the stables, the smoke-house, and the ice house. Beyond that, another mansion was visible. The sky was incredibly blue, with not a cloud

to mar it. She turned to look at Hannah, and she was
smiling.

"Lord, you're pretty when you smile like that," Hannah said. "Bet you're a looker without those glasses."

Grace blushed. She knew she was more than pretty. It
was the bane of her existence. She had always been considered a good-looking child, but by the time she was
eighteen, she was considered beautiful. It was frustrating.
As long as she was pretty, men would not take her seriously. She didn't want them looking at her, chasing her,
trying to feel up beneath her skirts—not when she was
trying to accomplish something with her life. For some
unknown reason God had given her all that hair and beautiful features and a slim body with full breasts, though
she'd bound them tightly in. It seemed a joke, because
every day she went to great trouble to hide her looks so
she could attend to life with the seriousness it deserved.

"Is this the new governess?"

Grace looked at the child who had to be Mary Louise,
the ten-year-old. She was the image of her mother.
"Hello," she said, with a friendly smile.

Mary Louise folded her arms. "That's an ugly dress."

Grace stared.

"Hush up," Hannah said.

Mary Louise smiled. "But it is. I'm making a pillowcase. The stitches are all wrong. Come and fix it."

Grace was still stunned. "Excuse me?"

"It's your job," Mary Louise said haughtily, "to help
me."

"Miss O'Rourke starts tomorrow, Mary Louise," Hannah began.

"Hush up, you dumb nigrah," Mary Louise said.
"Don't you have things to do? Why, if mama knew you
were standing here idle instead of working she'd send
you packing. And if it was a few years ago she'd whip you
good for you telling me what to do! Maybe you'll get
whipped anyways—by the night riders!"

Hannah clenched her jaw, but fear flared in her eyes.

"That's enough," Grace cried, grabbing Mary Louise by her wrist. "You apologize this instant—first to me, and then to Hannah."

Mary Louise stared at her, her blue eyes filled with shock. "What?"

"I expect an apology and so does *Miss* Hannah."

"First of all," Mary Louise said, in a strangled voice, "I'd sooner die than apologize to a no-good lazy darkie."

Grace stepped back. What did she expect? This was the Deep South, not New York. Mary Louise took the opportunity to dart out of the room.

"It's all right, Miz O'Rourke," Hannah said. "You come on down and get somethin' to eat when you're ready. John will bring your bags up." Hannah left.

Grace had never seen such atrocious manners in her life. She wondered if she would be allowed to discipline the children. Heavens, if she wasn't, how was she ever going to handle this one? She was relieved when footsteps sounded in the hall and John entered with her two small bags. Behind him, a small boy of about six was carrying her valise. "Oh, John, thank you, but that case is too heavy for that little boy."

"I done carried it all the way up here myself." The boy beamed, white teeth dazzling in a round black face.

"Don't speak unless you're spoken to," John said sternly to the boy. "Please don't be mad at my boy."

"Oh, I'm not," Grace said quickly. He had been so proud, but now he hung his head in response to his father's scolding. She smiled down at him. "And you are?"

"Geoffrey, ma'am."

"Thank you very much, Geoffrey, for a job well done."

He squirmed with pleasure.

"You need anythin' else you just ask me or Hannah," John said as he left, shooing his son out before him.

Grace went looking for the schoolroom, and found it down the hall. It was obviously the nursery. Margaret Anne was there, the image of her sister, except chubbier, sitting on the floor and playing with a very expensive-looking doll. She stopped playing to look up and stare.

Grace smiled and came forward to kneel next to her. "Hello, Margaret Anne. What a pretty doll. I'm your teacher."

"It's mine," she said, hugging the doll tightly. "And I hate school. I don't want to read."

"I hated school too, did you know that? Especially when I was your age."

"I hate school," Margaret Anne said, her eyes filling with tears. "I don't want to read!"

"There is no school today," Grace said calmly, standing. "But tomorrow we'll get started and I'll show you just how much fun we're going to have together."

"I hate lessons," Margaret Anne cried, throwing the doll so hard it skidded across the floor, its head cracking.

Grace stared at the beautiful, golden-haired doll with the broken head.

Margaret Anne screamed and ran out of the room.

Grace sighed, a headache beginning, and started after her.

"Mama, Mama," Margaret Anne sobbed, turning a corner.

Grace broke into a run. The last thing she needed was the child fleeing to her mother in tears with her not twenty minutes on the job. She turned the corner—and wham! She ran into a solid brick wall of warm, male flesh. Muscular arms enfolded her, pulling her against steel thighs and a rock-hard chest. Her face was buried against a soft white linen shirt, slightly damp with sweat. A heady, musky odor filled her nostrils. Large hands held her hips firmly, intimately, against his. A rich chuckle sounded.

"What do we have here?"'

Chapter 3

She came out of her state of stunned immobility.

She was pressed intimately against a man . . . a strange man. His hands were even more intimate, moving against her hips. Her heart was racing and her knees were weak; something liquid seemed to be collecting deep inside her. And then he laughed again, another warm, rich rippling sound. She pushed her arms up and braced herself away.

And looked up.

She recognized him instantly.

Not because of his gorgeous looks—the beautifully carved cheekbones, the straight, flared nose, the full, sensual lips, the sky-blue eyes and the sun-streaked hair—but because, of all the people who had been at the van Horne mansion that night two years ago, he had been the only one to find her amusing. He had been the one laughing, as if the issue of women's rights was a joke! Not to mention the fact that then, as now, he had handled her as if she were a sack of beans, hauling her out upside down while patting her behind—yes, she remembered that! She didn't know his name, but she knew him.

He was grinning. His eyes sparkled. At the corners of his mouth were two well-formed dimples. His teeth were white and even.

"How dare you!" Grace said.

He lifted a brow. "Oh, I apologize for running into you!"

His Texan drawl was thick and sweet. Grace blushed,

33

much to her chagrin, for as they both knew, it had been she who had run into him. She squared her shoulders ramrod straight and started to move past, but he blocked her way.

"Don't rush away in a huff," he murmured softly. "What's your name?"

She looked up, her face frozen in an expression of fury, and said, "Grace O'Rourke." And then she began to think, frantically.

Did he recognize her? It had been almost two years since their brief encounter and she had been wearing that concealing bonnet. Grace was trying not to panic, but who could forget a suffragette standing on a piano in the midst of a private soirée? If he recognized her, she would probably lose this job. He appeared to be an intimate in this house. Who was he? Brother? Cousin? Brother-in-Law? Oh Lord, let him be a guest—about to leave! She could not lose this job!

"Grace O'Rourke," he drawled, testing it. He appeared to like it, because he smiled a smile that made her throat tight. She started to push past, panicked. He blocked her with one strong arm, then winked at her, as if sharing some private joke.

"Miss Margaret Anne, do come out," he invited, looking Grace right in the eyes with silent laughter.

Grace stood stiffly still.

Margaret Anne appeared from a nearby doorway, looking belligerent and red-eyed.

"I believe you're looking for this little culprit?"

"Yes, thank you," Grace replied.

Margaret Anne glared at Grace and ran to the golden-haired stranger. "She broke my doll! She broke Lisa!"

He lifted her up, high into the air. "Oh no! Poor Lisa! But I'll bet Miss O'Rourke didn't mean it, now did she?" He held her close to his face, nuzzling her affectionately. He was impossible for even a little girl to resist. "I'll bet she feels awful about the accident; and you, princess, are going to be charitable and forgive her."

"I did not break the doll," Grace said, trying hard to control her outrage. "She threw it on the floor herself in a fit of temper."

He looked closely at the child. "Margaret Anne!"

She started to cry.

"Hush now, sweeting," he crooned, rocking her. "I think maybe we had better get Lisa to a doctor, what do you say?"

"She's broke," the child sobbed.

He shifted her to the crook of his arm and Grace followed them unwillingly down the hall to the nursery. He set Margaret Anne down and knelt, inspecting Lisa. "Why, it's nothing a good doll doctor can't fix," he pronounced cheerfully.

"Really?" Margaret Anne asked cautiously.

"Would I lie?" he coaxed, dimpling.

Grace gritted her teeth. He was turning his potent charm on a child of six! And the child, already susceptible, was softening, smiling. "I love you, Rathe," she said, hugging him.

He laughed, hugging her hard. "And I love you. Now, I'll take Lisa and she'll be fixed up in no time. But I expect you to be nicer to Miss O'Rourke in return. Ladies are always polite and well-mannered, and you, darlin', are a lady."

Grace was incredulous.

Margaret Anne frowned.

"Don't pout," Rathe said. "It causes ugly wrinkles."

He tucked the doll in one arm and turned to Grace. His eyes twinkled. "You shouldn't pout, either."

She realized she was clenching her fists. This man . . . this philistine was molding the child into a simpering Southern belle already. Grace felt ready to explode, but because she didn't know who he was and didn't dare jeopardize her job, she remained atypically silent.

"I'm going to go tell Hannah about Lisa," Margaret Anne shouted, and ran out.

Grace looked after her—it was safer than looking at

Rathe—until she had no choice but to lift her gaze to his.
His eyes were searching her from the top of her red head
to the tip of her toes, moving very slowly and deliberately
along the way. She felt another blush rise—her fairness
caused her to blush too easily and too often. She lifted her
chin, trying very hard to ignore his blatant assessment of
her. The problem was, her body had a mind of its own,
and her heart was trying to leap right out of her rib cage.
"That child is only six, not sixteen. Wrinkles? Please,
don't go putting any more vanity into her head than already exists there."

"Why not?" Rathe asked easily. "She's a beautiful
child and she's going to be a gorgeous woman. Do you
have something against flattery, Grace?"

Her jaw muscles went tight. His gaze seemed to be
penetrating her through and through; it was as if he was
trying to see inside to all her deepest secrets. "It's not
flattery I have a problem with," she replied coolly.

At that, his dimples deepened. "Good," he said, staring. His gaze had become very warm. His hand came up,
slowly. Shocked, Grace realized he was reaching for her
glasses and she found herself leaning backward against the
wall.

"Because I'm going to take off those ugly spectacles
and look into your eyes," he breathed, his forefinger
touching her face. "And then I'm going to tell you just
how beautiful you are."

Grace literally jumped. "Please," she cried, aware of
being breathless, "spare me your chauvinistic attentions."

That stopped him dead in his tracks, puzzlement crossing his features. "Chauvinistic attentions?"

It was men like this who were responsible for the plight
of modern women—men who saw only a pretty face and
a warm body to serve their needs. She felt the hot surge
of victory for having outmaneuvered him. "I have no need
of flattery, not from you, and not from any man."

"Ah, I see. Independent, are we?"

She flushed, lips tightening. "Yes."

He stared at her, then smiled slightly. "Are you afraid of me, Grace?"

She was so angry and shocked she was speechless.

"Or are you afraid of a well-deserved compliment?"

She gasped. "I, sir, am afraid of no man and certainly of no words—at least, no words in your vocabulary! But please, let me ask a question." She was glowing triumphantly. She rushed on, both barrels about to blast. "You, of course, are an expert on which subject—flattery or women?"

He chuckled. "Both, sweetheart, both."

His nerve made her jaw lock momentarily. "As long as women are treated like inferior, doll-like beings by men like you, sir, as long as we are flattered for being merely pleasant objects to look upon, we will never rise to enjoy all that God has blessed us with."

He stared, blinked, then grinned again. "Oh, no," he breathed. "You aren't one of those crazy women agitators, are you?"

She ignored him, although she was red-faced now. "It is men like you, sir, who are responsible for the downtrodden plight of women today!"

"The downtrodden plight . . . I was only trying to make you feel good, Gracie," he murmured.

"Flattery doesn't make a man feel good?" she challenged.

"Flattery makes a dog feel good, for that matter. I happen to enjoy petting dogs." He stared back, hard.

She flushed. "We are talking about men and women, not dogs."

He grinned. "Let's talk about men and women," he said, his tone dropping suggestively. "Although talking does get boring—sooner or later."

She gasped in frustration. "Do you or do you not enjoy flattery, sir?"

"Gracie, you can flatter me any day, any time, right now if you feel like it."

"I'm afraid," she said crisply, "the task you set me is impossible, monumental, and insurmountable."

He had the gall to laugh with obvious enjoyment. "And I thought my appeal was irresistible."

"We are not all blatant, naive fools," Grace snapped.

"You have an interesting assessment of womankind—not very *flattering*."

"I am not a hypocrite."

He grinned. "Grace, somehow I don't think you're in danger of being labeled that."

He would never take anything seriously. She turned her back on him abruptly. "I have to go."

"Wait a minute." His large hand closed around her elbow, stopping her. Her head turned back to him, she glared and pursed her lips. He was insufferable; he smiled. "So, Gracie, how about a stroll along the river?"

She stared, appalled.

He came closer.

She moved backward.

His dimples appeared.

Her heart raced.

His teeth flashed white against his skin. Her back found the wall. His hands, one still holding the doll, found her shoulders. "Dare I risk it?" he breathed. "You're pretty even with those ridiculous glasses."

She couldn't respond.

"And you know what?" His mouth seemed to have drifted closer.

She stared into his blue eyes and was barely aware of anything but the man whose breath, tinged with tobacco and brandy, touched hers. He stared back intently, the dimples having disappeared.

She opened her mouth to speak.

He leaned forward, his eyes dropping toward her mouth. "Your mouth . . . your mouth is beautiful . . . begging a man's kiss . . ."

He is going to kiss me, Grace told herself. She couldn't move.

"Rathe? Darling? Where are you?"

He smiled, with a shake of his head and a shrug, but did not move away. "Damn," he said softly.

"Rathe?"

He stepped back then, tucking the doll under his arm. "I'm in the nursery, Louisa." Still his eyes held Grace's warmly. Too warmly. Grace felt herself flushing to the roots of her scalp.

Louisa rounded the corner, looked at them without breaking stride, and as she reached Rathe, hugged his free arm close to her breast. "Darling, John said you were here. I was so hoping you'd come for supper. What are you doing upstairs?"

"Saying hello to the girls," Rathe said, smiling at Louisa. "And comforting Margaret Anne. She broke her doll."

"I see you met Miss O'Rourke."

"Yes indeed," Rathe said.

"Don't flirt with the help, Rathe," Louisa snapped.

Rathe laughed. "Don't be a shrew, sweetheart, it's not becoming."

She stared, her fine nostrils flaring.

He put his arm around her. "What kind of welcome is this?"

Grace felt like an intruder. Something sick welled up inside her as their relationship became clear to her. "Not the kind I had in mind," Louisa said suggestively.

Grace escaped with a mumbled excuse. She fled to her room and closed the door on the lovers. She was trembling and even angrier than before, if that was possible. The man was not just the worst kind of scoundrel, he was the worst kind of flirt—callous, insensitive, selfish. She detested him.

It just wasn't fair that he was so handsome.

Chapter 4

"What do you think?" Robert Chatham asked.

"I think," Rathe breathed, every nerve in his body tingling, his heart racing, "I think I am very, very excited."

It was a perfectly beautiful Mississippi morning, still early enough to be cool, a few picture-perfect clouds floating overhead, birds singing high in the dogwoods around them. Rathe stood with his hands deep in the pockets of his tweed jacket, one breech-clad knee braced against the white paddock fence, his high boots gleaming. He looked the epitome of a Southern gentleman as he watched Chatham's colt run across the pasture, intent despite his nonchalant poise. He'd come to Natchez not only to see to a few of his local business interests, but to have a look at this yearling. Now he was glad he'd made the trip, especially if it meant the colt would soon be his.

Suddenly, though, Rathe realized that his desire to possess the magnificent animal was obvious, and a carefully neutral expression crossed his face. He tore his gaze away from the horse with difficulty. "I hear your cook makes excellent fritters," he said, to divert the conversation and regain some degree of leverage for the bargaining that would come. He was not overly worried. He was used to success; it had followed him his entire life.

"She does," Robert Chatham said. A perfect host, he gestured toward his white plantation house sitting on the hill behind them. "Shall we?"

An hour and a half later Rathe left Chatham's home, the

proud owner of the colt, and at a fair price. He was not surprised. One of his friends had once said, somewhat enviously, that he was not just a charming scoundrel, but a charmed one. Rathe had laughed at the time, but his friend was right.

He had been born on a west Texas ranch. His father, Derek Bragg, was a powerful man, a half-breed who had also been a captain in the Texas Rangers. He had never hidden the fact that he had fallen in love with his genteel English wife at first sight, a fact which much amused— but hardly surprised—his children. As they grew up, their parents' love for each other was more than evident: it was a tangible thing.

As the youngest, Rathe demanded attention, and naturally received it. He was the apple of his parents' eyes, and his older sister and brother adored him also. It seemed he could do no wrong, even though, if truth be told, he was constantly in trouble. He neglected his chores, running off with a friend to shoot rabbits, or setting off firecrackers in the attic. He liked to steal out at night to play posse, and once sneaked along on the trail drive, only to be discovered too late to be sent home. He tried to break a bronco mustang, played hooky from school, spied on a Comanche camp—as a test of courage—and in Galveston when he was ten, almost successfully stowed away on a cargo ship. He had wanted to see Africa.

He was uncontainable. His energy, curiosity, and intelligence were limitless. He drove his family to distraction. His father, who had rarely had to raise a hand to his other two children, walloped him frequently, if halfheartedly. ''I pray and thank the Lord every day that you were born under a lucky star,'' his mother once confessed, ''otherwise, you certainly wouldn't be long for this world.''

As an adult he enjoyed the same luck he had as a child. He nearly always won at cards. His first investment, in an ironworks, with money won at poker, quadrupled itself. In his hands, several hundred dollars became a thousand, a thousand dollars became ten thousand. Investing became a challenge to Rathe, a game that wasn't very different from poker—except that the stakes were much higher. The thrill came from the possibility of losing—and the staggering amounts that could be won. By the age of twenty-four Rathe had made his first million.

With women, it was the same story; his successes were legendary there, too. He had discovered sex at the tender age of thirteen, and couldn't remember having been rejected by a woman ever since.

As he cantered his horse back to his hotel, he savored his most recent success in purchasing the colt. Now that it was his, however, he realized that his business was concluded and there was no real reason to remain in Natchez. The thought unsettled him somehow, and made him think about Grace. Suddenly he was imagining her with her hair down, her glasses off, naked. Her hair probably came to her waist. She was undoubtedly beautiful without those spectacles—he was too experienced not to be able to see past something so superficial. And as for her body, he had held her, and he knew she was tall and small-waisted and long-legged, and that she fit against him perfectly.

Of course, she was not his type of woman.

But he was undoubtedly attracted to her; a mere fantasy about her could arouse him. He knew it was ridiculous for him to be feeling lust for her. She was a spinster and a prude, somewhat shrewish, and on top of all that, a crazy, man-hating suffragette. She was also as cold as ice, certainly a virgin. Rathe always stayed away from virgins, just like he stayed away from proper ladies. Just like he knew he should stay away from her. He was leaving Natchez soon anyway, wasn't he?

The only time he had ever seduced a virgin was when he was thirteen. Lucilla had been the fifteen-year-old daughter of their closest neighbors. In the back of his mind, Rathe had known better, but he wasn't exactly thinking with his mind. They'd been together a dozen hot, sweet times before being discovered, and he had gotten the thrashing of his life. His father had been furious. He had shouted at him, and Rathe would never forget his words: "What if it was your sister who had been taken by some young jackass?" The lesson had been very clear, and Rathe had avoided innocent, well-bred young ladies ever since.

Technically, Grace fit into that category. On the surface she might be cold and prim—but as a man, he knew instinctively that the ones who were the hardest to thaw flamed the brightest.

Next to Grace, the thought of Louisa Barclay somehow annoyed him. She'd been pursuing him ever since they first met several years ago at a Natchez ball, his willing mistress whenever he rolled into town. But now he felt as if he'd prefer Grace's haranguing to Louisa's manipulations any day. Perhaps he'd best avoid the widow Barclay in the future. . . .

Still, at noon, instead of tossing his valise on the stage as he'd planned, Rathe found himself riding out to Melrose. Only this time, it wasn't the dark-haired lady of the house he planned to visit—it was her fiery-headed employee.

Grace decided to explore at dinnertime.

She left the girls eating, with a feeling of freedom and relief. For one thing, the morning had been difficult. Both girls seemed to go out of their way to circumvent her efforts to be a good teacher. And Louisa's curriculum drove her to despair, insulted her. To have the bulk of their studies devoted to medieval pursuits like embroidery infuriated Grace. She intended to broach the subject of a change with Louisa Barclay at the first suitable opportunity. The girls simply had to learn arithmetic, as well as stitchery!

She strolled beneath a pair of willows and tried not to think about her charges and the difficulties facing her. Although it was quite warm, it was a beautiful day, and Grace took a deep breath, inhaling the scent of magnolias. She was wearing a loose brown cotton dress with a hint of embroidery at the cuffs and neck. The color was dark for this climate. She felt hot and damp. She removed her glasses to wipe a small amount of moisture form high on her cheeks. From somewhere to her right, a male voice said, "You should break those glasses in two."

Grace jumped in surprise.

Rathe smiled his broad, dimpled grin from the back of a big, black stallion. "Good day, Gracie," he drawled softly, his blue eyes caressing her face, sweeping quickly over her bodice, then lifting to lock with her gaze.

She felt herself flush and hated the reaction.

"What . . ." She slipped on the spectacles, frustrated. Her heart had already taken wings. "What are you doing, sneaking up on me?"

He laughed. "I didn't mean to frighten you." His look was pointed.

Grace knew he was thinking about their conversation yesterday, and the question he had posed: *Are you afraid of me?* Of course she wasn't, but why was her heart beating so uncontrollably? "Let me reiterate," she said. "You didn't—and don't—frighten me."

Her back was stiff and straight, shoulders squared, lips pressed tightly together. "Good day." She nodded shortly, turned her back, and walked away.

In seconds, the horse appeared alongside her, making her a bit nervous, for she was unused to animals. "That's good," he murmured. His tone was very sensual, and before Grace could react, he was on the ground beside her. "That's very good," he drawled softly, "because now we can start over."

She was assailed by his masculine scent, mingling of leather, sweat, and horse. "There is nothing to start."

"You don't think so?"

She shot a glance at him, and found that there was laughter in his eyes. That he might find her amusing angered her. "I know so."

She stared straight ahead and ignored him. But it was impossible to ignore her own physical reactions to his

proximity—a tightening of her breasts, an uncomfortable, yet delicious tingling of her loins, a breathlessness.
Nerves, she told herself.

"How has your first morning gone?"

"Just fine."

"The girls give you any trouble?"

"Not really."

His hip bumped hers. She shifted immediately away.
"If they do," he said, unaware of the touch of their bodies,
or so it seemed, "you come to me. I'll straighten them
out."

"Thank you, Mr.—"

"Bragg," he cut in quickly, "Rathe Bragg, at your service, Gracie."

"Yes, well, thank you, Mr. Bragg, but no thank you.
I've been a teacher for years, and I know exactly what I'm
doing."

He took her hand, stopping them. "I'm sure you do."

His hand was warm, damp, hard, and very large. Aghast
and angry at his nerve, she yanked her hand away. "How
dare you! And stop calling me Gracie! It's Miss O'Rourke
to you!"

"How dare I call you Gracie or take your hand?" He
chuckled. "I dare both, easily." He leaned toward her.
Her hand was suddenly in his again. His breath, when he
spoke, was soft and warm, his tone low and husky. "Your
hand is so small and delicate, and soft—like silk."

Grace stared, speechless.

He smiled slightly, raising her fingers to his lips.

At the touch of his damp, firm mouth on her flesh, she
reacted. With a gasp she pulled her hand away, her eyes
blazing. He lifted his head, and she found herself staring
at his beautiful mouth, lips still slightly parted.

Her temper flared. "You are going to jeopardize my
job! I don't think Mrs. Barclay would like you plying your
charms on me! So please, ply them elsewhere!"

He stared, then threw back his head and laughed. "You
have a bad temper, Gracie, but you know what? I like it,

I truly do! It definitely proves a point! Why do I rile you so when I'm only being friendly?'' With superb grace he swung onto the stallion. "Is it just me that you so dislike," he asked, "or is it all men?''

"I don't think you would care for the truth," she flung over her shoulder, striding away.

"I can handle the truth, all right," he said chuckling from behind her. Grace whirled to fire a retort, but he was faster. "But I wonder if you can.'' He winked and cantered off.

Insufferable and conceited.

Impossible and arrogant.

Never had she met such a man.

That afternoon both girls yawned frequently, pretended not to listen, or actually didn't. Grace could tell that they were several years behind in their lessons. Margaret Anne, at six, had not the foggiest idea of the alphabet. Mary Louise spelled like a first grader, and her reading was equally atrocious. Of course, her handwriting was as dismal as her stitches.

Halfway through her task of writing the word *cage* twenty times, Mary Louise threw her pencil aside. "Pooh! I hate this! This is stupid! I don't need to spell, my husband will do all my writing for me!''

"I hate this, too," Margaret Anne yelled, throwing her pencil aside. With Grace at her elbow, she had been learning the alphabet from A to G. Patiently Grace stood up.

"Miss Mary Louise. Will your husband pen your ball invitations?''

Mary Louise blinked.

"Will he pen invitations to a ladies' tea for you? Will he write your letters to your sister when she is married and lives in Memphis and you are married and living in New Orleans?''

"But Mama never writes," Mary Louise blustered.

"Your mama does not strike me as the type to have teas," Grace said recklessly. "Now, think on what I said."

"I guess you're right," Mary Louise replied, and picked up her quill. Margaret Anne followed suit.

"D is for?" Grace prompted, sitting back down next to her youngest charge.

"Dog!"

The triumphant voice came from the doorway, and all three looked up to see a grinning Geoffrey.

"Geoffrey, do you know your alphabet?" Grace asked.

He hung in the doorway. "No ma'am. Only what you been teachin' Miz Margaret Anne today."

"Why, he's been spyin'!" Mary Louise cried.

"Come here, Geoffrey," Grace said with a smile.

He came in, half eager and half bashful.

"Now Margaret Anne, let's start again. D is for?"

"D is for dog." Margaret Anne bit her lip.

"And E?"

It was no use. Margaret Anne had not retained anything, and she shrugged dramatically.

By her side, Geoffrey was wriggling, barely able to restrain himself. Grace looked at him. "Geoffrey?"

"Egg!" he shouted. "F is for fun! G is for good! A is for apple! B is for . . ." he broke off. Then his face brightened. "Bad! C is for cat!"

"That is very good," Grace said, stunned that he had remembered the letters, when she and Margaret Anne had only drilled through them a half a dozen times. "Start from the beginning," she cried, excited. "Try again."

Mary Louise gasped. "You can't teach him! He's a nigger!"

"Be quiet, Mary Louise," Grace said sharply. "Go on, Geoffrey, try again, this time from the beginning."

Proud and excited, Geoffrey flawlessly recited the sequence of the alphabet which Grace had been trying to teach Margaret Anne all afternoon.

"Very, very good. A hundred percent. Do you know what that means?"

He shook his head, grinning with pleasure.

"That means you've gotten every one correct."

"Every one?"

"Every one. Do you want to learn to read and write, Geoffrey?"

"Yes, ma'am."

"Don't you go to the public school?"

He hung his head. "I got too many chores, ma'am."

Grace was exhilarated. She would teach Geoffrey to read and write! And she knew, in the precise instant, that there was such a thing as fate after all, and that the reason she had come South was far grander than she had thought—it was to educate, and thus liberate, at least this one little boy.

She thought of all the runaway slaves who had passed through their home in New York on the Underground Railroad before the War, when she had been just a child. Grace had been told what her parents were doing as soon as she was old enough to understand. She had seen them all, even the ones she wasn't supposed to, the ones who had been abused and beaten and starved. Grace didn't think she had forgotten a single, desperate face.

She had been shocked the first time she had realized that most colored people could not read—were not allowed to learn to read. She had been six, and to this day she could remember it so clearly. She had wanted to share her favorite story with a little boy of eight or so, who had picked up the book and opened it, upside down, curiously and uncomprehendingly. Her disappointment that she couldn't share the story with him had been as vast as her shock that he was not allowed to even learn to read. The unfairness of it all had struck her to the core, even then.

Grace's voice trembled. "Why don't you sit down, Geoffrey."

"No!" Mary Louise shrieked, standing. "My sister and me will not learn with a darkie! I'm going to go tell Mama! You're teaching a nigger to read! You'll be sorry!" She ran for the door, her face white with rage.

Grace leapt to her feet. "Wait, Mary Louise!"

Mary Louise fled.

Grace pressed her hands to her chest. What had she done? Oh, damn her impulsiveness. "Geoffrey, honey," she said, her hand on his shoulder, "I will see you later. You had better go before Mrs. Barclay gets here."

His face fell. "Yes ma'am."

It broke her heart to send him away.

"Are we finished today?" Margaret Anne asked hopefully.

"No we are not," Grace said, sitting next to her.

Grace spent the rest of the afternoon waiting for the blow to fall.

It did not come until much later that evening.

Chapter 5

It was eight when she was at last summoned to the library; she went dreading dismissal. Somehow, she had to avert that catastrophe, for her mother's sake.

Louisa was waiting for her imperiously, impatiently, and she was not alone. Grace did not look at Rathe, standing by the mantel, but she could feel his presence.

"Mary Louise says you were teaching Geoffrey to read." One glance at the mistress of Melrose was enough for Grace to see that she was furious.

Grace began carefully, "He showed tremendous poten—"

"Were you, Miss O'Rourke?"

She took a breath. "Not exactly."

"My daughter is a liar?" Her voice rose. Her face was flushed, and her eyes were dark.

"He was hanging about, and when Margaret Anne did not know her letters, I asked Geoffrey if he did. And he did. That's all."

Louisa paced forward. "According to Mary Louise, you invited him in to learn with them. Is that true or not?"

Grace's eyes were steady and unwavering. "Yes."

"That is not the way we do things down heah," she said hotly. "This is not New York, Miss O'Rourke. The damn Republicans may have forced schools down our throats, the damn Union League may be tellin' the niggers they've got rights, but down heah, Miss O'Rourke, it's well known that the niggers are not equal and have no

51

need to learn—even if they could. And they most certainly do not sit as equals with my daughters in my house!''

''The Negroes are free now, and they have every right granted the white man as citizens under the law and the Constitution and—''

''What Miss O'Rourke is sayin','' Rathe drawled smoothly, cutting her off, ''is that she is indeed sorry to have so upset you, darlin'.''

''They may be freed men,'' Louisa said harshly, ''and they may have gotten the right to vote, but they still till *our* soil for us, and if they didn't they'd starve to death, every last one of them! They are still inferior bein's. They certainly have no rights heah at Melrose and you have no right to teach them!''

Grace looked at the floor. She was trembling, her face crimson. She fought her anger at this bigoted woman, and then thought of the victim of this unjust system—a poor little boy who was unusually bright and doomed to life as a sharecropper unless he could rise above his fate. And it could happen! There were educated, literate Negroes out there, fighting for the Republican cause, like the congressman John R. Lynch. She kept her eyes lowered so Louisa Barclay would not see the anger and defiance there. She did not raise them until she had her emotions under control. ''Yes ma'am.''

''If I weren't so desperate I would send you packin','' Louisa declared. ''But I'm bein' charitable. You are a Yankee, you don't know or understand our ways. Let this be a lesson. You may go now.''

For the first time Grace looked at Rathe. His gaze was steady and sympathetic. He gave her a slight, reassuring smile, then a wink, as if to say, Don't worry, her bark is worse than her bite and we know how to handle her. She was exasperated even more for his taking the situation so lightly—or was it because he had come to her defense? She could certainly fight her own battles—she'd been doing so for years! Giving him a tight-lipped, furious glance, she left with hard, squared shoulders.

"Don't you think you were being a little harsh on her, Louisa?" Rathe asked.

"Oh, fie! She deserved it and worse. How dare she?"

Rathe smiled, thinking that Grace could, and would, dare just about anything. "Why doesn't little Geoff go to school?"

Louisa raised an appalled eyebrow. "I happen to need him around heah. An' damned if I'll let my niggers attend that school!"

"I think it's a good idea," Rathe drawled, coolly. "You need the boy heah, but he sure could be more helpful if he knew his numbers."

"Rathe! What do you mean, a good idea teachin' those darkies to read and write? It's bad enough we have to pay the taxes for their damn schools. Look at what's happened to the South with the niggers votin'! Those damn Republican Yankee carpetbaggers are runnin' everythin'!"

"Sweetheart, the coloreds are men and women just like you and me, and no, they're not white, but they're as human as we are," Rathe chided gently. "I do believe that bemoaning the fact that they are free, with civil rights, is pointless. Don't tell me you wouldn't be happy if the Negroes started voting Democrat."

Louisa stared, pink and flushed. "You are a traitor, Rathe, aren't you? A damn scalawag! Are you one of them Republicans, too? Did you even fight for the grand old South? Did you?"

"Do you really care which way I vote?" he drawled, mockingly.

"Did you fight for the South?" Her tone was high, strident.

Rathe leaned against the mantel. "The War is over, Louisa. It's been over for ten years. You're hanging on to illusions and dreams. It's time to let go and face reality."

"Face a carpetbagger reality? Yankee reality? Never!"

Rathe sighed, pushing himself off of the mantel. "Enough. I stopped by because I think I left a letter from New York here." It was, of course, only a half-truth. He'd really returned to Melrose to catch a glimpse of Grace O'Rourke.

Louisa stared. Then, softer, "Just tell me, did you or did you not fight for the South?"

"I fought for the South all right, Louisa," Rathe said expressionlessly. "But for my own reasons. I was sixteen when I killed my first Yank, and you know what? He was younger than I was." His gaze was diamond-hard.

"Oh, Rathe, I'm sorry," Louisa cried, coming to him and wrapping herself around him.

He politely disengaged himself from her. "Did you notice that letter, Louisa?"

"Yes, it's upstairs. Rathe, darling, why don't you sit down." She smiled brightly. "Are you hungry?"

"Is it in your room?" he asked, already striding into the hall.

Louisa followed him. "Yes. Rathe, aren't you going to stay tonight?"

"I'm afraid not." He bounded up the stairs.

"But you didn't stay last night!" she cried in protest.

Rathe stopped and took her hand. His smile was gentle. "There's a big card game tonight."

"That's what you said last night." She pouted.

"Perhaps another time," he said quietly.

"Promise?"

He just smiled slightly. It wasn't that Rathe hadn't enjoyed the two nights they had spent together since his arrival in Natchez. But now, for some unfathomable reason, he wasn't in the mood for Louisa Barclay. He found her attitude mean and petty and conniving—and he hated the way she had just treated Grace.

Grace. An enticing vision of the redheaded governess came to his mind, spectacles and all. He tried to shrug it away. He remembered how the glasses kept sliding down her little nose, revealing more of her big, violet eyes. Despite the glasses, he had been able to see her anger just now. He had to smile. Grace could bite her tongue with Louisa, but not with him. His smile faded and became a frown. Now this was silly. Grace absolutely had nothing to do with his not wanting to remain at Melrose tonight.

He leaned back against the trunk of the oak tree and gave in to the pleasure of watching her.

It was the next day at noon. Rathe had ridden out to Melrose without questioning the impulse. But he had enough experience with women to know that if he wanted to see Grace, he'd have to avoid Louisa in doing so. The idea of skulking around like a schoolboy amused him somehow, sharpened the adventure. He had found Grace and Geoffrey ensconced in a copse of trees at the center of a little meadow not far from the house. They were sitting on a blanket, both of their heads bent over the slate Geoffrey was working so diligently on. "That is very, very good," Grace said, her voice rich with pleasure and carrying easily to where he stood not far from them. He liked the sound of her voice. He liked a few other things about her, too.

She had taken off her glasses, and her tight bun had loosened. Strands of curling hair had escaped to frame her face. Now, when she was relaxed and intent on teaching, without those ridiculous spectacles, she was beautiful. Her full mouth, curving in a smile, did something to him. It sent a surge of hot lust to his groin. He looked at her body again as she bent over the slate, the sunlight making her hair glint with gold, and he wished he could dress her in a well-fitted, expensive gown. Amethysts, he thought. He would deck her out in amethysts, too.

He wondered how old she was, and what made a woman like this become a crazy radical.

They were still bent over the slate, Geoffrey practicing his letters as he came forward. Grace leapt up in shock, purple eyes wide. Geoffrey screeched with delight. "It's Mistah Rathe!"

As Geoffrey ran forward to greet him, Rathe watched her relaxed, natural poise disappear. He watched her lips thin, her shoulders square, her slender white hand tuck away the sensual wisps of hair, the glasses reappear on her little freckled nose. He caught Geoffrey in his arms and lifted him high, swinging him around. "Hello," he said, over the boy's head, to Grace.

"You're spying!"

He put Geoffrey down. "I saw you coming out here, alone, and I couldn't resist the opportunity of strolling with a beautiful woman," he teased.

She was on her feet, prepared to do battle. "Your charm will not work with me."

He cocked a doubtful eyebrow, grinning.

She folded her arms across her chest, trying to look stern when in truth her heart was banging madly in her breast. "Why are you spying on us, Mr. Bragg?"

"Rathe," he said, softly. "Rathe. I think we know each other well enough for you to call me Rathe."

She blushed beautifully. "We most certainly do not!"

"Not for my lack of trying." He grinned.

The blush deepened. "You can try till your dying day, *Mister* Bragg, but it won't change anything."

His smile was broad. "Is that a challenge?"

She took a breath, suddenly uneasy. "Take it any way you like."

"Is that an invitation?" He couldn't help it—he imagined "taking" her a dozen different ways. Grace, he saw, was impervious to the innuendo.

"An invitation?" she said blankly. Then, "I suppose you'll be telling Louisa about this?"

"Now why would I do that?" Rathe asked, riffling Geoffrey's hair.

He was pulling at Rathe's big, calloused hand. "Come an' look, Mistah Rathe. Look at my *A*'s an' *B*'s."

Rathe laughed at Geoff's enthusiasm and allowed himself to be pulled forward. "Ah ha," he said, squatting and studying the slate. "Why, I have never seen a finer *A* or *B* in my entire life."

"Really?"

"Really."

Geoffrey shrieked a cry of gladness, bouncing around in a little jig, while Rathe and Grace's gazes met—hers hard, his soft.

"Don't play with me, Mister Bragg," Grace finally said, stiffly.

He smiled at her innocent words, imagining vividly how he would like to play with her. He would start by loosening that bun and letting her glorious hair flame free. He stood. "I'm not playing with you, Gracie. When we play, you'll know it."

She stared blankly, frigidly.

There was absolutely no doubt in his mind that she had never been with a man. Her innocence, at her age, with her intellect, was astounding.

"Are you or are you not going to inform on me, Mister Bragg?" she said rigidly.

"Rathe," he coaxed. "Rathe. And I never tell on a lady."

This time she understood, and this time she blushed.

He grinned. "I give you my word."

She raised her chin, her expression one of utter contempt.

It amused him. "You doubt the word of a Texan?"

"I doubt the word of a scoundrel."

Rathe laughed, a rich rumble of sound. "Then you'll just have to trust me, won't you."

"I'd rather not."

Once again, he wondered if her animosity was directed solely at him, or at all men. "Maybe if you tried trusting me, you wouldn't be disappointed."

She laughed. "You are the last man on this earth that I'd ever trust!"

He was genuinely insulted. "Another challenge? Gracie, I think it's only fair that I warn you," his gaze held hers, "that I find challenges irresistible."

She clenched her teeth. "That is your problem, not mine. If you'll excuse us? Geoffrey, come on, we don't have all day. I want to see your *A*'s and *B*'s again."

Geoffrey came running and plopped down. Grace made a point of ignoring Rathe, who made no move to leave. She watched her student making near-perfect letters. "Very good. Do you remember what *C* is for?"

"*C* is for cat."

"That's right. And *C* looks like this. There. Now you do it."

She watched him make a large, irregular *C,* trying to ignore the man standing with his boot-clad calf in the peripheral range of her right eye. The boot cleaved to thick, but not squat, muscles, and was gleaming with polish. Her eye wandered up to a doeskin-clad knee, lingered at the edge of a powerful thigh. She quickly looked back down as Geoff gave a cry of triumph and shoved the slate at her. "Excellent. Let's see four more."

"Let me see," Rathe said, and Grace watched the boot move practically against her arm as he came to stand behind her. She realized, as he bent over her to look down, that she was holding her breath. She exhaled, and it came out in a large rush of sound.

"That is excellent, Geoff," Rathe said.

He beamed and began enthusiastically making more *C*'s.

Grace flinched when she felt a pair of large, warm hands cup her shoulders. It was getting hotter out; she was perspiring. She pulled away, then rose to her feet. "What are you doing?"

"Doesn't it hurt, holding them so stiff like you do all the time?"

Her shoulders went squarer. "You have no right to touch me. What are you even doing here? Why don't you leave? Or don't you have anything better to do with your time?"

"No."

"What?"

"I don't have anything better to do—that is, there is nothing I would rather do than be here with you."

"That is too bad," she said stiffly, thinking, of course, that he didn't mean it. Words, they were just words. *But what if he did mean it?* "Because the feeling is not mutual."

"Now why is that? You being the fair-minded person you are, it doesn't seem right that you've judged me without knowing me." His gaze was bright blue and teasing, even though his words were serious. "Haven't you ever heard of a fair trial?"

"I wasn't aware that this was a trial."

"You could have fooled me," he said, unsmiling now. "There was no evidence, yet the verdict is guilty."

"Your conceit is astounding. Contrary to what you might think, I have not given you one thought." She stared, feeling secretly appalled by the immensity of the falsehood.

He started to smile knowingly. "Not one?"

"Life is one big joke to you, isn't it?" she said gravely.

"And you take it too seriously," Rathe said, reaching out a hand and touching one forefinger to her smooth, alabaster cheek. He'd known it. Like silk. Her skin was flawless.

Her mouth parted in shock.

His gaze was inexorably drawn to the full, open lips.

She stood frozen, unable to move.

Unable to resist, he bent forward.

For the briefest moment, his lips brushed hers with the delicate touch of a feather. Then he pulled back slightly, to stare into her wide, purple eyes framed by the ugly little glasses. He saw the slap coming but only turned his face slightly. The blow was surprisingly hard and it stung. He guessed he deserved it.

"How dare you!"

He didn't smile. "The question really is, how could I not?"

"You're worse than the others," she gasped. "Much, much worse! The worst sort of rake, a perverted philistine who wants only one thing from women. We're all your toys, aren't we? And the world is just one big playroom to keep you amused, isn't it?"

He stared, riveted by her words and the vague memory of another time and another place. Perverted philistine . . . Rathe suddenly cupped her face.

"Stop it!" she cried furiously, trying to twist away.

"Be still." He held her face in one large hand, studying it. He twisted his hips to avoid her sudden kick. "It was you!"

He released her and she backed away, panting and frightened. She had seen the light of recognition in his eyes.

"Grace—it was you! In New York! You're that crazy suffragette who shot up van Horne's home!"

"I don't know what you're talking about," Grace said tensely.

He threw back his head and roared. "It was you! Damn! I knew there was something familiar about you!"

He was laughing at her—again. "You bigoted pig," she said furiously.

"Male tyrant?" he supplied helpfully, eyes twinkling, dimples deep.

"Yes! Pig, tyrant, philistine, you sicken me!"

He laughed again, then clasped her shoulders, ignoring her struggles. His hands were so very strong—so uncompromising. "Gracie, what in hell are you doing way down here?"

She stopped struggling, flushed with anger and other dangerous emotions. Her glasses were slipping down her nose, but she couldn't raise her hands to push them up. "That, sir, is none of your business!"

He grinned. "I guess not." He released her, then suddenly swooped down on Geoff. "Hey, Geoff, what's wrong?"

Geoffrey was close to tears. "You done hurt Miz Grace."

"Oh, no, never, Geoff, I'm a Southern gentleman and I'd never hurt a lady." All his attention was on the little boy, and perversely, Grace was peeved.

"It's okay, Geoffrey," Grace said, reaching out to

smooth his hair. "He wasn't hurting me. We were—having a disagreement."

"Truly?"

"Truly," Rathe supplied. "Now, let's see those *C*'s."

Reassured, Geoff handed the slate to Rathe. "Perfect," Rathe announced.

Geoff looked hopefully at Grace.

"Yes, they are perfect. Geoff," Grace said, "I want you to practice these letters tonight in secret. Okay?"

"Yes'm."

"Now, I have to get back, so why don't you run on ahead. You can keep the slate, but don't show it to anyone."

After Geoffrey had gone, Grace turned a serious regard on Rathe, who was grinning. Before she could speak, he reached for her. "Can't wait for us to be alone?"

She dodged his eager hands.

"What are you going to do with—with the information you found out today?"

Rathe's expression grew bright with comprehension and his grin widened. "Ah. I don't know."

"Please," Grace managed, hating having to beg. "I need this job. She doesn't know—about New York."

"I see."

"No, I doubt that you do. I'm asking you nicely to stay out of this."

Rathe's eyes sparkled. "What do I get in return for my silence?"

"What do you mean?" she asked cautiously.

"What do you think?" he said recklessly.

She was breathless, blushing.

He was breathless, throbbing. "The price of my silence is a kiss."

She bit off a gasp of outrage. "You, sir, are impossible!" she cried, and turned away furiously.

"But irresistible," he said softly, close behind her, too close.

"Not to me!"

"When do I get my kiss?"

"Certainly not now," she said, moving away and facing him. "Not ever! You are despicable. If you were truly a gentleman you would keep your silence without a price."

"Then you must be right. I'm a scoundrel, a rake, and a—what was it? A perverted philistine?"

He was making fun of her again. She lifted her chin. "I must get back."

"When do I get my kiss?" he persisted.

Her bosom heaved. He had no scruples. She had no doubt he would reveal her secret if she denied him. It was a risk she could not take. "Tonight."

Chapter 6

The thought of seducing her had crossed his mind, once or twice. But it wouldn't be right, and he knew it, because he knew that if he seriously set out to seduce her, he would succeed. She would have no defense against his well-practiced, superior tactics. That knowledge definitely raised some guilt. If he were smart, he would ride out of Natchez now, this instant, instead of lurking by the barn waiting for their rendezvous. And their kiss.

Did she really think him such a cad that he'd tattle on her to Louisa Barclay? That upset him. Apparently, she really did think the worst of him—and she didn't even know him. He tried to remember someone in his past, especially a woman, who had not liked him. He couldn't think of a single one—up until now. Grace really didn't like him.

Well, one kiss did not make a seduction. And one kiss would not hurt either of them. And one kiss was certainly the least he deserved . . .

But would she show up? He waited impatiently. Somehow he figured she was scared enough about him keeping her secret, that she would. She had agreed to meet him behind the third barn at ten o'clock. He heard footsteps and turned.

Even if he hadn't been expecting her, he would have recognized her in the dim glow of the moonlight from the stiff, squared set of her shoulders. He smiled at the familiar sight. She stopped a few yards from him, and he could just make out her expression—tensed and grim. He wondered what he would see in her eyes if it were lighter out. Anger? Apprehension? Excitement? His own body had begun a slow, delicious, steady throb. Damn. He wanted this woman. Of all women, he wanted her.

"Come here," he said softly.

She didn't move.

He smiled, a flashing of white in the darkness. "Then I'll come to you," he whispered. He moved forward slowly, four easy strides, until he was standing an inch away from her. She looked up.

Oh Gracie, he thought, if you relax you'll like it.

Oh dear Lord, she thought, I just cannot believe I'm doing this.

Her eyes were dark liquid pools, at once anxious and angry. They glittered. He wanted to see them glaze with desire—with desire for him. "Don't be mad at me," he whispered. "It's your charms that are at fault." His voice was a soft, heavy caress. "I can't seem to help myself."

"My charms?" she said sarcastically. "Oh no, Mr. Bragg, I think it's your rutting proclivities that are entirely to blame."

His eyes widened with shock.

Hers narrowed with triumph.

"Grace," he managed, "you do have a way with words."

"Is the truth too much to bear?" she asked, too sweetly.

"Why don't we test my rutting proclivities," he said grimly.

She stepped back.

He stepped forward.

"I've changed my mind," she gasped.

"Too late." His hands closed over her shoulders.

"Then just get it over with," she snapped. But a tremble swept over her.

He winced at her reaction and with his fingers spread, began kneading her muscles softly. "I know you're not cold," he murmured, his blood thickening deliciously in his groin. He heard her breathe and felt her body stiffen. "Relax," he whispered. "This is supposed to be pleasurable." His voice was very husky. "Give me a chance. Let me show you just how good this can be."

"I detest you and what you stand for," she said, choking on a sob.

Rathe froze at that particularly female sound of anguish. For some insane reason, he thought of Lucilla, the fifteen-year-old he had deflowered when he was a boy. Unlike Grace, she had wanted him as much as he had wanted her. Grace was trembling beneath his touch. Rathe suddenly hated himself and his lust. He removed his hands. "I guess I'm more of a gentleman than either of us thought. You have my silence," he said with heavy disappointment.

He turned abruptly and left.

Allen arrived promptly at nine as they had arranged. He swung down from the buggy, beaming, dressed in his Sunday suit. "Grace! I've been looking forward to this all week!"

Grace hurried to him with a fond smile, genuinely glad to see him. Although her first week was shorter than normal because she had arrived on a Tuesday, she was already exhausted emotionally. The girls had begun to settle down and were improving both their literary skills and their manners, to her relief. But there was the constant strain of teaching Geoffrey on the sly and of worrying about that scoundrel, Rathe Bragg, knowing her past. He hadn't appeared again since the night he had almost kissed her, which suited her just fine. So it came as something of a surprise, when Allen drew back after pressing his lips to her cheek, to see *him* sitting on his stallion, staring with what distinctly looked like a frown. Their gazes met, and Grace was angry with herself for blushing as if she were guilty of some trespass.

She clearly remembered the promise in the tone of his voice when he had been about to kiss her—and the obvious disappointment when he had not. She herself had stood frozen, watching him disappear with long, hard strides, unable to believe that he had changed his mind, that he had actually done the right thing. She had felt a wave of triumph, but it was mingled with regret. The salute he had sent her as he rode away was somehow both mocking and bitter.

"How are you, Allen?" she said, still clasping his hand, tearing her gaze from Rathe with difficulty.

"Just fine, Grace. I've been counting the days like a schoolboy." He grinned.

Grace attempted a smile in return as he helped her into the buggy. Allen climbed in after her, spotting Rathe for the first time. "Hello, Rathe. A beautiful day, isn't it?"

Rathe's eyes had drifted from Grace, who looked fetching even with the silly spectacles, dressed in a green print gown, to Allen, puffed with pleasure, arranging a wicker basket and red checked tablecoth on the seat between them. He stared at the picnic basket a beat longer before managing a slight smile at Allen. "Allen, I didn't know you were acquainted with Melrose's new governess." His drawl came out thicker than usual.

Allen beamed, taking one of Grace's hands in his. "Grace and I share a bit of history," he explained cheerfully. "In fact," he shot her a warm look, "one day I hope she'll do me the honor of becoming my wife."

A heavy silence, filled with the scent of magnolias, the whisper of the dining-room fan, and the drone of bees, descended. Then Rathe smiled. "Well," he drawled, "the best of luck to you both."

"What's wrong?" Allen asked as they departed. Grace silently watched Rathe swing down from the stallion, clad in his indecently tight doeskin breeches. She hastily averted her gaze from the sight of his hard buttocks and thighs, flushing. She had never before thought men's breeches indecent.

"How do you know Rathe Bragg?" she asked carefully.

"Why, he's an old friend of the woman I board with," Allen replied. "A family friend, I believe. I've chatted with him a number of times. He's an interesting man—but no progressive thinker, as far as I can make out." He shifted his eyes from the Melrose driveway toward Grace. "Are you all right?"

"Of course," she responded too quickly. "Allen, I wish you hadn't said that—about marriage."

He looked at her. "But it's how I feel; and I'm proud of it."

"Your wanting to marry me should be private, just between the two of us."

"I'm sorry, Grace."

They traveled without mishap down a long, shady thoroughfare, the elaborate planters' homes giving way to more modest clapboard ones. Allen amused her with stories of his students and Grace found herself telling him about her own remarkable pupil, Geoffrey.

The church service seemed interminable. Grace fidgeted, eager for it to end so she could get to work and begin organizing the ladies. She hadn't mentioned her plans to Allen, but she was positive that she would have his support. As soon as the service was over she hurried outside and hovered by the exit.

"Grace, what are you up to?" Allen demanded.

She smiled at him. "I just want a chance to meet a few of the ladies."

He looked at her. "You told me you were going to stay out of trouble."

"Oh, Allen," she cried. "I just can't sit back and do nothing!"

He sighed. He knew her so well.

A middle-aged couple emerged. They smiled at Grace, and she beamed back. The congregation filed out and began milling about the churchyard sociably. Neighbors chatted with those they hadn't seen all week. Grace waved at Martha Grimes, the woman she had met on the train, who was standing with another woman, undoubtedly her daughter. "Allen, mingle with the men," she ordered, and he shook his head but went off to do her bidding. She went over to three women chatting animatedly in the shade of a huge magnolia tree. "Hello."

"Hello," said a plump, matronly woman. "You're new in Natchez, aren't you? Are you the new governess at Melrose?"

"Yes, I am," Grace said, "My name is Grace O'Rourke." She held out her hand, then wanted to kick herself, but it was too late to withdraw it.

The women stared at her hand. Finally the plump woman took it. "So women shake hands up north? I'm Sarah Bellsley, and this is Mary Riordan and Suzanne Compton."

Grace shook the other women's hands too. "I was wondering if we might have a women's meeting one night this week."

"What kind of meeting?" Mary asked.

"A meeting to discuss some issues that are very important to today's modern woman," Grace said, holding her breath.

"Oh, I think it's a wonderful idea," Suzanne said. "And that way we could introduce Miss O'Rourke around."

"Oh, I would so appreciate that," Grace put in quickly. "And please, call me Grace. It's so very hard to move to a new place where—"

Sarah laughed and patted her arm. "I will organize a ladies' social for Wednesday evening, dear."

"Oh, Sarah, thank you," Grace cried, clasping her palm.

When Grace climbed into the buggy forty minutes later she was flushed with exhilaration. Allen picked up the reins. "All ends accomplished, Grace?"

She grinned at him. "So far, Allen, so far."

Allen chose a beautiful spot for their picnic. The meadow was green and fragrant with honeysuckle. Tall, stately oaks provided shade, and oleanders crept along a fresh white fence in a riot of pink. Nearby, a spotted cow chewed its cud and eyed them lazily. Grace leaned back on her elbows and laughed.

Allen grinned. "You're feeling mighty pleased with yourself, now aren't you, Grace O'Rourke?"

Laughter bubbled out of her. "You know me too well."

He raised his glass of lemonade. "Natchez will never be the same."

Grace lifted her glass. "Amen."

They sipped in companionable silence.

Then Allen said, "You do realize the ladies here are more concerned with finding husbands for their daughters than attaining the vote."

"I realize."

"Natchez is especially conservative, Grace. I think it's because there's so much old money here. Even the War only put a dent in it. Why, there isn't even a temperance union here."

"That's sinful," Grace said. "Is Silver Street as bad as they say?"

Allen laughed. "Now how would you know about Silver Street?"

"I have ears," Grace said.

"Yes, it is," Allen said seriously. "And it's no place for you to explore."

She smiled. "Plenty of saloons and gambling halls and dens of iniquity?"

"What's going on in that sharp mind of yours?"

"Maybe the ladies will find temperance easier to swallow than suffrage."

Allen shook his head with a fond smile.

At the sound of riders coming down the road, they looked up curiously. Two big chestnuts and a bay came into view. Grace saw Allen stiffen. "What's wrong, Allen?"

The riders veered off the road, toward them.

Allen got to his feet.

"Allen? Do you know them?"

"They're a pack of Southern riffraff," Allen said, low,

"even if they are the old planter class. Rawlins is one of their leaders. I want you to stay out of this, Grace."

She was on her feet. "Allen, you're worrying me!"

"Hey, look at this," drawled a blond man. Clad in breeches, a fine linen shirt, and gleaming boots, astride a magnificent thoroughbred, he was every inch a Southern aristocrat. He was flanked by his companions, who were equally well-turned out. "If it isn't the schoolteacher!"

"Hello, Rawlins," Allen said levelly.

"What a surprise," drawled Rawlins. "Hey, Johnny, Frankie, ain't this a surprise?"

"Hello, Johnson," Allen said neutrally to the dark-haired man on Rawlins' left. "Frank."

"Looks like he's courtin'," said Rawlins. "Another Yankee? Hey, Yank, you courtin'?"

Grace clenched her hands, frightened by the man's boisterous lack of courtesy. Allen gave her a warning look. "This is Miss O'Rourke, the new governess at Melrose."

The men looked at her and nodded, Frank even removing his hat. Then the brief moment of politeness was gone. Rawlins spurred his chestnut forward, as if to ride Allen down. Allen didn't move, or even flinch, as the big horse knocked against him. Rawlins moved his gelding behind him. Frank moved his bay to the left, and Johnson came in on the right, encircling Allen with a ton of horseflesh.

"You remember our conversation last week, Allen?" Rawlins drawled.

"I believe so."

"Really?" Rawlins was incredulous, and looked at the others. "You sure aren't acting like you remember."

"Maybe we should remind him," Frank suggested.

Rawlins laughed. "Let's remind him," he said, and spurred the chestnut into Allen.

Allen stumbled into the bay. He stepped back to avoid getting hurt, right into Johnson's chestnut. The young men laughed, using their horses to push him this way and that, while Allen grew first white and then red, sweat streaking down his face.

"Stop it," Grace cried out.

"Hey, nigger-lover," Rawlins snarled, hatred etched clearly on his handsome face, "you better pack your bags and go on home. Got that, nigger-teacher?"

Allen didn't answer. He was breathing hard.

"We heard," Rawlins spat, "you been talkin' to them niggers about the election this fall, tellin' them to make sure an' vote. You keep out of our business, Yankee. 'Cause if you don't, you're gonna be real sorry." He reached down and shoved Allen hard, so that he stumbled into Frank's bay. Frank laughed, raised his crop and slashed it down on Allen's face. Grace screamed.

"You're gettin' off easy this time," Rawlins shouted. "Remember this—we don't like nigger-teachers down heah. An' you stir them up to vote, we'll break every bone in your body."

Rawlins whirled his mount abruptly around, and the three riders galloped away, raising a cloud of red dust.

"Allen, oh God!" Grace cried, rushing to him.

He touched his face where it was bleeding. "I'm all right, Grace."

"You're hurt! Who are those men? We have to go to the sheriff." She was dabbing frantically at his face with a napkin.

Allen caught her hand. "I'm all right," he said calmly.

Grace took a deep breath. "Let me clean that cut."

He allowed her to do so, wincing slightly. "Is it bad?"

"You need one or two stitches," Grace said, furious. "Let's get you to a doctor. Then we're going to the sheriff. I thought that kind of behavior was outlawed with the Ku Klux Klan." She began energetically gathering up their things.

"Grace, every single man arrested and convicted for Klan activities was given a suspended sentence."

She froze. "What?"

"Here in Mississippi," Allen said, "there were over two hundred of them in '72 alone—all let go."

Grace was stunned. She knew that a few years ago Congress had investigated reported acts of terrorism against the Negroes and the Republicans. Their findings had made headlines, shocking the North. A wave of arrests and prosecutions of Klan members throughout the South had followed—which was why Grace could not believe her ears now. More than two hundred Klansmen in Mississippi had been given suspended sentences? "You mean, they got off scott-free?"

"Scott-free."

"Why? How?"

"Most of the public is behind them. You saw them, Grace, young planters' sons, well-educated, well-heeled. Most of Southern society refused to believe that these boys had committed the crimes they were accused of. They chose to believe that their confessions of guilt—and most of the defendants did plead guilty—were lies of convenience. You see, once they pled guilty, a deal could be made, resulting in a suspended sentence. So the defendants went home and resumed their activities. Those who knew that the defendants were actually guilty, who were against the Klan, were afraid to speak out, Grace."

"What are you telling me?"

He shook his head sadly. "They don't even bother to wear masks anymore."

Her eyes were wide. "You mean—they're still hurting people for exercising their rights?"

"For less, Grace. Not long ago a Negro was whipped for answering a question the wrong way. He was impertinent, not in what he said—it was his tone and the light in his eyes."

"Oh, God."

Allen put their tablecoth and basket in the buggy, then guided her to it. "Come on, get in."

"What about the sheriff?" Grace demanded as Allen turned the buggy down the road.

"Ford's a joke. He's not only a night rider, but proud enough of it to brag about it. He's one of their leaders, one of the worst, Grace."

Grace sat stunned and appalled. "Will you be all right? Why were they warning you?"

"I'll be fine," he assured her.

She bit her knuckle. "Will they come after you again?"

"No," Allen said, too quickly.

Grace did not believe him for a moment.

Rathe moved away from Louisa's hand, staring out of the window at the darkening sky.

"Rathe, darling, what is it?" Louisa asked, gazing at his back. She was a vision in magenta silk. "First you disappear, then when you do appear, you're moody as a cat."

Was Allen kissing her? He stared grimly out at the driveway, obsessed with the same thought that had tortured him all day. It didn't seem likely, did it? Grace was prim and proper and a prude. If she had rejected him, she would certainly reject Allen, wouldn't she? Or would she? Why, of all men, Allen Kennedy? He was nice enough, but—Rathe stopped his thoughts. Actually, he not only liked Kennedy, he respected him. He was a man of integrity. Was he kissing her right now?

He had a fleeting image of Grace in Allen's arms on the red and white cloth he'd seen tucked under their picnic basket. Would Grace marry him? Was he proposing right now? He found himself angry with the thought—for it was none of his business. In fact, Grace and Allen would make a perfect couple.

"You are impossible," Louisa cried furiously.

Rathe didn't even turn, although he heard her skirts whipping about as she rushed from the room in a temper. He wasn't being very subtle, he realized, coming back here on the pretext of a visit, staying most of the day, enduring Louisa's company when in truth he was waiting for Grace to return.

He poured himself a bourbon then paced back to the window. His heart went still for a fraction of a second when he saw the buggy approaching; then it began speeding madly. Rathe stepped closer to the window. The green velvet drapes shielded him from view.

Kennedy stopped the carriage and for a moment they just sat there, looking at each other. Grace was the first to move. She flung herself at him. *Flung* herself, madly, passionately, hugging Allen fiercely. Rathe could not believe his eyes. She wouldn't even give *him* one little kiss.

But she could fling herself at Kennedy.

Kennedy held her, then tenderly touched her face. Rathe wished he could see their expressions more clearly; they were lust-filled, no doubt. Kennedy bent his head forward, blocking Rathe's view. Seething now, Rathe moved into the window so he could see better. Kennedy was kissing her, but all he could see of Grace was her white hands on his shoulders. She didn't, however, seem to be putting up much of a struggle.

"Damn," he exploded, and downed the entire glass of bourbon. When he looked again, they had separated.

Grace sure had fooled him.

No woman had ever fooled him like this before.

He'd known there were fires hidden beneath that prim exterior, but he hadn't expected them to burn so close to the surface. Or was it that Allen's wanting to marry her entitled him to a few kisses? That thought was immensely appealing in one respect, for it soothed his wounded vanity. On the other hand, it carried grave implications. Did this mean she had kissed Allen before? And would she kiss him again? He was furious.

He watched her leave the buggy, saying something loving no doubt, judging from the way Allen clasped her hands. Finally the buggy moved away. Rathe folded his arms, turned to face the open doorway, and waited.

The front door closed. Her footsteps sounded. She appeared in the doorway as she went down the hall. He called out, stopping her in her tracks. "Good evening, Miss O'Rourke."

She turned and looked at him.

And the first thing that he noticed was that she was pale,

not flushed. He looked more closely—specifically, at her lips, for signs of a passion-filled afternoon. There were no signs there. Maybe Kennedy wasn't the world's best kisser. Maybe he should give her something to compare his kisses to.

"Is there a reason you're staring? So rudely, I might add?"

Rathe smiled, but it was not a particularly pleasant smile. "Do you object also when *Allen* looks at you?"

She shook her head. "What are you talking about?"

He ignored her. "How was your picnic? Did you and Kennedy have an enjoyable day?" He expected to see a romantic melting in her eyes. Instead, she tensed, her lips narrowed, and her eyes grew suspiciously wet. Instantly, the jealousy was gone. Rathe was at her side. "What's wrong, Grace?"

She looked right into his eyes, and yes, hers were wet, and getting wetter by the second. "Oh, dear, dear Lord," she murmured.

His hands found her shoulders. She was soft and firm, a woman's wonderful constitutional contradiction. "What is it? What's wrong?"

She shook her head, tears falling now, unable to speak.

He pulled her into his embrace. "It's okay," he crooned softly. "Everything's okay now, Grace. Shhh."

She trembled against his shirtfront.

He had intended to comfort her, but was instead assailed by the feel of her breasts against his chest, and her hips against his. Blood filled his loins—a slow, delicious thickening.

"I was so afraid," she gasped, and he tried to check his lust. His success was only partial.

"What happened to so frighten you, Gracie?" he murmured into her hair. "Tell me."

"Allen," she said in a strangled note.

Maybe he did hate Kennedy. Rathe moved her away from his body so he could look at her face. She wasn't wearing her glasses. Her eyes were violet and veiled by long, auburn lashes. Tears streaked her cheeks. "Allen's in trouble," she said earnestly, "and I'm so afraid for him."

"Of course."

At the dry note in his voice, she pulled free. "What am I telling you for? You're probably one of them!"

He didn't like her tone, or her overwhelming concern for her fiancé. He was sure, by now, that she had accepted Allen's proposal. "One of them?"

"One of those hate-filled, bullying bigots!" she shouted. "You are, aren't you?

It took him a moment to understand what she was talking about. "Are you referring to night riders and such?"

She wiped her eyes. "If you hurt Allen . . ." she warned.

Rathe was so furious at the slur that he momentarily couldn't speak. Then his tongue loosened. "What happened, Grace?" he commanded.

"They threatened him. They told him to go home—back North. They cut him with a crop."

Rathe was grim. "Kennedy should know better than to be encouraging the Negroes to vote this fall."

"They have every right to vote," she said, her eyes blazing. "Oh, I'm too tired to fight anymore!" She turned and ran out.

Rathe wasn't sure whom he felt like strangling—her or Kennedy. The latter, he decided, for jeopardizing her. Kennedy was a fool. If he was preaching to the Negroes about their rights and encouraging them to vote Republican, he should at least be discreet about it. As for Grace— she thought he was one of the night riders.

He decided strangling was too good for her.

Chapter 7

On the following Wednesday, Grace spent the whole day excited over the prospect of the meeting planned for that night. Lessons seemed endless, and Grace had trouble concentrating on her pupils; instead, she was planning the best approach for winning as many ladies as she could to the cause of women's suffrage. As soon as Mary Louise and Margaret Anne were sent to their rooms to wash and change for supper, Grace went flying down the stairs and out the door, clutching her reticule and a sheath of pamphlets. On the veranda she ran smack into a very familiar wall of male muscle—Rathe.

"Are you all right?" he drawled, chuckling, his hands on her arms, holding her so close their bodies touched.

Grace wrenched backward. He reluctantly let her go. The pamphlets were scattered all over the porch, and she dropped to her knees to begin gathering them. Her face flamed. Worse, her traitorous heart was slamming madly around in her chest.

"Here, let me help," Rathe said, kneeling beside her. "Where are you off to in such a rush? Or did you see me coming up the drive?" he teased.

"Hmph," Grace said. She made the mistake of looking up at him.

His bright blue eyes were trained steadily upon her, and when she met his gaze, everything seemed to stop. For a long moment, she was unable to tear her glance away. He squatted inches from her. There were flecks of gold in his

77

irises. His lashes were short but thick and the darkest of browns. Laugh lines fanned from the corners of his eyes. As she stared, she watched the amusement in his eyes fade, while something else flared. The blue visibly brightened, growing hotter, darker. The look was so unmistakable that Grace was shaken right out of her trance; she reached wildly for the papers nearest her hand, looking down, anywhere but at him.

His hand clamped over hers, stilling it.

She froze again. She could hear her own breathing, feel her own careening heart. Damn, she thought, damn. She was aware of his hand, large and hard and calloused, of his knees, inches from her breast. The breeches clinging obscenely to powerful thighs, strained from squatting. Grace's glance wandered upward, settling unavoidably on the soft, conspicuous bulge of his crotch. The instant she was aware of where she was looking, she jerked away, standing. Immediately, he was on his feet too.

"Calm down," he murmured. "Relax, Gracie."

She would not, absolutely would not, meet his gaze again. "I'm late," she said, feeling utter confusion. With new resolve she began gathering the pamphlets. What was wrong with her?

"And where are you off to?" Rathe asked, helping her. Then he glanced at the title of the paper in his hand, *Elizabeth Cady Stanton Speaks on Divorce,* and laughed. She snatched the pamphlet back, glaring. He reached out and chucked her chin.

She drew back, shoving everything under her arm and huffed past him.

"You forgot this, darlin'," he called, retrieving her reticule and following her. "Where are you going, Gracie? Do you need an escort?"

That thought horrified her. "I most certainly do not," she cried.

"How about a ride then?"

Because she had to walk, the offer was tempting. But she'd sooner die than accept anything from this impossible scoundrel. "No, thank you," she said glacially, striding down the drive.

"You're walking?" Rathe asked incredulously, pacing alongside her. "Where are you going? You can't walk. Did you know that the whole reason I came to Melrose was to see you?"

She snorted. "I have two good legs, Mr. Bragg, and an excellent set of lungs. I most certainly can walk."

He grinned, looking sideways at her, "I'll vouch for the excellence of your 'lungs'."

Grace caught the glance and the innuendo and went crimson. She decided to ignore him. He wasn't worthy of her attention. Maybe that was the problem—instead of disregarding him she let him bait her, which he seemed to thoroughly enjoy. Then she realized he had stopped and was no longer following, and she had to check herself to keep from looking back to see what he was doing. She managed to keep marching down the drive, and refused to be disappointed that he had given up so easily.

But she did look back ten minutes later when she heard a carriage approaching. Rathe smiled, sitting relaxed as you please in the open vehicle, looking very much the Southern gentleman in his coat, breeches, and polished boots. Grace could not believe his audacious persistence. She resolved to ignore him as the buggy drew alongside.

"Come on, Gracie, let me drive you to town."

She didn't answer.

"How are you going to get back later? It'll be dark in a couple of hours. You can't wander around here alone at night. You might get lost, or worse."

"Something 'worse', as you put it, would most likely occur if I were to ride with you!" She felt quite smug and pleased with that retort.

"Ah, Gracie, that's not fair. Wasn't I the perfect gentleman the other night?"

"I really can't recall," she lied, cheeks burning. She doubted she would ever forget the sensual, rasping quality of his voice. Even now, thinking about it did something strange to her stomach.

"You wouldn't have forgotten if I had kissed you," he said tightly. "Look, Grace, I only want to give you a ride. And I really did come all the way out to Melrose just to see you." His coaxing smile flashed.

It was about two miles to Sarah Bellsley's house, and Grace would have dearly loved to ride. But she did not dare give him an inch. She did not trust him. Or was it her own self she didn't trust? "No thank you, Mr. Bragg. Would you please stop bothering me? Maybe you should think about Louisa. I'm sure she's wondering where you are at this very moment."

"I doubt it," Rathe said.

"I do not need a ride," Grace said firmly.

To her surprise, he acquiesced with a grin. "They're your lungs."

The night was balmy, soft and thoroughly pleasant. Rathe leaned back in the carriage, once again looking toward the lights of the Bellsley house. A dozen ladies had congregated. He had to smile at the thought of Grace arousing them with her incendiary talk. After having seen her at van Horne's, he could just envision her lecturing now—and it was too easy to recall just how adorable she was when she got excited.

Scraps of conversation had been drifting through the open windows to him all night. Initially, the women of Natchez had been shocked. They were not prepared for Grace's extremism. Grace's strident tone had carried. "But they make the laws! And we have to abide by them! How fair is that when we're principal parties, too?"

Hesitant murmurs had followed.

"We are equal! And with the vote we can pass new laws—laws that will give us a chance to obtain custody of our children in cases of divorce, laws that will enable us to keep our own property when we join in marriage . . ."

Rathe heard enough to know that the conservative and

genteel ladies of Natchez were intimidated by Grace's views. He found himself straining to hear everything she had to say, and realizing for the first time that Grace actually had quite a few good points. If all married couples had the relationship his father and mother or his sister and his brother-in-law had, the laws Grace wanted to change wouldn't really matter. But those kinds of relationships were rare, as he well knew. Many women were unhappy in their marriages and stuck there. But, he mused, many men were unhappy, too. Yet this was the point Grace was making—men did benefit from both society's double standards and the power they wielded through the vote. Women suffered.

He was still listening intently when she abruptly changed the subject to one more suitable for conservative ladies—temperance.

"It's disgusting," Sarah Bellsley cried. "The decadence, the sin, the shame! Why, I won't mention names, but three of the ladies here have husbands who pass every evening on Silver Street, spending all the family's income on liquor and—and—hussies!"

"Silver Street is abominable!" someone shouted furiously, and Rathe winced.

A chorus of rousing war cries greeted this statement.

"My Willard changes beyond recognition under the influence," a woman stated. "Normally he's so kind. But with whiskey in him he becomes a demon. I'm afraid of him. I can't—don't dare—even criticize him!"

Murmurs of understanding and affirmation rippled through the assemblage. The ladies agreed that it was their Christian duty to form a temperance union.

Outside Rathe shook his head. There were going to be a few unhappy husbands in the days that followed. Leave it to Grace to stir up Natchez.

Soon the meeting drew to a close. Rathe puffed on a cigar and watched the ladies as they left. Their goodbyes seemed interminable. As the carriages dispersed he spotted Grace, coming through the picket gate, walking slowly down the street. He watched her approach from the shadow of an ancient walnut tree. Did she really think she could walk back to Melrose alone at night? Did she really think he would *allow* her to walk back there alone?

He leapt down from the carriage in an easy, graceful movement. He didn't want to scare her, but when he moved forward into the illumination provided by a gaslight, she gasped and jumped.

"It's me," he called. "Rathe. At your service, madame."

She stared, then snapped, "What is wrong with you? Haven't I made myself perfectly clear?"

He shook his head with mock sadness. "Why did I suspect it would be like this? I'm driving you home, Gracie. Don't be a stubborn fool about it."

"I don't want *anything* from you," she cried furiously.

"I know you don't. You have made that abundantly clear. Bend a little, Grace. It's dark out, it's a long walk to Melrose, and there are always thieves and riffraff out at night."

"Ooooh," she cried.

"Does that mean yes?"

"Do you always get your way?"

"Until recently," he muttered.

She hadn't heard. "Oh, all right, I give up! If you're going to make so much trouble about it . . ."

He watched her march to the carriage, head high and shoulders stiff like a little martyr. He found himself smiling. Then he caught himself and ran forward to help her climb in. She ignored his hand, swatting it away, hoisting her skirts and starting to step up. She was too much to resist. His hands closed around her narrow waist. For an instant he paused, relishing the feel of her.

"What are you doing?" she cried, twisting to get free, as if a maniac was accosting her.

He sighed heavily and swung her into the carriage, then climbed in beside her. "Pretty painless, huh?"

She looked at him carefully, sitting erect and properly

apart from him, her hands clasped in her lap. He could feel her mind working. She said, "When does the pain begin?"

He threw back his head and laughed. When he met her gaze he saw that she was smiling, too—slightly, but smiling.

Miss Grace O'Rourke was thawing.

Chapter 8

Louisa Barclay met them on the veranda.

Her furious gaze went from one to the other. "Just what," she ground out, "is going on?"

Rathe was nonchalant, smiling slightly. "Good evening, Louisa."

Grace froze, silently cursing her fair coloring for another damning blush. Louisa saw it, and, if possible, her eyes became darker. "What is going on?" she repeated.

Louisa knew nothing about tonight's meeting, Grace told herself. But then why was she so angry?

"I gave Grace a ride back from a ladies' social," Rathe said easily.

She quickly added, "Sarah Bellsley was introducing me to some of the women in town."

Louisa burned her with a look. "Miss O'Rourke—I'll deal with you later. Leave me with our friend Mr. Bragg."

Grace did not want to go. She wanted to hear every word they said. She wanted to know whether Rathe would reveal the reason for tonight's meeting and exactly how much trouble she was in. She fled into the house—but lingered in the foyer behind the door.

Louisa whirled on Rathe. "Since when do you drive the servants around, Rathe?"

"Is Miss O'Rourke a servant?"

"She's the governess! And one more question," she cried. "Were you on your way to see me when you ran into O'Rourke and gave her a ride?"

"No, Louisa," Rathe said. "The sole purpose of my trip here tonight was to escort Grace safely home."

"You bastard!" She sensed then that she had gone too far, and clutched his sleeve. "I'm sorry." She tried to placate him. "I miss you." Her tone dropped to a husky, sensual note. "I couldn't sleep last night, thinking about you."

"I am sorry," he said, extracting his hand.

She smiled seductively. "You look tired. I think I know exactly the cure for what ails you."

Rathe softened with the knowledge that their affair had already ended. "I have an appointment in town tonight, Louisa."

"That's what you said last night—and the night before."

He smiled slightly, took her hand, and lifted it to his lips. Then he rubbed his thumb along her lower lip, which was starting to tremble. "I'm sorry."

"There's someone else," she accused. "I can feel it. Someone you're seeing tonight!"

He thought about Grace. "There's no one, Louisa. I'm playing cards tonight."

Her brows knit. "Just what were you doing with the governess? I wouldn't think you would like her, but . . ."

He felt anger rising. He didn't like scenes and he didn't have to answer to her, but so far Louisa had only managed to annoy him. The slur cast on Grace was another matter— one that made him surprisingly angry. He reminded himself of how much Grace needed this job, how he'd hate to be the cause of her dismissal. "I told you, I was giving her a ride back here. Leave it be, Louisa," he warned.

Louisa intuited all she needed to know; she could tell that something had occurred between her governess and her lover, and she felt a stunning fury. "That bitch."

"Louisa, you're wrong."

"I'm wrong? Oh, no, I'm not wrong. I know something's going on between you two. Have you been carrying on right here under my nose?"

"There's nothing between us," Rathe said, too grimly.

"I hate you," Louisa hissed.

Rathe sighed. "On that note, I think I'll leave. Tell the girls I'll be back to say goodbye to them, will you?"

"Don't you dare set foot on my property again," Louisa shouted.

Rathe shrugged and left.

Inside, Grace bolted for the stairs.

Louisa picked up the nearest object she could find, a delicately wrought brass lantern, and flung it after him. It hit the ground harmlessly, spraying dirt and stones. Then she ran up the stairs, panting, and flung open Grace's door without even knocking. Grace was standing in the middle of the room, waiting, hugging her arms to her breasts.

"You are discharged," Louisa shouted. "Get your things and get out now!"

She was trembling so violently she felt faint.

Grace sank down onto the bed. She was in the midst of packing up her two bags and valise. Dear Lord, what was she going to do?

She only had a few dollars left. Most of her meager savings had been spent on the ticket to come south. She had been counting on her income from her position at Melrose—her mother's hospital bill would be due shortly. Now she would have to find employment, when the whole country was still struggling out of an economic depression. And the South, because of the War, was far worse off than the North. Damn! Double damn! Damn that rogue for chasing after her! Here she was, stranded in a strange city with no income; and most likely even two jobs, should she have the luck to find them, would not be adequate. Of course, there was Allen.

Allen. She would go to his boardinghouse and talk to him. He was her dearest friend, and she knew he would help her. Of course, what she would really like to do . . . A very satisfying image rose in her mind: herself slamming a fist into Bragg's charming, dimpled face. This was all his fault. If only he had stayed out of her affairs in the first place—oh, damn him!

She finished packing her bags. The valise she managed to sling over her shoulder, despite the short strap. It dug immediately into her collarbone, but she ignored the pain. She gripped a carpetbag in each hand, and carefully made her way downstairs. Despite the need to focus all her attention on taking each step without losing her balance, she thought about the children.

It wouldn't be hard leaving Margaret Anne and Mary Louise, yet she knew she'd always feel sad that she hadn't been able to reach them and open their minds to the joy of learning. But Geoffrey? She felt a terrible pang of regret. She would have to talk to Allen about him. Maybe there was some way she could still tutor him in secret. He was too bright to condemn to a miserable life of sharecropping.

Pebbles seemed to work their way into her shoes. Her hands stung and ached. The strap of the valise dug deeper and deeper into her flesh. She had to stop to catch her breath and rearrange herself, and she was only halfway down the driveway. Tears came to her eyes, tears of anger. She was fighting mad.

Grace picked up her bags and stumbled on.

Rathe found himself sitting on his stallion outside of Harriet Gold's boardinghouse.

He was deep in thought. There was no poker game, of course. He was staying at the Silver Lady Hotel on the cliffs overlooking the Mississippi River and he was on his way back there. There was no reason for him to be here, except that he was, once again, thinking about the unfathomable, indomitable Grace O'Rourke, and this was where Allen Kennedy roomed. He'd toyed with the idea of stopping in and visiting with Harriet, but couldn't quite make up his mind. He now found himself recollecting the events of the evening, specifically Grace's fervent efforts to convert the good ladies of Natchez to her goals. Remembering her words and tone made him smile. "Ladies," she had shouted, "we must unite. We must stand together. Otherwise there is only defeat at the hands of our oppressors!"

Did she really see men as oppressors?

He chuckled into the night. He had no doubt she did—that she believed every word she spoke. Grace was no hypocrite. She would cling to her beliefs until she took her dying breath. Had he ever met anyone, man or woman, with such integrity?

Had he ever been so fascinated with a woman? What was it about her that held him so enthralled?

His stallion shifted restlessly beneath him, and Rathe put a soothing hand on the thick, corded neck. He thought of Allen Kennedy—of Allen Kennedy and Grace. He knew how right they were for each other, but that knowledge did not ease him. And what would Louisa Barclay do? She was proving to be a consummate bitch, capable of spending her jealous anger on Grace. If she actually discharged her, Grace would have every reason in the world to blame him. What's more, it would certainly drive her straight into Allen's open arms.

A cry of pain made him twist his head sharply around. A dark, shapeless form had paused on the street, then moved forward awkwardly, laboring under an indistinguishable burden. Rathe was about to look away when the person stepped into the gaslight. "Grace!"

She froze, eyes wide.

Rathe jumped off his mount and rushed to her. "Are you all right? Here, let me take those. What are you doing out here alone at night? Dammit all! I left you not two hours ago at Melrose!" The last was shouted with growing fury as he realized she was in exactly the position he had worked so hard to avoid earlier—out wandering the streets alone at night.

"You!" she cried. She was flushed from exertion. "Let go! Put down that bag! I don't want your help! Put that down!" She grabbed the valise he had taken and yanked it so hard that Rathe let it go, surprised. Grace stumbled backward; Rathe reached to steady her.

"This is all your fault!" she panted, pushing him away from her. "Don't touch me. You've done enough!"

His shock at seeing her had worn off, and now it was all too evident what had happened. "So Louisa terminated your position," Rathe stated, a sick feeling of guilt starting to gnaw within him.

"Yes! Because of you!"

"That's not fair," Rathe said quietly, but he was already blaming himself.

"She's your paramour!" Grace cried. "I didn't want to be driven to Melrose, I didn't ask for your attentions!"

"I could not let you walk alone at night," Rathe said softly.

"You mean you could not resist the challenge I provided!" she spat.

He stiffened. "I'm sorry."

"Sorry," she echoed. "Why, that helps. That will pay all my bills." She began picking up her bags resolutely, first the one over her shoulder, then the others. Rathe removed the two valises from her hands to carry them for her, very grim and guilt-ridden now. She gave him a look which he expected to be withering; instead, he saw she was close to tears. She started marching up the path to Harriet's. With her bags in hand, he followed.

It was still early, about eight o'clock, and not only were lights flooding from the parlor out into the street, there was a soft hum of conversation from the veranda, where several of Harriet's boarders were enjoying the night air. All discussion ceased as Grace and Rathe stepped onto the veranda, the two elderly women staring openly. Rathe managed to sling the two bags into one hand and push the door open for Grace. She ignored him as she entered.

A rag rug lay at their feet; a chipped white banister rose directly to their left. Old, well-worn draperies lifted ever so slightly in a whisper-soft breeze. The place was in need of repair, that was obvious, but it was clean and cheerful and Harriet had the well-deserved reputation of being a good-natured, motherly woman who made the best flapjacks in the entire state.

Harriet Gold was a middle-aged widow. Before the War, the boardinghouse had been her family's Natchez home where they stayed when not in residence at their plantation across the Mississippi. Her husband had died a natural death in '64; two of her sons had died on the battlefield, and her youngest was now studying law back East. She had opened Fairlief to the public years ago when high postwar taxes had left her no other choice. At that moment she came bustling in, a pile of linens in her arms. "Rathe!" the plump, gray-haired widow cried.

He smiled. "Good evenin', Harriet. Beautiful night now, ain't it?"

"Why, of course it is. What are you up to, you young scoundrel? I see a gleam in your eye." She smiled warmly at Grace. "And you must be the new governess at Melrose."

Grace flushed. "Yes, well, I . . ."

"Miss O'Rourke has decided to take other employment," Rathe interjected smoothly. "She is in need of a room. In fact," he abruptly decided, thinking about Grace and Kennedy, "I need a room as well." He ignored the incredulous look both Grace and Harriet directed at him.

"I have a few rooms left," Harriet said cheerfully, "but why you need one here when you keep that fancy suite over at the Silver Lady is a mystery to me. You're just like your daddy, full of no-good. Watch out for him, Grace, I'm telling you."

"Yes, Missus Gold."

"Are these your bags?" Harriet asked. Rathe instantly had them in hand. Harriet winked at Grace. "What a gentleman! Come on, let's get you upstairs. You look exhausted. And you can call me Harriet."

In no time Rathe was settled into a cozy blue and white room with a fine view of the treetops gracing the Missis-

sippi River. Harriet told him to come down to the kitchen
for a plate of leftovers, and Rathe agreed. He hung up his
jacket in the small wardrobe, removed his tie and unbuttoned the top four buttons of his white linen shirt. He
opened the window wider, inhaled his favorite scent, that
of magnolias, and was about to turn when he heard Grace's
voice coming from the garden below. He leaned over the
sill, straining to hear and see.

He could do neither from there, so he left his room and
went downstairs, pausing to check his speed so as to appear unperturbed, sashaying nonchalantly into the back
drawing room which he guessed, correctly, opened onto
the garden. He hesitated in the doorway, hanging back just
enough so she couldn't see him. He wanted to gage her
mood.

Suddenly he realized that she was with Allen Kennedy.
Jealousy rose in his chest.

"What am I going to do, Allen?" Grace was saying,
standing very close to him; in fact, Allen was holding her
hands.

"Darling, don't worry, there is a solution, such an easy
solution." He was gazing at her with such tenderness
Rathe couldn't stand it.

"I have no money," Grace said, sounding choked.
"Oh, it's all his fault! That no-good, philandering scoundrel . . ."

Rathe's eyes went wide—she was referring to him. She
was talking about him to Allen!

"Grace," Allen interrupted. "Grace, marry me. I love
you. I know you care for me. We suit. I'll take care of
you and you'll never have to worry about anything—"

Grace yanked away with abrupt, explosive anger. "How
dare you patronize me, Allen."

"Grace, I didn't—"

"I can take care of myself!"

"Grace, I didn't mean it that way!"

"You did! From you, of all men—I'd expect it from

someone like Rathe Bragg, but never from you!'' Her voice broke.

"Oh, Grace, I didn't mean it the way it sounded,'' Allen said, pulling her into his embrace. ''I meant I love you. I'm here for you, always. I want you to be my wife. We can teach together. It would be perfect. Grace?''

She gazed at him, and Rathe felt so positive in assuming it was with adoration, that her next words shocked him. ''Allen, you know I don't want to get married. Why should I? My life is just fine the way it is. Why should I become some man's chattel?''

"It wouldn't be that way with us, Grace,'' Allen said tensely.

"Oh, Allen, please, not now.''

"I know you care for me.''

"I do. Very much.''

"I'd make the perfect husband, Grace. We share the same beliefs, the same morals, and best of all, a deep respect and friendship. Think about it. Really think about it.''

"All right,'' Grace said.

Rathe stared at her, a disturbing sensation cramping his guts—an unfamiliar, shaky feeling. Grace was considering Allen's proposal. Apparently she had never really considered it before. And she cared for him. He had heard her say so himself.

She had paced away wringing her hands. Allen stared at the ground. Rathe remembered how she had flung herself into his arms last Sunday, how they had kissed so passionately, gazed at each other with such desire. The shaky feeling increased. Grace was going to marry Allen . . . unless something happened.

She turned to Allen. "I have just enough money to rent a room for a few days, and hope I can find work. I don't even have the means to go back to New York.''

"I don't want you to go,'' Allen said. Rathe echoed his sentiments silently.

"Allen, I'm so worried about my mother. I need to

work. If I can't pay the hospital bills . . . tomorrow morning I will find work, even if it's scrubbing someone's floors.''

"Oh, Grace," Allen said, "let me lend you some money."

"You're very kind," Grace whispered. "Maybe. But not right now, thank you."

Rathe barely heard. An exciting thought occurred to him, penetrating his thick jealousy. She needed money. He had money. His heart beat wildly. He had the perfect solution. He would take care of her.

He would make her his mistress.

Chapter 9

It was mid-afternoon, but Natchez-Under-the-Hill was just coming awake when Grace's hunt for a job finally brought her to the notorious district's outermost edge. At the end of Silver Street she hesitated, but not for long.

Curiosity, more than the prospect of a job, drove her forward now, for she never even entertained the thought that there might be suitable employment in a neighborhood that was nothing more than a den of decadence for the worst sort of lowlives. Contrary to what she had told Allen, she really had no intention of scrubbing floors, not if she could avoid it. The pay was far less than what she needed.

Unfortunately, she had not come across one open position of any kind all day long. Her first stop had been at the seamstress's, Mrs. Garrot, who she hoped might need help. However, Mrs. Garrot told her that there just weren't enough orders from the ladies of Natchez to warrant her taking on an assistant. "Business hasn't been the same since the War," she sighed. "No one has the money to buy beautiful clothes, no one except for a very few of Natchez' planters and the carpetbaggers, of course. It's terrible."

A pharmaceutical sales clerk repeated this theme, informing her that these were bad times. After that she had tried dozens of shops and stores in town, to no avail. She even inquired at the better hotels atop the cliffs, with the same results.

Grace stood now, watching a number of bleary-eyed sailors stumble through the twisting streets, a woman vendor trying to sell fresh biscuits, and a man smoking a cigar on the porch of a saloon, from which strains of raucous revelry already emanated. Three women lounged on a balcony clad in nothing but corsets and petticoats. Grace took a second glance at that last sight, staring with shock at such blatant marketing of their dubious wares. One of the faded, plump beauties caught her eye and waved. Grace blushed and looked away. Imagine appearing almost naked right out on a public street!

She whipped her head around and stared at the door of a house of ill-repute. Her heart climbed frantically into her mouth. Rathe Bragg closed the door casually behind him, glancing around. Grace had already turned away, her heart pounding. Fortunately, a huge dray moved right in front of her, blocking her from his view. Grace stood stiffly, flushed from her head to her toes. She couldn't help it—she imagined Rathe and the prostitute who had waved entwined together. A surge of righteous outrage flooded her. A man like him would consort with the lowest kind of women! Why, he had practically jumped from Louisa's bed right into the arms of a prostitute! And he was the one responsible for her dire circumstances right now. That man was the worst sort imaginable!

It was then that she really looked at the young, Negro woman vendor, and she was instantly, thoroughly, distracted. A man was holding her basket of biscuits tauntingly out of reach, while another fellow grabbed her by her waist. She struggled futilely, and Grace saw that she was close to tears. One of the men planted a hard kiss on her mouth, at which point Grace realized he was inebriated—not that that was any excuse. He then shoved the woman into his buddy's arms, laughing, the basket thrown aside, all the biscuits rolling out into the dirt, while the second man held her and shoved his hand down her blouse.

Grace didn't think. With her skirts held in one hand and raised to her knees, she ran toward the trio.

"Stop!" she shouted. "Stop it this minute! Unhand her, you pigs!"

The man kissing the young woman pulled her against his front, holding her firmly, while the other man started hooting. "Look at this, Able! A schoolmarm, from the looks of it. Jealous, sweetie?"

"Unhand that woman this instant, you perverted lout," Grace fairly snarled. She was so angry she could almost kill.

"Hey, Robbie, this one looks like fun. She looks like she's just dying for a man," the one called Able said, releasing the vendor. The woman scrambled away, grabbing her basket and clutching it to her breasts. Before Grace knew it, Able had grabbed her wrist and pulled her against his hips, locking her there with his arm, while he squeezed one of her breasts. Grace cried out, suddenly frightened, struggling. The man smelled like manure and stale sweat and sour beer. He yanked her closer. Panicked, she tried to twist her face away as his full, open lips came down on hers. She gagged at the feel of his tongue against her closed mouth. And then she felt his hands clenched on her buttocks, separating them, and something alien and hard pressing against her belly.

Suddenly, as fast as she had been grabbed, she was freed. The abrupt release sent her falling onto her hands and knees, panting, retching. She heard a sickening thud, a groan of agony. She managed to look up and saw Rathe landing a bone-shattering blow to Able's face, which was already streaked with blood. The man doubled over, but Rathe was holding him so that he couldn't fall forward. The expression on Rathe's face stunned Grace into utter immobility. Never had she seen such a look of murderous fury. Rathe hit him again, in his abdomen, and again on his nose, and yet again in an undercut that cracked resoundingly and sent his victim's head whipping back. Still holding him, Rathe viciously kicked his legs out from under him, and Able went flying onto his rear, in the dust.

Rathe turned to meet Able's cohort, and he was smiling. Grace had never, ever seen a smile like this one. It didn't reach his eyes, which were as hard and dark as steel. She saw the man's buck knife flash and choked on a sob. Then she cried out, her hands going to her mouth as Rathe stepped forward, his words cutting the air just before his arm did. "Come on, you bastard, just try it."

With one arm he sliced a blow at the sailor's knife-holding hand, while almost simultaneously landing a solid punch to the man's abdomen. As the man fell forward, his knife dropping harmlessly to the street, Rathe grabbed him by the shoulders and directed him down while his knee came up. There was a loud cracking noise as knee met nose. Robbie crumpled in slow motion. Rathe shoved him away. He was suddenly standing over the groaning Able, a knife in his hand, and Grace had never seen him draw it.

He spoke very softly, his drawl so thick it was almost slurred. "Care to try again, my friend?"

Able lurched unsteadily to his feet, swaying. He mouthed something incoherent, shaking his head and backed away.

Rathe stared at Able in disgust, and the knife in his hand disappeared. Grace hunched over, gasping for air, trembling. Never had she witnessed such violence. A long moment passed as Rathe stood, regaining his control, breathing hard. An animated crowd had gathered but his gaze never left Grace's huddled form. At last he moved to her and knelt. She felt his arms going around her, lifting her against his chest, cradling her. "Shhh," he soothed. "Shhhh. It's all right now. It's all right."

"Rathe, you want me to get the sheriff?" a man in the crowd asked.

Normally, Rathe wouldn't have cared, because the two men, sailors from the looks of them, would be out of jail in a night. But he was still angry enough to kill, or at least come close to doing so. *Grace had been in danger. Grace had almost been hurt.* "Yes."

He held her, offering her the comfort of his big body. His pulse started to slow. His reaction to seeing Grace being manhandled by those brutes had been instant and uncontrollable. Rathe had been taught to fight by his father, but he did not like it. It had been years since he had been in a fight. But today, with Grace in jeopardy, he had seen red. He had wanted to hurt, to maim, to kill.

As his blood slowed, a feeling of horror and dread began to well up in the pit of his stomach. This was the worst section of town. If he hadn't come along Grace would have been raped, right here on the street. The thought of the prim and proper Grace on her back screaming and crying and struggling beneath the sailor made him sick. His grip on her tightened.

The crowd milled about, chatting excitedly. Rathe looked at a familiar, brown-haired prostitute. "Betty, get some water and a brandy." He turned to Grace, still on her knees, her face buried against his chest. He pulled off her gray felt hat and stroked her tightly pinned hair. "Talk to me, darlin'. Are you all right?"

She raised her white face. "Yes, I'm fine."

There was a slight quaver in her voice. Then he felt her pushing away, trying to stand, and he helped her up. She raised a trembling hand to her face, touched her nose where her glasses should have been. "My spectacles."

He stared into her clear eyes and decided that nothing about her would surprise him, certainly not the fact that she wore glasses she obviously did not need. He accepted the brandy from Betty, and with an arm around Grace's waist, pulled her away from the crowd, into the shadow of an overhanging roof. He raised the glass to her lips. "Drink it."

"I'm all right."

She was, he realized, holding up very well—but he had already known how much grit she had. He forced her to take a few sips of brandy. She coughed, protesting. He smiled.

Their gazes locked. Hers wide and vulnerable and amazed, his calm, piercing, and triumphant. She was woman. He was man—and he had protected what was his. He stared at her, somehow not surprised by his own fierce possessiveness. Hard satisfaction glittered in his eyes. Seeing it, Grace flushed.

"Just what in hell were you doing down here, Grace?"

At his demanding tone, Grace drew away, her own eyes narrowing. The hostilities resumed. "Might I ask you the same question?" she said, sweetly. Then she pointedly lifted her gaze in the direction of the bawdy house.

He was almost amused at what she was obviously—and incorrectly—thinking. "I asked first," he said, dangerously.

"Looking for employment," she replied. "Not that I owe you any explanations."

His brows snapped together. "What?"

"My turn," she said. "Or are you afraid to admit where you were?"

"You were looking for a job down here?"

"Aren't you ashamed of yourself?" she whispered, all pretense of amiability gone.

He blinked.

"Don't you care that you resemble a rutting bull more than a thinking man? Are you so oblivious to anything other than your . . . needs that embarrassment and shame don't even occur to you?"

A wide smile broke out over his face. "Possibly," he mused, eyes sparkling. "Why, that must be it!"

"You don't take anything seriously!" she cried, furious.

"And you take everything too seriously." He captured both her flailing hands. "Are you trying to reform me?" he asked, a touch huskily, gazing deeply into her eyes.

She tried to pull her hands away, and failed. "You are undoubtedly not reformable," she said with a sniff.

"I don't know" he said, his gaze unwavering. "Maybe you could do it, Grace."

She opened her mouth, then closed it.

"Don't you want to try?" he asked, and there was no mistaking the rough timbre of his tone.

Something hot and wet and deliciously sinful unfurled in her body. His hands were so warm, dwarfing hers, his eyes so blue and bright. "What?" she croaked.

"Reform," he murmured, piercing her with his gaze. "We're talking about reform."

His face seemed to have drifted closer. "Reform," she echoed.

"You're going to try and reform me," he told her, his breath touching her face.

She opened her mouth soundlessly.

Rathe smiled slightly and leaned down, his mouth closing over hers. Grace gasped to feel the torrent of sensation that flooded her at the touch of his lips on hers. His tongue gently, softly intruded into the space she had granted him, thrusting ever so lightly, his mouth playing so tenderly. A raging storm of hot aching need washed over her, tightening her nipples, swelling her groin.

He pulled away without deepening the kiss, without releasing her hands. Grace couldn't move, couldn't breathe, couldn't even think. He stared into her eyes, and she couldn't have looked away for the life of her.

All at once, Grace realized he was still holding her hands, that he had kissed her, intimately, in public, and that he was now looking quite pleased with himself about it. She yanked her hands away, thoroughly discombobulated. "I think I'm going to like being reformed," Rathe murmured.

He was, in a word, impossible. Grace opened her mouth for a quick, angry retort, when she saw the sheriff striding through the crowd. She fought for some semblance of equilibrium, and seized on the first distraction she could think of. "Where are my glasses?" She started back toward the crowd, scanning the ground, brushing off her skirts in a no-nonsense manner.

Rathe reached down to retrieve the spectacles. Unfortunately, the glasses had not been crushed in the melee, just slightly bent. For the briefest of moments, he debated crushing them under his own booted heel before she saw that he had found them. Then the gentleman in him asserted itself and he handed them to her with a flourish.

Sheriff Ford was a tall, husky man in his late forties. His dark eyes were shrewd, his brow furrowed. "Rathe, what the hell happened?"

"Miss O'Rourke tried to stop these two sailors from accosting a woman vendor. They attacked her in turn."

Sheriff Ford looked around, then settled his glance on Grace. "That true, Miss O'Rourke?"

"Yes."

"Where is the vendor?"

"I don't know," Grace said.

"She run off, Sheriff," an orange-haired prostitute said. "She picked up all her biscuits and run off."

"She a nigger?" Ford asked.

Grace stiffened. "Yes, she was colored."

Ford looked at her. "You're not from around here, are you, Miss O'Rourke?"

Grace sucked in her breath with dread.

"You think that little slut don't give it out to the white boys when she wants?"

Grace gasped.

Rathe angrily planted himself between the sheriff and Grace. "Ford, there's no call for talkin' that way to Miss O'Rourke. She's a lady."

Ford nodded, looking past Rathe at Grace's face, which was now flushed with outrage. "Miss O'Rourke, I beg your pardon. But the boys were just havin' a little fun, you get my meanin'?"

"I most certainly do," Grace managed.

"Those boys attacked Grace," Rathe said in a low tone. His gaze met Ford's. "And I want to know what you're going to do about it, Sheriff."

"You threatenin' me, boy?"

"Now, would I do that?" Rathe mocked.

"Guess you wouldn't, not if you know what's good for you." The two men stared at each other, locked in a tense stand-off.

Then Rathe smiled, but it didn't reach his eyes. "I'll be down later to make a statement—since I saw the entire incident."

Ford's eyes glinted. "Before I make any arrests, I'll have to investigate."

"You do that," Rathe drawled. "You make sure you do that." His mouth curved in another humorless smile; then he took her arm. "Let's get out of here, Grace."

Chapter 10

"Where are we going?"

Rathe had his hand firmly on her elbow as he guided her up the street. "Back to the boardinghouse to clean up, then I'm taking you to supper."

That stopped her in her tracks. "Now listen! How you can even think of—"

He tugged on her until she'd started moving again. "I can, and I am." He flashed her his best dimpled smile. "Aren't you hungry, Grace? Won't you let me buy you a nice hot meal? After all I did for you today?"

That stopped her again, abruptly. "What you did for me? From what I saw, you got some perverse kind of satisfaction in pounding those two men to a pulp!"

His face went very still. "You're determined, aren't you, to fight me every step of the way?"

"I'm not fighting you, Mr. Bragg, for it's certainly not a *sport* that interests *me*."

"You little ingrate," he growled, grabbing both her arms in a viselike hold.

Grace tested it once then went motionless.

"You interfered with that young Negro and almost got yourself raped in the process. If I hadn't come along, right now you'd be flat on your back with your skirt up to your neck—do you understand?"

She blanched. Then a red tide of fury swept her. "That is circumstantial speculation!"

"Circumstantial speculation?"

"Circumstantial speculation!" Her hands were on her hips, balled into fists. "What's wrong, Mr. Bragg? Do you need a dictionary?"

His mouth went tight.

"What about that poor woman, Rathe? *What about her?*"

"What?"

"The vendor," she shouted. "There is an important issue here which you seem intent on ignoring."

"The issue which you seem intent on ignoring is one of safety, common sense, and propriety!" Rathe shouted back. He realized he had raised his voice, but didn't care. "Good women don't go barreling around the waterfront!"

"Propriety!" she shrieked. "You dare tell me about propriety when you're the one who lost me my job, thanks to your shameless attentions?"

That silenced Rathe momentarily.

"The issue," Grace cried, grabbing one of his hands to get his attention, "the issue is that colored woman being accosted on a public street by white men, Rathe, and no one giving a damn!"

"Damn." Rathe winced.

Grace felt the stickiness of blood at that exact moment and dropped his hand like it was a hot iron. "Oh, dear! Your hand is bleeding." Unconsciously, her own palm covered her racing heart.

"A bit," he agreed. Then, darting a glance at her and seeing her frozen countenance, Rathe winced again, this time with a slight groan. He checked her reaction. He was rewarded with brisk concern.

"Here, let me look at that."

"Ow," he said, pulling his hand back.

"Oh, dear," Grace said, feeling suddenly faint. His knuckles were raw and bloody. "We had better go to Harriet's and I'll clean up your hand. That dirt should come out immediately."

Rathe knew when he had a good thing going, so he wisely kept his mouth shut and meekly followed her. This course of action, however, did not stop Grace. Rather, it seemed to encourage her. "Rathe, something has to be done about that sheriff."

He didn't answer, and she didn't seem to notice. "This situation is scandalous. Outrageous. Allen told me Ford is one of those night riders. How can a man like that be in a position of power, which is given him by the public in good faith and with the utmost trust that he will uphold the laws and our Constitution? This situation cannot continue. I wonder if a letter to the governor would help?"

"He was elected, Grace."

"Elected! Well, he should be unelected! Or, at the very least, in the fall elections he should be ousted! Yes! That's a wonderful idea! We must encourage all the Negroes to vote against Ford this fall!"

Rathe looked at her. "Don't go getting involved in local politics, Grace," he warned.

"Hmm," she said, deep in thought. Then she focused on him as they walked along in silence for another minute. "You do realize, don't you, that the root of this problem is education? Values, Rathe, are instilled at an early age. The young white child must be educated to think for himself, to question what he is told and sees, not to blindly accept the injustices of the world. And as for the young Negro, well, there the answer is much more fundamental. He must learn to read and write. That is the key. I think it's a sin that Geoffrey doesn't attend the public school. There should be a law requiring all children, regardless of their age, sex, or race, to attend school until they have attained a certain level of proficiency. Here's Harriet's. Does your hand hurt very much?"

They had paused on the veranda. Rathe had not taken his eyes off her perfect profile through her entire discourse, while she had watched the street in front of them. Now she turned her gaze on him. "Well? What is it?"

"What makes you the way you are, Grace?" His words were low, soft.

She flushed. "What makes me the way I am? What kind of question is that?"

"It's a question that seems to make you very nervous," he murmured. "And it's one I intend to find the answer to."

He was right; it did make her nervous. She held open the door, but he insisted that she precede him in.

In the kitchen Harriet Gold took one look at Rathe's blood-spotted coat and shirt and cried out in concern, the supper she was preparing for her boarders forgotten. "Good heavens, Rathe, what happened?"

"Just a little scrap," Rathe told her, laughing inwardly at the gross misrepresentation, watching Grace while she pumped water into a basin. She set it down on the table.

"Harriet, do you have some clean rags I can use?" she asked.

Harriet looked from Rathe to Grace, then smiled broadly. "Of course I do." She returned from the pantry with some clean linen strips. "I'll be right back," she said, and hurried out, purposefully leaving the two alone.

Rathe didn't pay attention. He was sitting at the table, both hands palm down in front of him, intently watching Grace as she bent over him dipping the linen in the water. She had a perfect, angelic profile. It was deceptive because it hid a sharp intellect and moral fervor. He decided he had never met such an extraordinary woman. He also decided that her bravery scared him.

"You know, Grace," he said, "you never answered my question. What were you doing down at the waterfront? I know you couldn't possibly be such a Yankee greenhorn that you really thought to find work on Silver Street?"

"Well, no," she said, flustered. "Actually, I was exploring."

"Exploring!" That did it. Her bravery did scare him. Rathe knew she needed him desperately, in every way. When she was his mistress he would not just be her provider, but her protector. It was evident that she needed someone to keep her out of trouble.

Last night, when the idea had first come to him, he'd been elated, but that had rapidly given way to guilt and uncertainty. How would he ever get her to agree, and was it even fair to try to convince her? He had barely slept, his conscience warring with his baser needs. But today, there was no longer any doubt. She needed him more than he needed her. She needed him desperately to keep her out of danger.

Grace finally finished and looked up to find Rathe's intense gaze riveted upon her. She sensed the abrupt change in him and nervously straightened. "There, that's done." She quickly began gathering up the stained rags.

Rathe leaned back in his chair, following her every movement. She had a helluva body, even in the ill-fitting gown. So long and slender. He imagined what her legs looked like, imagined them long and lily-white and wrapped around his own hard flanks while he was pumping into her. That fantasy produced an instant hardening. He decided that it was because he'd gone for the past few days without sex, a very rare feat for him since he'd discovered that wonderful activity at the age of thirteen. Then he remembered how Grace had accused him of being with a whore this morning, and his grin widened. He had stopped by only to collect some money that he had lent one of the girls. He said, casually, to her back, "Shall I meet you down here then, in twenty minutes?"

She turned slowly. "Meet me here?"

"To take you to supper. I want to take you to supper, Grace."

Her every instinct told her that this was dangerous. She should wait until Allen arrived home, and have a quiet meal with him. She didn't want anything from this man. But then she met Rathe's eyes, his so very beautiful blue eyes, and felt that heated feeling uncurling deep within her. After all, she thought, she was decidedly impoverished. She hadn't eaten since this morning, and although Harriet's meals were very cheap, they still cut into her meager funds. Why not have a free meal? If she didn't

find a job, meals might soon become rather scarce. That
was, of course, the only reason she would dine with him.
"All right."

Rathe grinned.

Twenty minutes was enough to give Grace serious
doubts about her decision.

He was, she reminded herself, the antithesis of everything she believed in. To him, women were objects of pleasure. The fact that for Rathe Bragg, one woman wasn't
enough only made it worse.

He was also a prejudiced Southerner. After all, he was
from Texas. She clearly recalled the conversation between
him and Sheriff Ford. He had been preoccupied with what
had happened to her, a white woman, not what had happened to the Negro vendor. And while she had to be honest with herself and admit she was somewhat grateful he
had been there, he had not handled the situation in a way
she approved of. Violence was never the answer, though
she was certainly not surprised that that had been his solution. And she was sure he had exaggerated the consequences of the assault—surely someone else would have
stopped the sailors if he hadn't come by! Added to all the
charges against him was the blatant fact that he was nothing more than a wastrel, a drifter, a gambler, a complete
and unrepentant hedonist.

"Is something wrong, Gracie?" Rathe asked, as they
walked down the path to the street.

She didn't meet his gaze. I need this meal, she reminded herself, when some inner, traitorous voice piped
up: *He defended and protected you, Grace.*

"Grace?"

"I'm sorry," she said quickly, flushing from the thrill
she now felt; this man had been angry enough to come to
blows to defend her virtue. Good God! How could she be
thinking like this—she was an enlightened, modern
woman! She could defend herself!

Not that time, her inner voice snidely said.

"Grace?"

Then she looked at him, really looked, and noticed that he had changed from his breeches to a fine, dark suit with a silver brocade vest and tie. The faint hint of a pleasing musky cologne touched her nostrils. He had taken her arm. With the sun glinting in his thick, sun-streaked hair, he was not just urbane and elegant, but utterly virile and devastatingly handsome. She was suddenly miserably aware of her own drab appearance, and for the first time in her life wished she were wearing a nice silk gown. Then she stared at the carriage awaiting them.

She wasn't sure she had ever seen anything quite like it. A magnificent palomino tugged at the traces, shaking its head impatiently, its silver mane flowing past its shoulder. The carriage was varnished black, with brass trimmings, and gleamed brightly in the sunlight. The driver was liveried and holding open the door. Inside, it was all plush red leather. "Rathe, where on earth did you find something like this?"

He laughed, pleased. "Only the best for you, Gracie." His gaze held hers, bold and direct. She had to blush and look away.

He handed her in. Grace knew it was ridiculous, but she felt like a queen. She ran a hand over the soft, sensuous leather as the carriage dipped beneath Rathe's weight. She shot a glance at him and saw he was watching, smiling slightly; she quickly clasped her hands in her lap and squared her shoulders. The driver shut the door, climbed up to his seat above them and the carriage rolled forward. "It's yours if you want it," Rathe said.

"What?"

"It's yours if you want it."

She stared, thoroughly shocked.

His gaze was warm. "It would be my pleasure to give you things, Grace."

Her eyes widened. "What can you be thinking of?"

Ah, he thought, if only you knew.

He began pointing out the local landmarks, much to her

surprise. "That's Dunleith. It was first built in '43 by Jack Farrington, an Englishman. It was completely razed during the war. Farrington's sons have rebuilt it almost exactly as it was."

"It's beautiful," she said, craning her neck for a last glimpse of the massive brick, pillared home.

"That's Fairfax," he said, pointing out another plantation home, this one white and weathered. "It's another rooming house. It's also run by a widow, Missus Bergen. She's not like Harriet, though."

Grace looked at him inquiringly.

"She's old and a bit forgetful. I think she's almost ninety. Her servant, a freed Negro, is probably older. He's forgetful, too. But they're warm and wonderful people."

"Then it doesn't matter if they're forgetful."

He looked at her. "Not only do they forget to collect the rent, which no one, I daresay, minds, but from time to time they forget to feed their boarders."

Grace bit back a smile, or tried to.

He grinned.

"Oh, dear," she said. "What a hungry group they must be."

His grin widened. "I made that up."

She couldn't help it; she started to laugh.

She glanced out the window again, and this time gasped with delight, getting her first glimpse of a roundwheeler. It was white and red, with three decks, the paddlewheel huge. Her name was the *Mississippi Queen*. "Oh, she's beautiful! Where is she going?"

"To New Orleans," Rathe said, watching her.

"To New Orleans! How long does it take? Do the passengers sleep aboard?"

"Yes indeed," Rathe said, as the carriage came to a halt. "And it takes two and half days."

"Where are we going?" Grace cried.

Rathe grinned. "For a riverboat ride."

Grace was wide-eyed as Rathe escorted her toward the

plank with one hand possessively on her elbow. "But Rathe, I can't possibly go with you to New Orleans!"

He laughed. "We're only going to have supper. Our driver will meet us downriver." His look was both questioning and amused.

Grace put a hand to her rapidly beating heart. "Oh," she breathed. "Yes, yes, I would like that."

He seemed pleased as they strolled up the gangplank. "Let's take a turn around the deck."

"Yes," Grace said, turning to stare at a couple, the woman resplendent in white linen and lace with a matching parasol. They, too, were ambling along the deck, as were many other passengers.

"Come on," Rathe said, taking her hand.

She was too involved with her surroundings to notice the impropriety of it. They moved toward the bow. A blast of the ship's horn sounded, making Grace jump. Rathe clapped his hands over her ears as the atrocious, ear-splitting noise sounded again. He removed his hands. "Awful, isn't it?"

"Whatever was that for?"

"A warning. We leave in ten minutes," he told her, taking her hand again.

This time, because they were standing so closely together and all her attention was focused on him, she was aware of his palm, so large and slightly damp, holding hers. "Rathe," she protested, gently disengaging herself and trying not to notice his obvious disappointment. He was a gentleman, however. He touched her elbow and they walked on.

They stood at the bow, watching the docks and the stevedores unloading various cargoes, standing side by side. A whisper of a warm breeze touched them. "Look, Grace," Rathe said, putting his arm around her and turning her.

She forgot to object as she watched, fascinated, as the crew began untying the ship's lines and pulling in the gangplank. They worked quickly and efficiently. "Cover your ears, Grace,'' Rathe urged, and she obeyed, just in time, as the ship's horn blared again. Then the boat began edging away from the dock. "We're going backward!" Grace cried.

"Only to get out into the river," Rathe told her. "Right now we're under steam."

The shore receded. The bow began to swing slowly around, until they were facing south, and then the paddle-wheeler began drifting leisurely downriver. The breeze at once became cooler, and Grace lifted her face to it, smiling. "How glorious," she murmured.

Rathe could not take his eyes off of her upturned face.

Her hands were on the wood railing. She stood lost in the wonderful moment, until she realized one of his hands had covered hers. That brought her back to reality, and she pulled her hands away, clasping them together in front of her. She stole a glance at him. His regard was so warm it made her breath catch in her throat.

"Even in that bun," he said softly, "your hair is magnificent in the sunlight. Red and gold, like living fire."

The compliment was lovely and it pleased her almost as much as it unnerved her. "I didn't think to bring a hat."

"I wish I could see it flowing loose and free," he said.

He was so intense, she was held captive by his blue eyes. Then he broke the moment, taking her arm. "We had better get some food into you."

"Yes," Grace said quickly. "Yes, that's a good idea."

The dining salon was on the uppermost deck. It was as fine as any elegant restaurant, the carpets thick and Turkish, the walls brocade, the hangings silk. Rathe requested a window table and pulled out her chair to seat her himself. Grace stared at him as he sat, never having received such considerate treatment in her life. This was like a dream; it was as if she were some debutante who had grown up in a mansion in New York. She touched the white, spotless linen tablecloth and wondered if the glassware were crystal and the flatware silver.

"I've taken the liberty of ordering us a bottle of champagne."

Champagne. Grace had never had champagne before. She found herself unable to take her eyes off him.

"Do you like champagne?"

She felt her color rising. "Yes, of course."

"Good," he said, looking amused. "Because I do, too."

He reached out and covered her hand with his. Grace tensed, from deep within herself. She looked into his eyes and saw warmth again—not lust, but tender warmth. Confusion and a touch of panic roiled with other emotions too perplexing to identify.

"Grace?" Rathe interrupted her thoughts. He nodded toward the window. "Look."

Grace gazed past Rathe and smiled. The sun was hanging low in the west and two boys on a raft were paddling their way down the Mississippi. They were no older than thirteen or fourteen, barefoot, shirtless and in dungarees, tanned nut-brown. Apparently they were on a fishing expedition, for their lines were floating behind them. As Grace watched, smiling, they sat idly chatting and laughing and eating something from a basket. Then one of them leapt to his feet shouting, and Grace realized that one of the lines had become taut with the weight of a fish. "Oh, they've caught something!"

"Indeed they have."

She turned fully to watch. The boy was attempting to reel in his catch. He was straining from the effort, and his friend grabbed the pole to help. The boys became quite red. "Oh my," Grace said. "They must have caught a whale!"

Rathe chuckled.

The boys reeled in a log, their disappointment obvious.

Grace turned back to Rathe, smiling. "Too bad. I so wanted to see them catch something. It looked like such fun."

Rathe looked at her, then he grinned, his blue eyes twinkling.

"What is it?" she asked.

"You'll have to wait and see," he said, his tone teasing.

The champagne was poured. Grace watched, looking at the pale gold liquid with its tiny bubbles, curiosity and excitement racing through her. Champagne, she thought, awed. Rathe raised his glass. Grace realized he was waiting for her to do the same. "To an extraordinary woman," he said softly, his gaze holding hers. "To you, Grace. To you, to this day, and to the future." He touched his glass to hers.

Grace's heart was beating hard. She tried reminding herself that he was an experienced roué, and that these sort of words would come naturally to him. Yet he sounded so sincere. She took a small sip of the champagne and found it light and pleasant.

"Does it meet with your approval?" he asked, hiding a grin.

"It's quite good."

"This bottle is one of the finest in the world," he told her. "And, I admit, it's my personal favorite."

Grace tried another taste and found it more than quite good. She looked at Rathe and smiled.

"By the end of this day you will be a champagne aficionado," he said, chuckling. "What are you in the mood for, Grace? How about fresh fish?"

"Yes, that sounds absolutely wonderful," she said, sipping the champagne. Rathe was right, it was delicious. And very relaxing, too. She could feel her shoulders dropping, the tension slipping away, and it was divine. She looked up to find Rathe regarding her again, and she smiled at him. His eyes widened in surprise, and then he beamed. "What I wouldn't give for more of those smiles," he murmured.

"Then you'll just have to take me on more boat rides," she said.

He stared in mute surprise, then laughed. "Why, Miss O'Rourke! Are you flirting with me?"

Grace blushed, touching her hand to her lips. Had she just done that? She was saved from responding when something was placed in front of them—something suspicious-looking, jellylike and reddish-yellow. Seeing her expression, Rathe laughed. "It's caviar, Grace. A true gourmet treat."

"Caviar?" She cleared her throat. "Fish eggs?"

"Don't think of it that way." He placed a small amount on a cracker, Grace watching, fascinated. He held it out to her; Grace drew back. "For me?"

"You cannot possibly drink this champagne without trying caviar." There was something in his eyes, something too intimate. Grace looked at the cracker, so close to her mouth—close enough that if she opened her lips he could slip it inside. She took it from him and nibbled cautiously. It was terrible. She didn't want to hurt his feelings, though, so she finished what he'd given her, then took a long sip of water.

"Well?"

"It's quite—er—interesting."

"You have to acquire the taste."

"Undoubtedly. Whyever would one want to acquire a taste for something so awful?"

Rathe laughed. "I have no idea. And I'll let you in on a little secret—I can't stand the stuff myself."

Grace laughed. "Then why . . ."

"I wanted you to try it." His gaze lingered, all lightness vanishing.

Grace's smile disappeared, too. She was ridiculously touched. "Thank you."

"You're welcome."

Their glances held.

"I have a confession to make," Grace said later, over their excellent sautéed redfish.

"Ah, a confession. What could you possibly have to

confess?'' He was teasing. "No, wait! Your desire for
me?''

She laughed. "No, not my desire for you.''

"Ah, but you did say my desire for you. Dare I dream
it exists?''

"Rathe! Do you want to hear my confession or not?''

"I am dying to hear it.''

She leaned forward. "I've never had champagne before.''

He laughed, taking her hands in his and holding them
tightly. This time, Grace did not attempt to remove them.
"I know,'' he said softly.

She blushed slightly. "You do?''

"Of course.''

"You seem to know too much.''

"There are advantages to being with a worldly man.''

She couldn't look away, even though she knew she
should. She could easily imagine the advantages—wonderful, exciting afternoons like this, afternoons that should
be endless but unfortunately weren't. And she thought
about the way he had kissed her earlier that day. His lips
had been firm but gentle, and even now, remembering,
something tightened and spiraled deep inside her.

"Grace,'' he said, his tone no longer light but husky.
"You're beautiful.''

She knew it wasn't true. It was on the tip of her tongue
to protest. Instead, she said nothing, held enthralled by
the magnetism of the man before her.

"More champagne?''

"No, thank you,'' she said, leaning back in her chair.
"I'm feeling a little euphoric as it is.''

"Euphoric?'' He chuckled. "I love the way you use
words, Grace. I also like seeing you so relaxed.'' His gaze
slid casually over her.

It took her a moment to realize what he was referring
to. Not just their easy conversation and camaraderie, but
to the fact that she was sitting in a very improper manner—she was slouching! Had she been slouching all after-

noon? She sat abruptly upright, shocked. She darted a glance around the room, but no one was paying them any mind. "Oh, dear!"

He took her shoulders in his hands and pushed her back against the chair. "Relax. Today is for you, Grace—solely for you. For your pleasure. No one here cares that your spine isn't straight. Doesn't it feel good?"

She hesitated. "Yes," she admitted. "It does feel good. To be like this, with no cares. But Rathe, this isn't real. The life we left in Natchez is real."

"Oh no, Gracie," he said softly. "This is just as real, and just as important. Crusading is fine. But so are idle afternoons, and that's something you have to learn."

She blinked at him, thought of arguing, then decided against it. Not only was she feeling too fine, but maybe, just maybe, he had a point.

He was studying the tablecloth, his face downturned, his long fingers stroking the linen. Grace looked at his thick, gold hair and had the insane urge to touch it. She stared at his hands, at his strong fingers, moving so lightly now, toying with a spoon. She knew the strength he harbored in those hands—and the gentleness. She found herself wishing he would cover her palm with his again.

"Grace," Rathe said, raising his gaze to hers. The intensity of his tone commanded her full attention. "You do things to me."

She stared, perplexed.

He leaned forward. "My life hasn't been the same, not for a moment, since I met you."

Every fiber of her being tensed, and at the same time, her heart was beating with sudden joy.

"Do you realize that?" It was a demand. "Do you realize I finished my business in Natchez last week? Do you know why I've stayed?"

She was wide-eyed. "You can't mean . . ." She couldn't even say it. He was being the charmer again; nonetheless something inside her was full with yearning.

"Yes, I've stayed because of you."

Her hand touched her heart.

"I can't sleep at night, my thoughts are so full of you."

She managed to recover. "You can't sleep at night because of your various paramours."

Despite himself, he grinned, then sobered and reached out, touching one thumb to her cheek. "There's been no one since I met you."

Grace knew her disbelief was written all over her face.

"I mean it," he said urgently. "I want you, Grace. I want to hold you and take care of you, day after day and night after night. I want to clothe you in the finest silks and satins and the most beautiful jewels. I want to provide for you, protect you. I want to take you with me, to New Orleans, to New York, to Paris." He smiled. "I want to lose myself in loving you."

Grace's heart was lifting uncontrollably against her breast. She could not believe that this gorgeous man was proposing to her. "You want to marry me?" she heard herself ask incredulously.

For a faint instant, his eyes went wide. "Darlin'," he said huskily, his balance instantly recovered, "I'm not ready for marriage, not yet. But I'm mad for you, completely mad for you. Let me take care of you. I want to take care of you."

Confusion had risen tumultuously, only to suddenly be replaced by stunned insight. "You don't mean . . ."

"I'll make you so very happy, I promise," Rathe said, cupping her face. "Look at today, how good it was. As my mistress, you won't lack for anything, not ever. And you'll also have my protection, a man's protection, which is even more important. Grace, you won't be sorry."

Grace found she was clutching the edge of the table for support. She wished she hadn't drunk the champagne, which she wasn't used to. It was dulling her reflexes, making it difficult for her to react.

He leaned forward, still cupping her face, his eyes brilliantly blue. "Say yes," he said hoarsely.

Despite the anger—and disappointment—unfolding

within her, there was also a tightening in the deepest pit of her belly. He pulled back to regard her searchingly. Grace's hand closed around her water glass. "You bastard," she hissed, tears filling her eyes. "How dare you! I would never be your mistress!" And then she flung the contents of the glass right into his face.

Chapter 11

Grace ran out onto the deck, almost falling on the stairs in her haste. She was suddenly very sober. She was also spitting mad and completely upset. Instinct made her glance over her shoulder—to see Rathe leaping down the stairs and coming after her with pure determination. Instead of continuing her flight, Grace stopped short, whirling, fists clenched, ready to do battle.

"I do not think," Rathe said, his voice tight, "that there was any cause to throw the water in my face!"

Her brows shot up. "No? You insulted me! You made me the most indecent offer! I have never been so outraged in my life!"

Somehow, Rathe doubted that. "I insulted you?" He was incredulous. "To the contrary."

They glared, their eyes blue and violet fires, flaming inches from each other, so close their noses almost touched.

"It's not an insult when a man wants a woman, Grace, especially when he wants her the way I want you."

"I am not flattered," she snapped.

"Should I be a hypocrite and deny my feelings? Pretend to you, and even to myself, that they don't exist? That's not my way, Grace."

"And your way," she said glacially, "is not my way, Mr. Bragg!"

His face went dark. "Do you think I make that kind of offer every day? Well, let me set you straight! I've never

123

kept a mistress before,'' Rathe informed her tersely. "I meant my offer as a compliment, Gracie.''

"A compliment?'' She could not believe her ears. "You, Mr. Bragg, are the most antiquated specimen of the philandering male sex I have ever had the misfortune to come across!''

His jaw clenched. "Just tell me something, Grace. I know you need money. I can give you all you need. It would be my pleasure. And believe me, you would find pleasure in our relationship, too. I can make you happy, Grace.''

"You?'' She wished she could laugh in his face, but she was too distraught. "You are entertaining some grand illusions if you think a man like yourself could ever make me happy!''

"I see.'' Rathe gritted his teeth, his eyes gleaming coldly. "You have no trouble showering Allen with your kisses. Do you love him?'' he demanded. "Are you going to marry him?''

She blinked. "I do not shower Allen with anything.''

"Don't lie to me, I've seen the two of you together.''

She stared, speechless.

"Grace, I know you're no fool. You haven't even bothered to think about this. There are other benefits to such an arrangement besides money.''

"Other benefits!''

"Such as protection,'' he said stubbornly. "You need me, Grace. Today proved it.''

"All today has proved is that you are one callous, arrogant, bigoted male, ruled by your basest needs!''

Rathe inhaled. "That wasn't very nice, Grace. Was I ruled by my baser instincts this afternoon? I'm trying to help you.''

"Help me? By getting me into your bed? Hah!''

He grabbed her chin. His eyes were cold. "I haven't called you names, Grace. But maybe I should.''

She shrugged free. "Go right ahead,'' she said, but something inside her tightened with dread. She knew what he would say. *Prude, shrew, spinster.* The words she hated most.

Rathe opened his mouth, then closed it. "I could awaken the passion in you, Grace."

She actually felt relief that he hadn't used those detestable words. "I do not intend to give you a chance."

"Are you going to give Allen a chance?"

"That," she retorted, "is none of your affair!"

"I'm making it my affair. If I hadn't made you my affair today, Grace, you would have been raped. You think about that!"

"I have. And I think that's a gross exaggeration."

"And that is why you need me," Rathe said grimly. "That attitude of yours is going to get you killed!"

"I will take my chances."

"I think, Grace," Rathe said slowly, deliberately, "that you're afraid of me."

She froze.

"I think you're afraid of me because I am everything your dear Allen is not."

She clenched her fists, hard.

"I think you're afraid of me because you want me."

She was so furious she could barely think. "I care for Allen because he is everything you're not!"

"That is your mind speaking," Rathe said, "not your heart."

"I could never want someone like you!"

"Liar."

"No." Tears came into her eyes. "You're the liar! This evening was a lie! Nothing but a lie—it was all leading up to this!" She lifted her skirt, and began running down the deck.

For a moment Rathe stood and watched her, his expression agonized, and then he turned to the railing. With his fist he hit it, relishing the pain. Then he went after her. He had to.

She was at the stern, staring blindly at the paddlewheel, ignoring the spray of water that touched her face and neck and arms. His heart tightened at the sight of her tears. He wanted to pull her into his arms, but knew with certainty that she would not let him. He went to the railing beside her, standing half a dozen paces away. He too watched the river. "I'm sorry, Grace."

She sniffed.

He handed her a handkerchief, but she wouldn't take it. "This evening was not a lie, Grace."

"Yes it was," she said, not looking at him.

"It was not a lie," he repeated firmly. "I wanted you to have fun. Such a little, simple word: *fun*. And you had fun. You can't tell me you didn't."

She brushed away a tear and gave him a quick glance. "You were trying to make me relaxed enough so that I would accept your scandalous proposition."

Rathe had to smile. "If I hadn't asked you to be my mistress today, I would have asked you tomorrow, or last night." His tone softened. "I wanted us to share this day, to enjoy it together. Don't take away what we've already had."

She clutched the rail and looked at the banks of the river, thick with swamp and cypress. "It was a nice day," she admitted.

"There will be more nice days for us, Grace."

"No."

"Why not? We had fun together."

"Because it isn't right."

He came closer. "No? Why? Because I'm honest? Because I've told you I want you? Now you know the truth. I said I was sorry, Grace, and I am—for upsetting you. But not for asking you to become my mistress. I'll ask you that again and again."

"And I'll say no again and again."

He smiled slightly. "I have incredible patience."

She looked at him, and wished her anger hadn't evaporated. He smiled and touched her chin. "Your face is stained," he said, wiping the tears gently away. "The one thing I never want to do, Grace," he said, very seriously, "is make you cry."

She looked at him. "Then try to understand who I am," she said.

"Gladly," he replied.

He gazed at her as she slept.

The instant they had entered the carriage after they'd left the *Mississippi Queen,* Rathe had watched, amused, as Grace took the seat across from him. He had patted the spot next to him. "No?" he had asked hopefully.

She smiled at his tone. "This is quite fine, thank you." Moments later, she was asleep.

Her nose and cheeks were pink from the sun, even though they had spent most of the late afternoon indoors. Her head was on the back of the seat, where it joined with the side of the carriage. It looked distinctly uncomfortable. The carriage hit a rut in the road, and Grace shifted without awakening. Rathe began removing his jacket.

He rolled it into a pillow of sorts, then knelt in front of her, lifting her head with his big hands. Her eyes fluttered open. She started to protest. "Shh," he murmured, slipping the garment beneath her neck. "Better?" He smiled.

She smiled back sleepily and closed her eyes.

She had rejected him. He supposed he should have expected it. But, as he had said, he was patient, or he would force himself to be so, at least where she was concerned; and he had every intention of waiting for the one word he wanted to hear from her. But how best to convince her to accept his proposition? So far logic hadn't worked. There was always seduction.

He started to feel guilty. Rathe knew he should forget about her. He knew he was being a cad. Grace was right— he was selfish, ruthless. Yes, she needed his protection and she needed his money, but she was an aging, very proper spinster, and he should leave her alone. The problem was, he couldn't. In fact, he wanted her now more than ever.

He could never leave Natchez now, not as long as Grace was here. Until she gave in, he decided he had better keep a very close eye on her. He thought about the close call she'd had this afternoon and shuddered. He thought about what she'd said about the sheriff. More trouble was coming, he could feel it. Ford was a bastard, and an evil one at that. But if Grace tried to change things, she was going to wind up seriously hurt, if not dead. Ford was not a man to take lightly. It was one thing to organize the ladies into a Christian Temperance Union; it was another to try and turn the town upside down by stirring everyone up and taking on the sheriff.

He thought about the way she had smiled at him this afternoon, not once, but many times. A riverboat ride—such a simple thing. You're going to loosen up, Gracie, he thought warmly, and I'm going to be the one to teach you how to enjoy life and yourself.

Grace was such an enigma. She didn't act like any woman he had ever known. He was fascinated.

The carriage hit another rut and Grace moaned softly in her sleep, shifting again, the bundle that was his jacket slipping from beneath her. Her head was tilted at what had to be an uncomfortable angle, yet still she slept, exhausted from her long day of job-hunting, the events of the afternoon, and the champagne.

Rathe suddenly moved to the seat beside her, replacing the ledge of the backrest and window with his own body. Grace blinked once. "Go back to sleep," he crooned, one of his arms around her and his fingers stroking her shoulder. He gently pushed her head to his chest. She snuggled against him, sleepily seeking the best position, and then her head was on his lap and she was curled up on the seat. Rathe adjusted her shawl more securely around her shoulders, his thumb moving across her temple. There was no doubt about it. This woman moved him in a way no other ever had.

She slept for the entire trip. There was no way Rathe himself could sleep, not with Grace warm and soft against him, making him hard and hot, making him want her, making him fantasize about what the first time would be like. He tried to think other thoughts, gazing out the window, but it was impossible.

They approached Natchez after midnight. Rathe shook Grace gently. "Wake, up, sweetheart. We're almost home."

She blinked, sitting up groggily. Rathe smiled at her. He still had his arm around her. As sleep left her, she realized how they were sitting. She drew back, away from him, to the other side of the seat. "Have I been sleeping on your lap?" she gasped.

"I make a very comfortable pillow."

She went red. She turned to stare out her window, into the purple starlit night. "Good heavens!"

"You were very tired and the road is very bad. I was afraid you'd get a stiff neck, the way you were contorted."

She looked at him. It was dark in the carriage, with only one lantern casting dim illumination. Dark and intimate. She had just spent several hours sleeping with her head in a man's lap. Grace didn't know what to think. And now, now it was worse, for she was awake, and the distance between them was so small she could smell his masculine scent. He was no longer touching her, but she could almost feel him. She realized her heart was racing madly. And he was staring at her.

She glanced out the window, clearing her throat. "Today was very nice, thank you."

He didn't answer.

She wrapped her shawl more firmly around herself, suddenly very grateful that she had been asleep for the past few hours. How else would she have survived the trip back to Natchez? She didn't dare look at him, but she knew he was still staring at her. "I wonder where the *Mississippi Queen* is now," she said, unable to think of a single intelligent thing to say. She knew she sounded foolish. But why didn't he respond?

"How far are we from Natchez?" She dared a glance at him. His blue eyes were so intense. He was golden and gorgeous in the lantern's soft light. She swallowed and looked away.

"A few miles," he said, his tone lazy and languid and distinctly sensual. Suddenly she felt short of breath.

"A few miles," she echoed. "I can't believe I slept the entire way! How long did I sleep?" She turned her head to look at him.

It was a mistake. The way he was gazing at her made her heart stop. His beautiful mouth was parted, and he touched his middle finger to her cheek. The lightest of touches—but Grace trembled.

A sound escaped him, a sound of need, a hoarse groan. Grace found herself in his arms.

For one instant, with his arms around her, he looked into her eyes with blazing intensity. Then he pulled her against him, against his hard, warm body, his mouth seeking hers. In that first instant, Grace put her hands against his chest and turned her face away.

"Please," he groaned. "Let me kiss you, Grace. Just a kiss, just one kiss . . ."

She could barely think. She knew this was wrong. His mouth wandered over the curve of her cheek, touched her ear. She gasped from the flood of hot sensations. Just a kiss, a little voice said. Surely you can give him one kiss!

For the first time, Grace responded. She turned her face back, opening her eyes. At the sight of his strained, aroused countenance, all coherent thought fled. And when his mouth touched hers, she thought she might faint.

"Grace," he said, harsh and low. "Open for me, darling, open your mouth—let me in."

Blindly, she obeyed. His tongue touched hers. Grace shuddered. Her hands, clenched into fists against his chest, relaxed, unfurled. Her breasts tingled and hardened against his chest. Rathe's grip tightened. His mouth moved softly, but it was deceiving, because his tongue thrust into her, again and again, picking up a rhythm that sent waves of pleasure flooding to her groin. Rathe slid his hands down to cup her buttocks.

She gasped at the feel of his large hands spread and clutching such an intimate part of her. His touch was like nothing she had ever dreamed possible—making her burn. She touched her tongue to his tentatively, shyly, and was shocked at his shuddering response, the tensing of his entire body, and the tightening of his hold on her. Her hands found the fabric of his shirt. Their tongues sparred, entwined. Rathe's hand slid up her hip, her waist, kneading with frantic urgency. Then higher, making no pretense, covering her breast. His hand paused. Grace was trembling, wanting him to keep touching her.

"What's this," he said, his fingers edging underneath her garments to find the linen binding she wore.

Through the hot fog of their passion, Grace heard and was too embarrassed to even discuss something so intimate as her underwear. She touched his wrist to stop him from further exploration, but his hand closed over her breast anyway, squeezing gently.

Grace's head went back against the seat, her eyes closing, red-hot desire, agonizing pleasure, the only thing she was cognizant of. His thumbs traced little circles beneath her nipples, now tight and hurting, straining against the cotton of her clothes. She whimpered with need.

"Yes, darlin," he whispered, and his thumbs touched the taut peaks gently.

Grace gasped.

He was suddenly, fluidly and dexterously, unbuttoning the many tiny shell buttons down the front of her bodice. Grace knew she had to protest. But when she opened her mouth, his was there, covering hers, his tongue entering her and flooding her with more wonderful, unbelievable hot sensations.

He parted her dress and pulled the binding down.

"God, Grace," he said, exposing her full, voluptuous breasts with large, coral nipples. "Why do you hide yourself?" And he lowered his head, inhaling sharply. His tongue flicked out, teasing her. Grace gasped. And when he took a nipple in his mouth and began to suck, she cried out.

She felt his hand sliding over the soft curve of her belly, beneath her skirt, with just two thin layers of cotton between them. Lower, without pause, with devastating intent, his fingers touching intimately between her thighs, then lower, cupping the swollen, wet flesh there through her undergarments. His grip tightened.

Grace's head came up, her eyes flying wide open. His head was still bent over her bared breast; he was still suckling one nipple. His fingers had slid into the wet folds of her flesh, oblivious to the cotton in their way. Rubbing, insinuating. Grace's hands came up and she pressed against his shoulders frantically. Panic gave her strength. They had to stop!

Rathe's head came up, his hand stilled. His eyes were blue and bright and brilliant. "Grace," he said thickly.

"Please stop," she pleaded desperately, panting.

He was panting, too. For a moment he did not move, struggling, she could see, with himself, and then he withdrew his hand and pulled her bodice together. "I'll do it," she cried, turning her back to him. She felt him moving away from her, to the seat on the other side of the carriage.

Her hands were shaking. She could not do up the tiny buttons. She tried again. She was breathless and feverish and panicked and terrified and ashamed and so utterly, unbearably confused! She choked in despair, a sobbing sound, when she realized she'd mismatched all the buttons. "Oh, damn!"

"Let me," he said, his warm hands closing on her shoulders from behind. "Please let me help."

Grace knew she was going to cry, and she fought it. His hands, both sensual and comforting, were going to be her undoing. "It's all right, Grace," he said. "Trust me."

"I don't understand," she managed, staring blindly at her lap.

His hold on her tightened. "You're a woman, Grace," he said. "You may have run from it your entire life, but I'm a man, and I can't let you run from it any longer."

That night she tossed restlessly, unable to sleep.

She was reliving every moment of the long day, from her fruitless search for employment, to Rathe's violent protection of her from the two sailors, to the riverboat ride and, finally, the shattering kiss in the coach. And it was on the last memory that her treacherous mind lingered.

His words echoed. "You're a woman, Grace . . . I'm a man . . . I can't let you run from it any longer . . ."

She turned abruptly onto her stomach. Of course she was a woman. And she hadn't been running from that fact, had she? Then why was she so uneasy, and so confused? And why did a part of her want to be back in his arms?

Never in her carefully constructed life had things felt so out of control.

She had to stop this nonsensical brooding over that man. Yes, that was certainly the solution. She very deliberately turned her thoughts to the problems facing Natchez, one of which was Sheriff Ford.

Allen had told her that Ford enforced the law with an iron fist. She was appalled but not surprised. After all, a man who led the night riders would certainly resort to intimidation and physical coercion. How could a man like that be stopped? She wondered just how many of the townspeople supported Ford, and how many didn't, but were afraid to speak out. Allen had suggested that there were local folks who were against the tactics and goals of the night riders. There must be a way of stirring those people up.

Grace rolled onto her side, her face on her arm. Both
Allen and Rathe would have her turn away, deaf, dumb,
and blind to the situation, but that was impossible.
Something had to be done to stop Ford from perpetuating
his reign of terror. The problem really was, she supposed, finding someone who could stand up to Ford.
Someone who wasn't afraid of him. Someone who could,
if need be, get down in the mud and give as good as he
got.

Someone like Rathe Bragg.

She sat bolt upright. How ridiculous! He was a Southerner, even if he did meet all the other criteria. She was
almost positive that he was a Democrat like most of his
class, and the Democrats were responsible for the likes of
Ford and the night riders. The political lines were very
clearly drawn. The Republicans were carpetbaggers and
Yankees and had legislated all the reforms and civil rights
following the War, while the Democrats had fought them,
desperately trying to hang on to the last remnants of the
glorious old South. Damn! It was too bad he wasn't a
Republican. Her heart started to pound.

People had minds. Minds could change. And somehow,
instinctively, she knew she could be instrumental in getting him to change his.

Oh, Lord! Was she being terribly arrogant in thinking
she could do that? Because if she could, he would be the
perfect person to pit against Sheriff Ford!

"You could reform me," he had said earlier, his tone
husky and sensual.

Her cheeks flamed. He hadn't been serious. Not at all.
Even though she wasn't an experienced woman, the sexual
innuendo had been unmistakable. *That* was probably the
only thing he was serious about!

Still, hadn't she dedicated her life to the enlightenment
of others? If she could ignore, just for the moment, the
fact that that handsome rake wanted her, if she could
look at him as she would anyone else, she wouldn't hes-

itate to try and make him understand some fundamental truths.

But he was handsome and he was a terrible rogue and he had asked her to be his mistress. Might that not make him more amenable to her suggestions? And what could it hurt to try? Her heart pounding, Grace hugged her knees to her chest.

She was going to try and reform Rathe Bragg!

Chapter 12

"Harriet, what do you know about Rathe Bragg?" Grace asked as casually as possible. It was the next morning. For some reason, all of her senses were as finely tuned as a quivering bowstring. Today she was going to begin her task of taming the lion!

Harriet, who had been refilling Grace's coffee cup as they sat in the kitchen, paused. Her eyes twinkled. "Well, what would you like to know?"

Grace blushed. "It's not what you're thinking." Then, growing redder: "Has he come down yet?"

Harriet chuckled. "Down and long since gone. Don't feel bad, Grace. You're not the first gal to have been snared by those dimples."

"No, really, it's not what you're thinking."

Harriet was eloquent. Grace found out that he had been raised on a west Texas ranch, that he came from a good family, and that he was a very successful businessman. "He's a good man, Grace, don't let his playful ways and his flirting fool you," Harriet advised.

Grace coughed to cover her own pleasure at Harriet's good opinion of him. She would have never believed that he had a responsible bone in his body—but apparently he did. "Just how well do you know him?"

"I've known him, oh, twelve or thirteen years. Since the War." Seeing Grace's mystification, she continued. "He rode with one of my boys in Walker's regiment."

137

Grace stared. "Are you telling me that Rathe was in the War?"

"Of course he was."

"But he must have been a young boy!"

"Ran away and followed his big brother when he was fifteen, that he did. Ask Rathe the story sometime. He doesn't like talking about it; none of them do, but I've heard him tell that episode more than once."

Grace turned away, confused. On the one hand she was dismayed that he had actually fought for the South and its institutions, for that would make her task even more difficult. At the same time, there was something so endearing about a young boy following his older brother off to war. "Harriet," Grace asked. "Would you mind very much if I hang a seamstress's sign under your post?"

"You going to take in some sewing?"

"I didn't have very much luck yesterday looking for employment."

"I don't mind your putting out a sign, but honey, I don't think you'll take in enough work to pay your rent, much less send something home for your Mama."

"That's what I'm afraid of," Grace said grimly.

At dinner she met with the ladies at Sarah's to organize their first temperance march, which they scheduled for Saturday afternoon—prime time for the saloons. Normally, this kind of planning and organizing would have absorbed Grace. Today, however, she was preoccupied, for that afternoon she intended to seek out Rathe and begin the task of both reforming him and setting him against Sheriff Ford. For that very reason, she took the long route from Sarah's house, so she could pass the Sheriff's office on Main Street.

She finally found Rathe at the Silver Lady Hotel. It graced the top of the cliffs above Silver Street, looking down over the sluggish waters of the Mississippi. She'd heard Harriet say that he kept a room there. This made no sense, until she found herself standing in the open doorway peering in. The beautifully appointed room, rich with brocade and silk furnishings and a four-poster bed, Aubusson rugs, and velvet drapes, also contained a massive rosewood desk. The desk was covered with papers, mail, files, and folders. Obviously he had made this suite his office.

He was leaning back in his chair, eyes momentarily wide with surprise, staring.

She began remembering intimate details from last night—his sensual touch, the erotic invasion of his tongue, his mouth on her breast. Now was not the time for reminiscing. She blushed, but did not have the will to break free of his bright gaze.

He was on his feet, smiling. The smile was intent, even predatory, and she knew he was also recalling their kiss. She wanted to turn and flee. Instead, she squared her shoulders and took a deep breath.

"Couldn't stay away?" he teased.

She could hear the loud thumping of her heart, and wondered if he could, too. She found her voice. "I have some business to discuss with you."

His face fell with an exaggerated look of little-boy disappointment. "You didn't miss me?" he asked, huskily.

"Rathe," she said briskly, trying not to look at his mouth, at the finely chiseled lips, and remember how they had felt and tasted. "First of all, let me thank you for supper yesterday, and the boat ride."

He approached, with a slow, deliberate stride. Grace forced herself not to step backward. "Thank me again," he said, his gaze holding hers, piercing hers. His hands closed around her arms; he pulled her into the room and nudged the door closed with his foot.

Her hands came up to ward him off. But, for some reason, her fingers closed around his wrists, clinging. He was staring at her mouth and Grace found that all she could think about was kissing him. "We have to talk," she gasped, her heart careening madly.

He smiled slightly, and released her. "I suppose talking is second best."

She flushed.

"I was looking for you earlier," he said. She watched him move away, pull a chair to the front of his desk and then gesture to it. Grace let him seat her. She expected him to take his own chair behind the desk. Instead, he lounged carelessly on the edge of the desktop, right in front of her. Once gain she noticed that his breeches were indecently tight, clinging to his strong legs, molding his sex. She quickly looked at the floor.

"You were looking for me?" she asked with her breath caught in her throat.

"Yes, I wanted to take you to dinner. Have you eaten?"

"Yes, at Sarah Bellsley's."

"Oh. You're not here, by any chance," he said hopefully, "to discuss my offer?"

It took her a moment to gather her wits. "Your offer? To become your mistress? Oh! No, absolutely not!"

"Grace, do you know that I always get what I want?"

She met his gaze. He was not bragging, but making a statement of truth, or at least one he believed to be true. That worried her. Or did it thrill her? "Not this time," she said firmly.

His grin was lightning-quick. "Another challenge? Don't you ever learn?"

"That's not a challenge," she said, with more calmness than she felt. "But a mere statement of fact."

He laughed. He slipped to his feet. "Come on. We can discuss your business in a more leisurely manner." He took her arm.

"Where are we going?" she asked, with some consternation and even more excitement, thinking about the hours they had shared yesterday.

"I have a surprise for you," Rathe said cheerfully. "And if you don't like it I promise to bring you right back."

She bit her lip and cast a glance at him as they went

downstairs. "What kind of surprise?" She almost felt like a child of six on Christmas Eve.

"If I told you it wouldn't be a surprise." He tapped her sunburned nose. "Does it hurt? I see you're wearing a hat today."

"It's a bit sore."

"We'll get you some salve," Rathe said, taking her hand.

They were walking down the street. "Rathe," Grace whispered, glancing around. "We're in public!"

He smiled. "Aren't I allowed to court the lady of my choice?"

In that one, precise instant, her heart took up winged flight. And in the next moment, it fell tumbling back to her body with vast disappointment. He was playing games. He wasn't courting her. He wanted her to be his mistress; he had made that clear yesterday. She withdrew her hand. He regarded her quizzically.

They walked out of town in silence. "What's wrong, Gracie?" Rathe finally asked.

"Nothing."

He took her down a quiet street lined with homes until the Mississippi River came into view. The street ended; Rathe took her hand. "Where are we going?"

He didn't answer, just flashed her a charming smile. He didn't release her hand, either, but this time Grace didn't protest. The path to the water's edge was rocky and rough. She was grateful for Rathe's help.

The Mississippi lapped the sandy bank. Grace's eyes widened with surprise, for pulled up on the shore was a log raft. Another glance found fishing poles and buckets and a basket and blanket. "What's all this?"

"You said it looked like fun." He winked.

She placed her hand over her heart, which was jumping erratically. "Oh, it does, but Rathe—what can you be thinking of?"

"We're going fishing, of course."

"I can't."

He grinned. "Why not?"

"Why—it just isn't done."

He snorted. "Come on, Gracie, sit down on that log and take off your shoes."

She stared. "What?"

Rathe had already seated himself and was pulling off his high boots with obvious relish. "Come on. What are you waiting for?"

She didn't move. This was unbelievable! She watched his naked feet and ankles appear. He yanked his breeches right up to his knees. She stared at his legs, at the hard, muscular curve of calf. She blinked.

"All right," he said, proceeding to remove his jacket and tossing it carelessly on the ground. His vest followed. "Leave on your shoes. I don't mind." He rolled his shirtsleeves right up to his elbows and smiled brightly at her. "After you, my lady."

She looked at the raft and the gentle river rolling past. Oh, it had looked like such fun! But . . . "Rathe, I just don't know."

"I could always abduct you," he teased.

"All right," she decided instantly.

He placed all their equipment on the raft, spreading the blanket out on one end. He began pushing it into the water, the muscles of his shoulders and back standing out against his shirt as he forced it over the sand, even his buttocks tightening and straining, until it slid into the river. Grace turned her gaze away, belatedly realizing that she should have done so sooner. The raft floated in place, held by a line tied to a tree on the shore. Rathe waded out. "Okay," he said, reaching for her.

It was too late when she cried out in protest; she was already high in his arms. "What are you doing?"

"You wouldn't take off your shoes," he said, his mouth against her ear as he sloshed through the water to the raft.

She found herself clinging to him. "I didn't think . . ."

"Ummm," he said, his lips brushing her temple. "I'm glad you didn't take off your shoes, Grace."

Her hold on him tightened reflexively, her whole being alive with the feel and scent and sound of him. He placed her on the raft; she clutched him as it dipped and swayed.

"Better get on your knees," he said.

She did, hanging on.

His grin was wide and his dimples deep. As he started back to the bank, panic assailed her. "Where are you going?"

"I've got to unmoor us," he said. His breeches were soaking wet, and so was his shirt, clinging to his hard torso. Yet he seemed oblivious of the fact. Grace moved cautiously into a sitting position as he untied the raft and ran splashing back to her. Water sprayed her dress, and she smiled. He was pushing the raft out into the river, and as it caught the current, he hoisted himself on. The float dipped precariously, and for a moment Grace feared she would fall into the river. But then it righted itself and she relaxed. Rathe sat sprawled next to her, so close his bare foot touched her own ankle. Water glistened on his face. "Well? What do you think?"

She looked around, and smiled. They were drifting past houses and pastures and livestock. She raised her face to the sun and sniffed. The afternoon was gloriously fresh and fragrant. "What am I smelling?"

"Cows."

She jabbed him with her elbow, for there was not even the faintest scent of manure, and he laughed.

"No, really. Tell me."

"Honeysuckle. Have you ever tasted honeysuckle?"

"You can't eat honeysuckle!"

"No? You'll see."

She looked at him doubtfully.

He taught her how to bait her hook. Although Grace did not enjoy doing it, she was determined not to be squeamish. Then he showed her how to cast. The sun was high and bright. Their lines drifted behind them. Rathe casually worked open the buttons of his shirt, and Grace immediately looked away, anywhere but at the expanse of broad,

powerful chest covered with dark hair he had partially revealed. He was leaning back on his elbows, practically
lying down, completely at ease. She sat carefully upright
with her knees together, supporting herself on her hands.
It was very hot.

She looked at the tip of one black shoe peeping out from
beneath her skirts. She wiggled it. Wouldn't it be nice to
be able to go barefoot? She fingered the collar of her dress,
tight and scratchy against her throat. She glanced at the
sun. When she looked at Rathe, she saw he was watching
her.

He flashed her a smile, sat up, and stuck one bare leg
in the river. "Ummm," he said, grinning. "Nice and
cool."

She bit her lip and looked away, but she could hear him
splashing his foot in the water. Then a spray of waterdrops
dashed the side of her face. Startled, she turned. More
water hit her, and as it came, her indignation died. Oh, it
was cool and wet and wonderful!

"Nice, isn't it," Rathe said, smiling.

"Very." She looked at his leg, which he was still dragging in the river. Abruptly he raised it, sending another
plume of water at her. To her surprise, she heard herself
laughing. Her dress was quite wet.

"Take off your shoes, Grace," Rathe said.

She slid her eyes away from his. Should she? No one
would know—no one, that is, except herself and Rathe
Bragg. Oh, but it would be so much cooler!

"Well," she said, glancing at him. "I think I will."

He was still sprawled on his back with one foot in the
water and he didn't say a word. Grace made sure not to
look at him. She started unbuttoning her shoe. She began
to feel highly self-conscious. She knew he was watching.
When all the buttons were undone she hesitated. Then,
abruptly turning her back to him, she pulled it off, and
began working on the other. When that shoe had joined
its mate on the raft, she found herself facing a dilemma. She
wanted to take off her stockings, but she just couldn't reach

under her skirts to her knees to ungarter them. Her heart was racing. Oh well. She stuck a stockinged toe in the water.

Rathe made a noise. "I won't look. Take off your stockings. There's no one here but you and me, Grace."

She couldn't look at him. She was too red. "I'm fine, thank you."

"Grace," Rathe said, coming to kneel behind her. His tone was gentle. "I am not some farmboy."

For a minute, she was confused, and then she understood what he was trying to say. He was an experienced man. He'd seen more than a few ankles, and many garters as well. Why did that thought make her feel miserable?

He whispered in her ear, "If you don't take off your stockings I'm going to throw you in the river!"

She had to laugh. "You wouldn't dare!"

"You are getting very brave, Miss O'Rourke!"

He wouldn't, would he? "Close your eyes."

He sighed loudly, still behind her. Grace hadn't looked at him since she'd begun removing her shoes, but she was acutely aware of every move he made, and now she was waiting for him to retreat to his end of the raft. To her shock, he squeezed her shoulders and kissed the nape of her neck. Only then did he back away.

Her heart beat thickly in response to the tiny little kiss. She took off her stockings, carefully rolling them and placing them in her shoes. Then she dipped a toe in the water, wiggling it. She smiled. She stuck her entire foot in. She giggled.

Rathe shifted to sit beside her, dragging both of his feet in the river, one of his knees bumping hers. She glanced at him. He grinned back, kicking up and down. Grace put her other foot in and began swaying them aimlessly as Rathe was doing. It was truly glorious!

They drifted along in a companionable silence until the raft tilted. "Oh!" Grace cried, as Rathe threw his arm around her.

"You've got a fish," Rathe said.

She slid onto her knees to see that one of the lines was taut. "Oh, no, it's your line, Rathe!"

"No, it's not," he said, "it's yours. Quick, Grace, grab the pole. I'll help."

She was excited. She took up the pole and felt the weight of her catch at the other end. "Now what do I do?" she cried.

Rathe was behind her. "Move it back and forth until you can swing the fish out of the water."

It took some doing. The fish fought her. Rathe stood behind her, his hands on her waist, steadying her as she battled to pull in the fish. When it finally broke free of the water, an arc of silver, she cried out eagerly. "Look!"

"I see. It's a real grandaddy." Rathe grinned, catching the line and then the fish. He held it up for her. "Well? What do you think?"

She was glowing. "My first fish! Can we eat it? Is it edible?"

"Oh, we're going to eat it, all right," Rathe said. He removed the hook and placed the fish in the bucket. Grace began baiting her line again with concentration. She was so immersed in the process that she was not aware of Rathe's regard, suddenly serious and intense. When she looked back up after casting, he was his carefree self, flippantly winking at her, already sprawled out at her feet. She slipped down beside him, and thinking, *To hell with it,* she unbuttoned the top two buttons at her throat, baring her collarbone. Rathe turned his head away but she glimpsed his smile anyway.

The afternoon passed too quickly, and Grace was disappointed when they turned around to go upriver. She also found herself fascinated by Rathe's strength and stamina as he poled them back. He was tireless. He appeared to enjoy physical exertion. He put his entire body into it. A few times he caught her watching him but he didn't smile. His gaze held hers briefly, but potently.

When they arrived back where they had started, Grace didn't wait, she grabbed her skirts in one hand and jumped into the knee-deep water. Rathe stared in dumbfounded amazement as Grace waded past him. When she got to the shore her skirts were soaked to her thighs and clinging indecently. She wasn't sure she really cared.

"My amazing Grace," Rathe murmured from directly behind her.

She jumped, startled, not having heard him approach, and found herself in the circle of his arms. Instantly, her body responded, tightening, her pulse picking up its beat. "Rathe."

"Did you enjoy yourself today?" he asked huskily.

"Yes." She met his gaze fully, wanting to show him all her appreciation. "Yes, thank you, it was wonderful."

He didn't smile. He slowly lowered his face to hers.

Grace didn't know what to do. She shouldn't let this happen, not again, but . . . His lips brushed hers, teasing and tentative and so very seductive. Grace felt herself relax, felt her lips part. And mostly, she felt herself wanting more of his kiss, more of him. As if sensing her desire, his mouth opened on hers, searching and testing and tasting. Grace began shyly returning his kiss.

His strong hands moved over her back and hips, hard and then soft. He pulled her against him. The feel of his full, hard maleness for the first time stunned Grace. Heat and lightning swept her. He made no attempt to move his hips away, no attempt to hide himself from her. Shock warred with sharp desire. Remember last night, she warned herself. If he would stop at a gentle kiss, why, she could handle that. But she knew him now, and she knew he wouldn't stop. If she gave him an inch he'd take a mile, or even more. She wrenched away with sheer determination.

"Stop," she cried. "Stop it this instant, Rathe Bragg!"

He was breathing as if he had run a great distance. "I want you." Her body quivered. "Ah, Grace, damn." He ran a shaking hand through his thick, sun-streaked hair. "You want me too, you know you do."

"No." She shook her head. "I don't."

He stared at her, then sighed. "You just won't admit it to yourself. You enjoy my kisses and my touch as much as you enjoy my company. We're good together, Grace." His tone had dropped. "Very good."

She turned away, wringing her skirts. She was shaken and confused. Again. He was a rake, of that there was no doubt—times like these proved it. But what about the other times, and the other sides of his character? If she was very brave and faced the truth, she'd realize that she did enjoy his company and his kisses!

They walked back to town in silence until Grace remembered that she had never broached the subject which was the very reason she had sought him out. "Rathe, I've been doing some thinking—about what we were discussing yesterday."

He raised a brow.

"Our problem—Sheriff Ford."

"I wasn't aware that *we* had a *problem* with Ford."

"Ford is perpetuating all the injustices of the So—of discrimination, with intimidation and terror! You said so yourself! You agreed he has to be stopped."

The same eyebrow lifted. "If I recollect, you did all the talking. I was merely listening."

"Well," she managed, "I assumed, as you did not raise any objections, that you were in agreement with my views."

He smiled, showing off his dimples. "What you are up to, Grace?"

"Is it or is it not apparent that Sheriff Ford needs to be undermined?"

The smile faded.

She rushed on, clasping her hands tightly together. "Rathe! You could do it! If anyone could—you could! After all, whoever takes on Ford has to be as tough as he is and more importantly, unafraid! And you're not—"

"Whoa! What in hell are you getting at?"

They had both paused. "Won't you even consider helping me? I need someone to take a stand against Ford, to make him act in accordance with the laws, to let him know that he can't get away with intimidation and violence! I know you don't really care,'' she rushed on, despite his scowl, ''but you meet the most important criteria.''

''You are out of your mind,'' he said. ''Number one, Ford's got a lot of support. Number two, why in hell would I want to butt heads with the sheriff? And what criteria are you talking about?''

She looked at him with a vast, reproachful disappointment. He shifted uneasily. ''Are you afraid of him? That was the criteria I was referring to—I didn't think you were afraid of him.''

''I'm not!''

She cocked her head.

''You know damn well I'm not afraid of him, Gracie,'' he snapped.

She was very calm, calm with the sure knowledge that she was moving him in the right direction. ''You know, she said conversationally, ''I had dinner at Sarah Bellsley's today.''

He twisted away abruptly. ''What does that have to do with anything?''

''I passed by the jail on my way back,'' she said sweetly.

His gaze seared her.

''There were no sailors in there, Rathe. I asked the deputy. They were never arrested.''

It took him a moment to react. He cursed. Then he was striding down the street.

''Where are you going?'' she asked innocently, not that she didn't know.

He shot her a dark look.

''Rathe, don't be angry,'' she said, trotting alongside him. ''If you think about it, surely you will realize that I am right. There is such a thing as law and order. That is why we have a government, a democracy. It's a gift given us by our forefathers.''

No answer. They were going uphill now, and he was starting to outdistance her. Grace gamely lifted her skirts and lengthened her stride. "Don't the Negroes have the right to enjoy the benefits of our democracy? The War is over, Rathe. We are one country, one government, one people, with one set of laws! But Ford is imposing his own law and his own rule over this town! It is a perversion! He has to be stopped!"

Rathe bounded up the steps and into the Silver Lady Hotel. Grace was on his heels. "If you think about it," she said, puffing, "you'll see that I'm right!"

He slammed into his suite and went right to the rosewood desk. He withdrew a revolver from the drawer and checked the chambers. Grace's insides clenched. "What are you doing?" she cried. "Why do you need the gun?" She hated guns and she hated violence.

"You think I'm going to go up against Ford without protection?" he asked grimly. "Think again."

"But . . . but I didn't mean . . . violence breeds violence!"

He was striding for the door. "Too late, Gracie."

She ran after him. "Rathe, if you threaten Ford with a gun—"

"Go on home, Grace." His tone was harsh and resigned. "You've gotten what you wanted."

"This isn't what I want!" she cried, stumbling down the stairs after him. "Not violence!"

"You couldn't stop me now no matter what you did. You were almost hurt, Grace, almost raped, right on a public street. Because of how I feel about you, I take Ford's failure to act very, very personally." He strode across the lobby.

She ran after him. "But what about the vendor, Rathe? She was accosted too. She's not a slave anymore. She's a free woman, no different from me."

"Is she free? If you think so you're dreaming and you'd better wake up. Slavery still reigns, Grace. Just in a different form, that's all." He was moving down the street with long, hard strides, and she was skipping to stay abreast of him.

"What do you mean?"

"I mean, because of coercion, sharecropping, and men like Ford, the effect is as if there was no Emancipation Proclamation."

"That must make you very happy," she said bitterly.

He halted abruptly, eyes glinting. "Now what are you condemning me for? I'm getting tired of your judgments, Grace."

She flushed. "You don't care about the injustice those poor people have to face. You don't care if they're still enslaved, still chained to the same plot of land, the same *master*—after all, you fought for the Grand Old South! How could I ever have hoped to reform you!"

Rathe's expression was furious. "Let me set you straight, lady. Yes, I fought for the South, and I'm proud of it. If I had to do it all over again, had to face all the blood and death, all the destruction and mutilation, I wouldn't hesitate! I'm a Texan, Grace, and I'll fight for Texas without hesitating. I fought for her right to make her own laws, to decide her own future—not to have some Northern carpetbaggers telling us what to do! We never owned a slave in our lives. My mother is English and a firm abolitionist. So is my pa. We were all raised to believe that a human being owning another human being is a sin. But we had the right to decide ourselves whether or not to own slaves before the War, and we fought for that right in the War. We may have lost the War, Grace, but we didn't lose our pride! I'm proud to be a Texan, and proud to be a Southerner! And don't you ever think otherwise!"

"Are you proud of how the night riders terrorize this town?" she asked softly.

His eyes blazed. "Do you think I have anything to do with them?"

"Yes!"

He stared, incredulous and enraged all at once.

"I don't mean that you are one of those awful night riders," Grace cried. "I mean that by not trying to stop them, and Ford, and the discrimination, by doing nothing—you support them!''

He shook her off. ''Go home, Grace. And take your crazy ideas with you. I have something to settle with Ford—and it's personal.''

They rounded the corner onto Main Street, Rathe striding straight up the steps of the jailhouse. Grace hovered nervously in the doorway. Ford was sitting at a desk in the middle of the room.

''You didn't seem to take our last conversation very seriously,'' Rathe said, low. Grace could only see his back. He was leaning menacingly over Ford. But she could see the sheriff. He wasn't perturbed in the least.

Calmly, he spat a wad of tobacco at the floor. Then he grinned at Rathe. ''Now what conversation was that, boy?''

''Miss O'Rourke was accosted yesterday. Or have you forgotten?''

''I didn't forget, boy.''

''Looks to me like you forgot,'' Rathe drawled.

''Nope. I know how to do my job. Them sailors just up and disappeared. Guess their boat floated away.'' He chuckled.

''You had better say a prayer,'' Rathe advised, ''that that is the truth.''

''I'm shakin' in my boots, boy. An' jest what are you gonna do if it's not?''

''You'll find out,'' Rathe said. ''Don't worry about that.''

Ford's laugh followed them outside. Grace peeked at Rathe's face. He was really furious, but visibly restraining himself. Grace should have felt elation for having maneuvered him into standing up against Ford, but she didn't. She felt apprehension.

''Go home, Grace,'' Rathe said, not looking at her, his strides hard and purposeful.

Grace knew better than to test her luck. Meekly, she

slowed and stopped, watching his rigid back. "What are you going to do now?" she called after him.

There was no answer.

"Rathe! Where are you going?"

"Where the hell do you think," he flung back. "To the waterfront. And don't you even *think* about coming with me."

"Maybe Ford was telling the truth!" she cried, worried about his safety. "Maybe they really did leave town!" She crossed her arms tightly against her chest and gazed after him until he turned a corner and disappeared from view. "Oh, what have I done?"

Chapter 13

The next day the one dozen members of the Natchez Christian Temperance Union crowded into the open doorway of the Black Heel Saloon.

Grace, who'd recently been elected president, had the honor of being smack in the front, with Sarah Bellsley and Martha Grimes flanking her. For Grace, it was hard to focus on this event. Rathe had not appeared at Harriet's for supper last night. She had been frantic by the time all the occupants of the house had turned in for the night, and, feeling like a fool, she had waited in the dark parlor for him to return.

Then, just as Grace had tried to tell herself her fear was justified, that she would be frightened for anyone who'd gone to take the law into his own hands on that rough waterfront, he'd returned. It was midnight, and she hadn't alerted him to the fact that she was there, awake and waiting for him. Only after he had disappeared up the stairs to the second floor and all sound of movement had ceased did she go up to her own room.

He hadn't been at breakfast. Grace had assumed that he was sleeping late. She could well understand that—she was exhausted herself. But she was irked. She wanted to know what had happened. Had he found the sailors? Perversely, she couldn't help wishing that the sailors had left town— that Ford had been telling the truth.

Now, Grace surveyed the crowded saloon, pleased that they had chosen a Saturday, when the establishment was

155

full, to do their work. The ladies all carried pamphlets and
hymnals. They were also all wide-eyed, staring at the plush
furnishings, the vast, shimmering chandeliers, and the
massive rosewood ceiling fans. The floors were polished,
gleaming oak, covered with bright Persian rugs. The walls
were paneled with shiny mahogany. Grace was just as surprised as her cohorts at the elegant interior of this establishment.

A tall man hurriedly came toward them, having arisen
from one of the card tables. "That's Sam Patterson, the
owner," Sarah whispered in her ear. "And the big ox
behind him must be the one who keeps the riffraff out."

"Gentlemen," Grace cried loudly. "Gentlemen, please
give me your attention!"

The saloon was noisy with conversation, drunken
laughter, and music from an elegant Heinreich piano that
seemed out of place in the raucous saloon. Sam con-
fronted them, pulling on his sideburns. "Ladies, what are
you doing? Please, you can't come in here, it's not
proper!" He was aghast.

"Oh, but we can and we will," Grace assured him
sweetly. All around her the patrons were oblivious, playing cards, drinking and conversing, although a few men
sitting at the front tables had turned to gawk.

"There's my Benjamin," cried Beth Ferguson.

Benjamin, his eyes almost popping out of his head at
the sight of them, went red and hastily ducked.

"Oh my Lord," Martha whispered, and as one entity
the ladies followed her gaze.

A beautiful woman in a very short skirt that showed her
entire calf and her knees had arisen from a gentleman's
lap to saunter forward, laughing at the good women of the
Natchez Christian Temperance Union. Grace could not
prevent herself from staring at the prostitute. Despite her
scandalous attire, the woman was very beautiful. "What's
this?" the blonde cried. "Ladies, I do believe you made
a wrong turn somewhere."

A few men at the front tables laughed. The rest of the

saloon remained unimpressed at the historic event occurring.

"Sing, ladies. Sing now," Grace directed, determined to get everyone's attention.

The ladies broke into a harmonious, rousing rendition of "Glory, Glory Hallelujah." The laughter and conversation in the saloon died. The piano music stopped. Every man jack there turned to gaze upon the spectacle of some of Natchez' finest examples of gentility and motherhood crowded in the doorway of the Black Heel Saloon.

"Oh my God," Sam Patterson said when the song had ended.

"Gentlemen!" Grace cried. "The Christian spirit has descended. It is time for us to examine the evils of intemperance!"

"Oh, shit," a man at a front table said.

"I never thought I'd see this day in Natchez," someone else muttered.

"I want you out of my saloon," Sam cried.

"Let 'em speak, Sam." The blonde laughed. "They're just making fools of themselves."

"While you are here drinking merrily," Grace shouted, "where are your wives and children? Sitting at home, gazing upon a barren hearth, looking into an empty larder? Weeping with loneliness, with hunger! And why? Why? Because you are drinking away your family's income, leaving nothing but suffering victims and widowed hearts behind! Have you no shame?" She signaled to her women. They burst into another deafening chorus.

Sam Patterson moaned, and when finally the singing ended, he warned, "I'm going to get the sheriff."

"Go right ahead," Grace said pleasantly. "I do not think I need to tell ugly tales," she cried, then faltered abruptly for one moment when her gaze met a vivid, piercing blue one. Rathe did not look pleased. Grace tried to ignore him. Oh, why did he have to be here!

"But I will tell you ugly tales," she continued, her voice ringing loud and clear. "Tales of drunken men who spend every penny in their pockets, leaving nothing for their family. Men who are perfect Christian husbands until they imbibe. And then, they are known to assault their wives and children, sell off their property, even apprentice their own children to fill their pockets again—and for what? For more drink! Ladies, let's hear another chorus.''

"What do you want me to do, boss?" the big man asked Sam Patterson.

"Go get the sheriff," Sam said.

"We don't need the sheriff," a large redheaded man shouted, standing. "Ladies, I for one don't want to hear another goddamn word. You're interrupting my poker game and I've got the best hand I've had all day!"

"Yeah!" someone seconded. Soon the room sounded like a den of roaring lions.

Grace clenched her fists. "If we prize our loved ones," she cried, "if we cherish our homes, our American institutions, our country and our God, it is our Christian duty to overcome this evil!"

Some of the men had risen at the poker player's angry statement. Now he came forward to confront Grace, towering over her. "Listen, lady, we've had enough."

"You'd better go," Sam Patterson said nervously. "Please, ma'am, before there's trouble. Red can be mean."

"I am not afraid," Grace stated.

"We are not afraid," Sarah affirmed, although most of the ladies were white with tension.

Someone in the back shouted, "It's high time we had a temperance union in Natchez!"

A roar of male disapproval and fury sounded, all heads turning to spot the culprit. Grace's heart constricted. It was Allen. Dear, dear Allen. She should have known he would guess her plan.

"The ladies are right," he continued loudly. "If a man is irresponsible because of drink, he shouldn't imbibe. Isn't it up to us to protect and cherish our wives, the mothers of our children, the guardians of our Christian morality?''

There were a few hesitant murmurs of agreement.

''Ladies,'' Grace cried with aplomb. ''Another chorus!''

They sang.

''No-good Yank traitor,'' the man called Red bellowed.

''Get outta here, Yank,'' someone else shouted. The voice was familiar. Grace instantly spotted Rawlins, the young man who'd threatened Allen last Sunday, and felt sick with dread. Then, instinctively, she glanced at Rathe. He was standing tensed and ready, watching everyone.

''Get the Yank traitor outta here!'' a man in the back echoed.

''Get the ladies outta here!'' someone closer to the women added.

''Remember your Christian duty,'' a blond, bewhiskered fellow admonished. ''They are ladies and wives and mothers and the finest flower of Southern society.''

But this latter went unheard, for suddenly two men were swinging punches at each other, and for an instant, everyone stared. Then Rawlins leapt at Allen. Grace screamed. The saloon exploded into a free-for-all.

''Allen!'' Grace rushed forward. All around her men were wrestling and fighting. Grace could see that Rawlins had knocked Allen onto the bar with a series of hate-filled punches. Grace was afraid—Allen wasn't a fighter. She shoved through two pairs of wrestling men. Her foot hooked on someone and she sprawled onto the floor. She felt a hand in her hair, yanking, and she cried out, rolling over and twisting to get up. A strange man had one hand anchored in her hair, his fist raised for a blow. His eyes went wide when he realized he held a woman; then, with a whoop and a grin, he pulled her beneath him and gave her a wet, slobbering kiss.

Grace kneed him ruthlessly in the groin, then leapt to her feet, panting, ignoring her victim, who was now moaning in agony on the floor. The man directly in front of her received a violent blow, and he staggered with the force of a locomotive into Grace. She went flying backward, landing on a table, sending glasses of whiskey tumbling.

"Grace!"

For a moment she remained on the table, the only safe place in this sea of fighting men. She scanned the throng and found Rathe, who had called out to her. Their gazes met. He was livid. He jammed his hand at her, and somehow she knew he was ordering her stay put until he could come to her. Then she saw a man coming up behind him with a chair raised in his hands, about to send it crashing down on his head. "Rathe!" she screamed.

Just in time he turned and caught the man's hands, wrestling with him for the chair. Rathe finally yanked it away and sent it flying across the room. Grace watched it hit some unsuspecting duelist in the back and send him to his knees, leaving his opponent staggering above him in drunken shock. Rathe and his adversary were now exchanging serious blows. Grace searched the crowd for Allen, and swallowed a scream. A man was holding him while Rawlins hit him repeatedly.

She cautiously slid off the other side of the table, this time careful not to get into anyone's way. Furious, she picked up a whiskey bottle and shoved through the rioting crowd. Without even thinking, she slammed the bottle down on the back of Rawlins' partner's head. He crumpled at her feet.

Allen was only semi-conscious. Grace's gaze met Rawlins'. Rawlins grinned. "Howdy, lil' lady."

He grabbed her so quickly, Grace didn't have a chance. He kissed her ruthlessly. She felt her hair cascading free of its pins; she writhed like a wildcat, but he caught her wrists and jerked her hard against him.

That was when Rathe hauled Rawlins away. Grace went down on her knees, panting, as Rathe hit Rawlins hard, first in his abdomen, knocking the wind out of him, and then in his face, possibly cracking his jaw. Grace saw the redheaded poker player reaching out for Rathe from his left side. Still on the floor, she screamed a warning and dove for Red's feet, tugging wildly. It was as hopeless as trying to fell a California redwood tree.

Red kicked her off, sending her rolling away, a million shafts of pain shooting through her ribs. For a moment she lay still and stunned.

Rathe saw it. Fury might have given him the superhuman strength he needed to take on Red, but Rathe wasn't interested in finding out. As the man reached for him Rathe drew his knife. Red froze. Then the man behind Red raised a bottle and smashed it on Red's head. With a roar, Red turned to find this latest opponent.

Rathe reached Grace in a second and lifted her in his arms. "You damn fool," he shouted, as he shouldered his way through the crowd.

"Wait, Rathe, please," she cried. "I can't possibly leave all the ladies behind . . . and Allen. He was hurt; I saw it."

"The rest of the women have a lot more sense than you," he snapped as he carried her through the doorway, out into the bright afternoon sunlight. "They got out of there as soon as the punches started to fly. And I'll come back for Allen." The thought of looking after her Yankee beau irritated him, but then he reminded himself that he actually liked Allen.

As he hurried down the street with Grace in his arms, he saw the pain on her face and the tears welling in her eyes. Her long, impossibly thick, curly hair hung to his knees, tangling around him with every stride. "Hang on, Grace," he said hoarsely. "Just hang on a little longer."

After he saw how badly hurt she was, *then* he would kill her.

His heart was in his throat, practically choking him as he carried her up the stairs, and into her room, bellowing for Harriet. She was very still in his arms, and very pale. Her full, lush mouth was narrowed in obvious pain. When he set her on the bed, as gently as he could, she whimpered and opened her eyes. His hand moved into the untamable thickness of her red hair. "Everything's going to be okay now, Grace," he murmured.

Her eyes focused on his. "Allen?"

His heart clenched. Anger and jealousy swept over him. "Is it your ribs?"

"Is Allen okay?" she whispered.

"I don't know." He had slid his hands beneath her to unhook her gown. She didn't even protest. It was a sure sign of the state she was in and it made him even grimmer. He gently eased her gown off her shoulders and down to her waist.

"Grace, I've known you for less than a week," he growled, "and I've saved your pretty little hide more times than I can count."

"What are you doing?" she gasped.

She wasn't wearing a corset, just a chemise and the godawful heavy linen she used to bind her breasts. For the moment he ignored it.

"Rathe, what are you doing?"

"What do you think?" He cut her off. "Dammit, Grace, I want to see how badly you are hurt."

Her mouth closed. He pulled the chemise out from her skirts and lifted it to expose her torso. Ugly red bruises were already turning purple. The sight hurt him unbearably.

"How bad is it?" she asked tremblingly.

He gently slid his hands over her ribs. Her skin was like satin—not a timely observation. "Nothing's broken," he announced, feeling greatly relieved. "Just bruised." His look was dark. "You're lucky."

"Are you sure?"

"Not only have I seen my fair share of bruised, cracked, fractured, and broken ribs, I've had them," he said emphatically, hoping to get a smile out of her.

She did smile.

He did, too. Then, pulling down the chemise, he spoke her name. "Gracie." His tone was tight, full of vexation.

She just looked at him out of wide, pain-filled, violet eyes.

That stopped the lecture he so badly wanted to give her. He was close to her, his hand was still on her back, lost in her hair. She was pale but impossibly gorgeous. Her eyes held his. "Grace," he whispered, about to tell her how she'd scared the life right out of him, about to beg her never to do anything so foolish again.

"Please," she said. "Please make sure Allen's all right."

He stood abruptly, eyes narrowed, mocking. "Of course."

Allen wasn't all right.

Rathe delivered the news a little later. He'd brought him home just after leaving Grace, put him in bed, and summoned a doctor. He was now in a very serious condition, still unconscious. Grace trembled. "How bad is it?"

Rathe shifted uncomfortably. "He's had several blows to his head. Dr. Lang is worried he might not wake up."

Grace started to cry. "He did it on purpose," she choked. "Rawlins. Because Allen is teaching the Negroes."

"You're right," Rathe said softly. He sat next to her and pulled her into his arms. "If you believe in the Lord, Gracie, now is the time to pray."

She clung to him, weeping. "It's all my fault."

"It's not your fault." He held her tenderly, so overwhelmed with the warmth of his feelings for this woman that for a moment he couldn't think. He brushed away her tears with a delicate touch.

"If we hadn't marched on the Black Heel, none of this would have happened."

"It would have happened," Rathe said grimly, finding himself holding her face, so small and delicate, in his two large hands. "If not now, then sooner or later."

"I have to go to him," she cried, pulling away from Rathe.

"You're not going anywhere, Grace. Not today."

"I have to," she cried with panic. "Please, Rathe, I have to go and see him."

Jealousy rose again and he didn't like it. "There's nothing to be gained by your seeing him. He won't know you're there."

"I don't care," she told him stubbornly. "Please, Rathe, please."

He melted. "Only if you let me help you."

"All right," she agreed, starting to slide her legs over the side of the bed. Rathe lifted her in his arms. Though his timing was completely inappropriate, he imagined carrying her to his bed, with her warm and wet and eager for him. He shook his head to clear it of such thoughts.

Outside Allen's door, he paused. "Grace, he was beaten up badly. It's not too pleasant to look at. Are you sure you won't wait a few days?"

"I have to see him now," she said. "I have to let him know I'm here."

"He won't know," Rathe tried again. "He's unconscious."

"I don't care."

Did she care for him that much? He opened the door. Harriet rose from where she was sitting beside Allen. "Rathe," she said disapprovingly.

"She insisted," Rathe said quietly. "I was afraid she'd hurt herself if I didn't help her."

"Oh, dear God," Grace cried.

Allen was unconscious, his face battered and swollen, his nose bandaged. The covers hid the rest of his body. Rathe gently deposited her by the bed. Grace reached instantly for his hand, ignoring her own pain in the face of the terrible aching of her heart. "Oh, Allen, it's me, Grace. Allen dear, I'm here, and you are going to get well!"

Rathe felt like an intruder. Grimly, he turned away.

* * *

Rathe sat up late into the night, staring into Harriet's unlit fireplace, bathed in utter darkness. He knew he would never have the heart to chastise Grace as she deserved.

In fact, he thought that he was probably more shaken by her close call than she was. He couldn't get over it. He would never forget the feeling of sheer horror as he watched her fall on her face in the midst of the brutally fighting men, watching Rawlins kiss her while he was prevented from reaching her by the violent throng. And later, when he'd seen her kicked, the terror he'd felt was like nothing he'd ever experienced before. Right now Allen was lying unconscious in his bed, but it could have been Grace.

Dear God! How was he going to keep her out of harm's way? It was certainly a task he could dedicate his entire life to! And even then, the day he died he'd go to his grave worrying over her.

He shifted uneasily. Grace needed him, that had been abundantly clear from the moment he'd met her. He had no doubt that she would eventually become his mistress, for not only did he know the power of his own charm, but more importantly, Grace liked him no matter how much she tried to convince herself otherwise, no matter how hard she fought against falling under his spell. But how could he protect her until then? Ah, Gracie, he thought, the sooner you stop fighting me the better it will be for the both of us!

Again, he shifted uneasily. No matter how much he tried to convince himself that he would be as good for Grace as she would be for him, he had to recognize that his pursuit of her was ruthless. He thought of his parents, and knew they would be appalled at his behavior—at his relentless preying upon a virgin spinster. He would, of course, tell them that he could not help himself. They would tell him that, if he wanted her so badly, he should marry her. Rathe almost laughed.

His smile died a sudden death, as he realized that, if he had a decent bone in his body, he *would* marry her.

I'm not ready for marriage, he told himself quickly. And it was true. And I don't love her. That, too, was true. Wasn't it?

Of course it was! Rathe knew he was the last person in the world who would fall in love with a politicking harridan. The woman he had always envisioned as his wife was like his mother—genteel, well-bred, elegant.

Damn! He wanted Grace, and she wanted him . . .

He passed a sleepless night. The next day took him to Melrose, his heart light with anticipation, where he found Geoffrey and spirited him away without Louisa's knowledge. Back at Harriet's, Rathe was delighted to surprise Grace with her visitor. And her obvious pleasure increased his. "Oh, Rathe, thank you! I was about to expire from sheer restlessness! How I've missed you," she cried to the child.

He watched her hugging Geoffrey, a beautiful smile on her mouth, her eyes shining. "Don't I get one, too?" He asked, absurdly pleased.

"Are you eight years old?" she returned impishly.

"I guess not," he said, with mock disappointment. "But can't we pretend?"

Her lips twitched. She laughed.

Her laughter followed him back to the waterfront. Finding the two sailors who had accosted Grace had become an obsession. As yet, he hadn't determined that they had indeed left town. He knew, in his gut, that Ford was lying. Ford had made no effort to apprehend the two men. Rathe didn't appreciate Grace trying to manipulate him, but he realized he could probably forgive her just about anything, and certainly this. The fact that she wanted him to stand up to Ford meant nothing, not when he was determined to avenge her honor, no matter who stood in his way.

It was late, and he was tired from lack of sleep. But he couldn't afford to lose any more time, because eventually the sailors would leave town. And there *was* a principle involved here. It might not be the one Grace adhered to, but it was the one he would gladly fight for. He could not let those men get away with accosting Grace the way they had.

It was a shame the colored vendor had been accosted, too. But nothing he or anyone did was going to stop men like that from treating the Negroes as they saw fit.

Her words echoed, haunting him. "By not trying to stop them, and Ford, and the discrimination, by doing nothing—you support them!"

"Ah, shit," he said aloud. "Gracie, what are you doing to me?" It was then that he saw one of the sailors.

With the speed of a striking rattlesnake, he exploded into a run, after the man who had just turned the corner. He was ten steps away when the sailor, alerted by the sound of footsteps, glanced over his shoulder and saw him coming. He took off. Rathe dug his legs into the ground, running as hard as he could, the muscles of his thighs straining, his face a mask of determination. He was only a step away. The sailor suddenly whirled, a knife in hand, and lunged forward.

Rathe was coming dead-on, like a locomotive, but his reflexes were finely honed. He shifted his weight and the knife only grazed his side. With one arm and all the force of his momentum behind his body, he drove the sailor to the ground.

In seconds Rathe had disarmed the man and had him in a headlock. "Don't move."

"What do you want? Sweet Mary, what did I do?"

Rathe laughed, the sound both chilling and exultant. He got to his feet slowly, transferring his grip, keeping one of the man's arms twisted high behind his back. In this manner he led him to Ford's office.

The door was ajar; Rathe kicked it open. "Look what the tide brought in," he mocked.

Ford rose, glaring. "Just what in hell do you think you're doing, Bragg?"

Rathe smiled. "When I saw this fugitive, Ford, I just knew how glad it would make you to throw him behind bars. I couldn't resist helping you out. Let's just say I've appointed myself deputy."

"The hell you say," Ford shot back. "I got a deputy an' you damn well know it."

"Imagine the headlines: Sheriff Ford begins campaign to clean up the waterfront. I imagine the good ladies of Natchez would sure be moved to hear that! Bet they'd tell their husbands to vote for you this fall."

"Their husbands already vote for me," Ford sneered.

Rathe raised a brow. "Then imagine these headlines: Schoolmarm accosted; sheriff lets assailants go free."

"Just what the hell are you trying to do?"

"I want him thrown in that cell, and I want him standing before the county judge when he comes riding into town next week."

"You're asking for trouble, boy."

"No," Rathe corrected calmly. *"You're* asking for trouble. Look at it this way. You can either get some good publicity, or some bad. But if I were you I'd keep in mind that it's an election year."

Chapter 14

A few days later Grace went to the mayor's office and requested an appointment. She introduced herself as a friend of Allen's from New York. Natchez being a small town, Mayor Sheinreich had immediately guessed she had been the governess at Melrose who, town gossip held, had been dismissed by Louisa Barclay in a fit of jealousy over Rathe Bragg.

"I would very much like to substitute for Allen Kennedy while he is recovering."

Mayor Sheinreich was surprised, then, to Grace's relief, utterly pleased. "This is wonderful! I was despairing at the thought of finding a temporary replacement. You do know, dear, that there is some, uh, resistance to our new public school system?"

"I'm aware of it," Grace said. "But apparently you support it?"

"I'm Republican," Sheinreich said proudly, then paused. "I assume you've discussed this with Mr. Kennedy, and that he agrees?"

"Why . . . yes." She'd had to talk the recuperating Allen into it, but he'd finally said yes.

And so she had a job, or at least, a temporary one. The pay was atrocious, three dollars and fifty cents a week. She would, of course, have to supplement her income, and immediately, before the hospital began harassing her about her mother's bills. As always, thinking about her mother filled her with sadness and dread.

169

That night **Grace** was too excited about the upcoming day to eat. She toyed with the roast chicken on her plate, her mind on tomorrow's agenda. Charles Long, another boarder, who walked with a limp due to the War, asked her, "Are you looking forward to tomorrow, Grace?"

As Grace looked up, smiling and eager to share her feelings, she was aware of Rathe, in his usual seat across from her. He had paused from eating to stare. "Absolutely thrilled, Charles."

Rathe said, slowly, "You found employment?"

"Why, yes, I have," she returned, feeling worry burgeoning now. She cast her eyes down nervously, unable to hold his gaze, certain of his disapproval should he find out exactly what her new position was.

"You'll have to tell us, dear, " Harriet said, "all about your first day. Allen will be so pleased. I know it's a relief to him, what you're doing."

Rathe put down his knife and fork and leaned back in his chair, scorching her with his gaze.

"Yes, of course," Grace said, very apprehensive now. She was desperate to change the topic. Was she crazy to think she could hide her employment from him? Besides, what did she care if he disapproved? "Harriet," she said quickly, "this chicken is delicious. Could you give me the recipe?"

"Certainly."

"What," Rathe drawled, "exactly are you doing?"

She paled, then reached for her coffee. "I've taken Allen's place at the public school for a while," she said.

For a moment he didn't move, and Grace thought she was wrong—he didn't care, and that, perversely, dismayed her.

Then he stood. "Excuse me," he said to the room in general. Before she knew it, he had come around the table and was pulling her chair back, with her in it. She protested. "I believe we have something to discuss," he drawled, and because she knew him well now, because his words were so thick and slurred, like Southern honey, she knew he was very, very angry.

"Rathe . . ."

He hauled her to her feet and jerked her with him into the hall and out the back door. Outside, she twisted free, furious. "How—"

Rathe's look was murderous, cutting Grace off in midsentence. She took a nervous step backward.

"Are you out of your mind?" he demanded.

"This is not your affair."

He started for her.

She backed away.

"You need looking after," he said, stalking her.

"I can take care of myself."

"The way you did on Saturday?"

"I . . ." She backed into the wall with a gasp.

His arms came up on either side of her, closing her in. At this proximity he was even more intimidating, for she could see that he was madder than she had thought. "You could have been seriously hurt on Saturday," he said tensely. "Just like you could have been hurt that day on the waterfront."

"But I wasn't." She swallowed, her mouth terribly dry.

"Because I was there. Dammit, Gracie! The next time I may not be around to save your silken skin!"

"I can take care of myself," she shouted back. "I've been doing it for years!"

"You have nine lives," he snapped. "Ever since I've known you, you've just barely escaped seriously hurting yourself!"

"I cannot sit around and do nothing."

"Dammit! Can't you at least keep to one program? Do you have to go sticking your nose into everything you possibly can?"

"Is there only one injustice in the world?" she flung back.

"You know what you need?"

"I'm afraid to ask!"

"You need a thrashing," he said, his face inches from hers. "A real thrashing, the kind that will teach you some sense."

"Let me go," she ground out angrily, pushing against the steel wall of his chest. But he didn't budge.

"Then you need a protector," he said more levelly. "Face it, Grace, you need *me*."

"You are the most arrogant, conceited man I've ever had the misfortune to meet."

"You are the most unreasonable, lunatic woman . . ." he growled, then leaned forward, pinning her with his body, finding her mouth with his.

Beneath his onslaught, Grace froze. She tried to resist, she truly did. But it was hopeless. Her mouth softened, parting gently, and her body began a slow melting. She raised her hands and hesitantly put them on his shoulders. A deep, guttural cry of triumph escaped Rathe.

He didn't move his hands from the wall on either side of her neck, keeping her imprisoned with his big body. He pulled at her lush lower lip with his teeth, then licked the seam of her lips insistently. "Open for me, Grace," he breathed.

She opened. His tongue thrust in, hot, hard, urgent. His hips, at the same time, moved sensually against her, and he began rubbing his long, thickened arousal back and forth. Grace groaned, flinging her head back, leaving Rathe free to shower her throat with kisses, to seek the recess of one delicate ear. When his tongue began to trace its spiraling contours, Grace shuddered helplessly. In response, he rubbed himself more urgently against her, telling her what he wanted, and that he wanted it now.

"Damn," he cried, burying his face in her neck.

Grace could feel his entire body pulsating against hers. She didn't want him to stop. Not now. Not ever.

He separated his body from hers, but he took her firmly by the shoulders. "We have to go back inside."

She could not believe herself. She was disappointed, she wanted to fling herself back in his arms.

"Grace," he said, taking a breath. "You're getting in over your head. I don't want you teaching."

Her heart was still beating furiously. "Maybe," she said, wetting her dry lips, "maybe if this town had some decent law and order a person could teach freely and in peace. And besides, you have no right to tell me what to do—you of all people. You're the reason I was unemployed!"

Rathe raised his gaze to the heavens and swore. "Damn," he said softly. "You have more tenacity than anyone, man or woman, that I've ever met."

"It's the truth."

He stared at her. A muscle in his jaw jumped. "Do you want the truth?"

She bit her lip.

"The truth is you and me, sweetheart."

"I don't have to listen to this!"

He barreled on. "The truth is what I do to you—what you do to me. The truth is we belong together, and you know it."

The truth.

It was not the truth!

They did not belong together. It didn't matter that he was handsome. What mattered was who and what he was. He was a callous philanderer, selfish and self-absorbed. He was not the man for her, not the kind of man she should even look at. She didn't know why his kisses stirred her so, but hoped it was because of her lack and his wealth of experience.

There was no doubt about becoming his mistress! She'd never do it. He would have to be the last man on earth, and she the last woman! However, if he continued to be so persistent, she was going to have some problems. How could she keep Rathe at arm's length, and at the same time coax him into helping clean up this town?

Grace, you're playing with fire, a little voice said.

But what other options do I have? she asked herself miserably. She had a terrific headache.

After supper she adjourned to Allen's room with a book, intending to cheer him with a favorite story of theirs, and cheer herself as well. She was determined to forget, for the moment, Rathe Bragg, Sheriff Ford, all her worries.

Allen was thrilled to see her. He was still weak and sore, although he had sat up earlier that day. He turned his head to her, and smiled slightly, unable to do more because of his puffy lips. "Grace, hello."

"Hello, Allen," she said, sitting beside him and taking his hand. She clung to it. This man, who was good and just, loved her enough to want to marry her, understood her enough not to push her. Yet in his arms, she felt nothing at all. A terrible kind of despair rose up in her.

While *he, he* was the worst sort of philanderer, and *he* only wanted to make her his mistress—his toy, his plaything. *He* understood her not at all, and was pushing her remorselessly. And in his arms, she felt *everything.* Dear Lord, just one hot look was enough to make her pulse pound.

She began telling Allen about her day, too rapidly, rushing headlong in flight from her memory of Rathe. It took her a while to notice Allen's consternation, though at last, at the sight of his tensed countenance, she froze. "Allen? What is it? Are you in pain?"

"I don't want you teaching, Grace," he cried. "I've changed my mind." He tried to sit up. The movement made him gasp with pain, for two of his ribs were cracked.

"Please, Allen, you'll hurt yourself!"

Allen lay weakly back. "Grace, don't be a fool—worse, a martyr. You saw who did this. I don't want you involved. I was wrong to let you see Mayor Sheinreich . . ."

Grace felt tears rising, tears of frustration. She touched his cheek gently, and he turned his face fully into her cupped hand. "Allen," she whispered, "you are so dear to me. I love you very much."

"Oh, Grace."

"Being as I didn't get through to her," came a thick, rough drawl from the door, "maybe you can."

Grace gasped, whirling. "What are you doing in here?"

Rathe was standing with his arms crossed against the doorjamb. He didn't look charitable. "I should ask you that very question. What, no chaperone? Shame on you, Miss O'Rourke." His face was hard. "Tell her, Allen."

"Promise me, Grace, promise me you'll tell Mayor Sheinreich you've changed your mind. Please, Grace."

But Grace wasn't listening. "You!" she shrieked. "*You* tell *me* I need a chaperone when I'm with Allen?"

Both men looked at her.

"You dare to insinuate that Allen would be anything other than a gentleman—even as he's lying here hurt in bed?"

"Calm down, Gracie," Rathe said.

"Calm down! After you have just accused me of needing a chaperone? After what you just did out on the back porch? You dare to chastise me?"

Rathe reddened.

"What's going on between you two?" Allen asked.

Neither Grace or Rathe heard. "I apologize," Rathe said stiffly.

Grace had opened her mouth, about to keep on blasting him for his morals and his double standards. Now she swallowed air. "You what?"

"I apologize," he repeated.

"You're apologizing to me?"

"How many times would you like me to say it?"

"Once is fine," she murmured, dazed. Then she glared. "Wait a minute. Exactly what are you apologizing for?"

His gaze was level. "For chastising you."

She wanted to scream.

"The one thing I am not," Rathe said, "is a hypocrite. I will never apologize for what I've asked of you."

"Are you implying that I am?"

"Implying? Why should I imply something when I can state it openly."

"Me?"

"A hypocrite," Rathe said, at the door, "according to my dictionary, says one thing and does another." He gave her a look, then walked away.

"What is going on?" Allen said.

Grace flushed. Was she a hypocrite when it came to being in his arms?

"Grace? What's going on?"

Slowly, she turned to Allen. "That man is impossible." She tried a smile. "Nothing. I was hoping he might take on Ford, but instead we seem to be constantly at each other's throats."

"Rathe? What do you mean—take on Ford?"

"Someone has to stop him," Grace said. "Rathe may not have any morals, but he's tough and he's not afraid of Ford. Most importantly, he can hold his own against him."

"Grace, you can't go after Sheriff Ford! That is begging trouble! Is that why Rathe apprehended one of the men who accosted you?"

"What?"

"You never told me about that, Grace." Allen turned an accusing look on her. "I had to hear the gossip."

"It wasn't important. Rathe caught one of the sailors? What happened? When?"

"Yesterday. He's locked up, awaiting trial. The circuit judge will be in town next week. Grace, why didn't you tell me?"

Grace was stunned. "He's already made a difference, even if it was for all the wrong reasons." She bit her lip, apprehension filling her as she imagined the confrontation that had probably occurred between Rathe and the sheriff. "As you can see," she said slowly, "he is the perfect man to stand up against Sheriff Ford."

But there was no fervor in her words.

The next day, Grace was gathering up her books in the empty church where classes were held, as the last of her students left. Geoffrey was hanging about shyly, having appeared, to her delight, that afternoon. Apparently he had chores in the mornings that he couldn't escape. "Would you mind carrying these books for me?" Grace asked with a smile.

He was thrilled, taking the books with pride.

Suddenly, the door opened, letting in a stream of light, and Grace looked up, startled, thinking that one of her students had left something behind.

Rawlins smiled, sauntering down the aisle.

"Hello, Miss Teacher," he drawled, sitting down in a pew. "Got some time to give me a few lessons?"

Grace struggled to remain composed. Fear and revulsion swept through her. She remembered him viciously hitting Allen while another man held him. She remembered the feel of his hands on her—of his mouth. "Good day, Mr. Rawlins," she said, barely managing to contain a shudder. "I'm afraid classes are over."

He stretched. "That's okay. I wouldn't ever sit in the same schoolroom with niggers."

Grace had nothing to say to that hostile comment. "Let's go, Geoffrey," she said quietly, urgently.

As they started up the aisle Rawlins rose to follow them out. Grace's heart was in her mouth. Perspiration trickled from her temple down her jaw. Outside, Grace bent down to take her books and whisper in Geoff's ear. "Go get Mr. Rathe, *now*."

Geoff took off at a run.

Grace straightened, turning slightly. "If you'll excuse me, Mr. Rawlins?"

He blocked her. "An' if I don't?"

She tried to look cool and poised. "It's getting late," she said. She heard the quaver in her voice.

He grinned. "Mmm." He was staring at her intently. He reached out to toy with a strand of hair that had escaped her tight bun. "You are pretty, Miss Grace O'Rourke, do you know that? Especially with your hair down." His grin widened.

"Excuse me," she said stiffly, repulsed by his touch. She started away.

He caught her arm easily, swinging her around and pulling her very close to him, gazing down into her face. "I'm surprised that boyfriend of yours let you take this job," he said. "Real surprised."

"Allen will not be coerced," she exclaimed.

His brows raised in puzzlement. "Allen? Allen Kennedy?" He laughed. "I meant that no-good Texas sidewinder, Bragg."

She blanched.

"Miss O'Rourke, I've got to warn you; this heah is no place for a nice schoolmarm like you. We don't want no public schools down heah. We don't want them darkies thinkin' they can do more then they eveh can. They're not equal to white men no matter what the damn Republicans are sayin'. People down heah aren't takin' kindly to you Yanks, no sir, not at all. An' we don't like being taxed to send no niggers to school, to pay your salary. You think on all that, Miss O'Rourke, you think on it good."

She inhaled.

Before releasing her, he said, " 'Cause I don't want to have to come down here and do some teachin' of my own." With that he strode to his horse, mounted, gave her a perfect bow, and cantered off.

Grace sank down on the steps of the church, trembling. She rubbed her arms, hard. Then, breathing in deeply to regain some measure of calm, she stood, picked up her books, and started resolutely down the road to town.

A few minutes later she saw a horse galloping toward her and she froze up inside. Then she realized the horse was black, and that Rawlins rode a chestnut. As Rathe pulled up beside her, Grace gave a cry of relief. He slid down. "Grace? What is it? Geoff said you were in trouble. He was crying."

Before he'd finished, Grace hurled herself into his arms, seeking sanctuary in his powerful embrace. She felt him tighten his hold, and she burrowed deeper. He rocked her.

She felt his mouth on her jaw, the firm, soothing caress of his lips. For a long moment she clung and he held her. Then he set her gently away, cupping her face. "What in hell happened?"

"Nothing," she managed. "Thank heavens, nothing!" Tears glistened on her lashes.

He cursed audibly.

Feeling considerably braver now, Grace sniffed. "I don't think he would have done anything. I think it was just an empty threat."

"Who?"

"Rawlins."

This time she went scarlet as he paced around her furiously. "What exactly happened?"

Grace told him.

Rathe grabbed her shoulders, and his fingers dug in, hurting her. "This was your last day."

"Rathe, I can't quit now!"

"Dammit!" he exploded, whirling away. He twisted back. "Damn you, Grace!"

She clutched her hands to her breast.

"You're not going to see the light of day here, are you?" She shook her head no.

"Nothing I can do will change your mind, short of beating some sense into you?"

"Not even that."

"All right," he burst out. "I'm going to be here every day after school to pick you up. And don't even think of trying to talk me out of it!"

"I wouldn't dare," she said meekly. Secretly she was relieved.

That night, the more Grace thought about it, the more certain she was that Rawlins would never actually hurt her. After all, she was a woman, and Southern men prided themselves on their respect for the fair sex. Allen, however, disagreed.

Rathe had, unfortunately, gone directly to him to inform

him of her unwelcome visitor. Needless to say, Grace was furious with him.

Allen half-sat, gasping from exertion. "Grace, you're getting on the next train back to New York."

"I am not," she responded with pursed lips. "Allen, Rathe was exaggerating; he wasn't even there!"

"Don't underestimate Rathe," Allen warned. "He can be a dangerous man, Grace, and dangerous men recognize dangerous situations. You—"

"I'm a woman, Allen," Grace interrupted. "Rawlins is too much a Southern boy to ever harm a woman."

"Grace, I've never asked you for anything. But now I am. For me, please, go back to New York. I should never have arranged your employment down here in the first place, knowing you."

"I'm not running away."

Allen cursed, completely startling Grace, who had never heard him do so before. Instantly he apologized.

But Grace wasn't paying attention. "Besides, I have no money. None. I need to stay and get paid on the fifteenth of next month. As it is, I won't have enough for Mother's bills." At that grim thought, her lips thinned. Time was running out. She had to do something about supplementing her income. Yet she knew there wasn't a single job to be had in Natchez—not a respectable one, anyway.

"I have twenty dollars, Grace. I want you to take it. It's all I have. Teaching doesn't pay well, you know that. Besides, I've spent some of my own money on extra books. But what I have is yours."

"I'm not going to New York," she said calmly, while inside she felt dread, wondering if maybe she should borrow the twenty dollars from Allen; at least then she could pay most of her mother's bills. But she knew she couldn't. "Allen, you need your savings to tide you over until you're working again, and that won't be for a few more weeks. And what about Dr. Lang?"

Allen flushed. "He told me not to worry, that I can take my time paying him."

Grace managed a smile, though she felt sunk in the morass of her thoughts. So far, there had been no response to her seamstress's sign. And even if a position became available, she had already acquired a reputation in this town. Now, what with her teaching the Negro children, it had to be worse. The situation seemed out of control. It was like New York, where no one would hire her because of all the notoriety she had attained. And she promised herself that she would be discreet!

Maybe she could beg Louisa to let her tutor the girls part-time. She imagined herself groveling, and Louisa's spite at the power she would be wielding over her. Grace didn't care; if she thought she had a single chance of getting some extra income she would prostrate herself at that woman's feet. But she knew Louisa would never rehire her.

Just like she knew there wasn't a single respectable job in town.

As she closed her eyes, a horrifying thought occurred to her. *There's always work on Silver Street.*

Chapter 15

It was this worry that kept Grace awake past her bed-time.

There was a simple solution . . . Rathe.

She was instantly appalled.

She knew she would die before accepting Rathe's inde-cent, arrogant proposition. Unbidden, warm recollections rose to her mind, memories of his hard body pressed in-timately against hers, his lips soft and gentle and utterly seductive on hers. Grace buried her face in her hands. It wasn't fair! To have all of life conspiring against her, even her own traitorous body, pushing her into Rathe's arms. She felt trapped.

She was not going to become his mistress. She folded her arms across her breasts. Her mind conjured up Silver Street, with its row of saloons facing the broad, slowly moving Mississippi.

She tried to imagine herself in one of those short skirts, like the blonde had been wearing at the Black Heel on Saturday, and failed. She blushed. Before she would sink so low and compromise the beliefs she held so dear, she would check the hotels on the cliff again for a waitressing position. Even waitressing, as disrespectable as it was, was better than working on Silver Street.

She shut off her thoughts, her heart tightening uncon-trollably as she heard someone coming up the stairs. All the ladies who lived on this floor with her had retired, so who could it possibly be? She sat up, listening.

There was a soft rapping on her door. Immediately, Grace rose to answer it.

"Clarissa! she gasped.

Relief swept Geoffrey's sister's distraught features when she saw Grace. "Miz Grace, I don't know what to do!"

"What's wrong? Are you all right?"

"The night riders are riding tonight," Clarissa cried frantically. "I don't know what to do, an' I thought of you, bein' the teacher an' all an' so smart! Last time they almost killed my brother Jim!"

"Oh my God," Grace said, momentarily stunned. Then she snapped to. "Are you sure of this?"

"Yes ma'am."

"Do you know where they're riding?"

"On Shantytown. A Republican government man was down there today, spoutin' off, tryin' to make sure we all vote this fall, tellin' us not to be afraid—that there ain't no more Klan." Clarissa was clinging to her sleeve. "What are we gonna do?"

"We have to find Rathe," Grace said instantly. "He'll help." She was already yanking a skirt up over her night-gown and flinging a shawl around her shoulders. "Come on, Clarissa," she said grimly, running for the stairs. "His room is on the second floor."

He wasn't there. "Damn! He's probably at one of those saloons or brothels," Grace said. "Come on!"

Clarissa was on her heels, choking on a sob. "Now what are we gonna do?"

"Stop them," Grace retorted briskly. "We are going to stop them!"

In Harriet's study she paused in front of the beautiful mahogany gun case. Grace hesitated, thinking about how she abhorred violence—but only for a second. Lives were at stake. She tried to pull open the door. Clarissa gasped. "You can't stop 'em, Miz Grace. Not you."

"I sure as hell intend to try," Grace said, rattling the lock. "Damn, it's locked."

Clarissa grabbed her sleeve. "Miz—"

Grace picked up a paperweight and tapped the glass, shattering it. She grabbed the most modern-looking rifle she saw. "Let's go, Clarissa. Do you have a horse?"

"Jest Mary—a mule."

Outside, Grace looked at the big, skinny mule and shuddered. Sternly, she reminded herself that now was not the time to let her fear of horses interfere. Clarissa gave her a boost, then jumped up behind her. Mary laid her ears back at the double load, but with two pairs of heels kicking at her, she finally broke into a recalcitrant trot. Grace bounced wildly, clutching both the reins and the rifle, desperately trying not to fall off.

"I think we should go into town an' find Mistah Rathe," Clarissa said worriedly. "We's jest gonna get ourselves killed." Then she added, "Relax yore spine, Miz Grace. It'll be a lot easier on your hinny."

"I've always disliked horses," Grace said through clenched teeth, "but I've just discovered that I *hate* mules!"

A few minutes later, she asked, "Clarissa, just how do you know the night riders are riding tonight?"

She felt the young girl stiffen. "I heard it," Clarissa finally said.

"How?"

"When I was leavin' Treelawn."

Grace had been in Natchez long enough to know Treelawn was all that was left of the old Rawlins plantation, a big white clapboard house not far from Melrose. Her guts shrank. "What were you doing at Treelawn?"

Clarissa hesitated. "We needs the money, Miz Grace."

"Clarissa! You don't mean—you don't mean you gave yourself to that Rawlins boy?"

"I ain't got no choice."

"You have a choice!"

"No ma'am," she said stubbornly. "I don't. We's so in debt to the Barclays our children will never be able to leave this land, and God knows, my babies ain't gonna grow up heah, not if I can do somethin' about it."

"Babies," Grace said weakly. "You're pregnant?"

"No, I'm not. But one day I'll marry and I will be. When that day comes I'll have the money I need to get outta heah. Besides," she said defiantly, "I listen to Rawlins. Sometimes after a few whiskeys he talks open even to me. Tonight he had some friends stoppin' ovah. I heard them talkin' about what they plan to do. They's gonna make another lesson outta one of us, Miz Grace. They wanna win the fall elections and end Republican rule forever. They's real tired of the Yanks tellin' 'em what to do. Ain't nothin' gonna stop 'em this year, they said, not even if they have to kill half us coloreds and half the carpetbaggers to do it."

"Oh God," Grace said, "we'll have to get federal troops."

Clarissa didn't respond.

The back parlor of the Black Heel Saloon was completely private. Once the gentlemen who had booked the room were all comfortably settled, absolutely no one else was allowed in, except for the one waiter who freshened drinks and cleaned out ashtrays. By midnight smoke usually hung thick and heavy, despite the massive overhead fan. Unlike the front room of the saloon, where the hum of conversation and laughter, the whirring of the roulette wheels, and the melody of the piano made a constant cacophony, the back room was invariably soundless. And unlike the front room, where the beautiful hostesses charmed potential customers, absolutely no women were allowed in the back.

Rathe was losing consistently. He couldn't concentrate on his cards. An image of Grace grabbing her skirts in one hand, lifting them to bare her slender ankles, and jumping off the raft to wade to the riverbank, assailed him. And he smiled.

His smile faded as the memory continued. Her skirts had clung to her long, beautifully curved legs. For probably the thousandth time, he thought of Grace's sensual body, tall and slim with her voluptuous breasts, and felt an instant stirring in his groin. He thought of her lying beneath him, spread-legged, warm and wet, and an untimely erection was his reward. Then he recalled the latest development in the saga of never-ending crises Grace seemed to thrive on, her having substituted for Allen at the public school. His gut tightened. She was a fool. She was going to get herself killed if she kept on like that.

"Rathe, where the hell are you?" Tilden Fairbanks asked.

Rathe threw his cards on the table. "I'm out."

George Farris grinned. "You having a few problems tonight?"

Rathe's gaze was calm. "A few."

The door opened, but no one paid attention as the waiter came in with a trolley of drinks and clean ashtrays. Then, from behind him, a small dark body catapulted into the room, past the waiter. The bouncer, McMurty, appeared, panting. "Stop that kid! You, kid, you can't go in there!" He began cursing eloquently, red-faced.

Startled, the card play ceased as Geoffrey ran right into Rathe's arms. Rathe held him for a moment, then squatted, holding him by his shoulders, seeing that the boy was crying. "What now, Geoff? Is it Grace?"

"Yassir," he choked. "I followed my sister to Missus Harriet's. She was lookin' for Miz Grace. But then they left, and they had a gun. They's gonna get whupped!" He started crying helplessly.

"Where are they heading?" Rathe asked grimly.

'Shantytown."

Tilden Fairbanks spoke. "Hey Rathe, are you the only white man in this heah town who doesn't know what's happening tonight?"

He turned on his friend. "Spit it out, Fairbanks, *now.*"

"They're just gonna teach a few niggers a lesson, just in case anyone decided to listen to the Republican voterman who's been in town all day."

Rathe cursed and was gone before anyone could blink.

* * *

"Shall we make an example of him?" Rawlins cried, sitting astride his horse.

There were seven night riders, four mounted and flanking Rawlins, and two on foot holding a terrified Negro named Henry. "Yeah," came their roar of agreement.

They had rounded up a dozen frightened Negroes, forcing them to watch. "This is a lesson. You don't listen to your Yankee friends, 'cause if you do, you won't have any hide left at all," Rawlins stated. "Start whipping, Frank."

It was too much for Grace to bear, even though she was shaking from head to foot with fear. She sat atop Mary in the woods fringing the clearing where the flogging was about to occur. "How do I get this jackass to move?" she whispered to Clarissa, who was on the ground, trembling and crying soundlessly.

"Kick it," Clarissa said.

Grace kicked furiously. Mary craned her head around and gave her a look. Clarissa hit her in the flank. Mary bolted from the woods right toward the group of men as the hapless Negro was being tied to a stake.

Grace bounced wildly, trying to hold the reins, guide the mule, and point the gun threateningly at the same time. For the first time in her life she wished she knew how to ride. But maybe it was better that she didn't. At the sound of the charging, braying animal, heads swiveled toward her. Their horses shifted uneasily. Mary had the bit between her teeth and was in a mad gallop. Grace clung with her legs and one hand, maintaining her seat out of sheer terror, the reins trailing like streamers behind her. She found herself riding straight for Rawlins, and managed to keep the rifle pointed directly ahead.

"What the hell," Rawlins shouted, reining back to get out of her way.

Mary swerved, almost clipping Rawlins' chestnut. Rawlins fought to keep his frightened mount still. Grace started to slip sideways. To better right herself, she shifted her upper body. At that moment Mary stumbled. The gun exploded.

The shot came perilously close to Rawlins' chestnut, which screamed and bolted, running through the line of four riders, causing utter chaos.

The dozen Negroes forced to watch scattered and fled.

Grace landed on the ground in an ignominious heap.

Mary stopped abruptly and began munching weeds.

Rawlins regained control of his chestnut, whipping it around. "Get those niggers back here," he shouted furiously.

Grace was on her feet, leveling the rifle at him. She was shaking. "No!" she shouted back. "Anyone makes a move and he's dead!" The line, right out of a penny dreadful, sounded foolish even to her own ears.

But it worked. The night riders froze, waiting for orders from their leader.

He was incredulous. "You're not going to shoot me, girl," he leered.

"I almost got you the first time," Grace panted. "The mule made me miss. This time I'm not on some mule."

Rawlins hesitated.

"What should we do?" Frank asked, still standing by the tied man.

Anger flooded Rawlins' face. "No piece of nigger-lovin' Yankee trash is going to dictate to me," he said, spurring the chestnut into a trot—right toward her.

Grace prayed the gun had more bullets in it, and raised it higher. "Stop right there, Rawlins," she cried. "I mean it!"

He grinned and the chestnut picked up speed.

Grace swallowed. He'd been thirty yards away. Now he was half the distance and closing. He laughed. Grace summoned up all her resolve and squeezed the trigger.

Nothing happened.

Rawlins whooped and reached for her. His arms went around her just as a shot sounded. For one instant, Grace was trapped by the man against the chestnut's sweaty side. Then she felt him tense, heard his cry of pain, and he released her. She fell onto her knees.

"Try it, Rawlins," Rathe drawled from the shadows. "Pull that gun."

Rawlins froze. His shoulder was bleeding profusely, turning his sleeve red. For an instant everyone held their breath waiting for Rawlins to draw. But he must have realized the utter insanity of it, for Rathe had his gun leveled as cool as you please and couldn't possibly miss.

Contempt in his voice, Rathe said, "Get the hell outta here—now!"

The four riders broke first.

Rawlins held his ground, eyeballing Rathe furiously. "You're gonna be sorry, Texas boy. I'm gonna see to it."

"I'll be waiting with anticipation."

As Frank and the third man mounted, Rawlins leered pointedly at Grace, now standing and cradling the empty rifle. Rathe followed his glance with its implied threat and went rigid. Rawlins saw and his grin widened. Then he yanked his chestnut around and the three went galloping off.

Grace started for the tied man. One curt phrase from Rathe stopped her in her tracks. "Halt right there."

She froze.

Negroes materialized as if by magic out of the trees and two men began cutting their friend down. Clarissa came running. "You all right, Miz Grace?"

Grace squared her shoulders. It wasn't easy, due to the violent trembling assailing her body. She managed to nod to Clarissa, all the while listening to Rathe's horse approach, until she felt the heat of the lathered animal at her back. "Good question," Rathe said in that same icy tone. "Why don't you answer it, Grace?"

The sentence, although clipped, came out as rough and gravelly as sandpaper, and Grace knew he was enraged.

Her mouth was dry. "I'm fine," she said, intending to speak in a clear, loud voice. It came out as a fragile squeak.

"Is that man all right?" Rathe said.

"Henry, you okay?" Clarissa asked.

"I'm fine, suh," Henry said, coming forward and rubbing his chafed wrists. "Ma'am, I done got to thank you."

Grace was too apprehensive to feel any pleasure, but she managed to give Henry what she hoped was a smile. Then Rathe hauled her unceremoniously onto his lap, sidesaddle. She found herself looking as his taut, clenched jaw. She opened her mouth to protest. Rathe said, not looking at her, "Don't push me."

Her mouth closed.

His arm was iron around her waist. The black's trot was nothing like Mary's, and even though she was firmly anchored on Rathe's lap, she couldn't—didn't dare—relax. In fact, as she sat ramrod straight, trying to avoid all contact with his upper body, periodic tremors swept her. If Rathe noticed, he said nothing. The tension she felt in him terrified her.

He did not turn his stallion toward Upper Street where Harriet Gold's boardinghouse was. Grace was afraid to ask where he was taking her. Her eyes widened when they arrived at Silver Street, then turned left toward the cliffs. As if sensing her confusion, his grip tightened. Rathe pulled up in front of the Silver Lady Hotel. Grace stared, full of dread.

He slid to the ground, then pulled her down as if she were a sack of grain. For some reason her knees were very weak and they buckled the instant her feet touched down. Rathe was there, his steely arm going around her waist, and he held her in such a way that she had no choice but to walk with him as they entered the hotel.

"Rathe . . ."

"Shut up."

He led her up the stairs and to his suite. He didn't release her as he produced a key, and opened the door on the beautifully appointed rooms she had seen the other day. Grace found herself pushed inside. She stood unsteadily on a thick Aubusson rug, looking around, thinking, This is insane. Then she heard the door lock and her head whipped around. Her anxious gaze found Rathe's.

He was so grim and cold she took a step backward. "I'm going home," she quavered.

"Just who in hell do you think you are?"

"I'm going home now," she managed, and started past him.

He grabbed her, spinning her back around. She was in his arms. His entire body felt like a tightly coiled spring. "Does facing death excite you, Grace, is that it?"

She shook her head weakly, mortified with the knowledge that at any moment she was going to start bawling like a newborn infant.

"Do you even care if you die?" he demanded.

She choked on a huge sob.

"I brought you here to beat the hell out of you," Rathe rasped. "But I've never laid a hand in violence on a woman in my life!"

The words weren't even out of his mouth when he was lifting her and carrying her to the huge, canopied bed.

The sob blossomed uncontrollably in her chest, rising upward inexorably.

The bed sank beneath her body's weight, Rathe coming down on top of her. His hands caught hunks of her hair ruthlessly, anchoring her head, hurting her scalp. She tried to fight down the rush of tears. One of his thighs jammed crudely between hers. And then his lips came down, hard and hot.

He forced her lips open, and shoved his tongue thickly into her mouth. She tried to turn her head, and found herself trapped by his hands. His mouth ground ruthlessly on hers. He was already hard and huge against her belly. She knew beyond a doubt that he knew he was hurting her, that for some reason he was trying to prove his mastery over her—in the only way left to him. And she knew he was going to take her tonight whether she wanted him to or not.

The knowledge meant nothing.

He was warm. He was man. He was strong—he was life and safety. She had faced violence and terror, but she was secure in Rathe's arms. She wrapped her arms around him, clinging fiercely.

He buried his face in her neck, hugging her desperately.

Grace choked out loud on the first sob. The second sob was inhuman, sounding more like an animal in great pain. On top of her, Rathe went still. And she started crying—completely, hysterically, pitifully.

For one more moment Rathe froze, then he closed his eyes and rolled over, gathering her even more tightly against him. She wept then, against his linen-clad chest. "Grace," he said raggedly, "it's all right now."

She moaned, shaking, clinging. He held her, stroked her, rocked her. She wept uncontrollably, trying to burrow into his skin. When, a long time later, the tears rolled to a jagged stop, she found herself utterly exhausted, in his arms and between his thighs. His shirt was partially opened, and her cheek was somehow against his bare chest, wet from her tears, in a nest of surprisingly soft brown curls. One of his large hands was on her waist, sliding gently up and down from her hip to her rib cage. The other held the back of her head. Her braid had long since come free. The feel of him stroking her hair was exquisitely reassuring. She gave a long, drawn-out sigh.

"Better?" he asked, and she thought, although she wasn't sure, that his mouth grazed the top of her head.

She was so tired her answer was barely audible. She was so tired that she didn't care how she lay, not even the way her hip nestled intimately in his groin. She rubbed her face more fully into his chest, and immediately fell asleep.

The next morning when she awoke, she was still in his bed and still in his arms.

Chapter 16

Rathe woke up first. He didn't move. His entire body was burning with the same uncontrollable lust it had burned with all night. Never, in his entire life, had he slept chastely with a lush woman. And there was no doubt that the woman in his arms was lush.

They were on their sides, her back wedged into his front. Her soft buttocks cradled his throbbing groin, his swollen organ nestled deliciously and agonizingly in the warm valley she provided. He had his arms around her. Her breathing was steady and slow; his was harsh and loud. Cautiously, he raised himself up on one elbow and looked down at her.

So impossibly gorgeous. His hand stole to her slim, curved hip, slid higher, wrinkling the cotton of her nightgown, slid lower. He pulled her more firmly against his thickened manhood, leaned down, and nuzzled her jaw. She sighed.

"Grace?" he whispered, a hoarse, gravelly sound.

There was no response.

He rubbed his hips languidly against her, his eyes closed, his face contorted, pained. He bent over again, his mouth inches from her ear. "Grace?"

She pushed her backside against him.

He groaned and slid his hand up to cup her ripe breast. The nipple hardened instantly beneath his fingers. She shifted, still asleep, pushing herself more fully into his

palm. He knew he was being a cad. He opened the ribbons
of her gown and bared her beautiful breasts.

With his tongue, he touched one pointed nipple.

She whimpered, her lashes fluttering.

Rathe was clad only in his breeches, and they felt very
tight and constraining. He wished he had taken them off,
then instantly knew that would have precipitated a crisis.
He pushed his thigh between hers, moving it back and
forth.

Grace sighed, her lids drifting open.

His hand had its own volition. He found himself lifting
the hem of her gown, sliding his palm along the smooth,
firm yet soft contours of her thigh, her hip, to the soft,
slight swell of her belly. He raised himself up a bit more
to watch her face as his hand traced small, intimate circles on her stomach, roaming lower and lower. He
watched the haze of sleep leave her eyes. Their gazes
met, his bold, brilliant, hers soft, startled. His fingers
touched the outermost edges of a soft, red vee. Grace
gasped. Rathe threaded his fingers through the untamable
curls. She shifted onto her back with a deep breath, her
eyes closing, thighs opening. Rathe could barely breathe.
His third finger slipped down between thick, slick folds
of flesh.

She moaned softly.

He felt her swelling beneath his hand. She arched
slightly. Rathe couldn't stand it. But he couldn't, in all
conscience, make love to her while she was half-asleep.
Still . . .

He shifted onto his knees between her parted legs, kissing her navel, nuzzling her breasts. "Grace," he commanded. "Wake up, Gracie. Wake up."

"Rathe," she breathed, her lashes dark fans against her
pale skin.

He bent lower and touched her pink, glistening flesh
with his tongue.

Grace moaned and twisted languidly.

Rathe's arms went around her hips, locking them into

place. With his tongue he began a delicate exploration.
His heart threatened to pound its way right out of his chest.
And he wondered if he might split his breeches, he was
so full. She lifted for him, toward him, with another
whimper, a pleading sound that almost made him insane
with desire. He lifted his head abruptly. "Grace, wake
up."

Her eyes flickered open.

He bent to nuzzle with his mouth and stroke with his
tongue.

She gasped.

He raised up. "Grace, look at me."

Her glazed, unfocused eyes met his.

He felt a hot bursting of triumph at seeing her like this,
languid with desire for him. "Tell me what you want,
sweetheart," he commanded thickly. And, with strategic
timing, he flicked his tongue against her again.

She writhed, falling back against the pillows. Rathe
licked and explored, pressing his own heavy weight hard
into the mattress. He still wasn't satisfied and it gnawed
at him. He finally lifted his powerful body up and caught
a hank of her hair, his face inches from hers. "Grace,
dammit, look at me!"

She looked at him.

He kissed her deeply, dominatingly, rubbing the steel-
hardness of his groin against her wet heat. She moved
sinuously with him, seeking. He caught her chin. Her eyes
locked with his. "Rathe," she gasped.

He didn't give her a chance, but was back between her
legs, intent on devastating her. Grace touched his bare
shoulders as his tongue sought, found, and conquered.
She fell back, her grip tightening, her hips arching on a
long whimper. "Please," she cried.

She arched violently moments later, crying out, and
he felt the hard contractions against his face. He didn't
mean to lose control. She was still in the throes when
he felt his own explosion as he lay grinding against the

mattress, his face buried in her, his arms locked around her hips.

It took a long time for them both to subside.

Then he was rudely kneed in the face as she swung her legs over him in a panic. Still recovering, Rathe wasn't ready to move. He felt her bouncing out of the bed. "Get up," she said furiously.

He realized he had made a mistake. He should have recovered instantly, pulled her into his arms, and showered her with loving kisses. A not-so-soft blow landed on his bicep.

"Get up!"

Wearily, Rathe rolled over and sat up.

She was enraged, and gorgeous in her Irish temper.

"Grace . . ."

"You took advantage of me," she hissed.

He couldn't exactly refute that. "But it was so good, Grace. You know that."

"The only thing I know is that you are despicable!"

"I don't seem to have any control around you," Rathe said, intensely. "And it's been that way since the moment we first met."

She turned her back to him, arms folded tightly.

"It's the truth." He came up behind her. "Dammit, Grace, stop fighting me—didn't I just give you a taste of how good it can be?" He reached for her shoulders.

She turned and her hand swung out. He didn't duck, not because he was feeling charitable, which he was, but because he had hardly slept at all last night, which made his reflexes slow. "Ow. That hurt."

"Oh, dear Lord," Grace suddenly said, her flaming cheeks draining of color. Rathe rubbed his jaw. "Grace, can we be calm about this? Let's order up some breakfast and talk this over."

Her hand was clasped over her mouth, her eyes huge. "I spent the night here!"

"You fell asleep."

"This is all your fault! You should have never let me

stay! Why did you even bring me back here?'' she wailed.

Rathe blinked. ''You were hysterical, in shock . . .''

''You did this on purpose!'' She whipped around and this time he ducked her right hook, but caught her wrist.

''Grace, stop it. I'm sorry, I wasn't thinking clearly myself. It felt so right, holding you while you slept.''

''You've ruined me!''

He felt a sudden, terrible pang. He had the dreadful feeling he had made a mistake. ''Grace?''

She wrenched away and he let her go. ''Clothes,'' she cried. ''How will I get to Harriet's in my nightgown and skirt? And where *is* my skirt? What time is it? I'm going to be late for school!''

''I'll run to Harriet's and get you a dress,'' he said, feeling guilt welling up in him. ''Grace, I didn't think . . . when you fell asleep . . .''

''When have you ever thought with anything other than what's in your pants,'' she snapped.

That hurt. He went to the wardrobe stiffly and produced a shirt, then remembered the stain on his breeches. He shed them casually, ignoring her gasp. As soon as he had changed pants and donned his boots, he left without another word.

Grace sank trembling onto the bed. She hugged herself. Her reputation was ruined. Natchez was a small town where gossip traveled fast. She would never find respectable employment here—not now.

Her mind refused to dwell on that. Instead, it rehearsed in precise detail what he had done to her and her unabashed response. Grace was an intelligent woman. She understood the facts of life. But she had never, ever dreamed an act like the one they had practiced could exist.

An act? No, a perversion. She clenched her fists. Of course he would know all the perversions—even if they were wonderful!

She wanted to weep. She wanted to hit him. At the same

time, she wanted, traitorously, to crawl back into bed and wait for Rathe to return, hold out her arms to him and welcome him into her embrace. He was so warm, so hard, so male. So handsome.

Such a bastard.

She closed her eyes, picturing him as he calmly shed his breeches, not even bothering to turn his back to her. His shoulders were broad and strong, his chest well-developed and powerful-looking. He had arms and legs like the classical sculptures of Greek athletes. And his manhood . . .

She hadn't meant to look.

She hadn't been able not to.

She had to pull herself together before he returned, better yet, find a maid, borrow some clothes, and leave before he came back. Ten minutes later, Grace did just that.

It should have been a normal school day. Yet Grace didn't think her life would ever be normal again. As she stood in front of her students that day, Grace had great difficulty concentrating. *He* intruded upon her thoughts constantly. So did the events of the night before, the violence and the terror. Because of the role she had played in them, she had become something of a heroine, with her pupils hanging avidly onto her every distracted word. She was also remembering the pointed look Rawlins had directed at her, its lingering threat. She began to wish that she hadn't run out that morning without seeing Rathe again.

He had said he would come to school every day to escort her home. Would he? Or would he be so annoyed with her for that parting insult that he'd decide she could fend for herself? More importantly, did she have something to fear from Rawlins and his cohorts? As the day ticked away, her feeling of dread grew.

The church and yard finally emptied at three-fifteen. Grace stood on the steps, glancing around. There was no sign of either Rathe or Rawlins. The knot of fear loosened slightly. Of course, Rawlins wouldn't appear—he had been shot last night. And as for Rathe, obviously he hadn't meant it when he had said he would take her home every day. Obviously he didn't care, which was fine with her.

It was a blatant lie. She could not keep pretending, even to herself, that she was indifferent to him. At the very least, she was disappointed that he hadn't come.

She was halfway home when she heard the horse approaching from behind her.

Every muscle in her body went stiff and she turned, clutching her books. It was only a farmer with a buckboard. He offered her a ride. Grace was about to accept when she saw Rathe cantering up the road on his big black stallion. She froze, then quickly reached for the wagon, about to climb in. She had one foot on the sideboard when he spoke from behind her.

"I said I'd be here and I'm here." He moved the stallion closer, reaching out his hand. "Get up."

"No thank you," she said rigidly. "This kind farmer has offered to drive me to town."

"He going to defend you from Rawlins' buddies?" Rathe asked coldly. "Get over here, Grace."

"That's okay, ma'am," the farmer said nervously. "I doan mind you ridin' with the gent'man." He raised the reins and clucked his mule forward.

Grace glared furiously. "You intimidated him!"

"He probably found the threat of Rawlins more intimidating."

"I'm walking," Grace said.

"Fine."

She didn't look at him again. He rode his horse at a slow pace right behind her, so close that once or twice Grace could feel the animal's warm breath on her nape. She kept her shoulders squared and her head held high. *He* was angry! Well, she was just as angry—no, angrier!

When they arrived back at Harriet's she hurried ahead

of him into the house. She passed several boarders on the veranda when she went in. One of them flashed her a grin, a very lewd kind of grin. His rummy-card partner, an older gentleman, gave her a clearly disapproving look and picked up his hand. Grace hurried inside.

She was still smarting under both the censoring and the grin when she came face to face with Harriet. "Good afternoon, Harriet," she began warmly. "How—"

Harriet bustled past after throwing her a dark glance.

Oh dear, Grace thought. *The story is out.*

"Grace?"

She froze. It was Allen's voice; he was calling from his bedroom down the hall. He called again. Afraid he would try and get out of bed, she hurried to his room. He was sitting propped up, looking much better. Her chest was tight with anxiety. "Allen, hello. How are you feeling today?"

He didn't answer, just stared at her as she approached.

She made a fuss of fixing his pillows. "Can I bring you something?"

"Is it true?"

She blanched. "Is what true?"

"You spent the night at the Silver Lady Hotel."

She went red. What could she possibly say? It was true. But it wasn't exactly what it appeared to be—or was it? They had been intimate, even if in some unusual, perverted way. Biting her lip, she sank onto the foot of the bed.

Allen looked away.

"It's not exactly what you think, Allen."

"You spent the night with him, didn't you," Allen said, distraught and hurt.

"I fell asleep," Grace said defensively.

"Is that all?"

Color swept over her face.

"Oh, God," Allen moaned. "Do you love him?"

"It's not like that at all," Grace cried, standing. "I didn't mean for it to happen. I didn't mean to stay the night—oh, damn!'' Whether from the tension of the entire day, or something else, deeper and more insistent, tears filled her eyes.

"Grace, I'm sorry," Allen said, taking her hand.

She sank back down by his hip. "It wasn't the way you think," she sobbed. "I tried to stop a whipping. Rathe saved me. I was so afraid. He took me to that hotel. I was in shock. Then I fell asleep."

"I'm sorry," Allen said, easing her into his arms. "That wasn't fair of me. You must love him very much."

"No, I don't," Grace gasped, pulling back.

"How damn cozy," Rathe drawled from the open doorway.

Grace stiffened.

Allen glared. "If I was a whole man, Bragg, I'd break your nose."

"You could try," Rathe said with clearly false pleasantry. Grace didn't turn to look at him, but she could feel his smoldering presence. Then she heard him stomping away. She realized she was barely breathing.

"Are you all right?" Allen asked.

Grace nodded. But she wasn't. And soon it got worse, because a letter with the mayor's seal was waiting for her beneath her door. This time she felt absolute dread as she picked it up and opened it. Sheinreich was precise and to the point. She was dismissed, for reasons of moral unsuitability.

At the sharp rapping on his door, Rathe moved to open it. He felt his entire body go taut with anger as he stared at Grace. He hadn't forgiven her for what she'd said—or for the fact that she had left that morning without waiting for him to return.

"May I come in?" she finally said, staring back at him.

"Finished with Allen already?" he asked snidely. He couldn't help it. Since last night, feelings of possessiveness had overwhelmed him—and something else, something like dismay. He had overheard her vehemently telling Allen that she didn't love him.

"I wish to discuss a matter with you," she said, her chin coming up. "And I'd prefer not discussing it out in the hall."

Rathe stepped aside, making a grand gesture with his arm. Grace walked rigidly past him, paused in the center of the room, then turned to face him. Rathe folded his arms and waited.

"Could you close the door?" she asked.

He shrugged and complied.

"I believe you owe me some money."

"I do?"

A pink tide swept her face. "Yes."

"For what?"

"For—er—services rendered."

He wanted to hit her.

Rathe walked stiff-legged to the window and opened it, hoping for a cool breeze to ease his own burning anger. Unfortunately, only muggy air touched his face. He counted to ten—three times. Then he turned. "What services, exactly, are we talking about?"

"You know exactly what we're talking about," Grace snapped, her fists clenched.

He raised a surprisingly nonchalant brow. "Darlin', I do believe you're mixed up. A man does not pay for what occurred this morning—on the contrary."

She was confused and angry. "Don't think you can twist things around."

"If anyone owes anybody," Rathe said, wanting to kill her, "you owe me."

She blinked.

"I performed for you, darlin', not the other way around."

She gasped.

"I pleasured you," he said crudely, cruelly. "Quite thoroughly, if I recall." He paused. "Although not as thoroughly as I'd like to."

She took a step back, her face white.

Rathe felt like the cad she was constantly accusing him of being. But he couldn't stop, not when she had come prancing in here perverting his offer and everything he felt for her by turning herself into a whore. "If you would like, we can rectify that immediately."

"I didn't come here to be insulted," Grace said tightly.

"No? Tell me, Grace, why did you come? To insult me—to insult us? Again?"

"I'm leaving." But she didn't move.

"Why did you run out on me this morning?" Rathe demanded.

She flushed. "I was late."

"It was only seven o'clock."

"I thought it was later."

They both knew she was lying. "You could have waited for me to return with your clothes. I would have driven you to the school."

"I didn't want to wait."

His smile held no humor. "Yes, you made that very clear." His jaw tightened visibly. "Are you going to spend your entire life running, Grace?"

Her nostrils flared. "I am not running!"

"No? You've sure fooled me."

"I told you a long time ago, Mr. Bragg, that you do not scare me. Therefore, it is impossible for me to be running from you!"

"Ahh! So you admit you're running from me!"

"I did not admit any such thing!"

"You're thinking it or you wouldn't have said it."

"You're impossible—impossibly conceited."

"Go ahead and run, Grace," Rathe said harshly. "Run as hard and as fast as you can. But don't lie to yourself. You *are* running, from me, and from your feelings for me."

She was trembling, her chest heaving.

"And remember this," he said, his gaze searing, "I am a man. I can run faster, and I can run farther. You can't escape me, Grace, and you can't escape your feelings, either—not even if you run to China.''

For a beat, Grace stared at him. Then she turned and fled.

Chapter 17

Grace woke the next morning feeling desperate. She had no job, no money, and a fistful of her mother's medical bills that were all long past due. Thanks to Rathe Bragg, she had no prospects either, for clearly everyone in Natchez knew about the night she'd spent with him.

Nevertheless, she dressed to hunt for a job, thinking she'd check back in at a few of the clifftop hotels. She didn't hold out much hope, though, because even if one of them had an opening, she'd be viewed as a pariah. She stopped in the middle of brushing her hair, covered her face with her hands, and began to consider the worst.

If worse came to worse, could she bring herself to go to work on Silver Street? What a hypocrite she'd appear! But then, Natchez already considered her a branded woman, so what difference did it make?

Damn! It made a difference to her; she was a woman of principles who condemned the businesses conducted in those dens of iniquity along Silver Street . . . prostitution, gambling, drinking. But she needed a job; principles wouldn't pay for her mother's hospital care.

Grace was halfway to the cliffs, preoccupied with her worries about money, trying not to think of that impossible cad, Rathe, and agonized over the fact that now the Negro children had no teacher. How soon would a replacement be found? Would the mayor even bother to actively recruit one? After all, Dr. Lang had said that Allen could return in a month. But one month was one month, and those children needed their schooling.

That precipitated a dangerous thought. Who was to stop her from organizing an informal class? Wasn't her time her own to give? She grew excited, so excited that she almost walked right past Sarah Bellsley and Martha Grimes without seeing them. "Sarah, Martha, hello," she cried, realizing that the next temperance meeting was coming up very soon. "When is the meeting," she began, then stopped abruptly.

Martha was averting her eyes; Sarah was staring her down with pure contempt. "I'm afraid, Miss O'Rourke," she said frostily, "that our meetings are only open to *ladies*." She barreled past, with Martha on her heels.

Grace stared after her, feeling stunned and hurt. And even though she knew why she had been treated so rudely, she didn't want to believe it. With her chin up, her lips pursed, telling herself *It does not matter,* she marched to the first hotel on the cliffs—the Silver Lady.

Instantaneously, she was flooded with memories. It had only been yesterday that she had awakened in Rathe's strong arms. She could still feel his hard body against hers. Her blood began to race.

There was absolutely no way she could work there. She bypassed the establishment. On the next block was a sprawling brick edifice called the Southern Star. Since she had already tried all these hotels previously, she knew exactly who to ask for. The owner was a portly gentleman who had offered her tea the other day and shared some innocent gossip. Today, his expression was full of contempt. "Even if there was something available, Miss O'Rourke, I don't think you and the position would suit."

Even though she'd been expecting just such a reception, Grace was devastated. But fists clenched, she tried the rest of the hotels, with the same results. Outside the last one, she had to fight not to give in to tears.

Grace was tired and demoralized, but she could not give up. She knew she had to venture into Silver Street. This was the one area of town she had never attempted to find work in before—so the prospects were actually better. It was just so very hard to believe that she had been reduced to these straits.

Grace paused at the first hotel she came to, the Golden Door. She peeked inside, and panicked. It was dark, dank, the floors filthy, the furniture scarred and broken, and it stank of sweat, beer, and cigars. Clearly she could not work in this sort of establishment. She backed hastily out, aware of the frantic hammering of her heart. She ignored the rest of the hotels for the same reasons, then found herself in front of one of the saloons.

Oh dear, she thought, standing on the boardwalk and clutching the railing. Did she have a choice? Did it even matter? Didn't the way she had just been treated by Sarah and Martha and all the hoteliers on the cliffs prove that where she worked didn't matter? What did she have to lose, now? And why was she once again on the verge of tears?

She had already learned one lesson in the past hour, so it was easy to realize she had little choice when it came to the saloons, for most were as raunchy and rank as the Golden Door. She already knew that the Black Heel was the most elegant saloon in town, boasting the most elite clientele. But there was no way she would work there— not when *he* was a regular.

She strode resolutely past, finally deciding on an obvious runner-up as far as quality went—if such a word could be used in describing any kind of saloon. Max's wasn't bad. The floors were polished oak, the bar mahogany, although it lacked the fine brass trimming and the ornate mirrors of the Black Heel. Grace tried to ignore the paintings of lush nudes gracing the pine walls. She took a few deep breaths, and shoved through the swinging doors.

It was the middle of the day and the saloon was quiet, with only a half dozen customers, the bartender polishing glasses and bottles, and a man sitting in the back at a table with papers spread out before him. Grace approached the barman, feeling very self-conscious and very out of place. He looked up and studied her speculatively. "Lady, you lost?"

"No, I'm not," Grace said in her clipped northern accent. Knowing that now was not the time for her careful diction to emerge, she tried to soften her tone. "Is the owner or manager around?"

"Right here."

Grace turned to the man who had risen and approached. He was in his fifties, broad-shouldered and a bit portly, his dark hair streaked with silver. "I'm Grace O'Rourke," she murmured, wanting to back out now, before it was too late.

"Yeah, I know," he said grinning. "I'm Dan Reid. A redheaded schoolteacher isn't too easy to miss."

Her tension increased because she recognized the gleam in his dark eyes. "Mr. Reid—"

"Dan."

"Dan." She swallowed. "I'm afraid I am out of employment." She turned her violet eyes on him with a consciously appealing look. "I have a mother in New York who is ill and needs constant medical care. I'm desperate. Although I am a teacher, I need a job."

Dan's eyes were wide. "You asking me to hire you?"

"Yes." She quickly added, "But only to serve drinks, Mr.—uh—Dan."

He grinned. "He know about this?"

"Excuse me?"

"Bragg. He know you're here?"

Grace went crimson, her mouth tightening. "I assure you, I am my own woman."

"Yeah? I don't want any trouble with the likes of Bragg."

That possibility had not occurred to Grace. "There will be no trouble."

"Good." He looked her up and down. His gaze lingered on her breasts, flattened by their binding, then on her tightly pulled-back hair. "Take down your hair."

"Excuse me?"

"Take down your hair. I want to see how you look with it down."

She opened her mouth to protest. Only an angry exhalation came out.

He held up a hand. "You're pretty in a prudish way, even if you are a bit long in the tooth. I don't need a prudish-looking schoolmarm working here. My customers want to see pretty young girls."

Feeling like a cow at auction, Grace slowly pulled the pins out of her hair and let the wild mass fall past her hips.

"Holy Christ," Dan said, picking up a heavy strand and fingering it. "I don't think I've ever seen hair like yours before."

"Do I have the job or not, Dan?"

"You got it. You can start tonight. You come by at five an' ask Lisa for something to wear." He looked at her as she blanched. "You can't work like that."

"I realize that," Grace managed. "How much do you pay?"

"Five dollars a week and the tips are your own."

Grace was stunned at the generous sum. "Do—do the girls make a lot of tips?"

He gave her a look. "If they work hard enough." He grinned. "In fact, take the customers upstairs and you'll make a fortune."

"I think I already made myself quite clear on that point," Grace said.

He chuckled. "You really are pretty. But honey, you talk like some spinster schoolmarm and you won't make a cent. Take my advice. You got to be sweet and soft and make the customer feel like he's special."

"I'll try and remember that," Grace said stiffly, then escaped back into the street.

By that evening, Rathe had calmed down over Grace's attempt to collect money from him. Of course, he still felt

an urgency, a restlessness, a barely containable need—and
it all centered around her. He couldn't go on much longer
like this. He wasn't used to this kind of treatment. He was
used to women who wanted him and leapt at his beckoning
finger.

But Grace—Grace was an entirely different story. He
knew her well enough now to know that he could beckon
from now until doomsday, and she wouldn't give in. Even
if he had deflowered her last night and brought her to the
heights of ecstasy, she would still refuse him. He could
not wait until doomsday. As far as he was concerned, he
had waited long enough. His patience was gone. He
wanted Grace at his side.

Which was why he was sitting here thinking about marriage.

He had always intended to get married eventually.
Maybe now was the time for him to think about settling
down, building a home, raising a family. A wonderful
image came to him suddenly of Grace cradling their baby
in her arms. It moved him.

He would gladly give her anything and everything she
wanted. The finest home, in New York, London, Paris,
anywhere she wanted. Silks, furs, jewels, horses, paintings, sculpture . . . Then he grinned. *Am I thinking about
Grace O'Rourke?*

He tried to imagine being married to Grace. He figured
she would be perfectly content with a cottage and modest
clothes. Rathe knew he didn't have a modest bone in his
body. He imagined spending a lifetime trying to teach her
to be immodest—it was a wonderful thought.

He would probably spend the rest of his life extracting
her from danger, too. For some reason, the idea tempted
him immensely. God knew, someone had to look after her!

Rathe grew excited. He was truly sorry that he hadn't
been thoughtful enough to send her home the night before
last. But now, now he couldn't help being a bit pleased
with the way it had turned out. He knew that they were
the gossip of the town. That suited him just fine. Now it

was his responsibility to marry her, after being the instrument of her downfall. He grinned. The idea of marrying her was appealing to him more and more every minute.

Then he thought about Allen. His smile disappeared. Apparently, Grace had rejected Allen. A niggling thought invaded: she might reject him, too! Rathe refused to entertain it. It was one thing for her to reject his proposition, another for her to reject his proposal. He was one of the most eligible bachelors in the country, handsome, wealthy, and successful. No woman could possibly turn down his suit.

Rathe, his mind made up, went directly to the finest jeweler in town, to purchase the biggest diamond he could find. Stern's was renowned for its jewelry, having catered to the great Natchez planters for the last fifty years. There he found a twelve-carat yellow diamond that was nearly flawless. He tried to imagine her expression when she saw it. She would gaze at him out of stunned violet eyes. Then she would smile. Tears might appear. She would bite her lip in that nervous manner she had, then fling her arms around him, crying, "Yes, oh yes!"

That evening Grace did not join them for supper at the boardinghouse, and no one knew where she was. Rathe found himself unable to eat and thoroughly distracted, a hundred thoughts racing through his mind. Knowing Grace, he figured she was in some kind of trouble. He finally excused himself early and went straight to Allen's room.

Allen was reading, and he laid aside the book to greet Rathe quietly. Rathe nodded back. "Allen, have you seen Grace today?"

"Yes, twice," Allen said.

Rathe felt a surging of jealousy. He hadn't even seen her once. "When?" he asked, quite calmly.

"This morning and this afternoon," Allen said, trying to straighten further. "Is something wrong?"

"No, not really," Rathe said, not wanting to worry him, not when he was bedridden.

"Isn't she at supper?"

"I forgot," Rathe lied. "There's a ladies' meeting tonight."

"Of course," Allen said, smiling fondly. "Grace would never miss a ladies' meeting."

If only there *was* a ladies' meeting. Rathe prowled about the front and back parlors. His feeling of imminent disaster grew. No one, including Harriet, knew where Grace was. Frustrated and anxious, Rathe finally slipped out the door and headed to town, hoping to run into her. He finally stopped in at the Black Heel for a badly needed drink.

He was in that establishment for exactly three minutes when he heard the news. His friend and fellow card sharp, George Farris, bought him a drink with the funniest twinkle in his eyes.

"Thanks," Rathe said with grim preoccupation.

"You look like you need it."

"I do." He downed it in one swallow.

George chuckled. "Never thought I'd see the day."

Rathe scowled. "George, how come I get the feeling you're just dying to spit something out? What day?"

"The day one of your women wears the pants in your household."

Every nerve ending in his body went on alert. "What?"

"Or maybe she isn't your woman—is that it?" His grin widened. "I can't imagine you letting her work like that."

"Are we talking about Grace?"

"Yeah. If she's not your mistress, I sure wouldn't mind a crack at her myself."

The words weren't out of his mouth when Rathe was standing and hauling George to his feet, about to slam a punch into his face. George raised his hands in surrender. Rathe realized he was about to hit a friend, and released him. "Spit it all out. Where is she?"

"Down the street at Max's."

The dress—if it could be called a dress—was much, much worse than she expected. The skirt consisted of black lace over red satin. It came to her calves in the back but only to her knees in the front. The bodice was unadorned except for black pearl buttons and seams of inlaid black lace. It was most certainly too small. She knew she didn't dare bend over or reach down for fear of losing what little cover she had.

She didn't know if she could go through with this. It was not just that it was the height of hypocrisy. She was against saloons and the excess consumption of spirits. But . . . five dollars a week. It was a fortune, enough to pay her mother's bills. And if she made tips . . .

The problem was, she was scared. Scared to walk down the stairs in this costume. Scared of this job. Scared of those men. Just plain scared.

The high, narrow heels were treacherous to walk in. Grace descended the stairs with difficulty. She could not control the flaming of her face. She reminded herself that this was business; she was desperate for the money; and these men were ignorant wastrels, greatly inferior to herself.

She did not feel better, especially not when whistles and catcalls greeted her.

Dan came over, his gaze admiring, repeatedly returning to her voluptuous breasts. "Jesus," he said. "You sure know how to hide your looks, don't you?"

He was the boss, but she hated the way he was regarding her, so she ignored him. Unfortunately, as she sailed past, she caught her heel between the planking and fell on her face.

Ten men rushed to help her up before she could even move.

As they lifted her to her feet she checked her bodice—thank God it was still where it was supposed to be—and she tugged it up. She stared at the floor and whispered, inaudibly, "Thank you." She was in dire jeopardy of crying.

"You all right?" one of them asked.

"Honey, you look like you need a drink," another commented.

"You like to dance, gal?" came yet another hot, breathy voice at her ear.

The barrage was endless. Grace summoned up every ounce of determination she had. She lifted her eyes and managed a smile, a fragile one. She could feel that her cheeks were burning. Someone groped at her thigh. Grace sucked back an angry cry. The men dispersed, looking as hungry as starving wolves, none of them able to take their eyes off of her. Dan grabbed her arm. "Go to that table and get their orders," he said.

Grace was grateful to have something to do. She approached, very careful of her heels, avoiding all eye contact. She realized she was lucky she hadn't broken her ankle. It was just another example of female slavery, she thought. Put them in high heels so they can't walk—that will keep them in their place!

She was serving a tableful of admirers sometime later, careful not to bend over too far, ignoring a few indecent proposals, sidestepping groping hands the best she could, when a hushed silence fell on the saloon. Grace looked up . . . and held her breath.

Rathe stood in the doorway absolutely red in the face.

Her very first reaction was one of relief—she half-hoped he had come to rescue her. Then her chest grew tight with humiliation. She didn't want him here. She didn't need this on top of everything else. And why was he so angry? She had never seen his color so high. Then it dawned on her—she had enraged him by being here—and she felt a little thrill at her ability to provoke him so.

But then it hit her. They all know, she thought. They all know we shared a room in the hotel. They all think I'm his mistress. Oh, no!

Rathe walked stiffly to a table, pulled out a chair and sat down. He looked right at Grace. "I want service," he said, his voice ringing out.

Everyone started talking at once.

Rathe wasn't sitting at her table, and even if he was, she had no intention of waiting on him. She smiled at the men in front of her, despite the hollowness she was feeling. "Can I get you all anything else?" Her voice was octaves too high.

Rathe scowled at the pretty brunette who came to his table. "I want the redhead," he told her in a tone that was completely uncompromising.

The brunette tried for a smile. "But honey, she's busy. 'Sides, this ain't her table."

Rathe rose abruptly and pointed. "That her table?"

"Yes," the woman said, eyes wide.

A look of deadly satisfaction crossed his features and he changed tables, once more hushing the saloon. He sat facing Grace, and looked directly at her. "A double bourbon, the best in the house."

Grace clenched her jaw. She was not going to wait on him. He was doing this on purpose, to demoralize her. She turned her back and sailed away, forgetting her heels. Once again she went down on her face.

This time over a dozen men leapt to her aid, but Rathe didn't move.

Before she could catch her breath they were fighting for the honor of helping her up.

Meanwhile Grace yanked her bodice up to cover one almost bared breast, her face flaming, still sitting sprawled on the floor.

"You all right?" asked the man who seemed to have won the right to help Grace.

Grace blinked back tears. She didn't dare look at Rathe. She could feel his gaze burning on her. "Yes, fine," she whispered, letting him pull her up.

It was a mistake. The man was as much a rogue as a gentleman, and he deftly used the opportunity to maneuver her into his arms, holding her pressed there briefly. Grace quickly disengaged herself. She didn't mean to look at *him,* but she couldn't help herself.

He was blazing mad.

Grace turned her back to him, feeling both frightened and embarrassed, wishing this evening was over. She walked very carefully to the bar, ignoring a few of the girls' mean snickers.

At his table, Rathe sat with clenched fists. If he weren't the man he was, he would give in to the rage he was feeling, and haul her outside upside down and spank her soundly . . . then make love to her until she begged for mercy, until she was so sore she couldn't move—maybe even keep her a prisoner in his bed. The fantasy grew.

In a second, it vanished, leaving him humiliated. No woman had ever treated him this way before, much less *publicly*. And she was treating herself like a whore. He decided, in that instant, if she didn't bring him a drink immediately he would carry her out and fulfill every one of his dark, angry fantasies.

Dan clapped his hand on Grace's shoulder. "I don't care that you're having a lover's spat," he said. "He's sitting at your table and that makes him one of your customers. Get him his drink."

Grace went scarlet with frustrated, shamed anger, but she brought him his drink, her chin up. His blue eyes burned, unwavering, promising dire consequences. She slapped the glass down so hard half of it spilled. He looked at the puddle, then at her. "Looks like you'll have to bring me another one."

She glared.

He downed the glass. Grace turned to leave. He caught her wrist, yanking her around and pulling her abruptly onto his lap. Grace gasped, but couldn't disengage herself from his iron grip.

His hand caught a hank of her hair, like a leash, stilling her instantly. "What are you trying to prove?"

"Nothing!"

Dan came over. "Rathe, I don't want any trouble here."

Rathe smiled and thrust a wad of bills into Dan's hand. "This buy her time for the evening?"

Dan pocketed the money and walked away.

Grace felt sick. Rathe had just purchased her. She felt like a prostitute. "Let me up." She was very close to tears.

"What are you trying to prove?" he snarled. "Or are you just trying to humiliate me? Isn't that what this is all about?"

His breath was hot on her face. He smelled of bourbon. "No," she said, trying not to break down. "I need the money."

"Enough to whore for it?"

She tried to slap him. He caught her wrist without releasing her hair and crushed her more fully against him.

"I don't understand," he said with twisted lips. "Why here when you could be whoring for me?"

She cried out at his cruel words.

Rathe took a deep breath. He cursed. Then he was on his feet, pulling her up with him. He half-dragged her outside. On the street he turned her to face him. He saw her tears and groaned. "Ah, don't cry. Grace . . ."

"Please don't do this," she whispered, wiping her eyes, looking at the ground.

Rathe sucked in his breath, then took her into his arms. He held her. "That was the stupidest thing you've ever done."

Secretly, Grace agreed with him. "I had no choice."

He stroked her hair. "You have a choice. The perfect choice." He tilted her face up. "Marry me."

She stared, shocked.

The question had popped out. Rathe was suddenly flustered, apprehensive. "I'm a wealthy man, Grace. I can take care of you and your mother. I can buy her the finest care there is, give you anything you want—anything."

"You're serious?"

"Yes."

She blinked at him. "I—I don't understand. You want to marry me?"

"You're a beautiful woman, Grace," he said huskily.

"I don't know what to say."

Rathe stared, his hold on her loosening. "What?"

Grace was overwhelmed. "I don't understand this. I thought you wanted me to be your mistress."

"I've had a change of heart."

Somehow, Allen's proposal had never felt like this. Her heart was racing madly. "I'll have to think about it," she heard herself say. Her eyes went wide—was she actually going to consider marrying this man?

"Think about it?"

Grace touched her temple, stepping away from him. Oh, dear! She had never expected this! She couldn't marry him—could she?

"You have to think about it?" he asked, strained.

"This is such a surprise," she managed. Her insides were fluttering. Did he love her? *Grace, don't be a fool! He's thinking with that male part of his anatomy again—it's only lust!*

"Do you know," Rathe said, "just how many women would jump at a proposal from me?"

She blinked. "Why, quite a few, I'm sure."

"Quite a few! Every debutante in New York City! Do you know how many debutantes there are in New York?"

Grace lifted her chin. "No, I don't. But I have a feeling you're going to tell me."

"Damn right! Hundreds. And we're only talking about New York." His eyes were blazing.

"I see," Grace said, so very calmly. "We haven't counted Paris or London yet, or New Orleans. Oh—and Texas. Why, I bet there's swarms of debutantes in Texas just waiting for a proposal from Rathe Bragg!"

He gritted his teeth.

"Well, you could always marry one of them."

He grimaced. "I have never proposed before."

Grace instantly felt horrible, despite his arrogance. "I'm sorry. I apologize. I will think about it, I promise. I'll let you know, soon."

"You'll let me know . . ." He stared. "Soon."

He was clearly upset. "Yes, soon. I really do need to consider this, Rathe."

He clenched his fists.

How can you even consider this proposal? she asked herself desperately. She looked at him standing before her, glowering. *The man has just proposed. This gorgeous man—to you!* "Rathe." She touched his sleeve. "I'm flattered, I really am. Thank you." She suddenly became aware of the saloon behind them, and stole a guilty look over her shoulder. "I'd better get back."

"You're going back in there?"

"Why, yes."

"No, you're not, Grace." It was a warning.

"You cannot tell me what to do."

"No, you're right, I can't. You want to go on in there and be treated like a whore—*when you could be my wife*—go right the hell ahead."

That was the problem. She didn't want to go back in there. Just the thought of it repulsed and scared her. She took a deep breath, for courage. She managed a smile for his benefit, because he was watching her so intently. She squared her shoulders and returned to the saloon.

Rathe moved, like lightning. He was in the saloon and approaching Dan. Grace was halfway to the bar. The conversation abruptly ceased. Grace froze, turned, saw him. Rathe halted by the owner. They exchanged a long look. Rathe never said a word.

Dan threw up his hands, an ingratiating smile on his face. "I thought she had your permission. When I hired her she said there wouldn't be any trouble. I don't want any trouble." He turned toward Grace. "Grace, I'm sorry, but you're discharged."

Grace gasped.

"Trust me, Grace," Rathe said. "This isn't the place for you."

She didn't bother to think of the consequences—or the fact that he was right. "But being your wife is?"

Rathe went red.

"I wouldn't marry you if you were the last man on earth!" She ran past him and out into the balmy Natchez night.

Chapter 18

Despite her exhaustion, she couldn't sleep.

Rathe had asked her to marry him.

She hadn't meant to embarrass him in the saloon, but she was finding it hard to believe he could want to get her into his bed so badly that he would actually offer marriage. He obviously didn't love her. That word had never been mentioned. She remembered how he had said he liked challenges—how his eyes had glinted. Was she just another challenge? One he would stop at nothing to get?

Grace tossed restlessly. After her outburst at Max's, did his offer still stand? She sat up, flipping her braid over her shoulder. Why was her heart pounding like this? There was no way she could marry him! Why, tonight had been the perfect example of how he would circumscribe her independence! He was wrong for her—in every way. Then she thought about how it felt to be in his arms, and she actually blushed.

What would it be like to be Rathe's wife? She had a fantasy of herself, elegantly gowned with diamonds in her hair, greeting Rathe in an elegant foyer as he returned home for supper. He was smiling, as was she. He held out his hand and she rushed to him. Then, from behind his back, he produced a magnificent bouquet of bright pink roses. As Grace accepted, overwhelmed, a little red-haired child suddenly ran into Rathe's embrace, shrieking, ''Papa, Papa!''

Oh, dear! She didn't even know if he wanted a family,

or where he wanted to live, or anything! And if she wanted to get married, she should marry Allen. In fact, wasn't she supposed to be considering Allen's proposal? She hadn't given it a single thought! She'd thought more about Rathe's proposal in the past hour than she'd thought about Allen's all week!

She might as well get it over with, she decided, and tell him tomorrow that they just didn't suit. She tried to imagine his reaction. He would become as angry as a bear. On the other hand, perhaps he had changed his mind. For some perverse reason, she didn't like that thought.

An inner voice said, *He's the answer to all your problems.*

"He is not," Grace said aloud. Yes, she needed the money, and she wanted him to stop Sheriff Ford from perverting the law, but that was no reason to get married. After all, she didn't love him. Slowly, she lowered her head back to the pillow. For a woman who was not in love, it seemed strange that she spent most of her waking hours thinking about him.

It's because he provokes and irritates me so thoroughly, she told the darkness.

If anything, she would rather be his kept woman than his wife. Marriage was forever, but if she was his mistress their relationship would eventually end.

Oh dear, she thought. I can't think straight, because of *him,* and I'm losing my sanity!

Next week's rent was due tomorrow. She would have to ask Harriet if she could be a few days late, which she hated doing. Harriet needed the income. She supposed she could borrow a few dollars from Allen, at least for another week's rent, but then what? Allen needed to support himself while he was recovering. She was in a terrible situation. If only Rathe hadn't gotten her discharged.

She couldn't be angry. She had hated that job. She was glad it was over.

Grace slept fitfully. She dreamed about Rathe, chasing her. At first she was running as fast as she could. But then her steps slowed, and she actually wanted him to catch her! And catch her he did. When he pulled her into his arms, to kiss her hungrily, it was so real, Grace awoke and thought it was actually happening. Her heart was pounding, her breasts throbbing. There was a wet heat between her legs, and she lay in the darkness recovering—with a sense of disappointment she refused to face.

Grace purposefully came to breakfast late, wanting to avoid Rathe. As soon as everyone else had left, Grace bit her lip and began. "Harriet . . ."

But Harriet interrupted. Clearly she had something she was anxious to say. "Grace, I just have to say my piece. I know you're different from the Southern ladies, bein' a temperance worker and a Yankee and a big-city gal. But I've got to warn you. You can't let the likes of Rathe Bragg walk all over you. He's a good boy, I know that, but you are a lady and you can't let him think otherwise—or treat you otherwise."

Grace didn't know what to do. A part of her felt defensive, the other part guilty. "What do you know about him, Harriet?"

"I know that he should know better than to be fooling with you the way he is," Harriet stated fervently. Then, "I know his folks. He comes from a good, lovin' family."

"Yes, you've mentioned that before."

"His daddy used to ride through these parts and have the same effect—set all the gals to swooning. 'Course, it was different back then, not so built up, no law and such."

"Back when?"

"In the forties and fifties."

"And his mother?"

"A beautiful little gal. I only met her once, but it was enough to know why Rathe's daddy never even looked at any of our gals. Look, Grace, I was very upset when I heard the gossip, but then I got to thinking—you can just make him marry you, you can.''

Grace bit her lip. What would Harriet say if she knew Rathe had proposed? She said, "We just don't suit, Harriet.''

She snorted. "No? He's crazy about you and you're not exactly indifferent. You're no Louisa Barclay, an' Rathe knows it. He was raised right.''

Thinking of his outrageous womanizing ways, Grace said, a touch bitterly, "You wouldn't know it from the way he acts.''

"Honey, Rathe is the youngest, and he's told me himself, he was spoiled with all the loving and attention he got from his family. Ask him about them some time. He loves them. You can tell a man by his folks, Grace, remember that.''

Grace had to ask Harriet about this week's rent. She couldn't put it off, no matter how curious she was to know more about Rathe Bragg. "Harriet? I know this is a terrible imposition, but I was hoping I might be a few days late with the rent.''

Harriet looked uncomfortable. "Grace, normally that would not be a problem.''

Her hopes sank.

"Grace, honey, try an' understand. I run a public place here, a respectable place. My ladies are very, very upset. They've told me they'll leave if I let you stay. My business is running a boardinghouse. I can't afford a bad reputation. What if my ladies leave? Other ladies won't come, either. I'll go out of business.''

Grace felt faint. "I understand.''

"Honey, I hate asking you to leave, I really do, and I put it off long as I could. But I'm going to tell my mind to that Rathe Bragg—this is all his fault—and you watch, he'll come around! In the meantime, you'll be better off at one of the hotels.''

Grace wanted to cry. "Harriet, Rathe has already asked me to marry him,'' she said, wanting to share her burden.

Harriet stared, then threw back her head and chortled with glee. "He did? That's wonderful! I knew it, the instant I saw the two of you together. Why didn't you tell me?"

Grace didn't smile. She could not tell Harriet that she would not marry Rathe. Harriet was harboring some romantic fantasies about the two of them. Harriet would try and change her mind. The older woman hugged her warmly and left.

Grace stood unmoving, realizing that now she had no choice. She would borrow ten dollars from Allen, exactly half of his savings. She knew he would lend it to her without hesitation. That would be enough to pay for a very cheap room for a couple of weeks; she would only eat one meal a day, as well. Something would just have to turn up before this money ran out.

"Hey, Rathe, you got yourself a telegram here."

Rathe swiveled his head. It was only ten-thirty, but he was sitting at a front table in the Black Heel, morosely. He sipped both a coffee and a bourbon, unable to decide which he really wanted. Actually, he wanted neither. He knew what he wanted. He wanted Grace.

But Grace didn't want him.

He was still in a state of disbelief. He had offered marriage. *Marriage.* And she had to think about it? Apparently she wasn't impressed by who and what he was. She wasn't even impressed by the fact that he had never proposed before.

His face grew red every time he recalled how she had thrown his proposal back in his face in front of the entire saloon. Well, there were thousands of women he could marry, but damned if he'd ever offer marriage to her again—not unless she came crawling to him on her hands and knees.

Somehow he could not picture Grace ever doing that!

He shifted very uneasily in his seat. Was it possible that, for the first time in his life, he was going to be thwarted? Never had he wanted anything as much as he wanted Grace. He kept thinking she would come around. But was he wrong? Was Grace really going to evade him? Would she walk out of his life, never to appear again?

That last thought made him sick, and he knew he could never let it happen. He would kidnap her first.

He looked at the telegram, and realized it was from his family. If his mother knew he was thinking of treating a woman like this, she would give him one rousing lecture . . . and maybe a smack or two. Rathe couldn't even smile at the picture of his tiny mother trying to hit him when he was six feet tall, built like an oak, and thirty years old, to boot. He knew his parents wanted to see him. If he had any common sense, he would pack his bags and leave Natchez and never come back. He picked up the telegram.

DEAR RATHE,
    WHEN ARE YOU COMING HOME STOP STORM AND BRETT
AND KIDS ARE HERE STOP HAD HELLUVA TIME FINDING
YOUR WHEREABOUTS STOP WE WANT TO HEAR ABOUT NICK
STOP COME SOON WE LOVE YOU STOP DEREK

His sister, Storm, and her husband, Brett, were at the ranch with his niece and two nephews. That alone was the best reason there could be to get going. It had been almost a year since he'd last been home, and that was too long. And he hadn't seen Storm in more than that, because she and her husband lived in San Francisco. If only his older brother Nick, were there. But Nick was in England, at Dragmore, the estate he had inherited from their English grandfather.

Rathe had been in England earlier that year on business, and the rest of the family was clearly anxious to hear his report about Nick.

But he knew he couldn't leave Natchez now, not with Grace here, not when he was so obsessed he couldn't even get randy around other women. If Nick or Derek knew they'd be howling with laughter, telling him it served him right.

Rathe shut off his thoughts.

Grace felt awful as she departed Harriet's with her two valises and single carpetbag. Allen had gladly loaned her the money. Grace had not told him that she was leaving, nor had she told him she had been asked to do so. She didn't want to upset him. After she was established someplace else, she would let him know, explaining that she had left in order to take a cheaper room. Two of the women who were boarding at Harriet's were sitting on the porch, watching her every move as she huffed down the path to the street. "Good riddance," she heard one of them say. "To think baggage like that claims to be a schoolteacher! It's a sin!"

Grace raised her chin, firmed her lips, and walked on.

Of course, the hotels on the cliffs were too expensive. On the edge of the waterfront she paused, putting down her bags, massaging her hands. Sailors were unloading a barge. Drays moved down the street. A couple of drunks were stumbling out of a saloon. The line of hotels, with their shabby facades and faded signs, stretched from where she was standing out into the distance and out of sight. She saw Dan Reid on the boardwalk in front of Max's, and flushed thinking about last night.

Just then a boy, barefoot and dirty and about thirteen, ran into her, almost knocking her down. Grace cried out.

"Oh, 'scuse me, ma'am," he said, steadying her. "Are you all right?"

"Yes, I'm fine," she said, shaken. "Thank you." She gave him a warm smile.

He grinned back, apologized again, and took off.

Grace picked up her bags and continued down the street. It wasn't until she was standing inside one of the hotels, registering, trying not to notice the dirt in the corners and a mouse scurrying across the floors, that she reached for her reticule and realized her money was gone.

She had been robbed.

The night was warm. She had nowhere to go. She knew she was in a desperate situation. She could not ask Allen for the last of his money. He would give it to her. Then he would have nothing.

She sat on a tree stump in a clearing in the woods on the outskirts of town, shivering despite the balmy temperature. Her bags were at her feet. Through the trees, she could just make out the sluggish, meandering Mississippi, shining in the moonlight. Two men on a raft drifted past her, poling along. She was shielded by trees and shrubs; nevertheless, she held her breath until they were out of sight.

Every snapping twig, every rustle of leaves, made her jump and crane her head around. What was she doing? Did she really think she could spend the night out here? It was so dark. She told herself there was nothing to be afraid of, that this was better than a street corner—and in the daylight, when she had arrived, it had seemed safe. In town she would have certainly been accosted. But what about the wild animals? Were there snakes out here? Lions? Wolves? Oh, God! She knew nothing about the wilderness! And even if she survived tonight, what about tomorrow, and the day after, and the day after that?

Tomorrow will bring a job, she told herself firmly. All you have to do is survive this night. Tomorrow you will find a job, a job with room and board. No one can see you from the road or the river. Just be still and quiet and you'll be safe.

There was a movement in the bushes behind her. Grace jumped to her feet, clamping a hand over her mouth to still the shriek that wanted to escape. It was only a gray tomcat.

* * *

Rathe paced the confines of his room at the Silver Lady Hotel. He knew Grace didn't deserve his concern, but he couldn't help it—he wanted to know where the hell she was.

He had been shocked by Harriet's response when he had casually asked her, just before supper, if she had seen Grace—not that he had anything to say to her, because he didn't. But he hadn't seen her since yesterday night at Max's, and he couldn't help wondering where she'd been all day—and if she'd changed her mind—not that he cared!

Harriet told him she had left her establishment.

"Left?" he echoed blankly. His first thought was a horrified one: She had left town, disappeared from his life!

Harriet was confused. "You haven't seen her? I thought you two were getting married."

"What?"

"Rathe, honey, she had to leave. I run a respectable place. But seein' as how you asked her to marry you, I figured it would all work out for the best. She didn't go to you?"

Rathe managed to piece together what had happened. Grace had been asked to leave because of the night she had spent with him. She had also borrowed ten dollars from Allen. Ten dollars! Two of the ladies had seen her leaving with all her bags, heading for town. How far could she get on ten dollars? And just where the hell was she going?

He reminded himself that she had practically rejected his proposal outright. Still, he marched to the train station to see if she had taken the afternoon train east. She hadn't. Immensely relieved, he returned to his hotel and decided she could surely stay out of trouble for one night. She had obviously taken a new room somewhere. He'd find out about it tomorrow.

He was expecting room service. He had a brandy in one hand and was clad in a dark blue robe. When the knock

came, he opened the door. He had the vaguest image of
the blur that was Grace. Before he could get a better look,
she catapulted into his arms, where she clung, shaking like
a leaf.

He held her, shocked. "Grace, what is it, what's
wrong?" He was terrified, for he knew that only the most
unimaginable of horrors could make her leap into his embrace like this.

She whimpered, pressing against him. "Oh, Lord, it
was so awful, so awful . . ."

Firmly, he moved her back so he could look at her. Her
face was stark white. Three long, bleeding scratches
marred its perfection. There were twigs in her hair, brambles on her arms and bodice, mud on her skirts. "Jesus,
what happened?"

She gripped his lapels, almost tearing the silk. Her
hands shook. "Lions, Indians, and then there was this
owl . . ." She started to cry.

He blinked, cupped her face. "Grace, were you attacked?"

"I think there was a wolf, but maybe it was a dog . . ."

"Were you attacked?"

"I was in the woods and I was running and I couldn't
see. I thought I was running back to Natchez, but I ran
for hours and hours! And I think there were snakes! I
wound up in the swamps!" She began sobbing. "Something slithered over my shoulder!"

Rathe put his arm around her and led her to the bed.
He sat and held her. "It's all right now," he crooned. He
stroked her hair, then began removing brambles between
the caresses. "What were you doing in the woods at night,
Grace?"

Her face was pressed into his chest. When she spoke,
her mouth moved against his flesh, and he could feel her
breath. "I was robbed, I lost Allen's money. I had nowhere to go. I found this little spot—it was so pretty in
the daylight. But at night . . ."

He bit back a smile. He decided not to tell her that there

were no wolves or lions in this area, and that there hadn't been in years. His hand curved around the back of her scalp, holding her head close. "Everything's all right now, Grace. I wish you'd come to me first."

She sniffled.

He couldn't resist, he brushed his lips over her temple. Slowly, she raised her red-rimmed eyes to his face. "You think I'm silly, don't you."

With one forefinger, he touched her adorable nose. "No, I don't. The woods are a frightening place at night, especially if you're a city girl. But you're safe now, Grace." His voice was a caress, a rich murmur. "Don't you know I would never let anything harm you?"

That made her sit up fully, putting distance between them. She studied him seriously, then removed some moisture remaining around her eyes away with her knuckles. Rathe wanted to bend over and flick the tear away with his tongue. Then touch it to her lips, part them, glide past. Instead, he sat unmoving, waiting.

She took a breath. "I've—I've been thinking . . ."

He didn't smile. "Yes?"

"About your offer."

His heart began to hammer. His face remained carefully expressionless.

"I don't think marriage is a good idea . . ."

He stared. Disappointment overwhelmed him.

"But Rathe?" Her voice was small and too high. "I've changed my mind about the other—the other offer."

He could not believe this.

"About being your mistress." She coughed.

"About being my mistress," he repeated foolishly.

"Yes." She took a breath, then managed a smile. "If, that is, the offer still stands, I've . . . decided to accept."

"I see." He got to his feet, looked at her, then walked to the window. Should he ever expect the ordinary from Grace? And why in hell was he upset? He hadn't wanted to marry her to begin with. Now he would have her—without paying the price of marriage. So why were his fists clenched and his temper roiling so dangerously? He turned back to her. She was watching him anxiously. "Of course the offer still stands."

She sighed in relief.

"Just as a point of interest," he said, "would you mind explaining one thing to me?"

"Of course."

"Most women would have chosen marriage. Instead, you chose to be my mistress. I'm having a little trouble understanding your logic."

She bit her lip.

"Grace?" There was warning in his tone.

She lifted her chin and gazed at him. "Marriage is a permanent union. The other is a temporary."

"Ah, yes, how foolish of me."

She clasped her hands and shifted uneasily.

"Perhaps I should make a few stipulations. I expect your services for the next year."

She flushed. "For the next year?"

"At which point," he continued, perversely satisfied to have been derogatory, "we will make a mutual decision as to whether to renew our liaison or not."

"A year?"

"Certainly you can manage to bear my presence for one year? After all, it's not a lifetime." His eyes flashed. He could feel himself losing control of his temper.

"A year. Well, yes, I guess so."

"Thank you. You do understand, don't you, that I have exclusive rights."

"Exclusive rights." Her eyes filled with tears.

"Ah, shit," Rathe growled.

"I'm sorry," she said, wiping her eyes. "I guess I'm just tired. Do you think we could possibly wait until tomorrow to begin our—our liaison?"

"Tomorrow. Yes, that is definitely a good idea." Rathe

knew he had to leave, now. He did not want to make her cry, yet he was furious and doing just that. With very stiff strides, he crossed the room and opened the door. He tried not to slam it closed behind him. He failed.

Chapter 19

Rathe quietly entered his room at the Silver Lady Hotel. It was several hours later. He leaned heavily against the door, his eyes adjusting to the darkness. Then he pushed himself off with an effort.

He was drunk, quite thoroughly, and he knew it. He navigated around the furniture in the room with some difficulty, bumping into a chair, causing it to scrape against the floor. He froze, not wanting to wake Grace.

He found a lamp and lit it. He wanted to look at her, really look at her, feast his eyes on her. He stood over the bed, holding the lamp up, staring. She was so beautiful. His heart did a series of the strangest somersaults. Beautiful and extraordinary. He smiled at that thought. After Grace, an ordinary woman would bore him to death.

He was no longer mad. In fact, he had trouble remembering why he had been so angry. What did it matter that she hadn't wanted to marry him? Most men would consider themselves lucky. Right now, watching her as she slept, curled up on her side, her hair streaming over her shoulder, he was feeling very lucky too. Lucky and lustful.

He eyed her breasts, swelling out of her thin chemise. He methodically stripped off his clothes, barely taking his gaze off of her, until he was stark naked. He crawled into bed beside her, taking her into his arms from behind. She stirred.

This woman was his. It was an overwhelming thought.

He nuzzled her neck and hugged her hard against him. He ran his hand down her torso, to her waist, and over her hip. No woman had ever felt this good.

He thought about how frightened she had been after her escapade in the woods. She was sleeping so soundly she must be exhausted. And he had promised. His body was hard and demanding satisfaction, but he had promised. He nuzzled her jaw, whispering her name, not to awaken her, but saying it as an expression of deep, nameless emotion. Tomorrow was almost here, and tomorrow he would make her his.

Grace hugged her pillow, resisting the inexorable pull of morning.

"Good morning, sweetheart."

The voice was a rough drawl, sensual and familiar. Grace thought that she must be dreaming. Then, as the last stages of sleep fled, she remembered, and she blinked her eyes wide open. Last night, stricken with terror, she had run to Rathe and agreed to become his mistress.

He grinned at her. He was standing beside the bed, clad in a barely belted silk robe. Her gaze was level with his pelvis. Gasping, she darted it to a more respectable point, behind him and to his right.

A linen-clad table was laid out resplendently with crystal and china. A bouquet of violets the exact color of Grace's eyes adorned its center; a bucket of the finest French champagne cooled in a stand on the floor. Enticing aromas were emanating from a multitude of silver-lidded dishes. "I've ordered us breakfast," Rathe said. "And I also ordered you a bath."

Holding the covers tightly to her chin, she looked past him at the steaming tub. This was it. She was taking the final step. She was going to become a man's mistress, and not just any man's—Rathe's. She peeked up at him.

His gaze was warm. Before she could make a sound, he sat on the edge of the bed by her hip. His hand touched her face. "What are you doing?" she squeaked.

"Don't be nervous," he said huskily. His thumb moved slowly over her cheekbone.

Grace couldn't look away. Her thoughts were a mass of confusion. *Yes, no, no, yes.* And his thumb, his big innocent thumb, it was making her heart race.

"Grace." His voice was hoarse. Grace recognized why that was. Their gazes locked.

His palm was infinitely tender and sensual on her face. She wanted to look away from him, but she couldn't. With his free hand, he gently dislodged the sheet she was so desperately gripping and pulled it off of her body. Grace couldn't move.

He looked at her. His gaze, warm and intense, slid over her chest, down the length of her chemise and down her bare legs. His lips were parted. In the opening of his robe, she could see his chest rising and falling heavily.

His hand on her face moved down her neck, like a whisper-soft breeze, just barely there. Her skin flamed and tingled. An urgency began to manifest itself in her breasts and loins, throbbing and electric. His fingers played over her throat. Grace's eyes closed of their own accord, the lashes floating gently downward. Her chin elevated, her head arched back. His thumb slid across her jugular vein.

"So beautiful," he whispered. "So soft. Grace, I'm going to make this so good for you . . ."

She heard his words, but didn't open her eyes, partly out of cowardice and partly because the drift of his fingertips was so exquisite. His hand moved lower, touching her collarbone, gliding, gliding . . . It paused, fingers splayed, just above the soft swell of her breasts.

Grace gasped as he grazed the top of her breasts lightly, teasingly. She realized that she could hear him breathing. His fingers danced to the side of one breast, and then she felt his thumb, beneath her nipple, sweeping back and forth. The bud grew tight and hard, throbbing against the coarse cotton of her chemise.

"Grace," he murmured.

She felt him grasp her straps, and she opened her eyes

abruptly. His gaze was on the delicate, lace-edged bands as he moved them off of her shoulders. He slowly pulled her chemise down over her breasts, his eyes following the trail of cotton and fixing on the white shimmering flesh he had bared. Reverently, he touched each breast, and then his hands closed around them. "Lush," he whispered. "Grace, I've dreamed of this . . . of you . . ."

She moaned as he lifted her and lowered his head at the same time. His tongue darted out, flitting over one swollen nipple. Grace cried out, throwing her head back. With his tongue he began a slow, deliberate, erotic teasing, touching and tempting, flicking, again and again. Then he pulled her nipple into his mouth and began to suck.

Grace was lost. There was no more coherence. She was in the throes of pleasure, pure, exquisite pleasure. Her head moved back and forth. She clutched the corners of the pillow, wishing it were fistfuls of his hair. His suckling was hard and then soft. She heard a tortured whimpering sound—and then realized it had come from her own throat.

His hand was still drifting languorously down her body, memorizing the smallness of her waist, the fullness of her hip, the soft curve of her belly. He threaded his way through thick curls. Grace heard herself cry out. And then he was touching her damp, hot flesh, stroking down into glistening depths, rubbing gently back and forth. Her hold on the pillow tightened.

Rathe lifted his head, his mouth covering hers, his tongue urgently thrusting through the lips she parted readily, eagerly, for him. His fingers never stopped in their shattering quest. "Darling," he gasped against her mouth, "you're so hot, so wet, so ready for me . . ." A finger entered her. Grace gasped. "So tight," he groaned, probing now. "But you'll open for me, won't you Grace? For me, darling?"

Grace thrashed helplessly, forces within her building, carrying her relentlessly, urgently along. She felt his mouth leave her and she cried out in protest. His hands moved beneath her, closed over her buttocks, lifting her. She felt his breath, warm and moist, and then he was nuzzling her swollen pink flesh. Grace's eyes flew open, her mind managing to form a protest, her lips refusing to voice it. His tongue touched deep, slick recesses, and then began to languidly lave over them.

The pillowcase tore beneath her hands. Her world tightened, tightened, tightened, and then exploded—a mad, mindless bursting of sensation. And when it subsided, she heard her fading cries of pleasure, still echoing.

He was there. Rathe covered her with his big body, holding her, his mouth seeking hers. "Grace, Grace," he chanted desperately. She tasted herself on him and was stunned. She could feel his maleness between them, hot and slippery and huge, and was both afraid and excited. He reached down between them, positioning himself against her entrance. "Grace, don't be afraid," he gasped. She felt her flesh stretching. "Darling, open for me. Let me in . . ."

She closed her eyes and tensed every muscle in her body.

He moved slowly, entering her, then paused. "Grace, darling, relax," he whispered. His hands moved over her body, light, like a butterfly, raising the hairs and making her skin burn. "Yes, darling, that's it," he murmured, pushing against her maidenhead. His fingers grazed her breast. He touched her nipple. She whimpered, and with his mouth, he caught the sound, his tongue taking hers. He entwined slowly, gracefully with her, and Grace relaxed, became fascinated, tentatively sparred with him. "Yes," he said, and his teeth touched hers. "Open for me, darling."

Grace opened her mouth, allowing him a full, leisurely entry. Languidly, he explored; languidly, she met him. And then his body shook and he moaned, a long, male sound of anguish.

"Grace, now, let me in now," he ordered, and he plunged through her barrier.

Grace cried out in pain. They both froze. He was huge, and she could feel all of him, encased tightly in her sheath.

"God," Rathe cried. "Oh, God, Grace." He kissed her hungrily and began to move.

The feeling of being stretched taut eased. The fullness became pleasant. He began moving harder. "That's it," he gasped. "Open, open wide, take all of me, all that you can . . ."

Her hands found his back, shyly lying flat on hard, steel muscles, throbbing with power beneath her. He was moving rhythmically now, determinedly, and Grace felt the pressure building again. Her fingers tightened on his skin. "Yes," Rathe cried, surging deeply. Grace felt the out-of-control spinning begin again. She heard herself cry out gutturally. She was aware of him surging deeper and deeper, and then his arms tightened convulsively around her and he collapsed, moaning her name.

She could feel him watching her.

Eyes closed, Grace gripped the sheet she had rescued from around their feet and held it tightly to her neck. Then she blinked and turned her head slightly.

He was watching her, raised up on one elbow. Grace was expecting anything but the look in his eyes. It was warm, not lustful. It was warm and sparkling and tender.

A slow smile curved along his beautiful mouth, and Grace became fascinated. His lips had a sensual line that intrigued her. Studying them now, she remembered how they felt on hers—and on her body. He leaned over and kissed the tip of her nose.

"Blushing?" he drawled. "What are you thinking about, Grace?" His tone was light, teasing.

His question brought forth a very graphic image of his sun-streaked head in a place it had no right being, and she felt her face burning.

He chuckled. "Cat got your tongue?"

She met his gaze. Hers wasn't exactly wary, more intensely curious. She did not know what to expect, now that her status had been established. And it was very hard not to look at this beautiful man who had just made her feel depths of passion she had never dreamed existed.

He was grinning, showing off his deep dimples. "Come here," he coaxed, the rasping quality of his tone reminding her of everything she had just experienced.

She looked at him. The sheet barely covered his hips. The muscles rippled beneath his dark, golden skin. Sleek he was, and powerful, the way she imagined a mountain lion. He patted the space between them.

Grace took a breath, and shifted slightly—about an inch.

He grabbed her and pulled her up against his warm, hard body. "Umm. This is much better, don't you agree?"

She looked at the hairs on his chest. She felt his hand on the back of her head, pressing her forward, until she let her cheek come down to rest on his shoulder. "Much, much better," he said, stroking her nape.

It was better. This was . . . quite nice. Comfortable. Safe. Warm. His palm moved down her back along her spine. Exciting.

She didn't know what to do with her hands, caught between their bodies. She was careful to keep her feet and legs on her side of the bed. Suddenly the mattress shifted and rolled as he moved abruptly. And then he was sitting and she was on his lap.

She stared, almost but not quite stricken, into his eyes. One of his strong arms anchored her waist. He met her look calmly, then bent and nipped her ear.

She gasped. "What are you doing?"

He pulled back, smiling. "Wondered if you still had a tongue!" Then, with his, he probed into the shell of her ear, and bit it gently again.

Hot delight raced through her, while, at the same time, her hands braced against his chest. "Rathe! What are you doing?"

He chuckled. "Playin'," he drawled. "Remember, Gracie? I told you when we played you'd know it."

She recalled their conversation, and now, understanding the meaning, went red in horror and—yes—pleasure. Then, before she had quite absorbed that, he was on his feet—with her in his arms. "Rathe!"

He was carrying her across the room, the both of them stark naked in the light of day. "Put me down!" she demanded. Her heart was racing wildly. But its beat accelerated when he leaned over to nuzzle her breasts with his beard-roughened face. "Put me down," she faltered, her nipples tightening dangerously.

"Bad timing, Gracie," he said, as he carefully lowered her into the steaming bathwater.

She gasped. Before she had adjusted to this turn of events, she saw him lift a hard, muscular leg—and stick it inside with her. "What are you doing?!"

Half of the contents of the tub sloshed out as he settled himself opposite her. Grace blinked, for she had seen it, his maleness, stiff again—so big. She was thinking, We couldn't possibly, could we? Knowing it was wrong, not now, in the daytime, in the bath. Yet her body was feeling tight and hot and traitorously yearning for his touch.

He got to his knees and, gripping either side of the tub, leaned close, his mouth inches from hers. "I'm sorry," he said, and he kissed her.

Shyly, she opened her mouth. She accepted the deep probing of his tongue, then began returning his attentions with growing boldness. He groaned and ended the kiss. "God, Grace, it's so hard. I need you again."

The heat in his gaze thrilled her. No matter how much she wished it didn't, it did. He lightly brushed his lips over hers. "But I'm afraid it will be too much for you. You're so small." He paused, then grinned wickedly. "And I'm not exactly that."

She went pink. Did other couples discuss such things? She had lowered her lashes, careful not to look at him, and she was finding it distinctly difficult to breathe. How could he talk so graphically? Slowly, newly aware of her body and what its heavy throbbing meant, she raised her glance to his. She found herself staring at his mouth. He inhaled sharply.

She looked at his chest. I'm sitting in a bathtub with a man who is not my husband, she thought, and I'm feeling lascivious toward him.

"Touch me," Rathe urged huskily.

Her gaze flew to his. That hot light was her undoing. Languidly, she lifted a hand and laid it on his shoulder. His body quivered like a finely tuned bowstring. She ran her palm down his bicep, exploring the rippling muscle, the hard male flesh and bone.

He kissed her again.

His arms were braced on either side of the tub while his mouth locked with hers. Grace clasped his shoulders, unable to let him go, gladly accepting his tongue and capturing it with her own, unwilling to release it. The heat racing through her body was more brilliant than the first time. Her heart was trying to rise out of her breast.

He lunged free of her, and before she knew it, he was out of the tub and walking away from her, putting on a robe. It clung to his wet body when he turned back, making her eyes widen and her breath catch.

He was so utterly aroused and so utterly magnificent.

"I'm afraid I'll hurt you," he told her harshly. "You'd better bathe alone."

"Oh," Grace said. Confusion gave way to disappointment.

Chapter 20

They had finished breakfast and Grace was playing idly with a spoon when Rathe broke the silence. "I just have to run out for a bit," he said.

Grace felt warm beneath his gaze. His look was hard to interpret, because it was so thorough and so very intent. Then he rose and pulled her into his arms, kissing her shamelessly, hungrily. When he finally left she was breathless.

Grace stared at the door, clutching herself.

She was this man's mistress.

She sank into a chair. Everything had happened so quickly. She wasn't even sure how she felt.

She looked down at herself, clad in his navy silk robe, without a stitch underneath. Indecent, scandalous, utterly improper. All through their meal he had touched her, his hand lingering on her arm, or her knee, or her waist. His gaze had been riveted on her face. Warm, bold. Yet soft, too.

She hadn't been able to eat more than a few bites. Her heart had been lodged somewhere in the vicinity of her throat. His scrutiny had embarrassed her, yet it had also made her pulse pound. She had been so very aware of him, as a man, sitting so close to her. In fact, never had she been so aware of another human being in her entire life.

Never had she felt so utterly alive. In his embrace, Grace didn't think, she only felt. How could she have ever imagined that a woman could experience such feelings in a man's arms? Such passion. It had not been the way she thought it would be. Never had she dreamed her own wild response. She also had not expected such tenderness from him.

Grace shuddered. She really did not know how she felt. A part of her, she supposed, was frightened; another part was shocked. There were other feelings, too, nameless emotions which she did not want to face. She had the uncanny fear that if she did try to analyze them, she would be irretrievably lost.

She looked around the room and realized she had absolutely nothing to do. He hadn't said how long he would be gone, or that she should wait for him to return. Well, it was the middle of the day, the perfect time to find Geoffrey and begin organizing a class.

She found half a dollar lying atop the bureau and used it to rent a buggy at Tom's Livery, just across the street from the hotel. As she prepared to go, she found herself wondering where Rathe was; then she thought about Allen. If he didn't know by now that she'd become Rathe's mistress, he would soon. She felt she owed him an explanation, but couldn't bring herself to do it today. She was a coward.

She had no trouble finding the home of Geoff and Clarissa's family, just north of town, on the outskirts of Natchez. Smoke curled from the chimney, a sure sign supper was on. Workers were trudging in from the fields carrying their tools, and she saw an old man sitting on the porch in a rocker. "Hello," Grace called, stepping down from the buggy. "How are you today?"

He got to his feet and smiled. "You're Geoffrey's teacher, ain't you, ma'am? I'm his granpappy. An' thank you, I'm jes' fine."

"I'm Grace O'Rourke," she said, extending her hand.

He stared, shaking his head, but he was grinning. "They says you is different," he remarked, taking her palm.

Just then Clarissa and Geoff came peeling out of the

cottage at the same time, the latter shouting her name in excitement. Grace beamed at the warm reception. After an exchange of greetings, she was led into the house by their grandmother, Maddie, who insisted she stay for supper. Knowing their fare was meager, Grace refused.

When she told them her plans to hold free classes, the entire family enthusiastically agreed to help her organize the children.

"Don't you worry about it at all," Maddie said. "Tomorrow at noon you'll have a churchful of children waitin' for you."

Grace was thrilled, but she knew she couldn't stay.

Rathe had intimated that he wouldn't be long. She had already been gone for a couple of hours; he was probably back. Was he waiting for her? Thinking of seeing him brought a strange, unexpected excitement. Warm, insistent memories tugged at her: his hard, driving passion, his delicate tenderness, the warmth in his eyes when he smiled at her. Don't think like this, she told herself sternly. He's a philandering rogue, and you're his mistress. It's as simple as that.

The sky was just starting to turn gray when she returned the buggy and mare. She found herself skipping across the street, her heart pounding despite her resolve to be nonchalant and even briskly businesslike. When she let herself into their room, her heart was beating joyfully.

His face lit up at the sight of her.

Grace stood still against the door, unable to prevent herself from gazing at him raptly, taking in every detail of his appearance, from his high black boots, his fine white doeskin breeches, to the casual lawn shirt left open at the throat.

He came to her. "Where have you been? I've been waiting for an hour."

His hands closed on her shoulder. Grace opened her mouth to reply, but it was no longer necessary, his mouth eagerly took hers. "I have something for you," he said huskily. He grinned with the eager look of a schoolboy.

Rathe hadn't been able to stop thinking about her for a single minute of the past few hours. He had experienced many infatuations before, but never one like this. If he didn't know better, he would think he was falling in love—which was silly. Still, his first and most insistent thought after making love to her, other than doing it again, was buying her a beautiful gift.

If he could, he was going to spend the next year showering her with beautiful gifts.

He had spent a long time choosing something for her. Now he couldn't wait to see her expression when she saw it. He couldn't wait to watch her lift stunned eyes to his—then glow with pleasure. He liked it when Grace glowed with pleasure. His heart was beating uncontrollably.

"Here," he said, reaching to the bureau behind him, smiling.

Grace saw he was holding out a long, flat jewler's box. An acute feeling of dizziness and nausea welled up in her. This was what she needed to remind herself of the exact nature of their relationship. To shake her out of her state of confusion. Respectable ladies did not accept gifts from men, other than their husbands. She felt a moment's pang, because they could have been man and wife. Then her lips firmed. She was being rewarded for her favors, which was to be expected. But it was so blatant and hurtful Grace did not want to take the box.

"Grace?"

She looked up at him, trying to contain the hurt behind a facade of coldness. It was so very hard to do.

Rathe stared at her expression. She was not glowing; she seemed upset. He heard his tone change, sounding almost apprehensive. "This is for you."

She wanted to fling it back in his face and tell him she didn't want it, that the deal was off, that she could not go through with it—she could not be his mistress. She wanted to weep. Instead, she resolutely took the box from his hands and opened it.

His gaze riveted on her face.

A brilliant necklace of amethysts and diamonds twinkled up at her. She thought of the men who gave their wives presents like this because they loved them. He was giving her this present because she had earned it by being his whore. Oh, God, it hurt.

"Grace?" he asked, not breathing.

She looked up at him with frozen features. "Thank you."

There was a stricken look on his face, but she only saw it for a second, for he turned away and walked to the table. Grace looked back at the necklace, and she had to admit, through the blur of tears, that it was beautiful. She would sell it the first chance she had. It would pay her mother's bills, maybe for the next year.

She had her back to him, and she used the opportunity to discreetly brush the few stray tears from her face. Then, elaborately, she tossed the box on the bed, knowing full well he was watching. "I think we should come to some sort of agreement," she stated, turning to face him.

His eyes left the black velvet case lying carelessly amidst the rumpled covers. They were singularly icy as they returned to her. "What sort of agreement, Grace?"

Her hands closed over the back of a chair. "In the future," she said, "I would prefer cash."

He sucked in his breath.

"Or a cashier's check will do."

He shook from head to toe.

Grace actually shrank back from the intensity of his reaction.

"In the future," he choked, fists clenched, face red, "you will most certainly have cash." Then he whirled and moved across the room in a maelstrom of rage. Grace was momentarily afraid to breathe.

He tore out of the room like a cyclone, slamming the door thunderously behind him.

Grace sank, shaking, into a chair. She was so confused. Why had he gotten so angry? She had every right to demand cash. And why did she feel guilty and awful, as if she were at fault? And why, oh why, was she crying?

She expected him to return, first for supper, and then to retire for the night.

But he did not.

"I'm out," Rathe said.

A groan greeted his statement. "You no-good bastard," George Farris said good-naturedly. "You've cleaned us up."

Rathe was sitting in the Black Heel with what was left of a full table of poker players. He pulled his winnings forward. He knew he had close to five thousand dollars, but he did not smile. He felt no pleasure, just grim satisfaction. A picture of her formed in his mind's eye, lush and pale and voluptuous and naked.

Anger, icy cold, froze in his veins.

He had been playing for twenty hours. His eyes were bloodshot, and there were circles beneath them from lack of sleep. His face was scruffy with a day's growth of beard. He was rumpled and worn-looking, his shirt opened, his sleeves pushed up to his elbows. But he wasn't tired. Far from it.

She wanted cash, did she?

Well, now she would have it.

He saw her tossing the velvet box aside, and the anger in him threatened to become red and hot. He began folding the bills carefully. Five thousand dollars took a while to fold and put away.

His first instincts yesterday had been to wire New York for money. But Rathe had a longstanding policy. Ninety-nine percent of his net worth was tied up in investments. He reinvested every dividend, living off his winnings at the card table. It was easy to do because he was such a successful player, and because he loved the game.

Yet yesterday he had actually gone to wire New York when he realized it was Friday. It would be days before he could throw the money in her face. He couldn't wait days. He was too furious. His desire to play her game the way she called it made this poker match the most important and hateful one in his life.

"You look like you could use a hot bath, honey," purred a lush blonde who'd been assigned to looking after the back room after the waiter had gone home exhausted several hours earlier. Players, too, had come and gone, though Rathe had been winning steadily. Even George had only joined in at ten o'clock last night.

"You're right," Rathe said, standing. He patted her shoulder. "A hot bath and a warm bed." He thought of Grace.

"I think I can take care of that," the woman said archly.

Rathe looked at her. "I've got a very expensive *lady* waiting." He felt another surge of fury.

"Oh, yeah," she spat. "That prissy redhead, I bet. You get tired of those boobs an' that hair, let me know." With that, she stalked off.

The anger boiled again. It seemed to be his perpetual state. He didn't like anyone casting slurs at Grace.

George had the good sense to wipe the smile from his face the moment Rathe turned a cold gaze on him. "Hey, go easy on her, okay?" he offered.

Rathe's icy blue eyes stung him. "If I want your advice," he ground out, "I'll ask for it."

George backed away.

Rathe strode out into the bright afternoon, blinking a few times in the sunlight. Then he strode across the street and up the hill and into the Silver Lady. Even though he moved with the coiled, tightly restrained energy of a mountain cat about to spring, his heart was hammering way too loudly. He imagined her expression when he paid her cold, hard cash.

She wasn't in their room.

He knew it the instant he stepped through the door. He kicked it shut, glancing around. Just where the hell was she? It took him a moment to realize that there was no sign of her in the room at all. He reminded himself that she hadn't brought anything with her the night she had appeared hysterically at his door. A lump of fear tried to worm its way into his anger. He insisted on ignoring it, on flinging aside the covers of the made-up bed, as if some sign of her might be underneath.

Furious, he kicked a chair over, displaced pillows, flung open the wardrobe and the drawers of the bureau. All his things were intact and as he'd last left them. Grace might have never been in this room.

They had a deal. There was no way he was going to allow her to run out after one night.

No way. Especially after it had been such an expensive night.

She wasn't at Harriet Gold's either.

"I don't know where she is," Harriet said, catching him as he was about to bound up the stairs. "And I want a word with you."

"Later," Rathe began. "Have you seen her at all since yesterday?"

"Oh no, Rathe Bragg. You're not diverting me. I'm too old for your tricks. Your mommy and daddy aren't here, but I am, and you need a good talking-to."

Resigned, Rathe let her lead him into the kitchen, where she shut the doors. She turned on him. "I hope you're proud of yourself."

Rathe, no fool, knew exactly what she was referring to, and he blushed like a guilty schoolboy.

"That's right, feel guilty. You've taken a good girl and ruined her, dragged her right through the mud. If your daddy knew of this, you know what he'd do?"

"I know," Rathe said grimly. "He'd thrash my hide."

"An' make you marry her," Harriet stated, watching him.

Rathe laughed in disgust. "Hah! Even Derek couldn't make that happen!"

"You underestimate your own pa."

Rathe gave her a look. "Grace isn't interested in marriage, Harriet, and no man, and no amount of talking, cajoling, or threatening is going to change that!''

"She turn you down?"

He felt more color rising. "She made herself very clear. She told me in no uncertain terms that she would not marry me. Not," he added quickly, "that I'd marry her either! She had her chance. I've changed my mind—I like things just fine the way they are."

Harriet glared. "Grace is too good a girl to be set up with you in that hotel and you know it. The damage is done, but it's not too late. You know what to do."

Harriet was right, and that knowledge made Rathe frustrated and furious. But he would *not* ask her to marry him again. "Harriet, when was the last time you saw Grace?"

Harriet pursed her lips. "You won't like it."

He was overcome by a wave of dread. He already knew what Harriet was about to say. "She was here—with Allen."

Harriet nodded. "Just after breakfast."

Rathe gripped the mantel as hard as he could.

"You tear that off the wall and you'll be putting it back up," Harriet warned.

He spun around. "How long was she here?"

"I don't know, I only saw her when she was leaving. I didn't even know she was here at all. It was a complete surprise when I saw her coming out of Allen's room." Harriet smiled serenely.

Rathe's eyes widened. "They had the door closed? Just the two of 'em?"

"You've got a filthy mind," Harriet said. "Just 'cause you treat her with no respect doesn't mean a good man like Allen Kennedy is the same. Besides, everyone knows he's got marriage on his mind."

Rathe curse, then turned on his heel and left. What had they been talking about? And where the hell was she now? He recalled the time he had seen them share that passionate kiss in the buggy in Louisa Barclay's driveway. The image loomed before him now, infuriating him. He had made it very clear that she was his exclusively for the next year. Yet she was already off traipsing around with another man.

He returned to the hotel. As he bounded up the stairs he couldn't help wondering if she'd returned. But his room was as empty as before. He ignored the disappointment, refusing to even recognize it, and drank his second bourbon in twenty hours. It went down like silk.

He could scour the town, looking like a fool, or he could wait.

He decided to wait.

Precisely three minutes later she walked through the door.

They stared at each other for a long, hard minute.

"Where have you been?" Rathe demanded, too aware of his heart's rapid hammering and the blood starting to course through his veins. "I don't want you to wear your hair like that."

She drew herself up as tall as possible. "Your dictating my hairstyle to me wasn't in our bargain. And I might ask the same question—where have you been?"

His eyes glinted. He wished she didn't look so damn gorgeous even with pursed lips and that awful bun. Even the damn gray gown couldn't diminish her beauty. If anything, the soft color made her skin look as pale as magnolias and magnificently translucent. "This isn't a two-way street, sweetheart," he drawled. "My whereabouts aren't your concern, but yours are most definitely mine."

She huffed.

He was glad he had made her mad. He wanted to make her as mad as he was—no, madder. He shoved his hands in his pockets and brought out fistfuls of cash. He flung them at her feet. She jumped back, gasping, as he proceeded to empty his pockets. Soon five thousand dollars' worth of greenbacks and gold lay strewn around her.

She stared at him, crimson. He felt very, very satisfied. "You can count it if you want."

Her color mounted, her chin went up, her eyes took on

a somewhat shiny look. "No thank you, it looks sufficient."

"Sufficient? Greedy, aren't we?"

She opened her mouth, to argue he knew, and he waited
with relish. Then she shut it abruptly.

"Where the hell were you, Grace?"

Her eyes glistened. "I was at the school. And frankly,
sweetheart, I really couldn't care who you spent last night
with!" Her voice rose sharply.

His eyes narrowed. She was jealous, and for an instance
that fleeting thought brought sweet triumph. "What were
you doing at the school?" His tone had lowered, become
dangerous.

"What do you think?" she snapped. "Sweeping the
floors?" Her head lifted. "I've organized an informal class
and—"

"You *what?*"

She stopped. "I've organized—"

"You're not teaching, Grace."

She stared. "You're not serious."

"Oh, I'm serious all right." He pushed himself off the
wall. "Take off your clothes."

She blinked.

"Your time belongs to me," he warned. "Take off your
clothes, Grace."

She was pale. "You can't mean it."

"Oh, I most certainly do." He waited. "Now."

Still, she hesitated, her gaze wide and tremulous. Rathe
suddenly hated himself. They both knew he was wielding
his power over her purposefully. Her hands trembled as
she touched the first button on her bodice, fingering it, her
lips white. Rathe moved. He caught her hand in his, stopping it. She raised glazed eyes to his. "I can't."

"I know you can't," he cried. "I'm sorry, Grace . . ."
He clenched her hand so tightly she made a sound of protest.

That little whimper was his undoing. He wrapped her
in his arms. She was very still and frozen, like a little,

trapped bird, and he could feel her heart winging frantically against his. His hold tightened. "I never want to hurt
you," he gasped into her neck. "I only want to protect
you."

Her stiff shoulders began to relax beneath his embrace.

"I only want to love you," he cried, rocking her. His
mouth formed the words against her ivory cheek. "Let me
love you, Grace. Let me."

He cupped her face. There were big glistening tears in
her eyes, and they spilled over. He caught one with his
mouth, kissing it away. He looked into her eyes, captured
her gaze, unwilling to let it go. Her mouth was open,
moist and trembling. He covered it with his. When her
hands shyly touched his back, he felt a surge of elation
and something else—emotion so vast he could not contain
it.

"Grace," he choked, against her mouth. "I love you.
Ah, I love you—let me love you."

In his hands she shuddered.

Kissing her wildly, holding her fiercely, he walked her
backward, urging her to the bed. She fell back in his embrace, clinging, opening, gasping beneath his onslaught.
His hands shook violently as he freed her hair. He lifted
her skirts, stroking her legs through her cotton pantalets,
his mouth on hers, soft then hard, hard then soft.

"Touch me, Grace," he cried, pushing her hands from
his shoulder to his back. Pausing on his side, facing her,
breathless, he watched her face as he moved her hand over
his shirtfront. She gasped when he moved it into the opening of his shirt. He groaned.

She met his eyes, startled, lips open and wet.

"Don't stop," he begged, pressing her hand against his
ribs. Then abruptly, he tore open his shirt, the buttons
flying about them, baring his torso for her touch.

Her hand was small and white on his bronzed skin, hovering uncertainly just below his chest. Rathe threw his
head back, closed his eyes, panting. "Please, Grace."

She didn't know what to do. Yet the feel of this man's

powerful body beneath her soft palm was overwhelming and exciting. Daringly, she looked at him, not moving. His ribs were stretched taut beneath his skin, barely visible. His chest was rising and falling rapidly, covered with thick, dark hair. His nipples were small and flat. She had the urge to touch one. Quickly, she looked away.

Her gaze met the full, straining bulge of his doeskin breeches. Her mouth was very, very dry.

"Grace."

Her gaze shot to his and she reddened to have been caught staring.

"It's all right," he breathed. "I love looking at you, too."

Her mind was spinning out of control with forces and emotions that were too strong for her to resist. She moved her hand up, across the slab of one chest muscle. His hair caught in her fingers. His entire body tensed beneath her hand. He groaned, took her hand, and moved it up over his small, tight nipple.

Her hand tightened. She couldn't breathe. Her body was throbbing shamefully, agonizingly, deliciously. Then he lifted his head to touch his tongue to her own nipple, mindless of the clothing covering it. Grace gasped when he tugged it into his mouth.

He pulled her down beneath him.

They kissed, open and wet, teeth grating and tongues touching. Her bodice opened effortlessly beneath his skilled fingertips, her breasts spilling into his hands. She was aware of him pulling down her drawers, and aware that she lifted her hips to help him. He thrust her skirts around her waist, stripped off his breeches. With a hoarse cry of joy he surged inside of her. Her hands found his broad back and held him closely. A part of her mind realized that her nails were digging into his flesh, that she must be hurting him, but she couldn't seem to stop. He was moving within her, slowly, beautifully, with precise restraint. Then harder, faster, answering the unconscious urging of her body. A long, drawn sound came from her, a cry of peaking pleasure. "Yes," Rathe gasped, "yes, darling, yes."

He lay and held Grace in his arms and knew, in a sudden revelation, like the striking of lightning, that life as he had known it was over forever. He knew, with utter clarity, that nothing would ever be the same again, that Grace had truly entered his life. It was chilling and frightening and glorious all at once.

Grace shifted in his arms. "Don't move away," he said, stroking his hand down her arm, gazing at her intently.

Her eyes were wide and soft. Rathe knew an intense determination, then, to put the past behind them. It wouldn't be easy; he only had to lift his head to see five thousand dollars strewn about the floor, evidence of the exact nature of their relationship, evidence of exactly what she wanted from him. "There's five thousand dollars on the floor," he said quietly, propping himself up.

She stiffened, nostrils flaring.

What would she say if I asked her to marry me again? He went red at that unwanted thought. She had rejected him once, firmly, and she would reject him again. "I'll open an account for you in the morning," he said, just as quietly. "From now on we won't ever discuss money again. Periodically I'll put money in your account."

She stared, eyes wide.

He felt grim and sad and very needy, too. He slid his hand down her arm. "But I want to remind you of our agreement," he said.

Grace found her voice, although she was still in a state of shock over the five thousand dollars. "What?"

"You agreed to a full year."

She sat up, pulling the covers over her bosom. "Yes, I did."

"I want that to be clear." His gaze was so solemn. "A year from now we discuss our liaison. Not before, not unless I change my mind and decide to let you go sooner."

Change his mind . . . let her go sooner? Her heart seemed to ache. The words hurt terribly. What was happening to her? If only he *would* change his mind, the sooner the better! She nodded, forcing the tears to stay checked.

"What's wrong? Why are you crying?"

"I'm not crying."

He studied her, not understanding her, wishing he did. But she was an enigma. Had he just done or said something to upset her, or were these tears of regret? He took a deep breath. "That is the last time we discuss money," he reiterated firmly. He didn't want to make a fool of himself by repeating what he had said—that she could not run out on him. But there was an aching deep inside, an aching from fear: he'd paid her well enough to know that if she weren't fair-minded, she'd be gone tomorrow. He slid off the bed and began gathering up the bills.

Grace watched, clutching the sheets to her chest. How long, she wondered, did she have before he'd tire of her? Oh, she was ten times a fool! If she was smart she would just take the money and return to New York. She owed him nothing.

It was time to face an awful possibility.

She wasn't sure, if she had a choice, she would want to leave this man.

Her eyes widened. Her face froze. This could not be happening.

He finished, placing the money on the table, while Grace hastily checked her eyes for any traces of dampness. Her heart was thundering inside her. He turned and looked at her, slowly, thoughtfully, and Grace's entire being tightened. He was so beautiful, so powerful, and she knew now that she had always thought so.

"What is it?" he asked, sitting beside her and putting his arm around her.

She didn't like his sudden perceptiveness. She forced a smile. "Just tired."

His smile was nothing like hers—it was devastating. "We could always spend the afternoon napping."

She did not respond to his teasing. She couldn't. She could only think of one thing. She could not be falling in love with Rathe Bragg—absolutely not!

Chapter 21

"What are you thinking about so seriously?" he asked, smiling.

"Nothing," she managed. She wasn't about to admit that she'd been entertaining the notion of being in love with him.

He was not, she reminded herself, the kind of man a woman like herself should ever entertain serious thoughts about.

Grace, he asked you to marry him, a voice inside her reminded.

Her resolution stiffened.

He's never asked another woman to marry him, not ever. You were the first, it continued. *The first and only one!*

Her fists tightened.

"What is it?" he asked, coming to her and kneeling, taking her hands in his.

Her heart began its insane beating. He was so close, even more beautiful at this distance. His gaze held hers. Then he lifted her to her feet and hugged her. She gasped at what rose between them—and felt triumph. See, he's only a rutting bull; he only wants to bed you!

"I'm sorry." He laughed shakily. "But we've only been together twice and it's just not enough." He caught her face in his large, rough hands. "I want to make love to you all day and all night and maybe then I can behave normally."

She blushed.

"But I'm afraid to hurt you," he said.

She stared. She crossed her arms, tightly. He was a cad—why wasn't he behaving like one now?

He smiled. "I wish you'd let me in there, Grace," he murmured, gently tapping her forehead.

She pretended not to know what he was referring to. She went to the mirror and began to brush her hair with long, brisk strokes. She could feel him watching, and when she looked at his reflection, their glances met. Her heart tightened again.

"We need to get you some clothes, Grace. I think Mrs. Garrot will make time for us."

Her hand stilled. "I don't need clothes."

He laughed, then wiped the humor from his countenance. "I'm sorry, Grace, but that was funny. You do need clothes—an entire wardrobe, in fact."

She clutched the brush. She imagined being paraded in front of Mrs. Garrot in her new role as mistress. She imagined being paraded in town for all to see in a mistress's flamboyant finery. "I don't need new clothes."

"You can't enjoy wearing those ra—dresses."

"What does enjoyment have to do with it?"

"Why not enjoy your clothes?"

She stared, imagining how he would dress her, in a whore's immodest finery, in taffeta and satins, imagining the scorn she would encounter from all who saw her. And then he was crossing the room with hard, deliberate strides. Her eyes widened. He took her shoulders and turned her back to the mirror. "Take a good look, Grace. Really look."

She looked into the mirror—at him.

He made a sound of exasperation. "Not at me—at yourself!"

Her gaze went to her own pale face.

His hands rubbed her lazily. "Look at how beautiful you are."

She started to protest, but he silenced her with a tightening of his grip. She stared at herself for another beat, trying to see what he did. She saw a woman in the prime of her life with the palest of skin. She had to admit her complexion was flawless. Her mouth seemed too full for her face, swollen from his kisses. Her eyes were absolutely glowing. Her red hair was a disheveled disaster. She hadn't really looked at herself in years. She had forgotten how pretty she was.

He nuzzled her ear. "I want you to see yourself the way I do," he said. "You're a gorgeous woman, Grace, but you do your damnedest to hide it."

He embraced her in a fierce, possessive hug. She watched their reflection in the mirror over the bureau. He felt so good. It was almost unbearable. He had closed his eyes, pressing the side of his face against hers, and for a moment she thought she saw the same agonized intensity on his face as she felt inside herself. But she knew she had to be mistaken as he straightened and met her gaze calmly in the mirror. "How long do you need to get ready?" he asked.

He didn't understand! Panic set in. "I don't want any clothes," she pleaded.

He folded his arms. They regarded each other steadily for a moment. "Why don't you want new clothes, Grace?"

She sought frantically for an excuse. She couldn't find one—other than the truth.

His tone was gentle, but tinged with frustration. "Grace, share what you're thinking with me."

She took a breath. "You want to flaunt me, don't you? In low-cut gowns, gaudy fabrics, high heels and expensive jewelry. Mrs. Garrot will know. Everyone will know. I don't want to look like that." She inhaled. "I don't want to look like your whore!"

He flinched. His mobile mouth tensed. "You're not my whore."

"No?"

He closed his eyes. "Dammit, all right then! You are my whore! And who the hell's choice was that?" he shouted.

She shrank against the bureau. She collected herself. "You're right."

He turned away, cursing. Then he looked back at her. "I offered you marriage."

She said nothing.

He stared. His eyes searched hers. Grace held her breath. She couldn't look away. Oh, Lord, he was going to ask her again!

He tore his glance away. "I never intended to flaunt you, as you put it," he said slowly. "I also don't want to introduce you to my family clad in rags."

She knew she had misheard. "What?"

"I'm not going to introduce you to my family dressed like some . . ." He bit off what he'd been about to say— like some virgin old maid.

She felt faint and sick. "What do you mean?"

"How many times do I have to say it?" he demanded, fully frustrated now.

"When am I meeting your family?" Absolute, unadulterated horror overcame her.

His glance was sharp. "I figured in a few weeks, maybe less, we'd head down that way. I haven't been home in a long while and my sister and her husband and kids are there."

She struggled for calm. A few weeks. She still had time. There was no way she was going to meet his family—not now, not ever!

"What are you afraid of, Grace? Other than the scorn? It is more than that, isn't it? Because if it really were condemnation, you would have never accepted my proposition the other night—you would have accepted my proposal. It is fear, isn't it?"

She folded her arms across her chest, hating this sensitive side of him. "No."

"You don't want to be beautiful. You're afraid of it. God knows why. You've spent your entire adult life running from being the attractive woman you are. I don't understand it." A look of bulldog tenacity crossed his face. "But I'm sure going to try."

"Rathe," she said, unable to stop herself from reaching out to him. "I don't want men to look at me and see just another pretty face."

"Why not?"

"Because I have things to do with my life! I can't be sidetracked by leering men with one thing on their minds!"

He stared at her. "You are the most unusual woman, Grace O'Rourke."

His tone warmed her, and filled her with hope. "Please don't make me go to Mrs. Garrot's."

His eyes softened. His smile was rueful. "Well," he said, "I suppose the mountain could come to Mohammed."

He returned an hour later with one of the hotel staff. They were carrying a trunk. Rathe tipped the boy and closed the door, then shot Grace a grin. "The mountain, my lady," he teased.

"What have you done?"

"And Mrs. Garrot is not hiding in this trunk," he told her, opening it. "Although she thinks this very unusual."

Her heart had sunk. Although at least he hadn't made her go to the seamstress, he was still going to insist on dressing her up like a kept woman. She blinked at what he pulled out—a soft gray silk gown, high-necked and completely modest. He looked at her.

Grace's heart started to soar.

He began unloading the trunk. Soft violets, forest and mint greens, quiet peaches and sky blues. "I personally think," he said. "that you would look magnificent in vibrant, deep colors—emerald greens, royal blues, deep purple. But—" He sighed and smiled. "I have a feeling you'll prefer these."

She fingered a delicate peach chiffon evening gown with the tiniest pearl buttons, the finest lace, and a fashionable bustle. It was utterly beautiful. Look what he had done.

"Try it on," he urged softly.

She lifted a bright gaze to his. She wet her lips nervously. "Rathe, really . . ."

"Go ahead," he said, smiling. "It's okay to want these things. I just wish you'd let me give you more."

She stared at the exquisite garment. She did want it. She wanted to own it, she wanted to put it on. It was the finest dress she had ever seen, ever touched. Suddenly, giving in to the impulse, she grabbed it and darted for the screen at the end of the room. His rich, warm laughter followed her.

"Do you need help?" he called.

She heard the teasing, lascivious note but was preoccupied with hurrying out of her own drab cotton clothes. "No," she said, stumbling out of her skirt and kicking it aside. She slithered into the peach dress. She pulled the bodice up, and was relieved to see that while it exposed her throat and collarbone, no cleavage was revealed. Even the most proper ladies wore scandalously low-cut gowns in the evening. She was ridiculously pleased with his choice.

She suddenly felt shy. She couldn't reach all the buttons, but that wasn't it. Would he like it? What would he think when he saw her in this? Her heart was beating thickly.

"Grace?"

She took a breath, then walked out.

His eyes glowed.

"How does it look?" she asked shyly.

"Gorgeous," he breathed. "You're so gorgeous."

He was exaggerating, of course, but there was no mistaking the joy surging through her. She turned to the mirror. She couldn't believe she was looking at herself.

"The hotel has a ladies' maid," Rathe said, moving behind her. His fingers automatically found the buttons she had missed, closing them. "Can I send for her to do your hair?"

She noticed her hair in its tight, prim bun for the first time. As if in a trance, she began removing the pins. Behind her, Rathe didn't move. With both hands, she lifted her hair and piled it high, holding it in place, turning her face slightly one way, then another.

"Can I take you downstairs to supper tonight?" Rathe asked softly.

Downstairs. Supper. She had seen the elegant dining room. He wanted to take her there, to a public place. Everyone, of course, would know she was his mistress. Yet . . . She imagined walking in on his arm, with her hair up, in this beautiful gown. "I don't know," she said uncertainly.

He was disappointed. "All right. Another time." His hands covered her silk-clad shoulders. He bent and kissed her neck.

She watched him. His lashes fanned out thickly on his face as his lips moved tenderly on her skin. Sometimes, he could be the gentlest man. She looked at herself in the elegant evening dress. Tears filled her eyes. She was his mistress, but he had clothed her as if she were his wife. "Rathe? I've changed my mind. Let's dine out tonight."

It was her first public appearance as Rathe's mistress, and she turned heads.

Grace knew a hundred eyes were on her and she couldn't stop the pink color from sweeping over her from her head to her toes. She was a bundle of nerves. Rathe's hand was firm on her elbow as he escorted her downstairs. He himself was magnificent in a black evening cutaway coat and trousers. She had felt beautiful a moment ago, when Rathe had worshiped her with his admiring gaze, but now she was wondering if she should run and hide. This was a mistake! Why, even the concierge was staring.

"Rathe," she whispered urgently, abruptly stopping on the bottom step. "Let's go back!"

"Grace, look at me. Do you want to hide in our hotel room for the next year?"

Her chin lifted.

"If that's what you want to do, we will," he said. His gaze locked with hers.

She was torn between fear and bravery. Then her glance flitted past Rathe, to land on the husky form of Sheriff Ford. Her eyes widened. At the sight of him standing in the center of the lobby, she was assailed by an image of Rathe and Ford squared off on Silver Street, both angry, both powerful, neither backing down. She had never been a coward before. She was not going to become one now.

"What in hell is he doing here?" Rathe muttered tersely.

At that moment, a black-haired beauty came through the front doors on the arm of an older gentleman. Grace went stiff at the sight of Louisa Barclay. Ford greeted the couple, and she smiled at something he said; then her flirtatious laughter rang out. She laid a hand on Ford's arm. Then she and her escort were leaving, passing through the elaborate rosewood doors of the restaurant's lobby entrance.

Ford looked at them.

Grace felt Rathe's body tense beside hers. "Rathe? Let's go, please. I'm starved."

He didn't answer. They moved off the step and into the lobby. Ford was approaching them. Grace tried to subtly guide Rathe toward the restaurant, but he pulled her firmly forward—toward the sheriff.

"Been lookin' for you, Bragg," Ford said easily. His glance raked Grace with lewd interest. "Howdy, Miz O'Rourke. You stayin' heah now?" He grinned.

Rathe was breathing hard, furious. "You have something important to say to the lady?"

"Lady?"

Grace grabbed Rathe's arm, but he shook her off. He swung, but her interference was enough to allow Ford to successfully duck.

"Stop it, he's the law for heaven's sakes. You could get arrested!" she cried frantically.

Ford leveled his revolver as cool as a cucumber, cocking it. "You assaultin' an officer of the law, boy?"

Rathe's jaw bulged with clenched muscles. He was panting. He regained a semblance of control. Casually, he lifted up his hands. Then he smiled. "Did I touch you, Sheriff?"

Ford grinned, holstering his gun. "Nope, guess you didn't. Hey, Bragg, I ain't stupid. I know you got more money than this whole town put together. I know you got some powerful people eatin' from your hands. But you provoke me, I will throw you in my jail. Your money may buy you freedom, but you spend a night in my place an' you ain't evah gonna forget it."

"Is that a threat, Sheriff?"

"Nope. That's a fact." He looked at Grace. "Maybe later, when the two of you are nice and cozy, you should remind him of it."

Rathe's arm tensed beneath hers.

"Please," Grace whispered, "please."

Ford was beaming. "I only stopped by to share some news. Thought you might be interested."

"What news?"

Ford looked sad. "That sailor, the one who assaulted Miz O'Rourke? Able Smith? He appears to have escaped. Can you believe that? What with the judge comin' an' all?"

Rathe stared.

Ford sighed. "You two enjoy yourselves tonight," he said. He turned to go.

Rathe's hand clamped on his shoulder, stopping him. Ford looked at the hand. But Rathe didn't remove it. "You're making a big mistake, Sheriff," Rathe drawled, "if you think you can come up against me and win."

Ford shrugged free. He touched his hat and walked away.

"Rathe, let's go into the restaurant—now."

He stared after Ford, then took her arm. Grace looked

at his profile, very worried. It was hard as granite. She laid her free hand on top of his. "Are you hungry?"

He forced his attention to her, but he still didn't answer.

As the maitre d' led them to their table, Grace was reminded that she had started this entire thing. Rathe pulled out her chair, seating her. He was very grim.

"What are you going to do?" Grace asked as he perused a wine list.

He didn't look up. "About what?"

"Rathe!"

He laid the list aside. "Isn't this what you wanted? Me to take on Ford? Stand up against him? Kill him?"

"No!"

"That's what this is going to come to, Grace. Either that or he'll kill me."

She clutched her hands. "No! There has to be a way to resolve this."

"I want you to stay out of it," he told her.

"What are you going to do now?"

"Order some champagne."

"No, I mean about Ford."

He looked at her, then turned and signaled to a waiter. "I'm going to find that sailor and bring him back."

"He's probably left town!"

"Undoubtedly."

"Rathe, don't pursue this. Let it go."

"What about the principles involved here, Grace?"

Grace looked at the tablecloth. "This is personal for you. You're doing this for all the wrong reasons! Just like you proposed to me for all the wrong reasons!"

His hand slapped the table, hard. "You're sitting in judgment on me again! And I don't like it!"

"Everyone's staring," she whispered.

"Everyone's been staring at you since you came down those stairs," he said tightly. "It's because you're stunning. Tell me something, Grace." He leaned forward. "Just how in hell would you know why I do anything?"

She swallowed.

"You don't know my thoughts, my feelings. You don't know them because you don't care enough to find out what they are! Instead, you've judged me as some sort of rotten cad—and for some reason, you won't look any further."

"That's not true."

"No?"

"Then tell me," she said, her heart pounding. "Why *did* you ask me to marry you?"

"Because I wanted you to be my wife."

Wanted. The past tense. He had wanted her to be his wife—he didn't want that anymore. Why should he? He had what he wanted—didn't he? Not that it mattered! She didn't want to be his wife—did she?

He was still staring at her, hard. Grace dropped her gaze, feeling miserable. She did not see the disappointment sweep his face.

How many times had he come close to proposing again? Rathe wondered. He kept giving her openings, but she wouldn't respond, wouldn't tell him she'd changed her mind. He was stunned, then, to realize he still wanted to marry her. And that he always would.

Oh, my God, he thought. He was in love with her. He hadn't faced it before—there had only been words spoken in the frenzy of passion. But he could no longer avoid the truth. He had fallen in love with Grace O'Rourke.

A crazy, red-haired, politicking spinster.

A wonderful, warm, blossoming woman.

And on the heels of shock came fierce resolution. He would marry her. No matter what it took, he would marry her.

"Well, isn't this a quaint, happy scene?" purred Louisa Barclay.

They both looked up, startled from their grim thoughts. Louisa was resplendent in bold purple silk, her shoulders and most of her white bosom completely bared. Grace suddenly felt dowdy and drab.

"Why, this is a surprise," she gushed loudly. "If it

isn't Rathe Bragg and—why—I almost didn't recognize you!''

Grace sat still and taut, wishing that Louisa had caught them gazing with rapt devotion into each other's eyes.

"Hello, Louisa." Rathe was standing politely. He took her hand and brushed it with his mouth, barely touching her skin.

"I had heard, of course—why everyone in this town has heard, but I just didn't believe it until I saw it with my little ole eyes! It *is* the governess—oh, excuse me—the darkie schoolteacher!''

"Louisa, stop it," Rathe said.

"Honey, I'll forgive you your trespass, as I can see that you're squabbling with your new par—ah, lady friend? An' how do you like the accommodations heah?''

Grace inhaled sharply.

"But darlin', " Louisa said to Grace. "Don't despair. You'll have such fun makin' up. Rathe is an *expert* when it comes to makin' women happy. But you already know that, don't you?''

Grace was red with humiliation and anger. Before she could take a breath, Louisa was kissing Rathe's cheek. He drew back rigidly, but too late. Grace had seen her full pink lips open and wet on his skin. Then Louisa sailed away. I will not cry, Grace told herself.

"Ignore her. She's a spiteful cat," Rathe said, sitting and taking her hand.

Grace yanked her palm away as if his touch burned. "You didn't ignore her. You didn't think she was spiteful enough to keep her out of your bed.''

"I never said I was celibate before you.''

"No, you most certainly didn't." She knew she could not contain the tears another moment longer.

"Grace!''

She leapt to her feet and ran out of the dining room. She knew he was behind her. She stumbled on her dress on the stairs, but managed to regain her balance. On the top step she fell, onto her hands and knees. Rathe called to her, pounding up the stairs. Grace stood and heard the fabric of her beautiful gown ripping. She began to weep.

He froze on the top step, but only for an instant. "She's not worth crying over," he said gently, taking her into his arms.

"I tore my new gown," she sobbed.

"It can be fixed."

"My beautiful new gown."

"I'll buy you another one."

"I don't want another one." She wept.

He rocked her. "Don't cry. Please don't cry."

"Hold me."

"I'm holding you."

"Don't let me go."

"I won't. Ever. I'll take care of you, Grace. I swear it."

"I'm afraid."

"Don't be afraid. Don't ever be afraid. Everything will be fine."

"How can you take care of me when you're going to get killed?"

He raised her tearstained face. "What?"

She looked into his eyes and her face crumbled anew.

"Would you care, Grace?"

"Yes, yes, I would care!" she sobbed hysterically.

His breath caught in his chest. His hold on her tightened. Together they swayed.

"I don't know what's happening to me," she said into his soaked chest.

"Just stop fighting me, Grace," he murmured. "Stop fighting me and everything will be all right."

Chapter 22

The first thing Grace was aware of was the morning sunlight spilling brightly, hotly, into their room. She opened her eyes, blinking, wondering why she had slept so late. Remembrance flooded her—Rathe carrying her into their room, holding her, touching her. Something had happened to her last night, an explosion of passion accompanying the realization that she was so very scared for him. When his mouth gently sought hers in comfort, still wet with her tears, she had clutched him fiercely, holding his big neck in her hands, never wanting to let him go. His gasp was one of surprise.

"Rathe," she cried, nipping his mouth frantically, demandingly. She could not control her need, her aggression, fed by horror and fear. She was desperate, and only his big body sliding into hers could still that desperation.

Grace rolled onto her side. She had started something, something she desperately wished she could undo. She did not mean the passion which she and Rathe had shared. How could she feel shame over her uninhibited behavior when there was so much more at stake? When an innocent man could be killed? When it was her fault for provoking Rathe to oppose Ford? And even if Rathe didn't get killed, even if it were Ford, she had never meant to put a match to burning coals, had never dreamed the result would be an uncontrollable conflagration.

The sheriff had threatened Rathe. She felt sick remembering. Previously, Rathe and Ford had only been hurling innuendoes at each other, but this time the sheriff had blatantly threatened him. If Rathe ever wound up in Ford's jail he would be in dire straits. Somehow, at all costs, that must not happen!

She found the note immediately. It was propped up on the night table by the pitcher of water. Shocked, Grace stared at his bold handwriting, the envelope addressed with a single word, Grace. Sitting up, she reached for it, filled with dread. Somehow, she already knew . . .

"I didn't want to wake you after last night," he wrote. "I'm on my way to New Orleans, which is the most likely place for Able Smith to have gone. I hope to be back in a week or so, with him. The room is paid for. Charge anything else you need, including meals. Everything is arranged. I've left you extra money, just in case. Rathe." There was a hundred dollars inside the envelope.

He was gone. Grace crumpled the letter and threw it on the floor. She would pray that he would come back empty-handed so that this ridiculous conflict would go no further. And even then, she had a feeling that nothing was going to stop the two men, not now.

Grace, you fool! If someone is killed it will be your fault! If Rathe is killed . . . She inhaled. The thought was unbearable. She cared for him. She really cared for him. Somehow, it was happening. She was falling in love with him.

And he hadn't even said goodbye.

Enough brooding. She decided she would take advantage of his absence in the best way she knew. She would devote herself full-time to her informal class. And if she could, she would think of a way to manipulate Rathe away from a confrontation with Ford. She had tried to manipulate him once; she'd try again. But why did she feel so awful just contemplating such action?

"Allen, you shouldn't have come today," Grace said.

Allen climbed slowly out of the buggy which Grace was driving. He had accompanied her to school that day and they had just returned to Natchez. It was late afternoon. "I had to, Grace. When I heard you had organized a class, I just had to. Besides, I'm feeling much better now."

Grace shifted in her seat uneasily. She had been too much of a coward to ever bring up the subject of Rathe with him. "I think Doctor Lang was being optimistic when he said you could be up and about. And he certainly didn't mean for you to spend an entire afternoon out of bed!"

"Do you care?"

"Of course I care," Grace said miserably.

"Do you love him?"

She paused, stricken. Then a burning blush began.

"I knew it," Allen cried, turning his face away. "I knew you would never have gone to him if you didn't." He turned a hot gaze on her. "Has he asked you to marry him?"

"I don't want to get married," Grace said, more calmly than she felt. And the moment the words were out she realized they were a lie.

"I can't claim to understand what's going on between the two of you, Grace," Allen said carefully. "I can't even tell whether you're happy with him. God knows, he's not a bad man, but he ought to marry you. Anyway," Allen added softly, "should you change your mind, I'll be here. Waiting. I still want to marry you, Grace."

He was so sincere and there was so much love in his eyes that Grace wanted to weep. "I don't deserve you, Allen," she said huskily, and then she clicked the buggy on down the street, back to the livery.

On the fourth day that Rathe was gone, Grace had visitors. The children were playing tag in the churchyard. Grace was eating her lunch beside Allen, who was getting better and better. Every day he insisted upon coming with her to school. He moved less stiffly now, and she was glad he was here, for he so enjoyed teaching. She had to admit, it felt good being with him; it felt good teaching together; it felt good sitting here like this at noon, discussing their

students, sharing their progress. This was what it would
be like if she married him.

She pictured Rathe. Her heart and soul took flight and
soared. There was no comparing her feelings—and she
knew it.

"Who's that, Allen?"

Allen looked up from the book he was reading. "I don't
know, I—" He suddenly stood. "Grace, don't say a
word."

She stood too, shielding her eyes from the bright sun.
As the two riders came closer, her heart sank. She would
recognize Rawlins' white-socked chestnut anywhere. And
then her dismay increased. Ford was with him.

"Well, well, if it ain't the little schoolmarm," Rawlins
drawled. "Teachin' all the little niggers with her Yankee
friend."

Ford grinned, his eyes on Grace. "Hear your man left
town." He edged his horse closer.

Grace was afraid. "Good day, Sheriff, Mr. Rawlins.
What can I do for you?"

Rawlins threw back his head and laughed.

Ford smiled. "She talks like she's all full of vinegar,
don't she? But I seen you the other night, all decked out,
pretty as a peach. You're with the wrong man, honey."
He reached out and touched her shoulder.

Grace inhaled. Allen stepped between them. "Sheriff,
what brings you all this way?"

Ford's eyes reluctantly left Grace. He looked at Allen.
"My friend here is all fired up. Thought he'd reached a
little understandin' with the lady, ya see. But 'pears he
didn't. So I thought I'd accompany him while we discussed
things." He grinned.

Rawlins, sitting negligently in the saddle, suddenly
threw his leg over and slid to the ground. He began walking toward them.

"What would you like to discuss?" Allen asked
hoarsely.

Grace reached for Allen, grabbing his arm. She whipped

her head around as Ford slid to the ground, put his arm around her and dragged her against him. "Let me go," she cried, trying to pull free and look at Rawlins at the same time. Ford easily wrapped her in his arms, holding her from behind. The man was husky and strong as an ox, and Grace went still, her heart pounding so fast she felt faint. Sweat gathered and made her dress stick to her body.

"This is my last warnin' to you dumb Yanks," Rawlins spat. "We don't want no nigger school in Natchez." He hit Allen, one punch, right in his cracked ribs. Allen cried out and fell to his knees, clutching himself.

Grace gasped and struggled furiously. "You bigoted bully! Let me go!"

"God, bet she's somethin' in Bragg's bed," Ford said, nuzzling her neck. One of his large hands closed over her breast. Grace froze, stunned, disbelieving. He fingered the nipple, then released her. She bolted to Allen, putting her arms around him. Rawlins and Ford mounted their horses.

"Are you all right?" she cried as they thundered away.

Allen was on his knees. "That bastard!"

"Allen, are you all right?"

"It could be worse."

Grace helped him up. He was sweating. "Bragg will most likely kill him," he stated grimly.

"No!" Grace was frantic. "Allen—we can't tell Rathe. Please!"

Allen looked at her sadly. "Oh, Grace."

"I don't want him hurt."

At last he nodded.

Grace began calling to the children who had gathered in a tight, frightened bunch. "It's all right, those dreadful men are gone and they won't be back today. Come on, everyone! Time for class!"

Allen grabbed her arm. "You are insane, Grace! You can't continue with this!"

"Someone has to teach them. And until you are officially back at work, I intend to do that."

"Grace, these men are not little boys. They have guns and whips. They hurt people, they kill them."

"I realize that. But I have an advantage. I'm a woman. And they might manhandle me a little, but I doubt even Ford would hurt me."

"I disagree!"

"Anyway, tomorrow I intend to have a trick or two up my sleeve. I am going to purchase a gun."

Allen stared.

"Not to use it," she said, flushing. Allen felt the same way about violence that she did. "Just to carry it."

"Oh, God," was Allen's reply.

"I don't believe this." Ford was on his feet.

"Believe it." Rathe smiled. It did not reach his eyes. He was hot, soaked with sweat, and dirty. But the man he shoved forward was even dirtier—and bruised as well. He had a closed black eye, a swollen mouth, and various cuts.

Ford recovered, and began to grin, thumbs in his pockets. "You don't quit, do you, boy?"

Rathe leveled a stare on him. "Never. Just think of how this is going to make you look, Sheriff. Prisoner escapes, prisoner returned. Good for you, don't you agree?"

Ford spat. "All over some colored trash."

"And a lady."

Ford just looked at him.

Rathe controlled himself. He did not want to fight with Ford now, not over Grace, not when he wanted a bigger victory—the sailor tried and judged guilty. He would sacrifice the battle for the war. "Later, Sheriff."

Ford laughed.

Outside, Rathe nodded to the Pinkerton man he had hired to guard the prisoner, then began hurrying with long strides to Cliff Street. He could not wait to see Grace.

She wasn't in their room, and he assumed she was out shopping. He hoped she was buying herself something pretty and extravagant. He smiled at the thought. He had brought home a few gifts for her, which he carefully placed on the table. One of them was something pretty and extravagant. He thought they had gotten close enough for her to wear it. But maybe not.

He had not been able to forget the last night they had spent together. Grace had been a tigress in his arms. He had been stunned by her fierce, demanding passion. And he had responded. He had imagined that Grace had deep, hidden fires, but never had he dreamed they could be so hot, so bright. Never had he imagined making love to her in such a hard excess of frenzy. She didn't know it, but she had actually left marks on his neck from her teeth and on his back from her nails. He had worn them proudly.

While he'd been gone he had worried about her, too, knowing the penchant she had for getting into trouble. But what trouble could she possibly get into? He knew she was no longer in the Ladies' Christian Temperance Union, due to her relationship with him. And she was no longer teaching. That was one thing he wasn't sorry about, that he was indirectly responsible for her having been dismissed. Fortunately he had found out about the informal class and forbidden it. That was one issue Grace did not need to be involved in.

He lolled in a hot bath, hoping she would return while he was in it. He would drag her down, clothes and all, letting her know just how much he had missed her. After the other night, she couldn't still be prim and proper—could she? He grinned. There was only one way to find out.

He had, however, just stepped out of the tub and was wrapping a towel around his waist when the door opened and Grace appeared, and then froze, eyes widening. He grinned. "Hello, sweetheart."

She was staring right into his eyes, her lips parted in a soundless exclamation, a vision in pale blue silk. Then her glance dropped, taking in his mostly naked body, and high spots of color began to form on her cheeks. He couldn't help it, he was having an instant erection from wanting her so badly, missing her so much. "Come here, sweetheart."

She did the unexpected. She rushed to him, throwing her arms around his damp body. Rathe hugged her fiercely. "I like this welcoming!"

She clung. He wanted to give her her gifts, but he also wanted to do something else, and his hands held her hips hard against his. "Oh, Grace, did I miss you."

Her lips met his. Her mouth was open, moist, eager. He cupped her face in his palms, so he could look into her eyes. "I don't think I can behave right now, Grace."

She smiled, mouth trembling, and he was startled to find tears in her eyes. "Now is not the time to be reformed," she whispered.

He whooped. He lifted her and carried her to the bed. She lay sprawled against the white sheets, holding her arms out to him. It was a moment he would never forget. A magnificent, breathtaking sight—Grace holding her arms out to him.

He laughed, and dove on top of her. She giggled in surprise. He yanked her reticule out from beneath them and tossed it to the floor, where it landed with a thud. He straddled her, still wearing the towel. "Now, you," he said, with laughter in his voice. "You are in big trouble!"

"I am?" asked amazing Grace. She reached for the towel, and pulled. "Oh dear," she said. "I guess I am!"

He showered her with the gifts.

The lightweight boxes and the wrapped parcels fell to the bed, sliding across her body. Grace sat up, clutching the sheet. "What are you doing?"

Smiling, he took a red, red rose out of the dozen in his hand, and tossed it at her.

"Rathe!"

He tossed another, and another. One fell on her belly, one on her hand. She started to giggle. He started to laugh. He tossed the roses until they were strewn all around her on the big, white bed.

"You're impossible!"

"And you like it like that," he said, sitting and kissing her lightly on the mouth.

She couldn't contain her smiles. They were like sunbeams and starbursts. "Open one," Rathe urged.

"What have you done?"

She opened a box and found a beautiful turquoise shawl, shot with silver and gold threads. "Oh." She lifted her eyes to his.

"Like it?"

"I love it." She hugged him, hard and fast.

Rathe knew he was grinning like an idiot. "Open another."

She did, and bit her lip to contain her pleasure. "How did you know I like chocolate?"

"Good guess," he replied smoothly, not about to tell her he'd never met a woman who didn't.

"You've done too much," she scolded.

"Open another."

She reached for a box.

"Not that one, the other one."

She looked at him, then smiled, and took the box he shoved toward her. She unwrapped it slowly, then pulled out a chiffon wrapper, lace-trimmed, the creamiest white. A wisp of nightgown followed. "Oh."

"Do you like them?" Rathe asked hesitantly.

She did. She had to admit it, she did. The material was sheer, but so finely made, the stitches exquisite. They were garments fit for a princess, not her. "Only a queen should wear this," she said, blinking back a sudden tear.

"You are a queen," he said, taking her hand. "My queen."

Their gazes locked.

If only he meant it, she thought.

Why won't she believe me? he wondered.

"There's one more."

Grace smiled, unable to contain an expression of eagerness. "This is too much!"

"Nothing is too much for you."

She looked at him sternly. "Words come a little too easily from those lips of yours, sir."

He bit back a smile. He placed a hand on his heart. "I plead guilty, madame."

She opened the box, and drew out the scantiest silk drawers she had ever seen. They were black. They would only reach the top of her thighs—if that. They had lace garters with red rosettes. With it came the shortest lace chemise Grace had ever seen. It was doubtful it would reach her waist. "Oh, how nice," she said, holding up the chemise. "A handkerchief."

Rathe started to laugh. He couldn't help it, and soon he was in tears. She was laughing, too. Extraordinary Grace! He had expected any reaction but this. He swept her into his arms, holding her tightly.

"You are so very bad," Grace said into his neck.

"I'm holding out. I need you, Grace, to reform me."

She touched his cheek.

He was sheepish. "Is it too much?"

"A bit."

"Can't blame me for trying."

"No, I can't blame you for trying."

Rathe got up and began to gather the empty boxes and wrappers. Grace watched, unable to take her eyes off of him, filled up with the unbearable pleasure of love. I'm in love, she thought, holding her chest. Truly in love!

"So what have you been doing?" Rathe asked, placing everything in one neat pile for the maid. Grace was about to reply when he spotted her reticule on the floor. He picked it up; she froze. "What the hell's in here, anyway?" he asked. "This thing weighs a ton."

"Rathe," she said, to distract him. But it was too late. He turned to face her, staring, shock giving way to disbelief and then anger, holding up a gun. It dangled black and ugly from his hand. She had purchased it after the incident with Ford and Rawlins.

"What the hell is this?"

"It's a gun."

"I know it's a gun," he said grimly. "Grace, why is there a gun in your reticule?"

"Because—" She wet her lips. "Because I thought I might need it."

He looked at her. There was a strange expression on his face—worry, agitation, dread. "Why do you need a gun?"

She didn't want to tell him about Ford and Rawlins. "It's just a precaution," she assured him cheerfully. "Going back and forth to the school every day, alone—well, I thought I should have a means of protecting myself, just in case. From robbers. And men like that sailor."

He stared.

She gave him a brave smile.

"You're teaching?" He couldn't believe it. He had forbidden it—even if, immediately afterward, they had become preoccupied with the issue of the five thousand dollars. He had forbidden it—and she had defied him. "You're teaching?"

"Yes."

"I don't believe it!" His hand slammed down on the table, so hard that the top tilted.

"Rathe!"

"I thought I told you," he shouted. "I don't want you teaching!"

She wished she were dressed so she could stand. Instead, she could only sit up straighter, holding the covers high. "Let's stay calm. You didn't tell me not to teach. And you can't—"

"I'm telling you now!" he roared.

She was on her feet, sheets or no. "How dare you! You can't tell me what to do!"

"You listen to me, Grace. I can and I will," he cried furiously.

"I'm a teacher!" she shouted. "It's who I am, what I do!"

"You're my mistress."

She inhaled. "You don't own me."

His jaw clenched. Thankfully, he did not reply, for they both knew the truth—he did own her; he had bought her for the next year. Grace tugged the sheet around her body. "You don't own me," she repeated stubbornly.

"You're not teaching," he said. "It's too dangerous, and that's the end of that."

"You're not being fair," she said thickly, swallowing a lump of tears.

"I don't want you hurt, Grace," he responded tightly.

"I won't be hurt. I'm a woman. They wouldn't harm me."

"You are deluding yourself. And I'm not interested in any further arguments. This conversation is closed." He turned and opened the wardrobe, reaching for his breeches.

"This conversation is *not* closed," she yelled.

He ignored her, yanking on his pants.

"Do you think you can really stop me, Rathe?"

He jerked his belt together. "I've made arrangements to move your mother to the New York Frazier Hospital. It's the finest in the city, and I'm close friends with the director. She'll have special care."

She understood instantly that he was changing the subject. Now he was being thoughtful, but she didn't care; it was too late. "I'll have her moved myself."

"I've also arranged for a private nurse."

"You gave me the five thousand dollars, remember?"

"I gave that money to you," he said. "It's for you, Grace. I'll take care of your mother."

Was he trying to buy her off? Why did he have to try and strong-arm her? Why did he have to be so damn stubborn? Her resolve reasserted itself. She could be just as stubborn as he was—especially when she was right, and he was wrong! Oh, she would keep on teaching, all right. She would just have to become a liar and a cheat to do so.

Rathe saw her fierce expression. "Grace," he warned, "don't even think of whatever's put that stubborn look on your face. I will not back down on this."

To his surprise, she smiled. "All right. I don't want to fight, anyway."

"Neither do I," he said harshly. He went abruptly to her and took her into his arms. She was stiff with anger. "Don't be mad at me, Grace. I'm only trying to do what's best for you."

She looked at him and softened.

"You know that, don't you?"

"Yes," she admitted, touching his cheek. "I do know that."

He looked at her and knew there was no way he could let her teach.

She looked at him and knew there was no way he was going to stop her.

He just could not allow her to place herself in such danger. He loved her too much.

She just could not allow him to dominate her. There was too much at stake.

Chapter 23

Rathe was in love. The next few days passed in an idyllic haze and the sun at the center of his universe was Grace. He had to restrain himself from buying her too many presents, from reaching for her too often, from tumbling her too frequently into their big four-poster bed. It was impossible. He loved to see her smile, to hear her laugh. Suddenly it was easy to make her happy. Grace was no longer fighting him. She had succumbed, and he knew it.

He still had the twelve-carat yellow diamond.

He was afraid to push his suit too fast and too hard. He was succeeding, wooing her into loving him. He could tell, not just because of her response in bed, but because of the way she smiled at him, and the look in her eye when he caught her unawares, watching him. Still, he would give her more time before he asked her to marry him again.

At first, in between their sweet morning lovemaking and their luxurious afternoon picnics, he was a touch suspicious. Grace had given in so easily. It just wasn't like her. But then he realized that, by now, he should know never to expect a specific reaction from her, that she would always be unpredictable.

If it weren't for her, he would have neglected his business affairs completely. He didn't want to leave her for a minute. But Grace was brisk and stern, insisting that he must devote a few hours each day to his vast concerns. "You don't want to be robbed blind, now do you?" she asked, hands on hips.

"No ma'am." He grinned, and a pattern was set. Every day from about ten to two he took care of his correspondence and oversaw his business interests. Grace would browse through the town, always returning with a new purchase—fresh muffins, lace gloves, a cameo pin. Once she even brought him a gift—a beautiful man's ring of onyx and gold. Rathe had been speechless. Although he had received gifts from women before, this was different— this was from Grace. He was overwhelmed.

"Do you like it?" she asked shyly.

"It's beautiful."

"I know I bought it with your money—"

He cut her off, sweeping her into his arms and hugging her fiercely. "The money I give you is yours. Thank you, Grace." He wanted to tell her he loved her, but he was afraid to reveal his innermost feelings. Of course, they weren't all that well-hidden these days. He was wearing his heart on his sleeve.

He made a decision. He sent a wire to his folks, telling them that he and a lady friend would be arriving in three weeks, on the fifteenth. He smiled at the thought. Within ten days he would propose and Grace would accept, which meant that when he returned home, he would be bringing his bride. He had no intention of waiting until they got to his parents' ranch to wed. The instant Grace said yes, he was taking her to the nearest cleric and putting that ring on her finger.

He had settled into a poker game at the Black Heel after supper. Grace had shooed him out, telling him that she had to write some letters and she couldn't think straight with him around. He liked that. He wanted to be a distraction to her, always. Even when she was doing something else, he wanted to be there with her, on her mind . . . like she was always with him.

He wanted to go back to the hotel and make love to her. However, he had just started to win heavily, and he believed in fair play. Farris and the others wouldn't be very happy if he left right now. Also, he and Grace had made love all afternoon in a glade by the pond. But if he kept on thinking about it, fair play or not, he was going to quit the game.

"Rathe, hey you! You in or out? You even here?" George waved a hand in front of his face.

Rathe cursed and threw down his hand. "Out. Sorry."

"Why don't you go back to that little love nest and itch that scratch—or whatever it is." He winked, and gave Rathe a lewd look.

"Hey, listen," someone at the next table said in an urgent voice.

A silence fell as everyone, including Rathe, listened to the night. Only crickets, the whinny of a horse, and the roll of someone's carriage were discernible. To hell with it! He pushed back his chair, about to leave, when the drumming of approaching hoofbeats became clear, getting louder. A chill raced up his spine.

It was late and there could only be one possible explanation for such a group of riders.

George said, "Night riders."

"Wonder who the poor bastard is they're after," someone murmured.

Rathe was thinking the same thing, indignation and outrage boiling through his veins. Suddenly he realized that everyone in the saloon was looking at him. Another chill swept him—one of impending doom. He wasn't wearing his gun, but he did have his knife. He slowly rose to his feet. He thought, *Would Ford dare ride after me?*

George was standing, too. "You better get going," he urged.

Rathe gave him a wry smile. "I have no intention of running."

George's eyes widened. "You fool! It isn't you that they're after! Rathe, how could you let her do it? Didn't you know it would come to this? Rawlins has been mouthing off for days about your little redhead."

"What?"

"He's pissed she's still teachin' the darkies," George

said. "He's pissed she didn't listen to the second warning. Real pissed."

It took him a second. *"Teaching?"*

A look of sympathy crossed George's face. "You didn't know? She got a whole new class organized an' they meet every day from ten to two. Rathe, I got this feelin' after hearin' Rawlins today—"

Rathe cursed and was running out the door. He knew George was on his heels and was vaguely surprised. He wasn't one step out of the doorway when the riders came galloping by, a dozen or so big dark horses, freezing Rathe in his tracks. The instant they were past he was leaping onto his horse, urging it into a gallop, trying desperately to think of a shorter way to get back to the hotel. There was no shortcut. As he turned the corner at a gallop, he saw the mass of horseflesh come to a wheeling, stomping halt in front of the Silver Lady Hotel. Half of the riders dismounted, and as one, they ran inside.

Grace knew she had made a mistake.

She had been lying to Rathe and she felt awful. But he would not back down about her teaching. So she'd sneaked behind Rathe's back to continue meeting with the children. She wouldn't back down, either. She couldn't.

The issue was deeper than the right of the children to learn. Allen would be able to go back to teaching at least part-time in a few more weeks. Then what was to become of her? She would be nothing but a man's mistress.

Even if he proposed to her again, how could she accept? Love wasn't enough. He was trying to force her to bend to his will, and she wasn't even his wife. He didn't have any hold on her, especially not a legal hold, yet he was dictating a decision that affected her entire being. It would be a miracle for them to marry without an issue arising over which he would try and railroad her again. And he would do so, repeatedly, because they did not think the same way, and it didn't look like they ever would.

Such speculation was pointless. He wasn't going to propose another time, and she should bless her lucky stars. Because there was a reckless part of her just dying to say yes!

Is this what love is? she wondered, her face buried in her pillow. Misery and heartache and a longing so intense it eats you up inside?

She loved him so much.

She felt trapped.

One day at a time, she told herself briskly. She had an agreement—she was to stay with him for a year. Because she couldn't handle this subterfuge, she would have to confess all. And take it from there. Grace was sure of only one thing. Her being forbidden to teach was not in the agreement. That had not been clear, and as far as she was concerned, if she had known, she would have never agreed to their liaison.

She had the awful feeling that sooner or later, Rathe would find out she'd disobeyed him, and that the truth was going to set off a chain of events culminating in her leaving him. Surprisingly, tears came, bitter, salty ones. The knowledge of what she had to do was devastating. Oh Rathe, she thought, come back and make love to me and wipe away all the hurt, even if only for a few moments. Hold me as if you love me. And I'll pretend . . .

She raised her head. The night had grown strangely still, when usually the rowdy sounds of the Silver Street saloons drifted up from beneath the cliffs, filling the air. And then she heard it—a rumbling sound like distant thunder. Could it be rain? She lifted up on one elbow. Impossible, there hadn't been a cloud in the sky all day.

Riders.

They were rapidly getting closer.

A terrible frisson of fear accompanied by comprehension raced down Grace's spine. They had to be night riders.

Her instincts were to curl up under the covers and shake. Instead, she threw her feet over the side of the bed and sat in outraged, frightened immobility, trying to think. Who

would be their next victim? It was almost impossible to
believe that they could ride so boldly right down Cliff
Street. What should she do?

If only Rathe were here!

The drumming of the horses' hooves was so loud that
they had to be outside her window. She heard the snorting
of horses, the clanging of bits, the creaking of leather.
Stunned, Grace ran to the window, to see several mounted
men holding six riderless horses right beneath her on the
street.

As the thought came, *they're coming for someone here,
in the hotel,* she heard the banging footsteps of men racing
up the stairs and she shrank, stunned, against the window.

Her door flew open, kicked off of its hinges, and she
stared at six men crowding the doorway, dimly outlined
by a raised lantern.

"Bragg ain't here," someone said with satisfaction.

Horrified, Grace numbly recognized the speaker as
Sheriff Ford.

"I told you, he's in the saloon," someone responded.

"Howdy, gal." Ford grinned, showing yellowish teeth.

Grace couldn't move.

"I'll get her." Rawlins shoved past, unsmiling.

With a frantic cry, Grace whirled and slammed the window, which was slightly open, all the way up. They were
on the second floor. Below her was a slanting shingled
roof, then nothing but the dusty street. She threw one white
leg over the sill anyway, panicked, but Rawlins' arms
closed around her, dragging her back, and she screamed.

He slapped her harshly across her face, silencing her.
"Shut up, teacher."

Grace barely had time to register the pain when he was
hauling her across the floor by her waist, like a sack of
potatoes. She began to twist and writhe, fighting with her
legs, trying to break free.

"Little hellcat," someone observed.

"Little nigger-lover," Rawlins spat.

"I don't know," a young voice said nervously, "a woman . . ."

"A fancy Yankee whore." Ford chuckled, yanking her through the door. "Hey, you think you want to whore for us, teacher? Think you can a handle what I'm gonna give you?" He mauled at her breast.

Grace leaned over his arm and sank her teeth into his forearm as hard as she could.

He howled, pulled her fully upright and backhanded her so hard she saw stars, then blackness.

He made no sound.

Ahead of him, the horses thundered north of Natchez, through the woods.

Rathe ran silently and effortlessly. Violence seethed in his blood and in his brain. In his mind's eye he saw one thing, and one thing only—Grace in her nightgown being dragged out of the hotel and thrown over someone's horse. She had been inert, lifeless.

He was going to kill tonight.

His strides came long and easy, despite his boots, which were not meant for running. In his hand he held George's pistol. He ran with a stealth learned in a childhood spent outdoors under the Texas sun, taught by his half-breed father. Not a twig snapped. Not a leaf rustled. It was dark, but he didn't stumble. It had been ages since he had run like this, not since the War, and then he had been the hunted. Now he was the hunter.

He heard them stopping, heard the drift of voices, excited, angry, arguing. Perspiration covered his body, causing his breeches and shirt to cling wetly to his skin. He paused, crouching behind shrubbery. He looked into the clearing, and the sight made every muscle in his body go rigid; and for the first time he made a sound—a sharp, indrawn breath.

Grace was on the ground on her hands and knees, shaking her head groggily, her long hair spilling all around her. Ford reached down from horseback and in a lightning movement ripped the nightgown from her. A stunned male silence fell, and then it was broken.

"Christ," someone gasped, "look at those legs."

"And those tits."

Ford laughed, the sound carrying in the night. Rawlins leapt to the ground and hauled Grace to her feet, pulling her back against him, grinning, one hand crudely squeezing her breasts. He opened his mouth to say something. It never came out.

The knife landed in the back of his neck. He stiffened, eyes widening, and crumbled.

"Run, Grace," Rathe shouted, standing and showing himself, and then he fired. The man standing closest to Grace fell before he could even react.

Grace was confused. She was slow to respond. She started to move moments too late. A barrage of gunfire was being returned, and Rathe was trying to meet it. He saw Ford leaping for her, spun to shoot him, taking his eyes off the fray. As he fired a bullet grazed his side, and he missed.

Ford dragged Grace aside, holding her in front of him, yelling for everyone to stop shooting. His men, crouched behind rocks and trees, obeyed. Rathe leaned against an oak, ignoring the warm trickle of blood at his side, watching Ford with Grace, wanting to kill again.

"I got your little lady, Bragg," Ford shouted. "Put down that gun or I'm gonna put a hole in her nice white skin."

Sweat trickled from his temple and into his left eye. The sight of Grace naked and vulnerable and being held by Ford threatened his control and his sanity.

"I mean it, Bragg!" Ford yelled.

Rathe tossed the gun out.

"Get it," Ford snapped. "An' get him."

Rathe stepped out from behind the tree and was promptly grabbed by two men. He allowed them to lead him into the torchlight. His insides clenched at the red mark on Grace's face, starting to turn purple, the flesh swelling. Then he saw Ford touch her breasts, and he went berserk. He struggled wildly, insanely, against the two men holding him and broke free. Ford's laughter died abruptly. Rathe felt an immense pleasure as he leaped for the man's throat, instants away from tearing it out with his own two bare hands. Grace's scream was the last thing he heard as an immense pain exploded in the back of his head, and everything went dark.

The water was warm. He choked as it streamed over his face and into his mouth, and then realized that it wasn't water but whiskey. Waves of pain coursed through his head, and with it, understanding and anger and fear. He struggled through the blackness as more liquor came cascading like a slap against his face. He sputtered and coughed and opened his eyes.

"Don't want you to miss the show, Bragg," Ford purred.

He met the man's gaze with hatred.

"First your little lady friend and then you."

Rathe's body convulsed against the ropes binding his wrists; with his powerful legs he pushed himself up to his feet. His eyes had already found Grace, tied face-down to a cross, naked and shaking. Horror almost incapacitated him, but when he spoke, his voice was very quiet and very calm. "Don't do it," he said, tearing his gaze away from her white body. "It's me you want. Not her."

Ford laughed. "We're only gonna hurt her a little," he said. "Enough so she packs up her bags and never thinks of comin' back. But you . . ." He stepped close. "You're gonna watch her pretty hide turn red. Then you're gonna watch me fuck her. Then you're gonna die, Bragg, long and slow, and no one in Natchez is gonna even care."

"She's a woman."

"She's your Yankee whore," Ford leered, laughing when Rathe jerked his arms impotently against his bindings. Ford reached out and shoved him back hard. Rathe fell onto his hands and buttocks, his head slamming back onto the ground. Pain coursed through him and he saw red and black. For a moment he lay stunned, fighting waves of dizziness and nausea. He heard Ford ordering someone to revive him. He couldn't pass out now. He had to save Grace. He shook his head to clear it as whiskey again splashed in his face. This time he was dragged to his feet by two men. When they released him he swayed precariously, and Ford snapped out another order. "Hold him, Frank, I don't want him to miss a minute."

"Get started," he said to the man standing by Grace with the whip.

It was like slow motion. Rathe saw her body tense, gleaming white in the torchlight, saw the man's arm drawing back, slowly, then coming forward, just as slowly; he saw the snake of leather thong unfurling toward Grace, taking an eternity to reach her. He heard a scream and was startled—it wasn't Grace's cry but his own. The whip flicked casually across the ivory skin of her back leaving a trail of red in its wake.

Grace's entire body contorted. Rathe pulled free of the man holding him. Ford laughed and another lash struck Grace again. This time she whimpered and sagged face-down against the cross.

A shot rang into the night. All heads turned, including Rathe's. The darkness was thick, but not thick enough to hide several riders just past the line of oaks. Another shot rang out and someone cried out in pain. The night riders ran for cover, Ford shouting futile orders. Rathe found himself abandoned. He fell to the ground, rolling as gunfire echoed and was returned. He twisted to see Grace, afraid she'd get caught by a stray bullet. He forced himself to his knees amidst panicked, fleeing riders.

"Doan move, Mistah Rathe," a small voice said behind him.

"Geoff!" Rathe gasped. "Can you cut me free?"

The little boy, as black as the night, had a knife and slashed through his bonds. Rathe was barely free before he was stumbling toward Grace through the last remaining riders. In the corner of his eyes he saw Ford cantering past and knew he would kill him soon. He reached Grace just as an eerie silence fell over the glade. "Grace? Gracie?"

"I'm all right," she gasped, a hoarse, raw sound.

He had his hands, which were trembling, on her white, unmarked shoulder, but he was sick at the sight of her bloodied back. Geoffrey was cutting her down with his knife, and Rathe took her into his arms. He didn't know where he found the strength to hold them both up. Then he was aware of George throwing his jacket over her, and Allen Kennedy saying, "We'd better get these two to a doctor."

Chapter 24

"I have to see him," she cried, trying to sit up.

"The doctor's with him. Just relax," Harriet soothed, trying to hold onto her hand.

Grace felt the threat of impending tears. All she could focus on was Ford's statement of how he was going to kill Rathe. "Oh, Harriet, please."

"He's out cold and wouldn't even know you were there," Harriet said firmly. "Stop moving about so or those nasty welts won't have a chance to heal."

Grace sank back down onto her stomach, cradling the pillow beneath her head. She was so utterly exhausted, and still so afraid. There was so much blood—and all of it Rathe's. She felt Harriet's hand on her head, stroking down her hair to her nape. Her eyes fluttered closed. "Promise me," she whispered, "if he needs me you'll call?"

"I promise," Harriet said.

Grace fell into the calming embrace of sleep.

His head throbbed. His first conscious thought was, God, what did I do? Drink myself under the table? Then came full, blunt awareness. His eyes flew open and he tried to sit up. Pain tore through his side and through his head.

"Good morning," Harriet said cheerfully, bearing a tray.

"Grace."

"She's fine, still asleep. Poor thing is tuckered out. Lie back down, boy," she admonished.

The effort to sit up was too great, so Rathe obeyed. He realized he was at Harriet's then, not at the Silver Lady. "Is Grace here too?"

"Yes, it was closer to bring you here." Harriet reached out and touched his forehead. "No fever. The doctor says you have the constitution of an ox. Says you should stay in bed all week, from the size of the egg on your scalp."

He grimaced ruefully. "Is Grace all right?"

"She'll have a scar or two."

Anger flooded his features.

"She's fine," Harriet soothed. "And it could have been much, much worse."

He did not have to be told. "I want to see her."

"You're not getting out of that bed."

"I have to see her," Rathe said, trying to sit again. Out of sheer perversity, he did.

"If I have to turn you over and thrash your bottom," Harriet said, "I will. But you're staying in bed like the doctor said."

Rathe had to smile, just a little. "Fess up, Harriet," he said, unable to resist. "You're just dying to get an eyeful."

"Oh," Harriet said, but she was smiling. "You are irresistible. However did your mama manage?"

The grin was full-fledged this time. "As I recollect, she had a tad of trouble."

"Rathe," Harriet said, sobering. "They burned the colored's church."

"When?"

"Last night sometime."

He felt more anger, deep in his gut. "Does Grace know?"

"No one's told her. Allen and I agreed she's been through enough. Now's not the time for more bad news."

At Allen's name, Rathe imagined him with Grace while she was recuperating. He couldn't help the small spark of jealousy, but it was outweighed by other, stronger emotions. "When you see Allen, can you ask him to stop by?"

"Too late," Allen said, from the doorway. "I'm already here."

Rathe looked at him directly. "How is Grace?"

"She just woke up," Allen said. He looked at Harriet. "Have you told him the rest?"

Harriet shook her head.

"The rest of what?"

Allen grimaced. "Able Smith—that sailor—is dead."

"What happened?" Rathe demanded, his jaw tight.

"A suicide, according to Ford."

Rathe cursed. He gazed grimly at the foot of the bed. Smith was dead. It was unbelievable. Rathe was positive the man had not committed suicide; there was no reason for him to do so. Did Ford really think he could get away with this, that he, Rathe, would now back down? If so, he had another think coming. Rathe intended to watch every move he made.

"How is Grace, exactly?"

"Tired, still a bit hysterical, I think. Shocked." He paused. He couldn't bring himself to tell this man, whom he both respected and envied, that she had been asking for him.

Rathe cursed. Then he looked at Allen. "I want to thank you. You and George. If you hadn't come . . ." He trailed off. Guilt flared. He had failed Grace when she'd needed him most. Farris and Kennedy were the heroes, not him.

"There's no need to thank me," Allen said. "You know how I feel about Grace and the public school system. But if it hadn't been for Farris I wouldn't have known what was going on."

"Still," Rathe said stubbornly, "you barely recovered from your own close escape. I thank you."

Allen nodded abruptly.

Rathe's gaze was penetrating. "Did you know she was teaching?"

"Yes." At Rathe's furious expression, Allen went on.

"I tried to stop her, but you know Grace. When she sets her mind on something, nothing will stop her. And she made me promise not to tell you."

Rathe swore. "Tell me everything, Allen. I want to know exactly what went on while I was gone."

"Grace," Harriet reproved.

Grace gave Harriet a determined look, then gazed past her at Rathe, asleep on the bed. His color was off; he was much too pale. Her face filled with consternation. She hurried to him. She sat on the side of the bed, by his hip, and not caring who saw, ran her hand over his cheek and through the thickness of his hair. He stirred slightly.

Her heart clenched. He was the bravest man she knew. She lowered her face and kissed him gently on the lips.

She watched his lashes fluttering, watched a slight smile tilt the corners of his mouth, watched his face turn toward her. He blinked. "Grace?"

"I'm here," she breathed, touching his cheek again. He turned his face more fully into her palm, closing his eyes. The next time he looked at her the sleepiness was gone from his gaze. "Are you all right?"

"Me!" She attempted a small laugh, and failed. "I'm fine. It's you I'm worried about."

His look became stern. "You could have been killed."

"They weren't going to kill me," she said as calmly as she could.

"Dammit," he cried, reaching out and grabbing her hand. He winced from the movement, but his grip was still like steel. "Grace, you lied to me!"

"I'm sorry." She trembled, stroking his hair again. "I am so sorry!" She bit back the anguish.

Her attitude was going to undo him. "How could you lie to me?"

"With great difficulty." She choked, tears glistening.

He closed his eyes on the brink of surrender.

"Oh, Rathe," she cried, hugging him. "I almost got you killed."

Later, he thought, carefully closing her in his arms. They would resolve this later. For now, being alive and together was enough.

A few days later, Rathe lay in bed and stretched—fully.

He heard footsteps and instantly lay prone, turning his face from the door and closing his eyes. He knew, by now, those footsteps belonged to Grace. He smiled, heard the door open, and wiped the smile right off his face.

"Rathe?" Her voice was tentative, as if uncertain whether she wanted to wake him or not.

He groaned slightly.

He heard her set the tray down and approach. He thought how lucky he was that she hadn't caught him downstairs at dawn looking for something to read—three days in bed, and if it weren't for her, he'd be going crazy. But she was here, and he wasn't going crazy. He groaned again and turned to look at her, blinking as if just awakening.

Her smile was so tender and warm he caught his breath.

She approached, instantly touching his forehead for a nonexistent fever. He had only had a slight temperature yesterday, but Grace's tender ministrations and hovering concern had made bedrest worthwhile. His only complaint was that Harriet refused to allow her to give him a sponge bath. When he'd suggested it, she had been appalled, exclaiming that there was enough talk already about the two of them, and that while they recuperated at her place there would be no carrying on! And she had added emphatically, "I hope you're going to marry her, soon."

"You look better and better every day," Grace said, sitting by his hip.

He sighed. "It's your nursing, Gracie. You know that."

"I'm wise to your flattery."

"How wise?"

"Very wise."

They were smiling. Rathe wanted to pull her into his arms and kiss her until they were out of breath. He reached for her. "Come here."

She resisted. "You have to rest, Rathe."

"I don't want to rest. I want you."

She shook her head, but she was smiling. "Only you, Rathe, could be sick in bed, wounded, and want to . . ." She trailed off with a blush.

"And want to what?" he teased.

"I don't think I have to say the words," she said gently.

He touched her hand. "Then I'll say them. I want to make love to you, Grace." He heard his own words— *make love.* It was easier to say it that way then to say what he really wanted to say—*I want to love you, Grace. I do love you. Let me love you. Stay with me—always. Marry me.*

Soon. He would ask her again, soon.

Rathe had not brought up the topic of their near-brush with death again or the fact that she had lied. The way Grace was caring for him now, made it all seem like a dream—a nightmare. She was so attentive, so warm, so tender. He realized that she was apologizing in the best way she could, by taking care of him. He rather liked the attention. And when they were married, well, there'd be time enough to deal with her penchant for stubbornly seeking trouble. Besides, she'd probably be too busy with his babies . . .

He suddenly had the uncanny feeling that even children wouldn't stop Grace from her crusade to change the world. He had to smile. How could he possibly want Grace any other way? Thank God there were normal teaching positions available, ones in normal towns where teachers weren't threatened with death by shadowy night riders. *Then he had a scary thought—even in normal, placid circumstances, he would bet his life she would find a way to place herself in jeopardy—and things would not stay normal and placid for long!*

She interrupted his thoughts. "Hungry?"

"Umm."

She was reaching behind him as if he couldn't sit up, fluffing pillows. He didn't move, didn't help her. Her breasts brushed his bare chest, causing his already aching groin more pain. "Lean forward," she ordered, and he gladly complied. As she fooled with the pillows behind his back he nuzzled the lush cleavage below his face. She gasped, withdrew, then laughed. "You *are* healing."

"My head still hurts," he lied plaintively.

She helped him sit up, her arms beneath his shoulders. He nuzzled her jaw and nipped it.

"Rathe."

"Mmm?"

"What are we going to do?"

Her tone, filled with anxiety, drew his full attention. "What is it, Gracie?" He clasped her hand.

"Rawlins' funeral was this morning."

Rathe grew grim. He met Grace's searching regard. She didn't have to voice her questions; he could read them in her eyes. "At least I don't see condemnation," he said. "At least this time you're wondering how I'm feeling."

"Yes."

He looked at her soberly. "I've killed before, Grace, and it's not something I take lightly, even when the victim is a snake like Rawlins was. The other night I had no choice. There were too many of them, and hatred and violence like that breeds death and murder. I had to react instantly. If I had to do it again, I would."

Grace squeezed his hand. "Rathe—I'm so afraid. Some of the townspeople are angry! They want you arrested!"

Rathe smiled slightly, his eyes narrowed. "Let them arrest me. I'll welcome it."

"What do you mean!"

Rathe laughed grimly. "Ford won't dare. I have money and power. My lawyers wouldn't just get me freed, they'd expose this entire town and Ford's reign of terror. There'd be a scandal. I'd make sure of it. Even though this kind of news isn't new, even though the North is fed up with the South's problems, I'd make sure it made headlines— and nationally. Ford would be finished. What he has been doing is against the law. If he arrested me he wouldn't just be risking his career, he might face prosecution."

Grace sighed. "I didn't think of it that way. I was so worried, thinking he'd arrest you."

"One thing Ford isn't," Rathe said, "and that's stupid. Unfortunately."

"Rathe? How do you feel about traveling?"

All around them bluebirds twittered, the grass trembled in the breeze. The sun was bright, the sky flawless. It was two days later. Rathe held her hand. They paused in the clearing. Grace carried a picnic basket.

Rathe smiled. "You know I love traveling. Where would you like to go? New York? London? China? Tibet?"

Her smile was forced. "I've never been to Europe." And she was thinking, *Is it going to be this easy?*

"Europe it is, Grace." He looked at her. "Don't you know I'd give you the moon and the stars if I could?"

Tears sparkled in her eyes. "Europe will be fine."

He took her hand. "Paris in the spring."

Grace realized she was holding her breath. "In the spring? But that's next year."

"When would you like to go?"

"Now?"

"Grace, even if we left right now, I have to stop in Texas. I'm so close, and . . ." He grinned sheepishly, "my mother would kill me if I didn't. Besides, I want my folks to meet you."

She was aghast. "Rathe, I don't want to meet your parents."

His pleasure faded. "They'll love you."

"Let's go to Paris—now." She was clutching his shoulders.

"Turning tail on me, Grace?" he asked quietly.

"No!"

"You wouldn't run from Rawlins' threats—you even lied to brave them. But now you want to run. Why?"

"I'm afraid," she breathed, clinging.

He held her close. "Don't be afraid. I won't let anything happen to you—I promise."

"It's not me I'm worried about! It's you! Ford is evil, Rathe, he's going to do something. Putting a bullet in your back wouldn't be beneath him."

He didn't smile. "You still don't have any faith in me, do you? From the moment we met, you pegged me a cad, a rogue, a philanderer, a gambler—am I missing any epithets?"

She wanted to tell him she loved him, but she was afraid. Instead she stood frozen with apprehension.

"Do you think me a coward, too?"

"No!"

"If I ran, that is what I would be. Things are not finished between me and Sheriff Ford, and until they are, I can't leave." He started to walk away from her.

Grace ran after him. "Rathe, be sensible. Cowardice has nothing to do with this. This is common sense! Why provoke Ford?"

"I'm not running from this, Grace. I won't run from any man."

"Damn you! You're going to get yourself killed!"

He turned slowly. She was sobbing into her hands. He was stunned. He went to her, took her hands, wet with her tears, in his. "You're afraid for me."

"Yes!"

"You care for me."

"Yes!"

"Enough to stand by me?"

She stared, her lashes thick and wet. The silence lengthened, and then she said, "Please, let's leave."

His tone was hard, bitter. "Enough to marry me?"

She gasped.

His gaze was diamond-hard.

"What are you saying?"

"Will you marry me, Grace? Do you care enough to marry me?"

Her heart was beating so hard she couldn't concentrate. "I—I—Rathe! I have to think."

His nostrils flared. "I believe," he said, as cold as ice, "that's what you said the last time."

"Rathe," she pleaded, grabbing his hand as he turned away. "We don't suit! You know we don't suit."

"We don't suit," he said. "Funny, I thought we suited very well."

"You know what I mean! You're twisting the words all around!"

"Am I? You're the one who is so precise with words— so to the point."

"Rathe, look at what just happened. Can you honestly tell me that you'd have let me teach the children if you'd known about it?"

He exploded. "What the hell does that have to do with us!"

"Everything!"

"You know damn well what you did was foolish. And you lied to me; you skulked around behind my back; you not only almost got me killed, but you almost got yourself raped in the process. You know damn well I would never have let you teach! For God's sake, Grace, Allen will be back at his job in a few weeks!"

"If we were married, you could have forbidden me to teach. And legally, I would have been bound to obey you."

"I ask you to marry me, and we're fighting about you teaching." His gaze was strained in his bitterness. "Nothing's changed. You've never trusted me, and you still don't." He turned and strode away, back toward the road that they had come from town on.

She was horrified. "Rathe, wait!"

But he wouldn't stop. His long strides ate up the ground. Grace began to run. "Please, wait, Rathe!"

She caught up to him, grabbing his arm. He shook her off, not looking at her. She halted, leaning against a tree, panting. "Please," she gasped. "Wait."

He didn't stop. Nor did he look back.

Chapter 25

It felt like she was mortally wounded. Grace slid to the ground at the base of the tree and wept. She had hurt him, and hurting him was worse than hurting herself. But, dear Lord, what should she have done? She hadn't even said no. She had been truthful in telling him that she needed time to think. And Lord, she did!

She knew she couldn't marry him.

He would slowly strip her of her independence, or try to, and their marriage would be one bitter fight. Eventually, wouldn't they start to hate each other?

He wanted to marry her. Did that mean he loved her? And if he did, how could he want to take away the most important things in the world to her? Worse, why was her heart begging her mind to acquiesce?

"I can never marry him."

Spoken out loud, the words rang with truth.

Resolute, she rose to her feet. *What should she do now? Leave.*

Grace hated herself. She did not want to leave. Should she stay here and play his paramour for the next year, until their agreement was up, waiting for the inevitable? Fighting like cats and dogs? Could she stand it, loving him, being with him, yet knowing it was doomed? And if she did leave, would he leave too? She was certain he would keep pushing at Ford as long as she was there to see it. But if she left . . .

It was the most hopeful thought she had had. She would

gladly sacrifice the remaining time left to them to assure his safety.

Grace found the picnic basket and bent to retrieve it. Just when she was feeling slightly less miserable, the sight of the abandoned basket brought forth fresh memories and fresh tears. If she were to be truly honest with herself, she'd admit there was only one place she wanted to be right now—in Rathe's arms, begging forgiveness, soothing away his hurt.

A few minutes later, she realized that she was not on the trail that would take her to the road to town. In her deep turmoil, she had taken a deer path of sorts. She hesitated, unsure of which way to go, then determined that the road did lie ahead, and that with luck, she would find it.

Grace walked for a few minutes, with growing worry, until she saw a clearing in the trees ahead. There was something familiar about the meadow ahead, and she felt relief. Then she stumbled to the edge, and clapped her hand to her mouth.

It was the meadow where the church she had taught in was—except the church was gone, destroyed. Nothing but cinders and dirt and scorch marks and the twisted lump of the iron wood stove remained.

Tears came to her eyes. Such violence, such destruction . . . such hatred. If Grace had more tears to cry she would have wept anew, but she didn't; instead, she leaned against a blackened tree and hugged herself in anguish.

She arrived back at the hotel with her heart in her mouth. She entered their room; Rathe did not look at her. He was wiping shaving cream off his face, clad only in his breeches and boots. A lump caught in her throat. "Rathe?"

No answer. He scooped up change from the bureau, putting it in his pocket.

"Rathe?"

He barely glanced at her, shrugging into his shirt.

Grace was terrified. He was leaving her. "Rathe?"

"What, Grace?"

He was so cold, it broke her heart. "Are you going out?"

This time he did look at her, with narrowed, frost-filled eyes. "Don't bother waiting up."

She choked on her own breath, watching him give her his back, full of anger and disdain, shrugging on an ice-blue vest and a tawny jacket. He walked past her as if she were invisible. The door slammed shut behind him, and he was gone.

He didn't return until close to dawn, when the sky was just changing hue. Grace had not slept at all, and her eyes were red from crying. She lay on her side, stiffly, pretending sleep, but listening to every movement he made. She could tell instantly that he was sober, as he methodically stripped off his clothes. Her heart was frozen in her chest, and she prayed that he would come to bed, take her in his arms, tell her that he loved her. Instead, he climbed in the bed, left a gaping two feet between them, and promptly fell asleep. Crying without making a sound was the hardest thing she had ever done.

The next morning was a repeat of the day before and Grace couldn't stand it. He was eating breakfast and reading the newspaper, giving her more of the same cold, cruel treatment he had given her yesterday. Grace had to know what he had been doing last night. There had been no fragrance of cheap perfume when he had come to bed, and she saw no rouge on the clothes she had so carefully set aside for the laundress. But she couldn't stand the thought that he had spent the night in another woman's arms. "Did you play poker last night?"

He didn't look up. "Yes."

She paused. "Did you win?"

He snapped the paper. "No."

"I'm sorry."

He threw the paper aside, his gaze burning. "Do you have something to say to me, Grace?"

"Where were you last night?" she cried. "Were you with another woman?"

His look was utterly uncompromising. "You have no right to ask."

She gasped.

"You're not my wife," he said, the muscles in his jaw rigid. "Only a wife has the right to ask a question like that."

She couldn't help it, her face began to crumple.

"Shit!" Rathe exploded, rising abruptly and knocking his chair over. Then he was gone.

She should leave now, while things were like this. Yet how could she, for that very reason?

Outside their room, in the hall, Rathe leaned against the door, fighting the urge to go inside and take her into his arms. Damn her! She didn't trust him at all! She didn't trust him enough to marry him, didn't trust him to be able to handle Ford, didn't think he could stay out of a whore's bed when he wasn't with her! What kind of man did she think he was?

He stayed out until sunrise, and this time came home drunk. He had lost a thousand dollars, and he didn't care. Of course, it was all her fault, damn the red-haired witch. Damn her for not believing in him. Damn her for refusing to be his wife. Now, under the influence of alcohol, the hurt was like a gaping wound, threatening to engulf him.

She was sleeping, looking impossibly beautiful, on her side, in the filmy nightgown he had bought her, her hair cascading all around her in fiery red waves. He was suddenly stricken with the wonderfully warm memories of the day he had returned from New Orleans. God, had she been happy, like a little girl at Christmas, unable to contain her delight over a few simple gifts. He had been happy, too. They had been so damn happy, and now they were so damn miserable.

Desire filled his loins until he was swollen and aching and wanting her so badly he thought he might die. But he wouldn't touch her, oh, no. Damned if he would show her how much he needed her, how much he wanted her.

She stirred and raised up on an elbow. "Rathe?"

Her eyes were so red and so swollen. *Am I doing this to her?* he thought with a terrible pang. He shoved the guilt and remorse away. He had offered her marriage, and she had been unsure, had told him she had to think about it, had proved she did not love him.

"Rathe?"

He steeled himself to ignore her, turning his back and stripping. Then he thought the better of removing his breeches—damn himself anyway for still wanting her! He made sure not to touch her as he crawled into the bed.

"Is every—" She gulped air. Her voice quavered, close to desperate tears. "Is everything all right?"

He closed his eyes and fought himself. He heard her ragged exhalation, and felt, rather than saw, her curl up into a little, self-contained ball. He cursed when she choked back a sob. He moved.

He leaned over her with a groan, touching her shoulders. She gasped, instantly launching herself into his arms. He held her. She cried. He stroked her. She clung. "Oh, damnit, Grace," he groaned.

She clutched his face. "Make love to me," she demanded, frenzied. "Rathe, please." Her lips covered his frantically.

He opened beneath their onslaught, melting, irretrievably lost. "Grace, Grace . . ."

"Oh Rathe," she cried, pushing him onto his back, straddling him, kissing his face, his eyelids, his neck, and his jaw. She grabbed hanks of his hair, anchoring him. "Rathe . . ."

He closed his eyes, arching back his head so her mouth could find his throat. Maybe, he was thinking, maybe this can be enough. If he could just be patient . . .

She stretched out on top of him, rubbing against him. Rathe was stunned at her blatant, aggressive desire. "Grace," he cried, taking her head in his hands and shifting his weight, about to roll her beneath him. He could not wait. Never had he needed anyone like he needed Grace. God, he had missed her!

"No," she gasped, on her knees, reaching down to unbutton his pants. Her hand closed around his hard, silk-and-steel length, the first time she had ever touched him there, and Rathe was helpless, lost, frantic. "Grace—please!"

She held him, rubbed herself against him, and then was impaling herself upon his full, thick length. Together, they soared.

She delayed leaving.

Rathe had sent another telegram to his parents, notifying them that he was postponing their arrival.

They were both clinging desperately to their new relationship. No longer were they simply man and mistress. Both were trying to endure a situation neither found acceptable, yet could not change. There had to be an end in sight, yet neither dared to consider it. It was easier to be together, and pretend that everything was as it should be, that things would never change. While their time together was as intense as before, both in bed and out, desperation and urgency underlay every moment they spent together. And they both felt it.

For this reason, Grace could not understand what Rathe was doing. The past two days he had disappeared mysteriously, claiming high-stakes poker that he couldn't afford to miss, leaving Grace alone and disappointed and hurt. Their relationship was in such a precarious state as it was, and his behavior now added to it. He was doing something behind her back—this she knew very well. Then one day Clarissa and Geoffrey appeared, a welcome relief to the unfamiliar boredom of an idle afternoon.

"You've gotta come with us, Miz Grace," Geoff beamed, tugging her down the stairs.

"Did you bring a bonnet, Miz Grace?" Clarissa asked

from behind them. "It's real hot out there. You sure need a bonnet."

"What is all this fuss about?" Grace asked, feeling their uncontained excitement. "No, I did not."

"You're going to need one," Clarissa stated. Grace ran back upstairs and retrieved a lavender hat that matched the stripes in her linen gown.

"Ah, my favorite mule, I see," Grace said, sighting Mary bridled to a small cart. Mary didn't bat an eye. Grace gingerly patted her—she did owe the mule something, after all. Mary craned her neck around to give her a look either reproachful or incredulous—it was hard to say which.

"Well," Grace said, "where are we off to?"

They climbed in, Clarissa picking up the reins. "It's a surprise," she said clucking smartly, "Giddup!"

"Mist' Rathe says," Geoff began, but Clarissa nudged him hard in the ribs with her elbow and he came to an abrupt halt.

"Rathe? What's he got to do with this?"

Geoffrey squirmed. Clarissa gave him a dark look, then proceeded to begin politely discussing the weather, then the upcoming cotton harvest, then the cut of Grace's gown. Grace finally leaned over and put a hand on her arm, silencing her. She was very, very curious.

They left Natchez behind, heading north. If Grace didn't know better, she would suspect they were heading for the burned-out ruins of the church. "Where are we going?"

"We'll be there shortly," Clarissa said, with a smile.

Grace sat with her hands in her lap. In the summer afternoon birds sang, the trees whispered, honeysuckle and lavender hung thickly around them. She heard voices, lots of voices, mostly male. As they approached, she could distinguish much laughter and singing. She would recognize the soulful, melodious singing of the freed men anywhere. And then she heard banging, steady banging. "What is going on?" Grace asked, straining to look around the bend.

And then she knew, of course, because this was where the gutted church was.

They rounded the corner and the mule came to a stop. Grace cried out. The shining wood frame of a new building, a bit larger than the old one, greeted her. Fresh pine floors were almost completely laid down. Men were in the rafters, on the ground, hammering nails. Mules and oxen were bringing in more lumber. A shingled roof covered half of the structure already. It was wonderful.

A hundred people must have turned out, not just men, but women and children too. A big barbecue pit was going, and tables were laid out with a multitude of food on colorful, festive cloths.

Then, shocked, Grace realized not everyone was black. She spotted George Farris, sleeves rolled up to his forearms, holding a hammer and grinning as he stood by what looked like a skeleton of steps. She spotted Allen, directing the placement of the contents of a wheelbarrow, and a few other white people, including Doc Lang, Harriet and Sarah Bellsley. There were only a dozen whites there, but it was a beginning, and her heart flooded with joy.

Then she spotted him.

Rathe sat in a right angle of the frame, high up at roof level. He wore work pants and boots, but no shirt. He was slick and shining with sweat, hammering steadily away. A bright green bandanna was wrapped around his forehead, keeping hair and perspiration out of his eyes. For an instant she was caught up watching the rippling of the muscles in his back, the contours of his biceps.

"Yore man did this," Clarissa said in her ear. "It was his idea. Now we got a brand-new church and schoolhouse, better than the ol' one."

Emotions too intense to be contained swept her, and tears filled her eyes. He had done this. He wasn't a rogue—he was wonderful. He was the kind of man who moved mountains when they stood in his way. Hadn't she sensed that from the moment she had met him? Wasn't that why she had so selfishly pitted him against Ford? Was it possible that she loved him more now than before? Was it possible she had begun falling in love with him the moment she had first seen him?

She couldn't stop staring. His hammer suddenly stilled in mid-motion. He shifted his weight and turned his head, searching the crowd. He saw her, and their gazes met.

A broad, dimpled grin broke out on his face. She saw that he had nails in his mouth. With the hammer, he waved. She was beaming back, and she lifted her hand.

"Be careful up there," she cried.

His answer was an insolent wink.

Then Grace was dragged by Geoffrey to his mother, Hannah, who greeted her with a plateful of food. Grace accepted it, her heart swollen to impossible dimensions. Her gaze kept flitting back to the rafters where Rathe was working. "That's some man you got there," Hannah said.

"He is, isn't he?"

"It took a bit of fast talkin' and sweet cajolin' an' even some hard words to get the folks goin'."

"Did it?"

"Everyone was scared. Rathe tol' em it's okay to be scared, what's not okay is bein' scared enough to run. He said Ford and the rest of 'em bleeds just like we do, same color an' all. He said if we unite, we stand, if we divide, we fall. He said a lot more, too. Said our children deserved a chance to grow up to be more'n farmers, that no matter what President Lincoln said, we're still slaves, tied to the land by debt and badness."

"He said all that?" Grace asked, trembling.

"I can't remember all he said, he said so much. He shore has a way with words, that boy does."

Grace smiled.

"Had everyone hanging their heads so low there were noses in the dirt. Then got everyone so riled up they were ready to pick up pitchforks and run Ford outta town. Finally he got everyone calmed and promisin' to show up heah for the church-raisin'."

Grace could not take her gaze off Rathe's bronzed, shirtless figure, vividly etched against the blue sky, one arm rising and falling repeatedly. Twenty minutes later he was scrambling to the ground, dropping the last ten feet. He sauntered up to her, putting a sweaty arm around her. Grace didn't care. She leaned close. He met her regard with a quiet, deep smile. "Thank you," she said softly.

"I didn't do it just for you, although you were definitely on my mind."

"I know."

"You do?"

"Anyone who went to the trouble to get these people together, and said the things you said, did it out of conviction."

"It's my turn," he said, huskily. "Thank you."

They looked at each other. Rathe lowered his face. Their lips touched. They both felt, at the same instant, the panic rippling through the crowd and the hushed agitation in the voices around them. Rathe lifted his head, searching. They saw Sheriff Ford mounted on his gray at the same time.

"Looks like we got a party heah," Ford drawled.

Chapter 26

Ford was not alone. Behind him, rifles casually cradled in their arms, were half a dozen men. Grace knew they were all night riders. She didn't realize it, but she was clutching Rathe's arm. Terror ran through her veins.

He stepped away from her, in front of everyone, until he alone was facing Ford and his men. He wasn't wearing his gun. "Care to join us, Sheriff? We can use a few more hands."

Ford laughed. So did the men behind him. "This heah is public property," he drawled. "It belongs to the town of Natchez. An' the good white folks of the town of Natchez got an aversion to seein' their coloreds in school when they belong in the field. Let's go, boys."

The riders started forward.

Rathe turned to the crowd, his eyes flashing furiously. "Damn it," he shouted. "You gonna let them burn your new school? There's only six of them and half a hundred of us! Six against fifty! Are we men, dammit, or animals, to be led meekly around by our noses?"

Grace wanted to cry, *Rathe, don't!* But she couldn't. He was so fierce and magnificent, and all around her, the crowd shifted uneasily, nervously. Rathe cursed.

Ford, on his horse, hanging back, laughed. "Them niggers don't have an ounce a courage in the lot of 'em."

"Sonuvabitch," Rathe growled, low. Then he moved.

He leapt at Ford, with the agility and power of a mountain lion, tackling him and taking him by surprise. Ford fell from the horse with Rathe on top of him, Rathe's fist slamming into his face. "For Grace, you bastard!"

The riders came surging forward, but before they could surround the two, the crowd changed, moving, rippling, blocking the riders—even the women and children. On the ground, Rathe was ramming his fist again into Ford's face, saying, "and that was for me, you bastard. Now this is for these folks—for all the people you've abused with your stink of evil."

A rider reached for his gun. Hannah shouted, "Stop him, stop him, now!" Someone threw a hammer. It missed the rider, but from the other side of his mount, a young boy grabbed his ankle, and then his elders joined in, helping, and the rider went tumbling to the ground. He disappeared beneath a dozen children and adults.

"Jesus Christ!" another rider shouted, panicked, the crowd surging against his horse, reaching for his legs and pulling the gun right out of his hand. His horse screamed and stumbled, jostled by the crowd, and almost went down. "Let's get outta here!" the rider yelled.

Already one of the riders had broken free of the crowd and was galloping away. In an instant, the others had followed suit. Suddenly, there was utter silence and stillness. The crowd parted, tension ebbing.

Rathe sat on top of Ford, unmoving. Grace rushed to him. "Are you all right?"

"Yeah," he said, standing. He shook his right hand, wincing.

Ford lay unmoving.

Grace stared at him. "Is he—?"

"No, I didn't kill him, Grace, as much as I wanted to." His gaze was black. "I thought you understood—I'm not a cold-blooded murderer."

"Oh, Rathe," she cried, putting her arm around him. "I do! And I think you're wonderful. I think what you just did was wonderful. And utterly foolish."

He softened. "Guess we're two birds of a feather, eh?"

She blinked.

"Tell me," he said. "Tell me just how wonderful I am."

She closed her eyes in relief. "Unbelievably wonderful."

He smiled, putting his arm around her. But he didn't say what he was thinking—*If I'm so wonderful, then why won't you marry me?* Instead, he shrugged that thought aside. "I'll just put the sheriff on his horse and see if he doesn't end up back in town," he said, then looked at the crowd. "Are we going to get this school raised today or next year?"

A mighty roar greeted his question; it was answer enough.

Like a thief, with one small carpetbag, she fled from their room and into the night.

She hurt so much she was crying silently, not daring to make a sound.

The school was finished, Rathe's gift to her and the freed people of Natchez, he had said. Tomorrow they were supposed to be leaving for Texas, but tomorrow would never come.

She knew now she had misjudged Rathe, because any man who had done the things he had done recently had to have had the right values all along. They had just been buried deep and ignored. But that didn't change the ultimate truth—that she was her own person, that she greatly feared for her independence. Rathe had made a public stand for all the right reasons, but he was still dictating decisions to her that should be hers alone. The issue of her teaching had never been resolved, for it could not—not to the satisfaction of them both.

She felt guilty. But staying only delayed the inevitable. His insisting they go to Texas precipitated her leaving. Because he was very perceptive and sensitive at times, she was surprised he did not realize she would be too ashamed

to ever meet his parents while he kept her. But there was
no point in revealing her feelings to him.

That afternoon, knowing it was their last, Grace had
made love to Rathe with a panic and frenzy born of
knowing it was their last time together. He had responded
as wildly, as frantically. Not just once, but again and again
they had come poignantly together, until somewhere
around midnight he had fallen into a deep sleep. "I love
you," Grace had said, bending over and kissing his still
mouth. To her surprise, he had grunted. His hand had
closed around hers and his mouth had opened beneath
hers.

Had he been awake?

She would never know.

She had left a letter, telling him she loved him, but that
it would never work out. In it, she tried to explain how
she felt about her independence, and how she could not
be with a man who tried to take that away from her. She
understood that he was trying to protect her. But just as
he had had to stand up to Ford, she had had to teach
despite Rawlins' threats. She could never marry and give
up her profession. Teaching was a part of who she was,
just as her belief in women's suffrage and the right of the
freed people to learn were. Both were deeply and irrevo-
cably ingrained in her.

It was a long walk to the next town where, far from
Natchez' curious eyes, she would take the first train
north, back to New York. She imagined Rathe's fury
when he found her gone. Fury? No, she knew him well
enough to know he would be hurt more than anything
else. Oh, Rathe, she thought, anguished, what a rude
awakening I've been to you! I wish we'd never met and
never fallen in love, so I wouldn't have to be doing this
to you! Instantly, she knew that wasn't true. She would
treasure the memories they had made until the day she
died.

She thought of her future grimly. She was leaving Rathe
but her life must continue. With the five thousand dollars

she could care for her mother indefinitely. She was already
a member of the National Woman's Suffrage Association
and on good terms with its leaders, Elizabeth Cady Stanton and Susan B. Anthony. She would go on the lecture
circuit. Throw herself back into the cause. Next summer
was the Centennial being held in Philadelphia, and Grace
already knew the National had big plans to lobby there.
She would be with them.

She paused when the road took her past the shining new
church. It still needed paint. Right now it gleamed blond
in the moonlight, and smelled deliciously of fresh wood.
Rathe had done this. Her Rathe. And one day he would
belong to someone else . . .

This time she heard the horses approaching with reflexes honed from experience. She didn't wait for them to
get closer; she fled into the woods. It couldn't possibly
be, she thought, agonized—but it was.

She crouched behind a thick oak, watching, trembling,
listening to Ford's voice. Tears of fury and impotence came
to her eyes as they rode around the building, dousing it
with something flammable, their voices low and harsh and
menacing. Moments later fire flickered from all four corners. Grace couldn't move, half-blinded by tears, as flames
cracked and crept higher.

She choked on a moan. Behind her, a deer leapt away,
into the brush.

"What's that?" someone hissed.

Grace froze.

"Someone's in the woods," a man responded.

"Probably a nigger," Ford said. "Flush him out."

Riders began coming at her. Grace screamed and
whirled to run away, but a rider was cutting her off. She
dodged past one horse, breaking out into the clearing
where the schoolhouse was now blazing.

"It's Bragg's woman—get her," Ford yelled.

Grace lifted her skirts and ran past the inferno and into
the woods on the other side.

She didn't think. She ran blindly, the woods as black as

pitch. Branches slapped and stung her. She stumbled, but
didn't dare fall. She ran into thorns, and cried out reflexively. She was almost sobbing, gasping for breath, as she
crouched, trapped in a wild rose bush. She listened and
heard only the Mississippi night, frogs, crickets, an owl.
It was some time before she caught her breath and decided
that she had, thank God, lost them. Gingerly she moved
out of the bush, becoming aware that she had lost a shoe.
Her foot started to throb. She pulled off her tattered stock-
ing and sank down onto the ground, shaking. Something
slithered against her ankle; she leapt up and ran. No end,
she thought, there was no end in sight, not to this violence
and not to this night.

She finally stopped to get her bearings. She had lost
her carpetbag with her few possessions. But the money
and the amethyst necklace were on her person. She
touched Rathe's gift beneath the fabric of her gown and
held it, closing her eyes, so glad he hadn't taken it back
when she had demanded money. It was all she had of
him except for memories. She was certain she was hope-
lessly lost. Just then, through the trees, she saw a large,
sprawling pillared home. An instant later she was overwhelmed with relief.

It was Melrose.

"I need your help."

Louisa, gorgeous in a frothy concoction of pink satin
and feathers, stared incredulously.

Grace swallowed. "I know you don't like me. I
know—"

"Whatever happened to you?" Louisa asked contemp-
tuously, taking in her torn gown and disheveled appearance.

"I'm leaving Natchez," Grace said quietly, no longer
hysterical even though there was an unswallowable lump
in her throat. "And I need your help to do it."

Louisa's eyes narrowed, and although she smiled, it was
not attractive. "You are kidding."

Grace only stared.

"You're leaving—in the middle of the night—on foot," Louisa sneered, glancing at Grace's bare, bloody foot. "You're running away!"

Grace didn't answer; she didn't have to.

"What happened?" Louisa demanded. "Rathe doesn't know, does he?"

"No."

Louisa threw back her head and laughed. "Tell me what happened. How did you lose your shoe? Why are there twigs in your hair and thorns in your dress?"

"On my way out of town I passed the church. They came and burned it and saw me. I managed to get away."

"Too bad," Louisa said. "Too, too bad."

"Would you lend me a driver and carriage, just to take me to the next railway station?" Grace was desperate. "I've got to be miles away from here before Rathe knows I'm gone."

"How could I possibly refuse?" Louisa asked. "I'll send for the driver instantly. I want you out of here before my guest arrives."

"Thank you," Grace said, wondering who Louisa was expecting. "Would you mind lending me some shoes? I also need to freshen up."

"You can use the kitchen." She waved a hand toward the back of the house. "You know the way."

Grace hesitated.

"What are you waiting for? I told you, I'm expecting someone at any moment."

"Please don't tell Rathe you've seen me."

Louisa smiled. "I wouldn't dream of it."

The triumph in her voice hurt, and Grace turned, stumbling down the hall to the kitchen. She couldn't help it, she pictured Rathe in Louisa's arms. Oh, she prayed he would not turn to her for comfort after she was gone!

Louisa did not bring her shoes, and using the back of a

platter as a looking glass, Grace tucked her hair back into place, removed the twigs and brambles, smoothed and straightened her skirts. Taking off her remaining shoe, she started for the front of the house. If Louisa had deigned to bring her the shoes, she would have secretly gone out of the rear entrance. Now—well, it was just too bad. Grace would be leaving anyway, so the identity of Louisa's lover was safe.

In the hall she froze, almost going into shock. There was no mistaking the voice coming from the parlor. Ford was saying, "An' Bragg's woman was there, but we lost her. Now what in hell was she doing runnin' around alone at night?"

"She's here," Louisa said bluntly. "She's leaving Rathe, and I'm helping her get to the depot."

There was silence, then Ford laughed.

Grace turned and ran.

"What in hell?" Ford cried.

He caught her before she even got through the massive front door, chuckling and holding her close. "Look at this! Look what I've got!"

Louisa stood, arms folded, scowling. "Just what are you doing, Will? Let her go! She's leaving town, and I say good riddance."

Ford's face was still swollen, scabbed, one eye black. "So you finally saw the light, huh? Too bad you didn't talk that Texas trash into leavin', too."

"Let me go," Grace panted, twisting.

"Oh, you can go all right, and Natchez'll be a better place, too. But not before I get a taste of what Bragg's been getting."

Both Louisa and Grace gasped at once. Grace's futile struggles increased. Louisa strode over, furious. "You listen heah," she snarled. "You got me—but if you lay a hand on this piece of white trash you'll nevah be welcome heah again—do I make myself clear?"

"Shit," Ford said, relaxing his hold on Grace.

"Remember," Louisa said, her nostrils flared, her

jaw taut, "he only turned to *her* because I got tired of him!"

Ford released Grace. "Not the way I heard it, but I think I can skin this cat another way. The hell with it." He turned his black eyes on her, fingering her amethyst choker. "This is yore lucky day, little lady."

Grace shivered.

Then he tore the necklace from her throat.

Chapter 27

He awoke with a smile on his face, sighed, and stretched leisurely, then reached for Grace. As he did so he was wondering if he had dreamed her declaration of love last night. He had been on the edge of sleep, but he could have sworn she'd said she loved him. Just recalling those words made his heart clench with joy and hope.

His hand moved over a cold, empty space.

Rathe turned his head and stared at the place next to him, where Grace should have been. He lifted his gaze to the room, but there was no sign of her. Bemusement was his first lazy reaction, but it was immediately followed by consternation. Her side of the bed was very cool, as if she'd been gone for hours . . .

Where in hell could she have gone in the middle of the night?

It occurred to him she had gotten sick, and he ran to the bathroom—but it was empty.

She must have gone for a very early morning walk. Either that, or—and he grew grim—she was off gallivanting about and getting into trouble.

He knew without a doubt it was the latter.

But at the crack of dawn? What could she be up to at the crack of dawn?

He had overslept. The sun was high; it had to be mid-morning. He glanced at his pocket watch and confirmed this. He quickly splashed his face with water, then soaped and rinsed under his arms. He would skip the shave. He felt a tiny tug of panic. Soon he was hopping into his breeches.

At the knock on the door he barked out a brusque, "Come in," expecting room service with their usual breakfast. He blinked once at Allen then he buttoned his shirt up too rapidly and mismatched holes and buttons. And he knew his worst fears were right—she was in trouble again. "What is it?"

"Rathe, I don't know how to tell you this," Allen said, shifting uncomfortably. His glance darted around the room, his face turning pink as it settled on the bed.

"Damn—where's Grace?"

Allen was startled. "Isn't she here?"

"You didn't come because of her?"

"No. Rathe, the new school's been burned right to ashes."

Rathe cursed. He slammed his fist onto the bureau, sending his wash water onto the floor. "Dammit all!"

"My sentiments exactly," Allen said dryly. "The mayor's sent a wire for federal troops."

"Do you think we can get them?"

"Not a chance in hell," Allen said. "The North is sick of the South's problems. The sentiment now is to let the South be, let it rebuild alone, to hell with it. Let's face it, Rathe. Without local popular support, we can't stop this. There were federal troops down here a few years ago, but they didn't stop it, and even if we could get them, they can't stop it now, either. It's going to take years."

Rathe looked at him. "You're not going to stay, are you?"

Allen met his gaze. "No, I'm not. I guess I'm a coward. That, and frustrated beyond endurance. I don't want my back broken next time. And—" He shrugged. He didn't have to say the next word. Rathe knew he had also decided to leave because of him and Grace.

Rathe was just about to depart to go find her when he saw the letter lying on the table. He froze. He reached for it, saw her name—and he knew. He knew she had left him.

He sank into a chair, reading, the hurt so awful tears shone in his eyes. She had told him he was wonderful, and last night, she had told him that she loved him. And now, in this letter, she was telling him again—yet it was goodbye.

But when he got to the end of the letter, he was no longer hurt, but angry. She had misjudged him again. He had already realized that she would never give up her career and her crusading—and he'd already accepted it! She was making another rash judgment about him, jumping to erroneous conclusions, without even bothering to ask him what he was thinking! If she had only asked! Yes, he didn't want her teaching here in Natchez, but there was a whole world out there, for God's sake. He understood, now, why she'd had to teach here, and if he had to do it all over again, he hoped that this time he would stand by her—as he expected her to believe enough in him to stand by him. But no, she had run away.

He was going to find her.

She loved him. He loved her. They were going to resolve this, once and for all. As he opened the door, about to rush through, he came face to face with Deputy Lloyd Baker. ''Sheriff wants you to identify some remains,'' he said.

He rode out to the school with Baker, feeling sick.

Grace was not dead!

But they said she was.

Grace was not dead! It was a refrain, a prayer, he kept saying over and over as he galloped headlong to the cinders and ashes that had been the new church.

He leapt off his mount before the stallion had even stopped. There was a large crowd, solemn, uneasy—and everyone was staring at him. Ford came forward, looking smug. Harriet was there, shaking her head, standing side by side with Hannah and John, and a few other colored families. Everyone was stricken dumb, except for one of the women, who wept openly and shamelessly.

"Where?" he demanded. Baker had said they'd found a burned body. Then he saw what Ford was holding—one of Grace's carpetbags and one of her dainty shoes. His knees became very weak. He felt faint. Someone held him by the arm, supporting him. It was Farris.

"Harriet Gold says these are her things," Ford said.

Rathe looked at him, eyes wide. Horrified. "They are."

"Body's by the fireplace."

Rathe turned to look, in a daze. No—it wasn't Grace— it wasn't! He started to move. Nothing felt real; it was like walking in a dream. From behind him, Ford's voice followed. "Can't tell much, 'cause of the fire and all."

The body was all charred bones—no hair, no flesh, just bones. Rathe felt relief. It wasn't Grace. And then the sun caught on something, drawing his eyes, and he stared at the amethysts and diamonds glinting on the skeleton's neck.

"No."

There was no gold, just the stones, in perfect, obscene order.

"No."

"Let's get you home, Rathe," Harriet said gently.

He didn't see her. He saw only Ford, gloating, hands in his pockets.

Ford lost his slouch. "I wasn't here," he shouted, backing away. "I was with Louisa—ask her—all night!"

Rathe stalked him, slowly, deliberately. Ford moved back farther. "You think I'm crazy enough to murder someone? After what you did to me? I told you—I was with Louisa."

Rathe was blinded with grief and anger, but he was still sane, and he could not kill Ford if there was any doubt. He fell to his knees. He raised his face to the heavens. The howl that sounded was blood-curdling, soul-shattering. It sounded again.

"Was he here, last night, all night?"

"Yes," Louisa said, reaching out to touch his sleeve. "Rathe, I am sorry . . .

He stared at her. "All night, Louisa?"

"All night. Rathe—" She came close, put her hands on his shoulders. "Darling, why don't you come in and have a drink?"

He looked at her. "I'm going to find out who was there," he said. "And I'm going to kill them all."

"Rathe, wait," Louisa called as he ran down the veranda stairs. "Rathe!"

His grief was such that it made him want to crawl into a dark corner and weep. Instead, he focused on revenge. He spent three days trying to find out who, specifically, had burned the school. Many of Natchez' young men were night riders, and while it was no secret who rode—for they all boasted about it—the night of Grace's murder no one was admitting to anything. Three days later, Rathe was in exactly the same place he had started.

"You're making yourself sick," Harriet said. She had come to his hotel room, where he sat, surrounded by Grace's things, still smelling her scent, half a bottle of bourbon in front of him. In his hand was her nightgown. He clutched it to his abdomen.

"I love her," he said hoarsely.

"You've got to start livin' again," Harriet said. "She's gone, Rathe, but you're still here. Go on home to your mama and daddy. Go home to your loved ones."

He looked at her, then drained his glass.

"Do you think I didn't want to hole up and die when my boys got killed? There isn't anything like losin' a child, honey. Nothin' is like that."

He hung his head. "It hurts so much, Harriet . . ."

"She'd want you to go on!"

Rathe brusquely wiped a small trickle of moisture away from his eyes. He hadn't cried; he would not cry. "Yeah, she would, but, damn, it's so hard."

For the first time, he looked at her. "First I've got some business to take care of."

Rathe began by rebuilding the church—this time, with

a whole separate room attached for classes. Then he spent the next three weeks mounting a campaign to destroy the sheriff, the crux of which was the sailor Able Smith's death. He hired the Pinkerton Agency to investigate the suicide. Although the evidence against the sheriff was only circumstantial, Able Smith had been a white man, not a Negro, and many of the townspeople who supported the night riders were indignant and even outraged at his suspicious death.

Rathe wrote letters to the local papers and the *Jackson Clarion* and *Aberdeen Examiner*. It didn't matter that the press supported the night riders and their methods. Soon the sailor's questionable suicide became a public scandal. A small group of local citizenry organized themselves to campaign for law, order, and justice—and against Ford. Sarah Bellsley's Temperance Union took part. Public indignation mounted, and Rathe fanned the fire through the press. It was only a matter of weeks before Ford came to him, furious.

"You're behind this," Ford snarled. "Do you think I don't know it? Do you think I'm gonna take this lyin' down?"

Rathe laughed. "I want you to know it, you sonuvabitch. I want you to know that I'm the agent of your destruction. You're finished in Natchez."

Ford was wavering, and Rathe knew he was afraid.

"You can't destroy me, boy," Ford said.

"No?" Rathe grinned.

"I still got most of this town behind me," Ford spat. "An' you have any doubts, why, you come to Cross Creek tomorrow night and see."

Cross Creek. It didn't take much for Rathe to learn that the night riders were planning another episode of intimidation; they intended to whip a sharecropper who was behind in his payment of goods to his landlord. And Rathe understood that this time it was very important for Ford to make a show of power and strength.

Concurrently, it was crucial for Rathe to stop him. And although much of the town was disturbed at Smith's death, Rathe knew he could not count on them to stop Ford in his nocturnal terrorist activities against the coloreds. This was the showdown. Rathe could count on a few men like Farris. More importantly, he hired his own men, all Pinkerton's. It was a small cavalry that rode out to stop the night riders that sweltering, moonless eve.

But there was no whipping. Ford and his men were not expecting an armed encounter with numbers superior to their own, and like the bullies they were, they turned tail and fled. Rathe rode after Ford. He chased him halfway to Natchez. Nothing and no one could stop him now, not when he was so close to destroying the man who had become his blood enemy. "Stop and fight, Ford," he shouted into the night.

Ford kept running.

Rathe caught up to him, their horses galloping neck and neck blindly in the darkness. He leapt at Ford. The two men went crashing onto the ground, rolling, struggling. It was Rathe who wound up on top, and it was Rathe who pummeled Ford to within an inch of his life.

That was the last time Ford was ever seen in Natchez.

Yet for Rathe there was no satisfaction, no victory, only the hollow emptiness of his heart and his soul.

"Hello, Pa."

"Rathe!" Derek Bragg's amber eyes went wide, and an instant later a smile of delight swept across his features. The next second Rathe found himself enveloped in a hard, fierce hug. The two men were nearly identical except for the difference of thirty years. They were the same height, the same powerful build, their faces mirror replicas of each other, one young and unlined, the other weathered but still unquestionably handsome. Derek released him and grinned.

Rathe smiled back. He watched his father's smile slowly

fade, saw the quizzical look in his eyes, and knew Derek had already picked up on the sadness that wouldn't leave him. *Don't ask,* Rathe silently begged, averting his gaze. He missed the look of concern that swept Derek's face, and it was gone by the time he raised his eyes. "Where's Mother?" With much effort, he managed to make his tone light. "And my big sister? And that no-good gambler she married?"

Derek threw his arm around his shoulder, leading him into the oak-floored foyer of the ranch house. "Miranda!" he shouted. "Storm! Brett!" He gave his son a grin. "Your mother's going to box your ears, son."

Rathe had to smile at that. "She's peeved, huh?"

Derek looked at him. "Peeved?" He threw back his head and laughed.

His sister, magnificently beautiful in the full flush of womanhood, five years Rathe's senior, came running down the stairs, her elegant silk gown, bustle, hoops and all, hiked to her knees, showing long, exquisite, silk-stockinged legs. This was the Storm Rathe knew far better than the one who had married and now lived on Nob Hill in San Francisco. She shrieked, a cry completely reminiscent of their childhood, and Rathe caught her as she catapulted into his embrace.

"I would have killed you if you hadn't come," she told him breathlessly. "All those telegrams! First one arrival date, then a new one! Mother kept preparing surprises for you! She's furious!"

Rathe smiled sheepishly and met Brett's gaze over Storm's shoulder. Keeping one arm around his sister, he reached out to shake his brother-in-law's hand. They exchanged genuinely warm hellos. They had come a long way from the day fifteen years ago when Rathe had refused to let Brett enter the house and had wanted to carve him to pieces—when Brett was hunting down his runaway wife.

His mother appeared in the doorway then, crying. Storm moved aside, into her husband's arms, smiling. Miranda was a tiny woman and Rathe dwarfed her as he embraced her. Since Grace, nothing had felt this good, and he felt such anguish welling up in him that he held her longer than necessary, so he could regain control. "Where are my nephews and niece?" He managed a very forced smile.

"They're asleep," Brett said. "Thank God." He exchanged a fond look with his wife. Something twisted inside Rathe, seeing their intimate exchange, when it had never done so before. Brett saw him watching, and flashed him a dazzling white smile. "My hands weren't full enough with just my wife," he said, winking.

Storm poked Brett in the ribs. "Don't let him fool you, Rathe, he's a wonderful father. How is Nick doing? And where is the lovely lady you were bringing?"

Rathe's expression froze. He became aware of a heavy, questioning silence. Storm quickly came over and held his arm. "I've just said something awful. I'm sorry, Rathe." She smiled at him tremulously.

Rathe couldn't return her smile. "Nick is fine," he said. "He's putting a lot of effort into restoring Dragmore." Had it only been a few months since he had been in England? It seemed like years, like a different lifetime—a lifetime before Grace. And now it was a lifetime without Grace. "As for my lady friend, she had an accident." He wondered if his voice sounded as hoarse to their ears as it did to his.

"Everyone into the parlor," Miranda said, throwing Storm a scalding look. "Derek, pour some brandies. Rathe, are you hungry? You're too thin."

This time his mouth curved. "No, Mother, I'm not hungry, but a brandy sounds perfect."

He clenched the fencepost and stared at the shadowy outline of Derek's prized stud stallion. The moon was almost full and very bright. All around him were the familiar Texas night sounds he had grown up with. Yet tonight, there was no comfort to be gained from them. An owl hooted. Rathe leaned against the fence and stared blindly into the dimness. Behind him, the ranch house was mostly dark, except for the lights in his room and the master bedroom.

In that bedroom Miranda stood with a brush in her hand, her beautiful features tense with worry. "He's outside walking, Derek. Something's so terribly wrong."

"I know," Derek said. "I could tell the instant I saw him. There's no sparkle in his smile, no light in his eyes." He looked at his wife, misery in his own gaze, sharing their child's sorrow. "Do you think she's dead?"

"I think he needs you," Miranda said, clasping his large hand with her little one. "I can't stand to see him like this. Rathe was always so full of love and laughter. It's like looking a a stranger!"

Derek went outside. He didn't try to disguise his steps as he approached. He knew Rathe heard him, not because he turned—he didn't—but from the mere fact that he was his son and he had trained him in the way of the Apache. Rathe finally ducked his head in some kind of acknowledgment as Derek paused at his side by the corral. A moment passed.

"He's a real beauty, Pa." His voice was raw.

Derek placed his hand on his son's back. "Rathe, what happened?"

Rathe made a protesting sound, looking at his boots, only now his vision was fogged. He blinked furiously. He wasn't sure he could speak even if he wanted to.

Derek didn't move his hand. He gripped his shoulder. "Get it out," he said. "You've got to get it out."

Rathe choked and took a long, deep breath, shaking his head no, but tears wet his face. He gulped air frantically. "Pa," he managed to say, "I need to be alone."

Derek's hand moved to his neck and tightened. "Did you love her?"

The warm pressure of his father's hand and the intimate question were his undoing. He convulsed over the railing and gasped on a huge sob. "Ah, shit," he moaned.

"I'm sorry, son," Derek said, pulling him to him, until

Rathe's hanging head touched his shoulder. Realizing their intimacy, Rathe started to tense and withdraw, but his father tightened his hold. "Dammit," he said, "I'm your father and I love you. Cry if you have to."

Rathe cried.

Chapter 28

Spring, 1876

Grace gazed out the window at the east Texas country-side, startled at the lushness of the pastures, the richness of the newly planted cotton fields, the thickness of the oaks and cypresses. She felt uncomfortable. She had been uncomfortable from the moment the train had entered Mississippi. And it had nothing to do with the weather, for it was a pleasant spring. It had to do with him. She had not forgotten him in the past eight months, but being in New York and knowing he was down South had made it a little easier. Now, all she could wonder was if he was still in the South, and if so, where . . . not that it mattered.

Fortunately, their lecture circuit had not included Natchez. Grace knew she could not have borne the memories had she even set foot in the town. She had wondered if he was still there—but of course he wasn't. And even if he was, by now there would be another woman, another mistress. It hurt too much to bear thinking about, even after all this time.

The National Association for Woman's Suffrage was planning to lobby in Philadelphia in July during the Centennial celebrations. This circuit was a well-organized and massive effort to recruit new members in the hopes that they would make the journey to Philadelphia to show their support. Susan B. Anthony and Matilda Joslyn Gage, while not on the official Centennial program, had grand plans of delivering a Declaration of the Rights for Women to Vice President Ferry. They intended to read a portion of it aloud from the platform before anyone could stop them. Other members of the National would be handing out pamphlets and copies of the Declaration to the crowd. But Grace could barely get aroused by the prospect. Excitement had long since drained from her life. It had fled the night she had left Rathe in Natchez.

Last November the Democrats had swept the Mississippi elections, ousting the Republicans once and for all from state and municipal office. She had read about it in the papers and felt sad at the thought. She wondered how many voters had been kept away from the polls through intimidation—if not sheer force.

But she had also read about events in Natchez. She'd followed Ford's fall with glee and had learned that the church had been rebuilt by Rathe after she had left.

Despite the fact that she had run out on him, he had stayed long enough to finish what he had started. She was so proud of him—but it was a bittersweet and heart-wrenching feeling. In a way, she wished he had just left Natchez in a fit of hurt anger. Instead, he had proven himself a hero. He had rebuilt the school, and it almost felt like he had reached out, through space and time, to touch her with his deed and his heart.

And there was more. Her mother was miraculously still alive, and at Frazier Hospital. She was stubbornly clinging to life, and the doctors had given her another few years. Grace was thrilled to see the deterioration had stopped, even if it was temporary. She had intended to stay in New York, to be with Dianna, except that her mother had adamantly pushed her to go on this circuit. "This is your life, Grace," she had said. "Or did you leave him for nothing?"

Grace had told her mother about Rathe. There had been no way she could hide her broken heart from her. But it

was no surprise to Dianna. It had been obvious that there
was a benefactor, because of the cost of Frazier Hospital.

And that was just it. Every month Rathe paid Dianna's
exorbitant bills. Grace didn't understand how he could find
it in his heart to do so after the cold way she had left him.
It was magnificent. It tore at her. It was a deed that, like
the rebuilding of the schoolhouse, stood blatantly for her
to see; and she felt as if he was still in her life, so close,
that if she just tried to reach out, he would be there, waiting.

But she didn't want him to be there. What she really
wanted was for him to leave her alone, so she could become healed and whole again. Instead, he was a shadowy,
insistent presence in her life.

She pressed her forehead to the window, forcing herself
to think about their Texas itinerary: Houston, San Anto-
nio, Fredericksburg, Austin, and San Marcos. It was
grueling, this tour, but she welcomed it.

"Don't tell me you're not coming?" Derek asked incredulously.

Rathe shrugged. "I'm not in the mood for a fair, Pa."

"We're going to spend the night in town. Fredericksburg's
got its share of wine, women, and song. Come on, son. I've
never seen you work so long and so hard. I don't know how
you're going to deal a deck of cards with all those new cal-
louses you're sporting."

Rathe had to grin. He knew his father respected his
sudden interest in ranching, his self-imposed isolation, his
austerity and celibacy, but he also knew his father felt that
after eight months, it was time for Rathe to return to the
living. Derek had even confessed that while he'd always
wanted him working the ranch at his side, he'd never
dreamed it would be under these circumstances. Rathe had
told them a little bit about Grace, just enough for his father
to understand his behavior. Now, subtly, Derek was encouraging him to revert back to his old ways, even if that
meant moving on.

"I'd rather see you roaming Europe," he'd said softly, one cold winter day over coffee laced with brandy, "instead of here in some kind of self-imposed exile."

Rathe hadn't responded.

Well, maybe Derek was right, maybe it was time to return to the living. Maybe he needed a good card game, a good drunk, and a woman—any woman. But even as he tried to convince himself of this, he felt no anticipation, and knew he would only be going through the motions. He tried not to think her name.

"Yeah, all right, let me pack a few things."

Derek grinned. "Your mother's already done that."

Miranda appeared, petite and dainty in a stunning pink traveling outfit. Derek's eyes brightened at the sight of her. "Have I seen that before?"

She smiled and turned slowly for him. "No, you haven't. Do you approve?"

He grinned and pulled his wife into a sensual embrace. "When do I ever not approve?"

Even as a child, Rathe, witnessing the blatant and hungry love between his parents, had sometimes felt like an intruder. But now, having experienced love himself, it stirred up too much agony to watch them, so he turned away to get his horse. But he was thinking of Grace. Her ghost wouldn't leave him alone.

They reached Fredericksburg as the sun was going down. After dining with his parents, aware of, but ignoring the flirtatious smiles from a dozen genteel young ladies, he settled into a saloon and downed five bourbons, half-heartedly attempting to enjoy a poker game. Hours later and several hundred dollars in the hole, he allowed himself to be led upstairs by a buxom whore with red highlights in her hair. He kissed her, the first woman he had kissed since Grace, and fondled her breasts academically. He was not aroused, and worse, the sight of her overly lush, even flabby body when she shed her clothes made him tender his excuses as fast as he could. He didn't want a whore. Full breasts and reddish hair did not make her Grace, not even a good substitute. He didn't want a substitute! Dammit, he wanted her, he was pining for her, he still loved her—and she was dead.

The next morning he was suffering from an acute headache when he joined his parents for a late breakfast. "Have a good time last night?" Derek asked, grinning.

Miranda jabbed her husband with her elbow in a very unladylike manner. "Don't encourage him to be a wastrel," she warned.

"It's good for him," Derek argued.

Rathe groaned. "I think I'm going back to bed."

"No, you're not," his parents said together. Derek let Miranda continue. "You're coming with us."

"Mother . . ."

"What do you intend to do? Drink yourself sober in a saloon all afternoon? Look at what a beautiful day it is!"

Rathe gave in. He was too tired to argue.

He trailed after his parents amidst racing children and milling adults. Booths sported the best of the county livestock and the best local homemade confections. A traveling salesman had set up his red wagon, showing off all his wares. Vendors hawked cotton candy. A gypsy fortune teller tried to lure him into her tent with a seductive smile, but he politely refused. A display of bright quilts, balloons, and puppy dogs completed the festivities. A young woman handed all three of them a flyer. The instant he saw the headline, *Support Women's Right to Vote*, his gut cramped and he felt sick. Would it never end? he thought angrily, crumpling the offensive paper. Would he always be tormented by memories of a dead woman?

"They have a speaker," cried Miranda. "And she's on now! It's Elizabeth Cady Stanton. Oh, I want to hear this!"

"Believe me, Mother," Rathe said, "you'll be bored."

Miranda turned on him. "Am I or am I not as intelligent as your father?" she demanded.

Rathe sensed trouble, met Derek's gaze, and saw that his father was trying not to laugh. "Of course you are." He meant it.

"Do you find me an inferior human being to your father?"

"Of course not."

"I think I've made my point," Miranda said.

"I think I've got a radical on my hands." Derek laughed, the two men trailing after the petite Miranda, marching ahead.

Rathe was afraid, but compelled. He knew he shouldn't go and listen to this speaker, it would only open all his wounds. But he couldn't stop his body's forward motion. Miranda, being short, worked her way to the front of the crowd, and her husband and son followed her. Rathe looked at the plain, quietly dressed woman standing on the platform, but didn't hear her words. There were a dozen chairs spread in a row behind her, where other speakers were seated. When his vision first caught the familiar pale profile and the glint of severely pulled-back red hair, he knew it was a mistake and it hurt so badly he couldn't breathe. It could not be Grace.

But then she turned her head toward him.

At that instant, his senses came painfully alive. It *was* Grace!

She paled, her violet eyes going wide with shock.

It was Grace! Grace—alive!

He shoved past his mother and father, a grim, frightening expression on his face. He started up the steps to the platform with hard, purposeful strides. The crowd murmured at his intrusion, the speaker stopped in midsentence. "What is this interruption? Sir! Excuse me . . ."

Grace was on her feet, eyes riveted on him.

Oh, God, she was alive!

Grace leaned toward him, as if she were going to come to meet him. Rathe's strides lengthened. She suddenly, abruptly, whirled and took two running steps. It was as far as she got. He caught her and slung her over his shoulder.

She cried out, "Put me down this instant!"

"Who is that man?" Elizabeth Cady Stanton said into

the bullhorn. "Can someone stop that man? He's absconding with one of my women!"

Rathe carried her through the crowd, which parted like the Red Sea at his feet, undoubtedly from the fierceness of his expression. He heaved her to her feet. She stared up at him, her eyes shining and bright. Rathe took a deep breath. It was as far as he got. She threw herself at him with a glad cry, and he clasped her to him, moaning. Eyes closed, he held her and rocked her, saying her name, over and over in a wondrous litany.

"Is it really you?" he cried, cupping her face. "Ah, Grace . . ."

She was crying. "Rathe, I missed you so . . ."

He kissed her, hard, possessively, bruisingly. She pressed against him wildly, clinging fiercely. The kiss changed tenor slowly. His mouth softened, his tongue slid between her lips. They drank of each other, their teeth catching in their effort to get as far into each other as possible. He wanted her so much he hurt.

He clutched her face. "Grace—how could you do this to me? I thought you were—"

"I had to," she interrupted, sobbing softly, her violet eyes pleading. "I love you, Rathe, I love you so much, I do! It tore me apart to leave, but how could I stay? I tried to explain it in the letter!"

"You didn't give me a chance," he cried, gripping her shoulders. "You didn't trust me, Grace! I never intended to take your career from you—never! But did you ask me how I felt—even try and find out? No. You ran away!"

"What are you saying?" she gasped, covering her mouth with her hands, eyes wide.

"I don't want you any other way than the way you are, dammit! I want you to teach, to crusade for what you believe in. I just want to be there to keep you out of trouble! I would never try and take away your career."

"But in Natchez—"

He cut her off. "Can you blame me?" His gaze locked on hers. "I'm a man. You're the woman I love. I could never stop myself from protecting you. There were two issues there, Grace, not one.''

"Oh, Lord," she moaned, and fell into his embrace.

"I should have made myself clearer, but Grace, God, how could you have done it? How could you have run out like that?''

"It was the hardest thing I've ever done." She wept. "I felt there was no hope for us, that you would always try to control me. I didn't trust you, Rathe, I was afraid to! I'm so sorry, because now I know if I had to do it over, I wouldn't! And I was terrified of meeting your parents." She was weeping. "I couldn't endure the humiliation, don't you see? And on top of everything else, I thought you might back off from Ford if I left. I was so afraid he'd kill you!''

He was starting to see. "But I thought you were dead!''

"What?" she gasped.

He couldn't, wouldn't, let go of her face. "I thought you were dead. There was a body in the fire." He stopped. He suddenly understood. His gaze pinned her. "Your necklace, the one I gave you, was there, and some of your things. The body was burned beyond recognition. I thought it was you.''

"No," she said, aghast. "I managed to escape the night riders and wound up at Melrose. I asked Louisa for her help. One of her drivers took me to the railway station. But Ford was there, and he tore the necklace from me. I thought he was stealing it because of the money—and because you had given it to me. I didn't know.''

Rathe closed his eyes for one bitter moment. "One day that Barclay bitch will be sorry. As for Ford, I'm only sorry I didn't kill him, that I only ran him out of town.''

"Oh, Rathe—I never meant for you to think that I was dead!" She flung herself at him, then stepped back. "Did it mean that much to you?''

He had to laugh, a raw sound. "Mean that much?" he echoed. "Only the difference between night and day, death and life. Grace, without you . . ." He hesitated, searching for words. "You are the light in my life, can't you understand? From the day I met you, nothing was ever the same. Without you, there's only darkness and despair."

She thought her heart might explode from sheer joy. She touched his beautiful face gently. "Are you telling me that you love me?"

"Love you? That word's not strong enough! I love you, I adore you, Grace, I want you." And suddenly he grinned wickedly, his dimples etched deeply in his cheeks. His eyes glinted. He pulled her close against him. "Right now, in fact," he said in a low voice.

Grace blushed.

"Marry me, Grace," Rathe commanded. "Now, today, this instant. Right here. And then I'm taking you to my hotel room and we're going to make love as man and wife."

"Yes," she said breathlessly.

He was smiling. "The lady finally said yes—on the third round! Does this mean you are no longer immune to my charm?"

"I was never immune to your charm," she chided gently, touching his face. "But where will we find a preacher?"

"There's at least a dozen men of the cloth here today. Do you think I'm ever going to let you out of my sight again?"

She smiled. "I hope not."

Rathe took her hand and practically dragged her to where his parents were standing a discreet distance away, yet unabashedly watching. "Pa, find us a preacher." He realized belatedly, then, that Stanton had never resumed her speech and the attention of the entire crowd was still focused on them. Now Stanton picked up her bullhorn. "Is there a minister in the house?"

Laughter greeted this, and a dozen preachers came rushing forward.

"We're getting married," Rathe told his parents,

proudly and unnecessarily. "Then I'm going to spend the rest of my life doing two things."

Grace held her breath, but she couldn't help shooting him an adoring glance. Just looking at him filled her up with love!

"What's that?" Derek asked, smiling.

"Keeping Grace happy *and* keeping her out of trouble."

Grace bit her lip nervously, but she was smiling. Miranda came forward and kissed her cheek. "Welcome to the family, dear." Grace's eyes flooded with tears.

"Okay, let's get on with this ceremony," Derek shouted, turning and pointing at a preacher. "How about you, good man?"

The minister grinned. "It will be my pleasure."

Grace and Rathe smiled into each other's eyes, Rathe taking her hand.

"Does anyone have a ring?" Derek addressed the fascinated crowd.

"Is this for real?" someone asked.

Rathe chuckled and Grace smiled, while Derek shouted that it was, indeed, for real.

A dozen people surged forth, offering to lend them their rings. Rathe accepted one with a hearty thanks and took Grace's hand. Derek and Miranda stepped behind the starstruck couple. "Go ahead." Derek grinned at the preacher.

"Dearly beloved," the preacher intoned.

Rathe and Grace shifted to face each other fully, gazing raptly into each other's eyes. "This is forever, Grace," Rathe whispered so only she could hear.

"Forever," Grace breathed back.

"I love you," Rathe mouthed. "I adore you."

Grace beamed.

"Soon," he murmured, giving her a pointed look.

Grace blushed.

"The ring, Rathe, give her the ring," Derek urged in a stage whisper.

Startled, Rathe recovered; the crowd laughed softly. Then Rathe placed the ring on Grace's finger.

"I now pronounce you man and wife. You may kiss the bride."

Rathe pulled her slowly and deliberately into his arms. "Finally," he murmured. And he lowered his head to hers.

Feeling his blatant erection, Grace came up for air and said, "You, Rathe Bragg, are incorrigible."

"I'm waiting for you to reform me, remember?" he said.

And they smiled and kissed again.

Epilogue

"Look! That's Mama!"

The little red-haired bundle of energy squirmed in her father's arms. "Can you see, honey?" Rathe asked. At the emphatic shake of her head, Rathe shifted his daughter up to his shoulders. "How's that, Lucy?"

"That's my mama!" four-year-old Lucy cried to the gentlemen in the crowd standing next to them.

Rathe smiled, holding her chubby little ankles.

"Mama says women must vote," Lucy declared loudly.

Despite themselves, the gentlemen smiled.

"Hush, sweetheart," Rathe said softly. "Let's listen to what Mama's saying."

"It is imperative," Grace cried from the platform of the auditorium, "that each and every one of you joins us in our quest! We cannot let Supreme Court decisions like *Minor* and *Bradley* deter us; to the contrary, they must spur us on! Never has the need for a Federal Women's Suffrage Amendment been greater; never has the law and the tyranny of men been so blatantly obvious. Our oppressors are scared, ladies and gentlemen. Why else would Mrs. Bradley be denied her rights as a citizen under the Fourteenth Amendment merely because she is a woman?" Grace paused, her violet eyes sweeping the crowd.

"I implore each and every one of you, not only to sign these petitions demanding a federal amendment, but also to take a blank petition to your neighbors, families, and friends. Exhort and implore! We need their signatures! The time is now!''

A moment of silence reigned. Then there was a smattering of applause. It was broken by a solitary boo, which was followed by a chorus of them. Someone shouted, ''Women belong in the home and I, for one, am sick of listening to you immoral, promiscuous free-lovers!''

More boos and applause followed.

''Ah, damn,'' Rathe said, tensing.

''Women are equal, we deserve the vote!'' a woman screamed.

''Lady, go home!'' a man shouted back.

Voices rose, a cacophony of protest and argument and imminent pandemonium. The crowd rippled and swayed, taking on a life of its own, its energy coiling, seething. Rathe pulled Lucinda into his arms. ''No, Daddy!'' she protested. ''I want to see!''

''Daddy has to rescue Mama,'' Rathe said, tucking his daughter under his arm and surging down the aisle. His eyes were on Grace. She met his glare. She smiled sweetly; his glare deepened. At that moment a ripe tomato went flying, and she ducked just in time. It landed on the woman standing directly behind her. Grace started to hurry off the stage.

People were shoving and shouting, and eggs and tomatoes pelted the stage as a dozen National members, both men and women, rushed off. Rathe never took his gaze from Grace as she stumbled down the steps at the side of the stage. He saw a man reach out and take her arm, shouting. A second later Rathe grabbed him, pulling him off with one hand, never releasing his daughter. He shoved the bewhiskered fellow into another man, knocking their heads together. They staggered groggily.

Rathe had Grace's elbow and was spiriting her out the exit when he felt something slap him on the back of the neck, cool and wet, then start oozing under his collar.

They hurried outside and onto the sidewalk. Rathe looked at her.

"Did you like my speech, darling?" Grace cooed to Lucy, forcibly taking her from Rathe's arms.

"We need mending," Lucy crowed. "We need the vote!"

"That's an amendment, darling," Grace cried, hugging her. "Oh dear, Rathe, you have tomato on your suit."

"Grace, do you have to train her this early?" Rathe groaned. "And whose fault is it that I have tomato on my suit?"

She blinked at him innocently, then leaned forward to kiss him. "Why, I just don't know."

He put his arm around her. "And to think I thought a baby would keep you barefoot and at home."

"You cad," she said.

"Let's not start another riot until next week," he said.

"All right," she agreed.

"We need mending!" Lucy shouted. "Daddy, I want to riot too!"

Rathe groaned.

Experience the Wonder of Romance
LISA KLEYPAS

STRANGER IN MY ARMS
78145-X/$5.99 US/$7.99 Can

MIDNIGHT ANGEL
77353-8/$5.99 US/$6.99 Can

DREAMING OF YOU
77352-X/$5.50 US/$6.50 Can

ONLY IN YOUR ARMS
76150-5/$5.99 US/$7.99 Can

ONLY WITH YOUR LOVE
76151-3/$5.50 US/$7.50 Can

THEN CAME YOU
77013-X/$5.99 US/$7.99 Can

PRINCE OF DREAMS
77355-4/$5.99 US/$7.99 Can

SOMEWHERE I'LL FIND YOU
78143-3/$5.99 US/$7.99 Can

NEW YORK TIMES BESTSELLING AUTHOR

Catherine Anderson

"An amazing talent"

Elizabeth Lowell

FOREVER AFTER
79104-8/$5.99 US/$7.99 Can

SIMPLY LOVE
79102-1/$5.99 US/$7.99 Can

KEEGAN'S LADY
77962-5/$5.99 US/$7.99 Can

ANNIE'S SONG
77961-7/$5.99 US/$7.99 Can

CHERISH
79936-7/$6.50 US/$8.50 Can